better with you

ALTERNATIVE COVER EDITION

BRIT BENSON

Better with you

BRIT BENSON

Cover Design by TRC Designs by Cat

Editing by Rebecca at Fairest Reviews Editing Services

Proofing by Sarah at All Encompassing Books

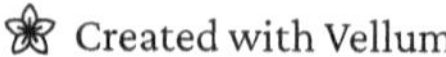 Created with Vellum

To all my fellow millennial babies who made mix CDs with songs you downloaded from LimeWire, spent too much of your money on Manic Panic and eyeliner from Hot Topic, and languished through every school year with only the promise of a Warped Tour Summer as your motivation. I hope my "punk rock pixie emo chick" speaks to your soul. I also left a few lyrical Easter eggs in here for you.
Let's see if you can find them.

To my husband, without whom there is no possible way I could have turned this book around so quickly. Thank you for putting up with my zombie looking, patience lacking, possibly-hasn't-showered-for-days, moody ass. Je t'aime.

By Myself- Christian French
buzz cut – lovelytheband, MisterWives
Grand Theft Autumn – Fall Out Boy
Starving – Hailee Steinfeld
The Rock Show – blink-182
Hero / Heroine – Boys Like Girls
sex – EDEN
FUCKBOY – Dixie
Dirty Little Secret – All American Rejects
forget me too – Machine Gun Kelly, Halsey
You're So Last Summer – Taking Back Sunday
Punk Rock Princess – Something Corporate
Head On Collison – New Found Glory
I Really Wish I Hated You – blink-182
Fat Lip – Sum 41
Everything Is Alright – Motion City Soundtrack
Memory - Sugarcult
Plot Twist – Marc E. Bassy, KYLE
10,000 Hours – Dan + Shay, Justin Bieber
I Think I'm In Love – Kat Dahlia

That's What You Get – Paramore
Lose Somebody – Kygo, OneRepublic
I Will Follow You into the Dark – Death Cab for Cutie
She Is Love – Parachute
Tell Her You Love Her – Echosmith, Mat Kearney
Hear You Me – Jimmy Eat World
Hands Down – Dashboard Confessional
Better Together – Jack Johnson

For the extended playlist, visit my website.

content note from the author

Please be aware: this book contains references to some difficult topics that could be upsetting for some readers.

Topics that take place on page are: death of a loved one, terminal illness of a family member.

Topics that are referenced in detail but do not take place on page are: transphobia, homophobia, bullying, forced outing of an LGBT person, deadnaming.

BETRAYAL.

That's what comes first. A painful, bottomless black pit rips open in my stomach, festering, stretching wider and wider until my body bends from the weight of it.

Then hatred. A blazing anger erupts in my chest, licking white hot flames around my heart and lungs, as my breaths grow ragged, and my eyes burn.

It's enough to consume me, to drive me mad, but it's doused quickly by a dark sense of despair. A soaking wet blanket covering all of my senses and stealing the light, rendering me lost.

I try to work through it, try to struggle my way out, but then anguish is joined by guilt. An iron fist wrapping around my throat as black dots blink in and out of my vision, and it hurts to breathe. It hurts to move. It hurts to exist.

Betrayal. Hatred. Despair. Guilt.

Separate attacks, but quickly they join forces until I am one raging battlefield of chaotic emotions, threatening to take my logical mind under siege.

I'm seeing red and the sound of blood rushes through my

ears. I want to scream, cry, run. I want to hide. Under the surface, I'm a mess.

I fight to keep my face neutral, to remain steady and appear calm, but all I can see is the date on the calendar. All I can think of is the deadline I won't reach, and the promise I'm going to have to break.

I let my guard down. I let someone in. And in doing so, I let *him* down. The only person worthy of everything good, and I've let him down. *Again.*

Tears burn the backs of my eyelids, welling up and threatening to spill, but I won't let them fall. I've had years of practice turning my outside to stone.

The man beside me shifts, and I can feel his attention on me. His pleading gaze with his dark, chocolate brown eyes. I see his hands moving in my peripheral as his big fingers fidget, and despite his size, the movement is delicate. I know how those hands feel on my skin. I know how soft his touch can be.

I try to fight it, the way my heart clenches and aches. I try to focus on my anger, on the betrayal. I try to keep my sadness for the boy I've let down.

But deep down, I know the truth.

Underneath the fury, buried under the newfound hatred, is loss.

Loss and longing.

Mourning for the man beside me, the man I thought I knew. The man who is not at all who he led me to believe he was.

bailey

Four weeks earlier

I SMELL like stale beer and french fries.

It's disgusting. I'll never let myself get used to it.

My shoes stick to the floor as I walk back and forth, wiping down counters and replenishing garnishes. Limes, lemons, oranges, green olives, and my favorite, maraschino cherries. I snag one before putting the garnish tray back in the ice chest.

"I'm about finished here," I call to my manager, wiping my hands on my bar towel.

"You're good, B. Thanks for coming in tonight. I know you've got a lot going on."

"It's cool." I shrug. "I can always use the money. Even if it is a slow Wednesday, cash is cash."

I grab a toothpick from the jar on the bar and steal another cherry from the tray in the ice chest. Popping it in my mouth, I wink at the guy two bar stools down. He left me a decent tip earlier. The least I can do is pay him one last bit of attention since he's likely to be back.

"Alright girl, well, head out and I'll see you on Saturday night. You're closing."

Jada pulls a draft for another guy and slides him the pint. A group of them came in to watch some live streamed coverage of the Butler University basketball team then stayed. I couldn't care less about the game, but it's the only reason I made any money tonight.

I say goodbye to Jada and head to the back of the bar to get my stuff. Switching out my hideous non-slips for my boots, I drop the shoes in my locker and grab my helmet and crossbody purse.

I should change my shirt because I know I stink like a bar, but I'm just too damn exhausted. I've been working more since Jada promoted me to lead bartender at Bar 31, my classes have been kicking my ass, and I've been spending all my free time trying to concoct the perfect cookie for the Bakery On Main cookie contest next month. My body is pissed at me and letting me know it, but if I can win that contest...the two-grand in prize money would be worth it. I don't even care about having my name and cookie displayed on their menu. Okay, that's a lie. That would be cool. But the prize money? That's the real appeal.

I duck out the back exit and walk to my bike. She's my Baby. A black 2012 Honda Rebel 250. I bought it used from the guy who owns the auto garage back home for $1500. It was a fucking steal, but I think he felt sorry for me and cut me a deal. Sometimes there are advantages to being the girl everyone pities.

Putting my purse in the saddle bag, I swing my leg over the bike, put on my helmet, and start her up. No matter how tired I am, the rumble of her engine always gives me a jolt of excitement. Something about the freedom and the danger, maybe. I rev her twice, just for fun, and then cruise out onto the street.

It's already a little past midnight when I pull into the

parking lot of Quick Stop, the small convenience store just off campus. It's late, I'm beat, and I only need one thing, so I'm braving it.

I hate having to shop so close to campus. I don't like running into people I know.

Working at one of the popular campus bars means a lot of people recognize me. Occupational hazard. Unfortunately, there are not a lot of jobs where I can make 500 bucks on a weekend fully clothed, so when I'm on the clock, I fake it. Makes me quite a damn peach when I clock out.

After locking my helmet onto the backrest and grabbing my purse, I pop in my earbuds—a whole other level of antisocial. I spent the last three hours being *on*. Any more human interaction and I might develop a twitch.

My 2000's pop punk playlist—the one I reserve for post-bar shifts—is blaring in my ears, and I head to aisle six, where they keep the baking stuff. I scan the shelf, find what I need and go to grab for it, then stop.

Shit. This store actually has pure vanilla extract. I drop my hand. I was gonna get the imitation stuff—it's what I've been using—but if I want to win this contest, I need quality ingredients.

Shit. Eight freaking bucks for two ounces? I can get eight ounces of the imitation for $1.99.

I groan. This hurts. Like actually flipping hurts.

It's that poor kid mentality. I'll probably never outgrow it.

I sigh, resigned, and reach for the pure vanilla, just as another hand snatches it from the shelf. I whip around keeping my eyes on the precious bottle—the only one this stupid convenience store has—and huff.

I'm about to pop off and put this snatchy thief in their place, but my attention is stolen by the hand that's holding the bottle. A big hand. A strong hand. *A sexy* hand.

Hmm.

I scan my eyes upward. A few woven bracelets are tied loosely around the thick wrist, and a dusting of hair covers the muscular, rigid, golden forearm.

That's a *nice* forearm, right there.

I move my gaze farther up, over a defined bicep and a broad chest covered in a blue and white baseball-style t-shirt with a silver necklace of some sort hiding just beneath the collar. The defined jaw is sporting a bit of dark brown scruff, and soft, chestnut hair feathers just above the shoulders.

I expand my focus, enough to study the whole hairstyle, to find it loose, kinda messy, with a bit of a wave to it.

Prince-haired Harry hair.

When the mouth moves, I flick my eyes down to it to find plump lips quirked in a bit of a smile, and they move again.

The hulking man is speaking.

"Huh?" All I can hear is Patrick Stump in my ears.

His mouth moves a third time, the tiny smile turning into a full-blown grin, showing off straight, white teeth.

Then I watch in slow motion as the other hand, the one not holding my bottle of pure vanilla hostage, rises up and tugs one of my earbuds out of my ear.

"You said Prince Harry," he says with a laugh.

"No, I said prince-*haired* Harry," I correct. "And I didn't realize I'd said it out loud."

"Oh," he says, voice low and playful, and raises an eyebrow in question. I raise mine in response but don't speak, and he laughs. "Are you okay?"

I bristle. "I'm fine."

"I wasn't sure. You're kinda just standing there staring."

"I was sizing up my new enemy." I tug out my other earbud.

"Enemy?" He laughs again. It's a good laugh. Deep and

vibratey. Yes, I just made up that word. The laugh is unique. It deserves its own word.

"You just stole that vanilla from me. I don't make it a habit to befriend thieves."

"I didn't steal it. I just got it before you." He's still smiling. It's an attractive smile, damn it.

"I was clearly here first. I was clearly reaching for that bottle when you jumped out of nowhere and snatched it." I put my hand on my hip and pop it out. My roommate Ivy calls it my power pose. She says it's how she knows when I'm in a 'take-no-prisoners' mode.

"You were here first, yeah. But you were standing there surveying the shelf for a pretty long time," he says with a smirk. "Some of us have places to be. It's not thieving to just sneak past ya and grab what I need."

"It's line jumping, which everyone knows is poor social etiquette, and it is thieving, because that bottle is mine."

"Poor social etiquette?"

"Mmhm."

"Is it poor social etiquette to blatantly check out a stranger at the grocery store, too?" He raises his eyebrows, grin still affixed to his mouth.

I huff out a laugh. "*Please.* I was not checking you out. I was surveying you for weaknesses in case I have to resort to violence."

His answering bark of laughter makes me lose my grip on my poker face, and I smirk.

Okay, maybe this particular social interaction isn't the worst.

"Resort to violence?" He laughs. "I'm like twice your size."

"The bigger they are, the harder they fall," I croon. "Don't underestimate me. It could be your undoing."

He watches me for a minute, eyes sliding over my face, my

body. I can actually feel his gaze on me, and I try to imagine what he sees. Tan skin, amber eyes, freckles, nose ring, Chap-Sticked lips, turquoise dipped black hair. The old Green Day shirt and plain black distressed skinny jeans I'm wearing are snug and show off what little curves I have, and, of course, I'm rocking my Docs (Thrift store find. Twenty bucks. Fucking treasure.).

For a brief moment, I wish I would have taken the time to change and at least peek in the mirror before I left work. I'm sure I have helmet head from the bike, and there's a damp spot on my jeans from a beer spill. Not to mention how I smell... I feel just a teensy bit self-conscious, but then it passes. If he doesn't like what he sees, screw him. The big, beautiful jerk.

When his eyes land on my lips again, I clear my throat loudly and force a frown.

"So, Butch, you gonna hand over my property or do I have to overpower you and take it myself?"

"Butch?" He jerks his head back, amused and confused.

"Butch Cassidy? Train and bank robberies? A famous *burglar.* Don't tell me you're a thief *and* uncultured."

He chuckles and gives me a shrug.

"Just a pretty face, then." I shake my head and sigh. "Such a shame."

"You think I'm pretty."

"I have eyes." I fold my arms over my chest and look away, feigning boredom. "Doesn't change the fact that you're a criminal."

"I'll tell you what." He mimics my stance and hits me with an all-business stare. "I'll trade you for the vanilla."

I purse my lips before asking, "What do I have to give?"

"I'll trade you this vanilla for your number."

Oh. Well, okay then. This is a no-brainer.

"I told you before that I don't associate with criminals."

"But if I give you the bottle, then I wouldn't be a criminal. I'm not stealing; it's all just one big misunderstanding."

"And what if this isn't your first offense? How do I know you're not trying to trick me? Get my number, then make off with the vanilla?" I squint my eyes at him. "You could be trying to set me up for a bunch of cold calling campaigns. Or planning to put my number on a billboard or a bathroom stall. How do I know you can be trusted?"

Pretty sure I've got this boy eating out of the palm of my hand. He's trying so hard not to let his smile take over his face, trying and failing, and his brown eyes are dancing with humor. He's amused. He's having fun, and I'm suddenly not tired anymore.

"You bring up good points." He pauses. "I don't suppose you'll take my word for it."

I huff a laugh and roll my eyes.

"Of course not." He chuckles. "I'll let you buy it first. You can buy it and put it in your car, and then give me your number."

I pretend to think it over.

"If we do it that way, you'll stay on the sidewalk until I've secured the vanilla, and then I'll shout my number to you."

He laughs, giving an amused shake of the head before nodding his agreement. "Deal. Shake on it?"

He sticks out his hand, and I narrow my eyes at it. Then I meet his gaze, pop a brow, and slowly reach out to take it.

It's warm and calloused. His grip is firm, but not crushing, and I have a feeling his hands could do some serious damage if he wanted them to. The thought sends a spark of lust through me. The way his eyes flash with heat tells me he noticed, so I drop his hand and head to the check out.

He follows me out the door, the bottle of vanilla and the store receipt clutched in my hand. When we're on the sidewalk, I turn around.

"You stay here," I remind him, pointing to the sidewalk where his feet are planted. "No moving."

"Cross my heart." He uses his index finger to draw an X on his chest, and I have to hold back my smile at how serious he looks.

I take my first few steps backward, keeping my eyes on him, until I'm a safe distance away. Then I pivot on the ball of my foot and sashay to my bike. I'm not ashamed to admit it. I might not have much by way of hips, but what I do have, I know how to work. When I reach Baby, I put the vanilla and my purse in the saddle bag, unlock my helmet, then turn back around to face the attractive almost-thief. I lean on my bike lightly and smirk at his shocked expression.

People never expect me to be riding a motorcycle. It's one of the reasons I love it.

We stare at each other for a moment, me with my smirk and him with his wide, surprised eyes. The connection creates sparks, even with a parking lot between us, and I have to breathe slowly to steady my heartbeat.

"Is the package secure?" he shouts from the curb, and I reach down and pat the saddlebag.

"Snug as a bug in a rug."

"Okay. I held up my end of the bargain. It's your turn to hold up yours."

"Hmmm, what was my end, again?" I cock my head to the side and watch as he grabs the back of his neck and smiles at the ground. It's so boyishly adorable, so magnetic, that I kind of hate him a little. This guy is *dangerous*.

"Your number," he reminds me.

"Oh yeah," I say with a grin. "Thirty-one."

"Thirty-one?" His handsome face scrunches up in confusion.

"Thirty-one." I stifle a giggle.

"Thirty-one is not your phone number."

"It's not," I respond slowly. "But you didn't specify what number you wanted." I shrug. "Thirty-one is the number you get."

As I swing my leg over my bike, I hear his rumbling laugh again. I'm just about to push my helmet on my head when he calls out.

"Sundance! Hey, Sundance," he shouts, and I can't help the huge smile that stretches over my face. That scoundrel said he didn't know Butch Cassidy, and here he is calling me Sundance. "I didn't get your name."

I look at him, smile wide, and roll my eyes. "Bummer for you."

Then I shove my helmet on my head, rev Baby to life, and cruise out of the parking lot without a backward glance.

When I get back to my apartment, it's past one in the morning, and I have a 9:30 a.m. class tomorrow. Ivy is probably asleep, so I move silently toward the kitchen. I put the vanilla in the cupboard and take a minute to admire it on the shelf. It's such a luxury. Makes me feel rich for a hot minute.

I flip off the kitchen light and walk to the sliding doors to our small balcony. I gaze longingly at my wicker bowl chair. I had plans tonight that included that chair, my new romance novel, and a glass of wine. Two of my favorite things: sexy romance novels and wine. Romance in real life, not my jam. But romance in books? Fricken love it.

If I hadn't been called in to work, and then gotten distracted by the sexy stranger with the Harry Styles hair, I'd probably would have been able to bust out maybe half the book. Definitely would have gotten some dick. *Fictional* dick, but that's usually better anyway.

I smile at the thought of my convenience store thief, Butch Cassidy, and my chest warms. That was an 'in real life meet-cute' if I've ever seen one. I didn't think that shit actually happened outside of books and movies. I guess forfeiting a few chapters of contemporary romance to flirt with the hot guy in the baking aisle isn't a big deal.

In my bedroom, I take out the cash I made tonight and divide it up. Fifty bucks is pretty decent for a Wednesday night. I put forty of it back in my wallet to be deposited in my bank account to help cover usual expenses, and I take the remaining ten and shove it into the Crisco can I keep in the back of my closet. I update the total on the pink sticky note inside the can and scowl at it. I've been saving for six months, and it's like I've barely made a dent in my goal. I'm hoping the promotion at work will help, but it's still taking too long. The sense of urgency, of guilt, is overwhelming.

It's been almost three years, already. Not for the first time, I curse myself for not starting sooner. For not thinking of it sooner.

If I can win this cookie contest... That two grand would be a game changer. I could make my deadline. He deserves *at least* that.

I have to win this contest. I kiss my fingers, press them to my chest, just over my heart, and murmur a promise. *I will win this contest.*

I shove the Crisco can back into my closet, grab a sleepshirt, and head into the bathroom that I share with Ivy. I need to scrub the bar smell from my body before I crash into bed. Then it's another day of classes and experimental baking.

Hopefully I can squeeze some fic-dick in there, too.

At least I don't have to work again until Saturday.

* * *

By the time Saturday evening rolls around, I've almost forgotten about the baking-aisle boy.

I did think I saw someone similar on campus yesterday, and once Thursday I thought I heard his laugh on the quad. But, otherwise, he's just a fuzzy image, fading from my short-term memory, never to be fantasized about again.

Saturday nights at Bar 31 are always hopping. I'm closing tonight, so I can make a cool $200 at least, and it will be easy money. Rum and Cokes, Vodka Cranberries, and way too many Jägerbombs.

College kids and our distinguished pallets. Ha.

Around 1 a.m., thirty minutes before I get to climb on a stool and shout LAST CALL into the bar microphone, a familiar hand slides into my line of sight.

A sexy hand.

With woven bracelets tied to a thick wrist.

I allow myself one small smirk before meeting his chocolate brown eyes.

"You found me," I shout over the music and crowd noise.

"I did. It wasn't too hard. I've been in here every night since Thursday."

I fight a smile. "So, you're a stalker as well as a thief."

His smile is immediate, his perfectly straight teeth on display.

"We've established I'm not a thief. And I consider myself more an investigator than a stalker. You told me thirty-one. I solved the riddle."

I nod. Gotta admit, his determination is hot.

"Does this earn me your *phone* number?"

His voice is quieter, no longer shouting over the noise, because we've somehow gravitated toward each other. I'm leaning over the ice chest, him over the bar top, and we're mere inches apart. I take a moment to study him. Thick eyebrows, thick lashes, thick lips. I wonder what else on him is *thick*...

A guy to my left is waving his card at me, so I give a "hold that thought" finger to the attractive man monopolizing my time and head to make a drink.

Or five drinks. Jägerbombs. And a five-dollar tip. *Score.*

I can feel my mystery man's eyes on me the whole time. I like it a little too much.

I walk back to him, and he's folding a napkin into a floppy origami crane. His long fingers are so precise and careful, exactly the opposite of what I'd expect. Those big hands, those calloused fingers. This guy is dangerous, but I think I could handle a little danger if it means having those hands on me for a night.

I reach into the back pocket of my tight jeans for my Sharpie, then I grab his hand and flip it over so his palm is up. I jot my phone number onto his palm, writing slowly, prolonging the skin-to-skin contact. When the last digit is written, I make eye contact and blow lightly on his palm to dry the ink. His pupils dilate, my core tingles, and then I walk away.

I make Jared, the other bartender, switch me sides, and I don't see Butch Cassidy for the rest of the night, but he left the floppy napkin crane on the bar for me.

When I finally get to my locker at 2:30 a.m., I have three text messages.

Unknown: Hey. I'm Alex.
Unknown: I'm putting you in my phone as Sundance until you tell me your name.
Unknown: Have a good night, Sundance.

My smile is bigger than it should be.

THE NEXT MORNING, I wake up to six more text messages from Alex.

> **Unknown:** Good morning, Sundance.
> **Unknown:** I have a question.
> **Unknown:** Something that I haven't been able to stop thinking about.
> **Unknown:** Can I ask it?
> **Unknown:** I'm taking your silence as permission.
> **Unknown:** Who is Harry and why does he have prince hair?

A small giggle bubbles up in me, and my lips are twitching with the urge to laugh outright as I respond.

> **Me:** Your hair is longish and wavey. Very princely. Similar to the Harry Styles prince hair era. Ask Google.

Three dots pop up, then disappear. I wait thirty seconds, watching the text box, and just when I decide to throw my phone down and get ready for the day, the dots dance again, followed by a string of photos of Harry Styles in all his prince-haired glory.

Unknown: Prince Hair Harry is fucking gorgeous.

I laugh out loud.

Me: Facts.
Unknown: You think I look like him.
Me: Whoa there, Butch. Rein in your ego. I said your hair was similar. That's where my comparison ended. Don't get ahead of yourself.
Unknown: Whatever you say, Sundance.
Unknown: Any comparison at all is a compliment.
Unknown: This man is a god.

He sends me a few more pictures of Harry Styles. My smile is unbidden as I flip through them, thinking up a witty retort, but my breath hitches and my eyes go wide when the final picture is a selfie of Alex.

The selfie is from the shoulders-up, but I can tell he's shirtless, and *whoa momma*, the traps on this one. His hair is loose and wavy, cascading around his defined, scruff-covered jaw, accenting a dimple in his chin, and dancing over the tops of his shoulders. His plump lips are pulled into a sexy crooked grin, and his deep brown eyes are crinkled at the corners. I'm so focused on the picture that I actually jump a little when the next text comes in.

Unknown: You think if I grow it out I can reach LHH status?

Unknown: (That stands for Long Hair Harry. Real fans know.)

I laugh loudly. This guy is ridiculous.

Me: I think you can try. But keep your expectations real-istic. The only person who can pull off the perfect LHH is LHH.

I throw my phone on the bed and head for the kitchen. Ivy programs the coffee pot at night, so I'm hit with the aroma of caffeinated goodness the moment I step out of my bedroom. Judging by the silence, she's already left for the library, which means I have the apartment to myself to spend the day baking before retiring to the porch to drink wine and read my newest romance novel.

After making my coffee and changing out of my sleepshirt, I pull out my cookie notepad and plan today's recipe.

So far, the favorite amongst my taste testers have been a caramel cheesecake bar cookie. It *was* delicious, but I don't know if it's unique enough to win the cookie contest with Bakery On Main.

I need something creative. Something that will wow the judges. That's not going to happen with some boring, run-of-the-mill recipe. No, I need a cookie that's going to stand out.

I survey my ingredients. I still have stuff from the cheese-cake bars, plus a bag of semi-sweet chocolate chips, and my brand new, beautiful bottle of pure vanilla. *Swoon.*

On a whim, I run into my room and grab my phone. I read the new texts from Alex asking about my plans for the day, and in reply, I snap a picture of the vanilla and send it to him. His responses buzz through immediately, one after the other.

Unknown: What are you implying, Sundance?
Unknown: Are you baking?
Unknown: Or are you doing something "vanilla"?
Unknown: You're welcome btw.
Unknown: For the vanilla.

I roll my eyes and smile. If he and I are going to keep up this text flirting, I might have to tell him to start condensing his messages. This firing squad of texts is a bit over the top.

My smile is huge the entire time I type out my response, and I can't help the giggle that escapes when I hit send.

Me: I don't need to thank you. It was mine first, and it
belongs to me. If anything, you should be thanking me
for convincing you not to continue your life of crime.
And in the future, you'll do well to remember something
about me.
Unknown: What's that?
Me: Nothing about me is vanilla.

I wait until I see the chat bubble dance on the screen before dropping my phone into the drawer of potholders and slamming it closed. Let's let the big flirt sit with that for a while. He really has no idea who he's playing with.

The entire time I measure, mix, and bake my latest cookie creation, my mouth is stuck in a smile, and it has nothing to do with the boy band throwback playlist I'm listening to.

Four dozen cookies and two new drafted recipes later, I'm ready to collapse in my bowl chair with my book and wine. I hope Ivy gets home soon, so she can be my taste tester, but she's spent the afternoon with our friend Kelley, so there's no telling when she'll show up. Those two drive me freaking bonkers. They've been friends for like nine years, and I'm pretty sure they've been in love with each other for most of them.

But, of course, they don't know it.

Me, our friend Jesse, and basically anyone else who's ever seen them together can tell they're head-over-heels, disgustingly gone for each other, but they're oblivious. It's as entertaining as it is annoying. One of these days, if they don't wise up soon, I might be forced to do something drastic—like lock them in a bedroom with a box of condoms and "Lovesick" by Banks on repeat.

I grab a glass from the cabinet and fill it with the box of wine we have in the fridge. Boxed wine is my new favorite thing. It's the alcoholic beverage choice of frugal bitches like me and Ivy. Classy bottle taste for a reasonable cardboard price. And you get like three bottles worth of wine in one box. It's amazing.

Just as I'm about to take my wine to the balcony, a buzzing sounds from the potholder drawer. Oh shit. I forgot that I tossed my phone in there. When I take the phone out of the drawer, a legit cackle escapes me.

Twenty-five notifications.

At first, I'm flattered, but then it's immediately replaced with suspicion.

If these are all from Alex, that's fucking creepy. I've watched enough serial killer documentaries with Ivy to know that stage-five clingers are a GIANT red fucking flag, especially this early on.

I take a deep breath, then a gulp of wine, and then I swipe at my screen to open my messages.

Oh, thank you, baby Jesus.

Two texts, two missed calls, and a voicemail are from my mom, and I delete them immediately.

I have a couple texts from Jesse, Kelley's roommate and the fourth member of our small friend group, informing me that Kelley took Ivy out to teach her how to drive a stick shift this afternoon. Jesse and I do this often, keep tabs on Kelley and Ivy. We like to speculate on when they'll finally pull their heads out of their asses and admit their feelings for each other. It started as a joke, but now J and I are weirdly invested.

I don't do relationships because I'm *hashtag jaded*, and Jesse has his own issues, so now we focus our attention on the sexual tension between our other two friends. And I can't speak for J, but I'd like to see Ivy and Kelley work out because at least then I'll know that kind of love—the real, true kind—can exist outside of the stories on my e-reader. And if anyone deserves that kind of love, it's Ivy. She's sweet, and pure, and *good*.

Ivy's love language is acts of service. It's obvious from all the little stuff she does for us; she's a nurturer by nature, our Mama Bear. She and Kelley are pretty evenly matched in that way. My love language is quality time. With myself. Because most people suck. And Jesse's is...hell, I don't even know. Are immature jokes and schoolyard taunts a love language? His text messages sure suggest they could be.

Jesse: 5 bucks says they get into an argument that leads to a make out sesh.
Me: Argument is likely, but no way on the kiss. V has been preparing for this driving lesson for weeks. Nothin is gonna distract her from it.
Jesse: Yeah u right. So a *waving hand emoji* *Eggplant emoji* in the passenger seat?
Me: Perv.
Jesse: *dancing lady emoji* *praying hands emoji* *water emoji*

I laugh out loud as Jesse and I exchange a few more messages, his mostly emojis that take some brainpower to decipher, and then I switch over to our group text thread. V sent a selfie of her and Kelley in the front seat of a truck. She's grinning proudly at the camera, and Kelley is, of fucking course, looking at her with a dopey love-drunk smile on his face.

Damn. They're so cute I could barf.

I read through the texts and send a few of my own, telling Ivy that I can't wait to hear about her NASCAR practice run, and then I close out of that thread and open the one I've been avoiding.

Alex has sent me a slew of texts, and none of them are selfies. *Bummer.*

Unknown: And what does that mean?
Unknown: Are you flirting?
Unknown: I think you're flirting.
Unknown: Sundance, you can't just send a text like that and then disappear.

I smirk. His reaction is exactly what I was hoping for when I sent my "vanilla" comment.

Unknown: You're killing me, SD.
Unknown: Well here's a confession for you.
Unknown: I already knew there was nothing vanilla about you.
Unknown: You're the furthest thing from vanilla.
Unknown: Absolutely nothing about you screams ordinary.

My smirk transforms into a smile at Butch Cassidy attempting to spit game my way. I'd be flattered if I wasn't sure he was feeding me a line. A good line, but still a line. I check the time stamp on his last text. Three hours ago. I think the guy's waited long enough.

> **Me:** You should really work on combining your thoughts into fewer messages. Condense. Sending multiple texts in such quick succession makes you look impatient and excitable.

His reply is immediate.

> **Unknown:** Maybe you make me impatient and excitable.

I snort and take a page out of Jesse's book by sending the face palm emoji.

> **Unknown:** I'm serious.
> **Unknown:** I'm usually much more calm and cool.
> **Unknown:** What are you doing right now?

Whoa, okay.

Wasn't expecting the "wyd" text so soon. I weigh my options. I could text back, give in, and be done with this whole thing after tonight. Or, I could string him along a little longer. Do the flirty texts for a few more days until I get bored or impatient and fall to the inevitable fuck and run. Can't get played if you're the one dealing the cards, after all.

I'm having fun with him, but I guess the sooner we get this over with, the better. Nothing good comes from dragging it out, and that text he just sent makes his intentions crystal clear. Not that I'm surprised. Maybe a little disappointed, but no harm, no foul.

I cover my wine glass with a piece of plastic wrap and put it in the fridge for later, then go into my room and change into a pair of jeans and a band tee. I run my fingers through my hair, swipe on some eyeliner and mascara, and then text him back.

Me: What do you have in mind?

It's just after seven when I pull Baby into the parking lot of Quick Stop and spot Alex standing outside the store entrance. He throws one hand up in a wave, and I look him over through my helmet shield before getting off my bike.

Damn it, he looks good.

Grey joggers, a Butler University baseball t-shirt, and a backward ball cap. His hair is tucked behind his ears, and I itch with the urge to run my fingers through it. I bet it's as soft as it is shiny.

Before it's obvious that I'm ogling, I swing my leg over Baby, lock up my helmet, and stride over to him. When I'm a few steps from the curb, his feet catch my eye, and I can't hold back my laughter.

"Oh my *god*." I laugh. "I did *not* peg you for a camo Croc guy."

He crinkles his nose with a grin and wiggles one foot at me. "These are fucking comfy," he defends. "And they're easy to clean, and durable, and convenient."

"Nope," I say with a smile as I walk toward him. "I will never, ever be supportive of that shoe choice. Especially not with joggers." I giggle again, and he shrugs it off, smile still plastered on his face. He's completely confident in his shoe wear. I bet he's completely confident in just about everything he does.

"Nice bike," he says when I step up on the curb.

"Thanks." I look back at her over my shoulder. "2012 Honda Rebel 250. Her name's Baby."

"Yeah? Like 'nobody puts Baby in a corner,' Baby?"

I raise my eyebrows in surprise. "Exactly like that Baby." First *Butch Cassidy and the Sundance Kid*, and now *Dirty Dancing*? This guy keeps surprising me.

"Is there a story there?" he asks, and I nod as we walk into the convenience store.

"The shop where I got her, she was tucked up in the back corner, forgotten. Neglected." I shake my head at the memory. "She didn't deserve that, being ignored. So, I rescued her. Fixed her up a bit, and now she's my Baby."

I see him watching me out of my peripheral, so I keep my eyes forward as we weave through the small store. Alex grabbed a shopping basket, and he's leading us to the baking aisle.

"That's fitting," he says after a breath. "Frances Houseman was definitely a rebel, too. Defying her dad and going against societal expectations like she did."

I stop in my tracks. "I've said the exact same thing." My smile is huge, and his answering proud grin is adorably sexy. "Crossing the class barrier when you're surrounded by a bunch of stuck-up pricks takes some guts, especially when you consider how close she was with her dad."

"She didn't want to disappoint him, but she was in love with Johnny." I roll my eyes at his *love* comment. He's not wrong, but it's a knee-jerk reaction when the L word comes up in conversation. Outside of movies, books, and my roommate Ivy's life, that shit just isn't real. I change the subject when we halt in front of the boxed cake mixes.

"Okay, Butch. I give. What are we doing here? You gonna steal something else?"

"I want cupcakes." He shrugs. "Thought maybe you'd want to help me make some."

I pop a brow. "You want my help making cupcakes?"

"Sure." His smile is playful, and he grabs the back of his neck again in that stupidly cute boyish way. *Ugh, fine.* I'll make cupcakes with him.

"Okay," I nod, "let's make some cupcakes."

He grabs a box of funfetti cake mix, a jar of fudge frosting, a container of colorful sprinkles, and a packet of cupcake liners and drops them all in the basket. I can't help but giggle at how childish his choices are. This guy is a beast, and he grabs funfetti cupcake mix. And a container of sprinkles. A-freaking-dorable.

I grab a jar of maraschino cherries and drop it in the basket, too. He eyes my choice and flashes me a smirk, and I shrug. "I like cherries."

After he pays, we head back out to the parking lot, and he takes out his phone.

"I took the campus bus here, but the next one isn't for another hour since it's a Sunday night. I'm gonna cue up an Uber."

"How far do you live?"

"Not far," he says, without looking up from his phone. "Three miles off campus."

I survey him. "How much do you weigh?" I ask after a second, and he chuckles.

"Like 210. Why?"

I freaking knew it. Dude's probably solid muscle, too. I look at his bicep, and he flexes under my gaze, making me laugh out loud. When I meet his eyes, he winks and flashes me a flirty grin. I shake my head at him.

"Baby has a weight limit, but I think I can ride you if we go slow." I try to keep the innuendo from my voice, but his smirk tells me he didn't miss it.

"Oh yeah?"

"On the bike, Romeo," I say with a laugh. "I can give you a lift on my bike. Might be a little wonky just because you're, uh, big. And I'm not." I scrunch up my nose and bounce my eyes between him and Baby. "And I might need you to help a little for balance if we hit a light, but we can try it."

"I can show you a way so there's no stoplights." He adds, "You sure?"

"Yep, just listen to me in case I need you to do something," I say as we head toward Baby. "I don't have a helmet for you, but they're not required in Indiana."

"It's cool. Just don't go crazy."

"I don't think we could go crazy even if we wanted to."

bailey

FIFTEEN MINUTES LATER, I'm pulling up to a small townhouse just off campus. There's a porch light on and a Butler University baseball flag hanging out front. The ride here wasn't too bad. Had to keep a steady pace and roll through a few stop signs, but otherwise, it was doable. Definitely not taking this breathing hunk of muscle onto any highways, though.

Alex unlocks the front door and walks us into the house. There is a pile of shoes just to the left of the door, and when he kicks off his camo freaking Crocs, I bend down and unlace my Docs. We bypass a staircase, walk down a short hallway, and enter a small living room. It's pretty much what I was expecting. There's a black couch and two recliners, and on the wall behind them is a Colts flag, a Bears flag, and another BU flag. A giant flat-screen TV is mounted on the opposite wall, and aside from a pop can, a few notebooks, and a laptop sitting on the coffee table, the place is clean.

"This way," he says, and leads me around a corner into a tidy kitchen. There's a blender and a few huge jars of protein powder on the counter next to the fridge, and several shaker bottles in the dish drying rack on the sink.

"You guys athletes?" I ask as he sets the grocery bag on the kitchen table.

"Oh, um, yeah," he says, following my gaze to the supplement stuff on the counter, then pulls a carton of eggs out of the fridge. "I have two roommates. They play baseball."

"Where are they tonight? It's a Sunday. Classes tomorrow."

"They're at the baseball house on campus. Sometimes they stay there." He grabs a cupcake pan out of a lower cabinet and sets it on the counter, then bends back down and pulls out a KitchenAid stand mixer. I force myself to shut my gaping mouth.

It's beautiful. Cobalt blue and shiny chrome. Probably new, from the looks of it. That's like a four hundred dollar machine, right there. I was using a hand mixer I got at the Goodwill until like three weeks ago when I finally broke down and bought a cheap stand mixer from the Wal-Mart. I reach out and brush my hand over the mixer's cool, blue surface.

"Nice, right?" Alex says, setting out a bottle of vegetable oil. "I just got it."

"I'm so jealous right now," I confess. "I could come just from touching it."

He barks out a surprised laugh, and I flick my eyes to his.

"I'm not kidding. The one I have gets overheated if I use it for more than ten minutes at a time, and I can't double recipes because the motor whines and jams up. This right here," I pet the mixer again, "is fucking luxury."

"Well then, I'm glad you came over tonight." He slides the box of cake mix toward me. "What's first?"

I crack the eggs in the mixing bowl, and Alex adds the vegetable oil. When he goes to measure out the water, I stop him.

"Let me," I say, and take the measuring cup from him. I pour the juice from my jar of cherries into the measuring cup first, then fill it the rest of the way with water before dumping it in the bowl. "Now it's better." I smirk at him.

"I never would have thought to do that."

I shrug. "I like to experiment."

His smile grows wicked, and he steps toward me, so I'm pressed against the kitchen counter, before asking, "Do you like to *experiment* with other things too?"

Goosebumps prickle on my skin. I hold his eyes, bite my lower lip, and give him another shrug. "Maybe." Then I brush past him and start opening cabinets. "I need a cutting board, a chef's knife, a spoon, and a mixing bowl."

He chuckles behind me. "Sure," he says, and he gathers the items I requested.

While Alex sets the cupcake batter up on the beautiful KitchenAid mixer, I dump the jar of cherries on the cutting board, pop two in my mouth, and chop the rest. Then, I dump the chopped cherries into the other mixing bowl and add the jar of fudge frosting. I stir the cherries in until they're perfectly blended.

"There," I say, "now that's better, too."

"What if I'm allergic to cherries?" His voice is light, playful, and I scrunch up my nose.

"Are you?"

He shrugs, and I laugh. He's full of shit.

After putting the cupcake pan in the oven and setting the timer, Alex turns to me and does that stupid thing with his hand on his neck that makes my tummy jump.

"Sooo, Sundance," he drags out, "you wanna hang in my room while these bake?"

My lips twitch at the corners. I want so badly to laugh, but I manage to tame it to a small smile. How is this gorgeous, Thorclone of a man adorably bashful right now? Confident in his Crocs, but shy as shit when trying to get a girl in his bedroom. So pure.

"Yeah, Butch," I say with a small grin. "Show me your room." For all my bravado, my heart is racing in my chest and my core is tingling with excitement. I might also be a little wet, which is absurd. But damn, I'm enjoying this high.

Alex leads me up a set of stairs and into what appears to be a master suite. A large king-size bed sits in the center, a walk-in closet is to the right, and a private en-suite bathroom is to the left. This room is *nice*.

There's a desk covered with papers, and a large bookshelf teeming with books as well. I walk toward the bookshelf, expecting textbooks, maybe canonized novels that he had to buy for freshman-level English classes or something. Instead, I find shelves filled with hardbacks of young adult fiction books, mostly fantasy and sci-fi, and decorated with random origami figurines. I've read a good portion of these books, and I'm giddy at the thought of him having read them too.

"This is the series I'm on now," he says from behind me, and he reaches over my shoulder to skim his fingers over the spines of four colorful hardbacks. "The final book just came out. You read it?"

"Yeah, actually." I grab one of the books off the shelf and flip through it. "I think it's one of my favorites. That battle scene at the end of book three was so intense that I couldn't read anything else for almost a month after."

"Oh man, same. I was fucked up. I literally preordered book four the minute it was available."

"I did too," I exclaim. "I'm kind of a sucker for Fae fantasy, anyway." I glance over my shoulder at him. "Even more if it's got some steam in it."

He chuckles. "This one's got some steam, alright. Caught me off guard, but I'm good now."

"Not a big fan of sex scenes?" I turn to face him and lean lightly on the desk next to the bookshelf. His eyes bounce between mine.

"I can take it or leave it. You like it though?"

"Yeah," I nod, place the hardback down on the desk, then lift myself up so I'm sitting on it, "I read a lot of romance, too."

"Romance?" He gives me a funny look. "Like mommy porn?"

"Mmmm, Butch," I shake my head slowly, "you just lost cool points."

He jerks his head back and scoffs. "You're saying you don't read it for the sex?"

"Oh, I definitely read it for the sex," I say on a laugh. "But I also read it because it's empowering and creative and feminist. It makes me feel good on many different levels." I raise a brow and flash a mischievous grin. "And romance incorporates two of my three favorite F-words—*feminism* and *fucking*."

He barks out a laugh and takes a step closer. "What's the third?"

"*Free.*" I widen my eyes and give him a *duh, what else would it be?* expression.

"What about *fun?*" He takes another step forward and puts his arms on the desk on either side of me, boxing me in.

A tingle of excitement skates down my spine, quickening my breath, but I cock my head to the side and play it cool. "What about my three words isn't fun to you?"

A wide grin spreads over his face. "Touché, Sundance."

"You a feminist, Butch?"

He nods seriously. "My momma would be disappointed if I weren't."

"That's a good answer."

"Maybe I should read some romance." His chest is inches

from mine. My fingers itch with the desire to touch him. On the bike earlier, I could feel his hard chest pressed up against my back. Now I want to feel it under my palms.

"I'll give you some recommendations."

"You do that," he breathes out, then runs his big hands up my thighs and, even through my jeans, I can feel his heat.

My heart is pounding, I'm trying desperately not to pant, and my core is on fucking fire.

When his eyes meet mine, the same desire that's flooding my body is reflected back at me. He wants me. I lick my lips, and his gaze falls to watch the motion. When he groans, I can't take it anymore, and I fist his t-shirt. As I rise up, he lowers, and we meet in the middle, our mouths colliding together.

His lips are so soft and warm and demanding. He bites my lower lip and I open for him. When our tongues tangle, he grips my waist tighter and pulls me into him.

"Fuck," he groans into my mouth. "Your tongue tastes like cherries." He dives back in with another devouring kiss. Like he can't get enough. Like he wants to eat me. And I want to let him.

I pull back and smirk at him. "Want to see how the rest of me tastes?"

"Holy fuck," he grinds out, then lifts me up by my ass. I wrap my legs around him instinctively, and he walks us backward before spinning and dropping me on the bed. He's on top of me before I can blink, and I explore his torso with my hands, taking special care to run my palms over his pecs and brush my thumbs over his nipples. His chest rumbles, and I can feel it running up my arms and through my body, like an electric current of desire.

"Take this off," I demand, and tug his shirt upward.

"Yes, ma'am," he replies, and uses one hand to reach behind his shoulders and pull his shirt over his head. Oh my god, why is that so hot? He tosses his shirt off the bed, boxes me back in with his arms, and I just kind of stare at his body.

"Shit, you're all solid planes and smooth ridges, aren't you," I breathe out, and run my fingers over his abs. "So this is what they mean when they say washboard."

He lets out a loud burst of laughter, and tries to resume kissing me, but I put up a hand to stop him.

"Gimme just another second. I'm committing this body to memory for later."

He laughs again and sits back on his ankles. "And what about me? Don't you think I should get the same opportunity?"

"Need spank bank material, Butch?" I grin at him, then sit up and rise onto my knees. Even mirroring his stance, I have to look up to see his face. And what a face it is.

"Yes, please." So polite. His eyes are on me with rapt attention, and I feel *powerful*. I play with the hem of my shirt, and his gaze is stuck on my fingers, waiting. Anticipating.

"Fuck, Sundance, don't make me wait any longer," he grinds out, without taking his eyes off my hand. His blatant hunger spurs me on, so I slowly pull my band tee off and drop it on the floor next to the bed.

"Christ," he whispers, and reaches out to palm my breast through my black lace bralette. It's nothing special, but he's staring like it is. He gives my breast a gentle squeeze, and I drop my head back and release a whimper.

He bends down and takes my nipple into his mouth, biting and sucking it through the lacy fabric of my bra, then meets my eyes and says in a voice thick with desire, "*Je veux te faire jouir.*"

Oh, okay.

That was sexy. I have no idea what he said—could have been "fancy a pb&j?" for all I care—but that was hot. *Hello,* French dirty talk. I'm a little stunned, head foggy with lust and need, so I say the first thing that comes to my mind.

"Voulez-vous coucher avec moi ce soir?"

His lips twitch, and I can tell he's trying to hold back a laugh. There's a sexy growl from his throat that makes me tighten my thighs.

"Oui," he says, his eyes dancing. Damn this man.

Alex grabs my waist, pulls me back to him, and attacks my lips with another desperate kiss. I pull back slightly with a smile, toying with him, and dip my tongue in and out of his mouth, caressing his tongue and then making him chase me. I reach my hand into the back of his joggers, gripping his tight ass and squeezing hard. He bites my lip, groans into my mouth, and moves his hands to the button on my jeans.

"I'm gonna fuck you so good you'll be thinking about it for weeks," he whispers as he drags my zipper down.

"Prove it," I taunt, and he tugs my jeans over my ass and down my thighs.

Then we're being halted by his phone alarm. It's one of the loud, foghorn-type ones, and I wince at how annoying the sound is.

"Cupcakes," he grunts against my lips. He rips himself away from me and walks backward toward the door. "Don't move. Not a single inch. I'll be right back." Then he darts into the hallway, and I hear the loud thumps of him running down the stairs.

Because he told me not to move, I stand up and take my jeans off. Then my socks. Because who the hell has sex with socks on? Not me. I drop them where my shirt has already been discarded by the bed.

Should I take off the bralette? I hear clanking in the kitchen and quicken my movements. *Yes, I should.*

I'm dropping the bralette on top of my pile of clothes when he comes rushing back into the room, and he skids to a halt. His gaze eats up my bare skin, turning my nipples to stiff peaks and setting me ablaze.

"I told you not to move," he growls.

I shrug. "Oops."

I put my hand on my hip and pop it out, power-pose, and wait as he looks me over. I'm almost completely naked, wearing just a pair of plain red cotton underwear, but I could be sporting the latest Savage X Fenti line with how slack his jaw goes, how scorching hot his eyes flare. When I feel his eyes settle on the tattoo on my chest, I speak up.

"I'm at a disadvantage here, Butch."

He raises his eyes to mine with a smirk. "Yeah?"

I nod. "Level the playing field." I gesture to his lower half. "Pants."

Alex complies without question, keeping his eyes on me as he lets his joggers fall to his feet and kicks them to the side of the room. Then he takes off his socks, thank god. When he stands back up to his full height, I lose my cocky smirk and literally gawk. His black boxer briefs are tight, really tight, and his hard dick is displayed perfectly down his muscular left thigh. I can actually see the ridge of his head outlined through the fabric.

"Holy dick print," I whisper, and his low chuckle vibrates through the room. He reaches down and grips his giant erection with his giant hand. I groan at the sight, and he squeezes and gives it a tug. I slip my thumbs into the band of my panties so I can slide them off, but he stops me.

"No." His voice is low and commanding, no room for argument, and he stalks toward me. "I'm doing that."

I gasp when he curls his hands over my ribcage, just under my arms, and brushes his thumb over my tattoo, then lower, over both of my nipples, and then the underside of my breasts, then lower still, tracking over my belly button to my hips.

When he drops to his knees in front of me, I almost come.

"You're all mine now," he says, deep and dark with promise, and he takes one of my nipples into his mouth. I plunge my fingers into his hair. God, it really is just as soft as I thought. And thick. I tug at a fistful, and he bites my nipple, making me cry out. His eyes meet mine, dark, dark brown with dilated pupils, and he grins at me.

This fucker *grins at me*, mouth full of my fucking tit, and drags my panties down to my ankles. I step out of them, then he lifts me up, puts me on the edge of the bed and spreads my legs so I'm totally exposed.

I lean back on my elbows and watch him, his wide shoulders settled between my parted thighs. It's so sexy; I can't even handle it. I'm tingling everywhere, ready and wanting. His eyes set me on fire, first on my pussy, and then up to my face.

"You're soaked," Alex says with a devilish smirk, and I roll my eyes.

"No shit, Sherlock. What are you going to do about it?"

"I've got big, *big* plans." He raises one eyebrow, smirk still on his face, and glides his thumb through my folds and over my clit.

"Yes," I gasp, and drop my head back. He rubs my clit in little circles with his thumb, and I'm just about to spur him on when he replaces his thumb with his mouth. "Oh, fuck yes."

I rise back up on my elbows and watch as he closes his entire mouth over me and licks with the flat of his tongue, never taking his eyes off me. When he sucks on my clit, I moan and raise my hips, wanting more. Needing more. He chuckles against me, and goosebumps erupt over my entire body. When I feel one of his thick fingers circling my opening, I drop back down on the bed and fist his hair in my hands.

Slowly, so slowly, he presses into me, first one finger, then a second, and with his tongue and lips attending to my clit, I can't separate the sensations. All I can do is rock against his mouth and pull on his hair, and soon, I'm riding his face as he fucks me with his fingers. The scruff on his jaw scrapes against my inner thighs, and when he flicks his tongue quickly on my clit, I feel him start to add a third finger. I don't think I've ever gotten a third finger before, and I want it. I want his.

"Oh my god, Alex." I press against him as he slides in, and after only a few pumps from his fingers, a few more licks and sucks, I can feel myself start to tighten and my hips start to quake. "Alex, I'm gonna come. Keep doing it just like that," I cry out, and he continues to flick and suck my clit as his fingers curl inside me, stroking my inner walls.

When I come, my orgasm blasts through me, bunching up all my muscles and making me quiver in a way I've never felt before. I clamp my thighs closed, but Alex uses his arms to press them back open, tonguing my clit until I start to jerk and shake, pulling harder on his hair.

"Oh my god," I say, "no more, no more."

He brings his mouth to my hip bone and bites, then sucks, and I know I'm going to have a mark tomorrow. When he stands, I sit up and immediately go for his boxer briefs.

"Off," I demand as I grip the band and tug down. From our position, the movement is awkward, but I don't care. I don't care about anything. I just need him inside me. I need to feel whatever it was I just felt again.

He takes a step back and replaces my hands with his, pulling his underwear down and allowing his erection to spring free.

And Ho. Ly. Shit.

"What the hell, Alex," I groan. "You're smuggling a freaking baseball bat in your pants." He laughs at me, loud and uninhibited, and for so long that he has to brace his hands on his knees.

"This isn't a laughing matter, Butch. You're gonna impale me with that thing."

He flashes me a salacious grin that I feel all the way to my toes. "I'll go gentle on you."

"Oh, no you won't." I want to prop my hand on my hip, but I can't because of how I'm sitting. "Get over here and fuck me so good I'll be thinking about it for weeks." The laughter vanishes from his face, and he stalks toward me.

"You want me to slide home," he growls as he climbs on top of me, boxing me in once more.

"Yes," and I grab his hair again and pull his mouth to mine.

Alex reaches in the drawer of his bedside table and pulls out a condom, and I take it so I can be the one to put it on him. I grip him and smirk when he thrusts into my hand.

"Patience," I tease against his mouth, and I slowly roll the condom down his thick shaft. Once it's on, I rub his head up and down my slit, and I'm so keyed up—so turned on—that I whimper at the contact. Alex places his hand over mine, guides his dick to my entrance, and pushes in. He goes slowly, allowing me to adjust to his size, to the weight and feel of him, and when he's fully seated, we both moan.

"I can feel you in my throat," I say on a gasp as he begins to move with long, deep strokes.

"Fuck, Sundance," he grinds out, "don't say shit like that." He hoists one of my legs over his bicep, and I can't hold back my shuddering cry.

"Oh my god, you feel so good."

He's barely moving, but the heavy, full feel of him has me reeling. When he starts to pick up speed, stars dance in my vision, and I move with him, chasing the high. Chasing the sparks.

"Fuck, you're sexy," he pants, and I grab onto his biceps—rock solid and smooth. I can feel them strain under my fingers as he pushes into me, and I squeeze. He kisses me, rabid and hungry, and when I bite his lip, he grunts and thrusts harder.

"Yes," I urge and buck into him. "Fuck me hard like that."

"You want it hard, Sundance?" His rough, rhythmic movements don't falter when he bends down and sucks on my neck, then rumbles onto my skin, "You want me to beat this pussy up?"

"Oh my god, yes."

He hoists my other leg up, so both are resting on his shoulders, then he shoves something soft under my ass. A pillow, maybe?

"Hold on tight, baby." He flashes me the sexiest grin I've ever seen, sweat dotting his forehead, his hair framing his face, and I clench around him just to see the lust in his eyes burn brighter. Before I can mirror his grin, he speeds up.

And *fuck me*.

He pounds into me so hard, so fast, that my teeth rattle and my pussy sings. The spot deep inside that he's hitting is torturously good. I watch where we're connected as he moves in and out at rapid speed. From this position, all I can do is watch and grip him, squeeze his arms and dig into his biceps with my nails. I want to move with him, to give him back what I'm getting, but I can't. He's in complete control, and I'm obsessing over it. It's amazing, the way he's owning me like this. The way he's hitting me so deep. I don't want it to end, but I'm not sure I'll survive it.

"Is this what you wanted?" he says as he does what he promised. As he fucks me so good I'll be thinking about it for weeks. "You're gonna feel me for days, Sundance."

I bounce my eyes between his dick and his face. I don't know what view is sexier—the picture of dominance on his features or the way he's stretching and filling me. How red and swollen and soaked my pussy looks. I clench around him, my walls start to convulse, and oh my god, I'm gonna come again.

"Yeah, baby," he says, never slowing, unrelenting, "come all over my cock. Let me feel that pussy choke my dick." *Holy whoa, the mouth on this one.*

"Oh fuck, Alex. Oh fuck, oh my god," I chant, and I clamp my eyes closed as I detonate. My cry is unrecognizable, animalistic and feral, and he continues thrusting until I'm shaking and shoving at his chest.

He drops my legs and kisses me hard, and I thread my fingers through his hair, pulling him into me. Our tongues tangle, and his hand runs up and down my body, pinching my nipple and squeezing my ass. Then he's pulling out of me and flipping me onto my stomach, so quickly I don't realize it happened until my face is in the mattress and he's pulled my hips up, so I'm on my knees with my ass in the air.

I rise up on my forearms and look over my shoulder, just in time to see him thrust back into me, his eyes on my pussy, and my responding moan matches his in desperation.

"Alex," I choke out, and he chuckles in that low, rumbling, devious way that vibrates through me.

"We're not finished yet, Sundance." He runs his palm down my spine and then smacks my ass. He strokes in and out of me, slower this time, but no less punishing, and despite my exhaustion, I rock my body back into him, feeling my ass hit his hip bones. When he speeds up, so do I, and I have to prop a hand on the headboard to brace myself. To meet him thrust for thrust with equal power.

"You're going to come again," he commands behind me and reaches around to rub my clit.

"I am," I say, and I don't know if I want to press back into his body or down onto his hand. When he pinches my clit, the decision no longer matters, and I come, for the third time tonight, on his dick as he fucks me, rubbing my clit and stroking inside me until I let out a sob and have to reach beneath myself to still his hand.

He laughs. The fucker *laughs*, and I'm too blissed out to care.

He grabs my hips and pounds into me a few more times, rhythmless and frantic, until he groans loudly with his release.

I faceplant into the mattress and he gets up to dispose of the condom. Then he drops down next to me, making me bounce from the impact, and for a few minutes, we just lie there panting. I have to wait to regain consciousness—for my soul to return to my body—because oh. My. *God*. That sex was phenomenal.

I mumble it out, to commend him on a job well done, and he smacks my ass again.

"You're unbelievable," he breathes, and I turn my head to meet his eyes. They're on me. Dark, chocolate brown and dancing with something I've never seen before. Some sort of post-sex magical juju or some such sorcery. Whatever it is, I blink and roll over. It's time for me to bounce before things get weird.

"Nope," he blurts and puts his giant hand on my thigh, "we're spooning."

"You want to cuddle?" I ask on a laugh.

"Fuck yeah, I wanna cuddle," he says as he pulls and maneuvers me so I'm curled in front of him. "Just give me ten minutes and we can go again." I feel him settle behind me, his arms draped possessively around my body and his breath warming my scalp through my sweaty sex hair. I barely did anything, but I feel like I just ran one of Kelley's marathons. My muscles relax despite the unfamiliar territory and my eyelids grow heavy.

"Ten minutes," I say on a sigh, and let my eyes drift closed.

• • •

I wake feeling overheated and trapped.

There's something large and heavy holding me down, and for a split second, I feel afraid. But then the surrounding room comes into focus, and I take note of the soothing deep breathing behind me, the familiar muscular arm that's wrapped around my body, and the large hand that's currently cupping my breast. I have to stifle a giggle. We're here, sleeping naked in Alex's bed, and dude is just casually holding on to my tit. Ridiculous.

Carefully, I remove his hand from my chest, slide my body slowly out from under his arm, then gently put his arm back on the bed. I start to gather my clothes from the nice, easily accessible pile I put them in, but I can't find my underwear.

Where the hell are they?

Shit, that's right. He took them off me. I huff.

I do a quick scan of the room but don't see my red cotton panties, and when Alex's big body rustles on the bed, I abandon my search and put my jeans on commando. Once dressed, I tiptoe to the door and take one last glance at the big, beautiful man on the bed. I feel a small twinge of something, a teeny tiny ache, and then I turn and walk out.

I slip on my Docs when I hit the bottom of the stairs, but before I can walk out the front door, I remember the cupcakes. My stomach rumbles at the thought. Damn it. I glance up the stairs and listen closely, but there's no sign of movement, so I make my way into the kitchen on light feet.

The funfetti cupcakes have been placed on a cooling rack on the counter, and the bowl of icing has been covered with a plastic lid. To say I'm impressed at the tidiness is an understatement.

I open random drawers until I find the one with silverware and take out a butterknife. Then I snag one of the cupcakes, pop open the bowl of icing and scoop some out onto the cupcake. I spread the icing on the top, then lick the excess off the butterknife. The fudge and cherries burst on my tongue, and I release a tiny hum of appreciation. I put the knife on the counter and peel back the cupcake wrapper, taking a giant bite and savoring it.

Damn, that's good.

"Now who's the thief?"

I jump at the rumbling voice behind me, and whirl to find Alex leaning on the wall, arms crossed, and wearing only a pair of joggers. His eyebrow is raised and he's smirking at me, and if I weren't so startled, I might gawk at how hot he looks.

"I helped make these," I say, and lick some icing off my finger. "Technically, I should be entitled to half of them." I take another bite and delight in how his eyes are drawn to my mouth. He watches as I chew and swallow, and when I peek my tongue out to lick my lips, he pushes off the wall and walks toward me.

"You dippin' out?" he asks, and I nod, placing my half-eaten cupcake on the counter beside me.

"Classes tomorrow."

He stops in front of me, eyes still fixed on my mouth.

"You've got icing," he murmurs, and when he reaches up and rubs my lower lip with his thumb, I can't stop the thundering of my heart.

He brings his thumb up to his own mouth and sucks on it, and I can't fight the tremble that runs through my body. His eyes are full of heat, my head filled with flashes of what we did in his bedroom just a few hours earlier, and I have to take a slow, steadying breath.

"I think cherries might be my new favorite, too," he whispers.

I give him a small smile, commit his brown eyes to memory,

then step around him slowly and make my way down the hall and out the front door.

When I reach Baby, Alex calls to me from the small front porch.

"I still didn't get your name."

I pause and cock my head to the side. "You did a pretty good job sleuthing out the last mystery, Butch," I say, and a grin spreads over his face. I swing my leg over my bike and ready my helmet. "Let's see if you can go two for two, yeah?"

He lets out a laugh, and then I drive away.

bailey

I DON'T HEAR from Alex all day. It's not a surprise, really. We both got what we wanted out of the exchange. And though I've caught myself dazing off, reliving moments of last night or absentmindedly brushing my hand over the mouth-shaped bruise on my hip, I'm cool with the silence.

It may have been the hottest lay of my whole damn life so far, but I'm a young, sexual being, and dicks are everywhere—both literally and figuratively. I'm not concerned.

I go to my classes and manage to avoid conversation with everyone, which means I thankfully don't have to explain to anyone that, no, I'm not scowling at you, that's just the way my face looks. Around noon, I grab a smoothie with my friend Jesse in the student union. As usual, he carries the conversation rambling on about his mom, his med school interviews, and the new knitting project he's working on. Then I head back to my apartment later that afternoon to knock out some cookie experimenting.

Ivy isn't home when I get here, but that's not unusual. She's been studying for the LSAT like crazy, and though I miss her, I'm so proud of her. She's come a long way from the scared, timid girl I roomed with sophomore year. She might be a little too chipper at times, might be a little too friendly and talkative, a little too obsessed with pros/cons lists, but she balances me. I like to think I balance her, too.

I was a mess when I transferred to Butler University sophomore year. Broken and sad and pissed off at the world. I'll admit that I immediately judged the gorgeous, curvy, blonde bombshell who was to be my roommate in the dorms. Thought for sure we would clash, would hate each other, and the year would end up being a continuation of the nightmare I was currently living.

But she surprised me.

I surprised me.

Turns out, we were both dealing with some shit—both trying to find our way out of a personal darkness, trying so damn hard to heal—and together, we helped each other find a glimmer of light. Now here we are, senior year of college, roommates once more and slightly less broken with each passing day.

Ivy is my kindred spirit. My sister of the moon. My soulmate. I love that girl, and I'll fight anyone who talks shit.

Well, I'll have some choice words for them, anyway.

Let's be real—I'm puny and unlikely to inflict much physical damage. Ivy made me go to self-defense classes with her one summer, so I know some need-based defensive moves, but I'm probably a goner in a street fight.

I sit down at the kitchen island with my notebook and a pencil. I've got cherries and a pair of chocolate brown eyes on the brain, and it shows in the cookie recipe I draft up. I don't have the ingredients to bake it just yet, but when I do, I think this one could be delicious. I write out a shopping list to get me through the next few recipes, tally up the approximate cost, and stick it to the refrigerator with a magnet. I'll have to ask Ivy if I can borrow her car—this much stuff requires a trip to the Wal-Mart, a few miles off campus, and I don't think I could carry it all in a backpack on Baby, even if I wanted to.

I resist the urge to go count the money in my Crisco can. I know the total hasn't changed since I last counted. The sticky note inside displays the same number it did before. But I feel like no matter how much I put in, I'm always having to take it back out again. I rub my chest. This is an important investment. Winning this contest would mean I could retire the Crisco can for good. I glance at the calendar on the fridge—the date of the Bakery On Main Cookie Contest is circled in purple highlighter, while two other dates, unmarked except for the ink on my skin, stare back me.

A promise and a debt.

Redemption-in-waiting.

I work on some homework for one of my accounting classes until my back and head ache. I luckily finished my required internship hours over the summer—any excuse not to have to go home—and all I have to worry about now are my final credit hours and business electives. Honestly, I really hate accounting. The internships were torture *and* unpaid. But I'm good with numbers, and this program guarantees a good paying job right after graduation. I glance at my pile of recipe notebooks—legal pads that Ivy gets for free from the law firm where she interns. Not all of us have the luxury of doing what we love for work. Sometimes, you just have to work so you can afford to do what you love.

Ivy texts around six to let me know she'll be home by eight, and she's going to bring home takeout from the burrito place on campus. My stomach rumbles, and I text her back a thank you. I didn't even realize I was hungry until I saw the words "steak burrito" on my screen.

I pack my shit back up into my backpack and drop it on the

floor of my bedroom, then take my glass of wine from last night out of the fridge, removing the plastic wrap lid and taking a sip. Snagging my phone off the counter, I walk out to the balcony and settle into my wicker bowl chair.

I'm reading this new enemies-to-lovers book on my e-reader app, and I'm just getting to the good part. I seriously love a good hate sex scene. Honestly, I enjoy them way more than the lovey-dovey sex scenes. Something about hate sex just seems hotter. Sexier. More enjoyable. My body tingles at the memory from last night that invades my head. The big hands that gripped me hard. The punishing, relentless pace. The deep, dark, commanding growls. The smattering of small bruises left on my skin.

Without thinking, I close out of the e-reader app and check my texts.

Nothing.

I go back to reading.

Ivy brings home dinner, and we eat it together in the living room while watching an episode of one of the true crime shows she likes. We don't talk much. She's exhausted, and I enjoy the silence. When she heads to bed, so do I.

I'm plugging my phone in on my nightstand when a text from Alex comes in.

I open it and find a single picture.

A picture of his thick wrist, adorned with woven bracelets, and his big, tan hand fisted around something red.

Red and cotton.

My underwear.

In spite of myself, I shiver.

Me: Where'd you find them?
Unknown: Under my mattress.
Unknown: Where I put them.

Unknown: Right before I made you come on my face.

Jesus. Now it's in my head. The whole night, every lick and bite and kiss. All of it.

My entire body warms, my face flushes, and I release a small puff of breath. I'm thinking of how to respond, of what I could possibly say to regain the upper hand, when he sends me one last text.

Unknown: Sleep tight Sundance.

I put the phone back on my nightstand without replying. Then I pull out my vibrator and turn off the light.

* * *

"Coffee," Ivy sings when I come stumbling out into the kitchen two days later, turquoise hair in a rat's nest and yesterday's eyeliner smudged. I'm fucking gorgeous in the mornings.

Ivy and I had some much-needed girl time last night, and I may have hit the wine a little hard since I don't have an early class on Wednesdays. I haven't heard a damn peep from Alex. Not a single word since he sent me that stupid picture of my underwear on Monday night. At first I was kind of bummed, and then I was pissed that I was bummed, but I'm good now. He was always temporary, anyway. I'm just mad I lost a pair of panties.

Ivy is already showered and dressed in her typical campus outfit—leggings and one of Kelley's old shirts—when I plop into the chair in the kitchen. She slides a coffee mug in front of me, already poured and doctored in the way I like, and leans her hip on the counter.

"How you feelin?"

I close my eyes and take a sip of my coffee, then release a pleased sigh. "A little fuzzy, but mostly fine."

I hear her slide something on the table and open my eyes to find two ibuprofens next to my coffee. I blink up at her. "I love you. You know that?"

"I love you, too." She smiles. "Any plans with the baking aisle boy?" She eyes me with a small, knowing smile.

I mentioned Alex briefly, very briefly, last night. It was maybe two sentences, tops. But she senses something—the tiny droplet of blood in the water of my calm, cool demeanor. It's that killer attorney instinct of hers, her mom-like intuition. Bitch is too freaking observant. For as oblivious as she is about her and Kelley's "friendship" (heavy on the quotation marks), she doesn't miss a thing otherwise. I'd be irritated if I didn't love her so damn much.

I pop the pills in my mouth and shrug off her question with another sip from my coffee mug. I feel her eyes on me, so I keep mine closed as I swallow. She waits another second, just long enough to determine that I am not, in fact, going to talk about it this morning, and then she changes the subject.

"Kelley's soccer thing is just drills tonight, but they've got a scrimmage next Wednesday if you wanna come with me. I asked Jesse already and he's down."

Kelley plays on an intramural soccer team that meets Wednesday nights. Ivy watches him play most nights, even when it's just practice, but Jesse and I usually tag along when there's a game.

It's a whole thing.

Kelley will kick ass on the soccer field, Ivy will unconvincingly pretend like she's not drooling over his hot bod the entire game, and Jesse will irritate the shit out of me with his constant bouncing, rambling, and immature jokes. Then we'll all go get tacos.

It's fun.

And anyway, is it really your found family if you don't want to pummel at least one of them from time to time?

"Yeah, I'll go. As long as I don't get called in to the bar, I'm there."

"Good." She hits me with one of her warm, concerned mom looks. Her voice is soft and low when she asks, "And how's your head? So far."

I resist the urge to rub at my chest, to look at the calendar on the fridge, and answer her honestly. "So far, I'm okay. It's already not as bad as last year."

She nods. "I'm here if you need anything, you know? Anything at all."

"I know, V." She's probably the only person who's ever said those words to me and meant them unconditionally. "Thank you. I promise to let you know."

Ivy smiles in that sunshiny way of hers, with her dimple on display and her blue eyes bright, and slips her messenger bag over her shoulder, just as my phone vibrates on the table beside me. I flick my eyes to the screen and my breath catches the teeniest, tiniest bit when I see a text from an unknown number. *Alex.*

"I've gotta go," she says as she walks toward the door. "Tell baking aisle boy I said hello, if you see him." She waggles her brows and I roll my eyes at her. Too. Freaking. Observant.

"Love you, V," I say as she opens the door.

"Love you back, B," she sings right before the door shuts behind her.

In spite of the pull to do so, I don't touch my phone. I finish my coffee. Eat a pop-tart. Take a washcloth to my disaster of a face and a brush to my bigger disaster of a head. I get dressed in a pair of black fishnet tights, black cut-off jean shorts, and a The Used shirt. Then I throw on some socks, apply my standard eyeliner, mascara, and ChapStick, and slip into my Docs. Despite being September, it still feels like summer in Indiana, so I forego a jacket.

After I slip my backpack over my shoulders, I pick up my phone.

Unknown: Thoughts on John Hughes movies.
Unknown: And not just if you like them or not.
Unknown: Deeper.
Unknown: Go.

Ok, well that's random. Lucky for him I have a whole drawn out response for this question, because I've thought about it a lot.

Me: I have a love/hate relationship with John Hughes. I used to really enjoy his movies, but the older I get, the more critical I get. I still can watch and enjoy them but I can't help but recognize the flaws.
Unknown: You mean the racism and sexism?
Me: Exactly that. I mean, Sixteen Candles is hella problematic. Long Duck Dong AND encouraging date rape. Not cool at all. They're full of stereotypes, too.
Unknown: Not to mention Andi should have chose Ducky.
Me: OMG YES SHE SHOULD HAVE. Blaine was a tool bag.
Unknown: How about Spielberg?
Me: Ugh I don't want to love him, but I do. Did you know E.T. was the first movie to use product placement with the Reece's Pieces? M&M's were offered the spot but they turned it down.
Unknown: I did not know that.

Me: The more you know. *rainbow emoji*

Alex and I exchange a few more texts, and then I put my phone in my bag and head to class. I'm grinning from the text exchange. Who'd have thought we'd have this much in common? Definitely not me.

Classes blow. I've got two this afternoon. A 90-minute lecture and then a small 45-minute discussion class. The professor in my lecture has a voice that grates on my nerves, so I spend most of it texting in my group thread with Ivy, Kelley, and Jesse and doodling song lyrics in my notebook. These lectures are always posted online, but the douche takes attendance, so I have to show up.

My discussion class isn't as bad. I make sure to speak up a few times to get my participation points. Having a 45-minute class after a 90-minute class makes me appreciate the shorter class more. By the time I'm done, I'm ready to be *done*.

I'm walking across the quad to the student parking lot, just about to shove in my earbuds, when I hear my name called.

"Bailey! Bailey Barnes!"

I halt my steps and look behind me to the voice. Well, what do you know? It's Butch Cassidy. I fight my smile and force a suspicious glare as he jogs to my side.

"Okay," I say on a sigh. "How'd you do it?"

He shrugs. "Facebook."

"Facebook?" I laugh. "No way. My profile is locked down tighter than Fort Knox."

"Yeah, but Bar 31's page isn't." He grins proudly, and I squint at him.

"I don't have anything connecting me to Bar 31. I don't have my job listed."

"On St. Patrick's Day last year, a one Jada Simmons has the whole bar staff tagged in a post about green lager and Guinness." He raises an eyebrow. He wants me to be impressed. I am, but I hide it.

"She tagged the whole staff," I say slowly. "That's a ton of people."

He nods. "Twenty-seven."

I widen my eyes and wave my hand in an *okay, continue* expression.

"Process of elimination."

I bark out a laugh. "How? My Facebook profile picture is of E.T. wearing a dress and a wig from the movie."

"Exactly." His straight white teeth are shining bright. I swear the sun glints off them with a little sparkle.

I pause a minute, searching for an explanation, and then it dawns on me.

"The texts. Spielberg." His grin is blinding, and he winks at me. "You're a sneaky bastard."

"I'm a clever bastard."

"It could have been anyone. What if I didn't have Facebook at all and you were creepin' on some rando?"

"Thought of that, but then you stopped when I called out Bailey, so that's when I knew for sure."

I shake my head, then continue walking.

"What are you doing tonight?" he asks as he falls in step beside me.

"I have plans." I don't tell him they're with my shitty Wal-Mart mixer and some baked goods.

"What about tomorrow?" I can feel him looking at me, so I shake my head with a playful sigh.

"Excitable and impatient."

He just shrugs with a smile. "I know what I like."

I pop a brow and slow to a stop.

"I've got plans, Butch. Tonight, tomorrow night, and the next night."

"Are you always this difficult?"

"Are you always this persistent?"

One could argue that I've been a grumpy bitch to him, but he's really digging in those heels. Big heels. On big feet. Jesus.

"When I want something, yeah."

"And I suppose that's me this week? Lucky me." I do my best to hide the flicker of excitement that shoots through me, but judging by the wicked grin he's sporting, I wasn't successful.

"This weekend, then." His unrelenting eyes search mine, and they dance with heat and suggestive promise. When he bites his full bottom lip, thoughts of Sunday night flash through my mind. His hands on me. His mouth on me. Him inside me. When his jaw clenches and his pupils widen, I know he knows what I'm thinking.

"Okay." I give in. "Maybe this weekend."

When I walk away, he doesn't follow, but he calls out from behind me. "See you soon, Sundance. I'm looking forward to it."

Yeah. Yeah, me too.

* * *

The past week and a half has been filled with classwork, bartending, and baking. A lot of irritation when it comes to my Crisco can, too, but it's been alleviated by my texts with Alex and our clandestine meetings.

We hooked up over the weekend, Saturday after my shift at the bar, and Sunday afternoon between studying and baking. Both times at his house, so I could leave right way, and both times his roommates weren't home. I've only told Ivy a little about him, mostly because she's been busy with the LSAT and caught up in her own little Kelley-fogged bubble. She can tell there's something I'm not saying, but she doesn't pry. She has her own experience with secrets.

Last night, she came home freaking out because Kelley almost kissed her, and—shocker—she wanted him to do it. She was going to avoid him, as V is apt to do when she's overwhelmed with emotions, but Jesse and I orchestrated a secret intervention at Keggers tonight, one of the other popular campus bars. It's hilarious and fulfilling to watch as they finally, *finally*, act on their repressed mutual attraction. And I have to admit, they make a seriously gorgeous couple. Kelley with his athletic build, auburn hair, and hazel eyes, and Ivy with her curves, blonde waves, and baby blues. They're so wholesome and hot. If they weren't my friends, I'd totally watch that porn. No shame.

After watching Kelley and Ivy eye fuck each other for the last few hours, I'm high on the sexual tension and horny as hell, so I text Alex and discover he's at Bar 31. He thought I would be working, and I warm knowing that he was seeking me out again. I would have been bartending tonight, but I switched shifts so I could go out with V. When V leaves Keggers, I walk the few blocks to Bar 31.

I find Alex at the end of the bar, chatting up Jared, when I walk in. His eyes find me immediately, like he sensed my entrance, and I get chills from his heated gaze. The man looks hot. His long hair is pulled half-up into a bun, and he's sporting dark jeans that hug his monster thighs with a black button down with the sleeves rolled a few times on his pornographic forearms. I know what's under that shirt, those jeans, and my mouth waters at the visions that flash in my memory.

"Sundance," he greets me, voice low and suggestive. One word and he's got me salivating.

"Butch," I rasp back.

"D'you ride Baby?"

I shake my head slowly.

"Wanna Uber back to my place, then? My roommates are at a party."

My lips stretch into a smile, and I hold his gaze for a breath, then two, letting the tension build. When he steps closer, attention zeroing in on my mouth as if he's going to kiss me, I grab his hand and tug him toward the door. "Let's go."

We're barely through his front door before I'm on him, pulling him down to kiss me while I kick off my heels. He squeezes my ass and I twist away, walking backward up a few stairs.

"You comin'?" I purr, and when he lunges for me, I squeal and run the rest of the way up the staircase.

Once in his room, he pulls my black bodycon dress over my head so I'm standing in just a green lace thong. He groans as he palms one of my breasts, and I'm attempting to tug his shirt up when he brushes his thumb over the tattoo on my chest, just above my heart.

"E.E. Cummings," he whispers, and my breath catches as my eyes snap to his.

"You know it?" I'm in awe. I can't help it.

He nods and, once more, brushes his fingertips over the inked script.

"Yeah. I do." His gaze is penetrating, searching, and before he can ask, before he can say anything more, I silence him with my lips.

Frenzied. Hungry.

Because this is what I want. *These* feelings are the only ones I can handle.

For now.

When I sneak out later, the grass is coated in early morning dew, and the first rays of light are breaking through the silhouettes of neighboring buildings. The moon is fading, but a few gallant stars are still holding on to their shimmer, grasping tightly to their patch of sky until the sun can break and take over.

I inhale deeply and turn back to the townhouse. In the fading darkness, I don't bother hiding my smile. I'm not exactly sure what it is. Maybe I find his persistence flattering. Or maybe it was the John Hughes text. Or the bookshelf full of young adult novels. Or the fact that he recognized the script of my tattoo. Maybe it was the cupcakes. Maybe, probably, it's that I don't hate the idea of more toe-curling orgasms. Of spending more time with him.

Whatever the reason, I take out my phone and put his name in my contacts. Then I shoot him a text before climbing into my Uber. My phone chimes when I'm unlocking the door to my apartment a few minutes later, and when I check the text, for the second time this morning, I don't hide my smile.

Me: Had to dip. See you later?
Alex: Looking forward to it.

FIVE

bailey

"YOU READY?" Jesse asks as we leave the student union on Friday, smoothies in hand. The cookie contest is tomorrow, and despite my attempts at calm, my nerves are through the roof. If I didn't have so much to do, I'd go home and hotbox the bathroom just to settle myself down.

So much is riding on this contest. So, so much depends on it.

I take a pull from my straw and consider his question, then nod once. "I think so, yeah."

"You're nervous, though," he states pointedly, surveying me with a steady gaze. I roll my eyes and puff out a breath.

"Yeah, I'm nervous as shit. I really wanna win this, and I think I've got a winning recipe. It's creative and unique, but it's also kind of classic and homey." I take another sip from my smoothie and shrug. "I've put so much thought into this. And practice. And money." *Fuck*, the money. "If I don't win..."

"Don't think like that, B. You're gonna win." Jesse bumps my arm lightly with his. "You've put in the work, and you're talented as fuck. Those lil carrot cake cookie thingies are banging. The judges will love them." He stops walking and turns to me. "Manifest, B. Manifest!"

Jesse gives his shoulders a little shimmy, and the corner of my mouth tips up the smallest amount. He's such a dork. Annoys the shit out of me more often than not, too, but he's a good guy to have in your corner. He's a genuine hype man and he's fiercely loyal to his friends. I'll never admit this to his face, but I'm really glad Ivy introduced us.

"We'll see." I sigh. "You really like the cookies?"

"Hell yeah. Me, Kelley, and V all told you they're great. We wouldn't lie."

I've decided to go with a carrot cake and oatmeal raisin cookie as my submission for the contest. I've reworked the recipe three times to get the consistency I like—it's eaten up all my free time this week—and I think I finally perfected it last night. Which is good because I have to bartend tonight, and the contest is tomorrow. Talk about cutting it close.

"Okay, well, I guess I've done all I can, you know?" I shrug and start walking. When my phone buzzes in my back pocket, I pull it out and check the screen. It's a text from Alex.

"What the shit is that?" Jesse gasps, and I whip my head to him.

"What is what?" I ask. His eyes are wide, and for a minute, I'm worried that something might be wrong, until he barks a laugh.

"A smile on Ms. Bailey Barnes's face!" He puts his hand on his chest, feigning shock, and swings his gaze from one end of the quad to another. "Is there a misogynistic frat boy being humiliated somewhere? The cancellation of a Karen?" I roll my eyes and start walking, but he doesn't miss a beat. "Wait! Is someone handing out free smut?" He puts his hand on my shoulder, halting my steps. "Is the local biker gang finally accepting new members?"

His face is alight with humor. He's so damn proud of himself.

"Shut it, Jesse." I shrug his hand off my arm and say in defense, "I smile."

"Yeah, when I stub my toe or hit my head on a door frame. I did neither of those things."

"You're dumb." I huff. It *is* funny when he hits his head on low hanging door frames, though. You'd think being so tall, he'd have learned to duck by now.

"You're hiding something," he croons. "Is it a guy?"

I don't say anything, but my face must give me away, because Jesse giggles. He fucking *giggles*. God, I hate him sometimes.

"Hot damn, it's a guy. Bailey, do you have a *boyfriend?*"

"It's just someone I'm talking to." I brush it off. "It's nothing."

"Yeah, okay. Liar," Jesse taunts, and I bristle. I should be used to his needling, but sometimes I still get the urge to nut check him.

We reach the end of the quad where Jesse usually goes left and I go right, and I've never been so thankful to see this crosswalk.

"Just drop it, J," I press, and toss my empty smoothie cup into the metal trash bin next to the sidewalk. "Don't make it something it's not."

"Yeah, okay. For now." He throws away his own empty cup, then winks at me. "But with my recent success with Kelley and V, I'm thinking of expanding my matchmaking services."

"Oh my god, J, stop. No." I prop my hand on my hip and narrow my eyes at him. "First, I helped with Kelley and V, so you don't get to bogart all the credit. Second, if you try to matchmake me, I will take a pair of scissors to all of your balls. And not just the ones made of yarn."

Jesse's eyes widen in mock terror, and he stumbles backward a few steps. Then he points an accusing finger in my direction. "You're evil."

"Yes." I nod once and raise an eyebrow. "See you tomorrow?"

He rolls his eyes. "Duh. With bells on."

"You better not mean that literally." I'm serious. Jesse would totally show up to my cookie contest wearing fucking bells.

"You shall see, B." He grins again, then throws up a peace sign and walks a few more steps backward. "Deuces."

I just shake my head at him, turn on my heel, and walk away.

Once I'm certain Jesse didn't double back to follow me, I check my text from Alex. It's stupid how much my heart speeds up in anticipation. I haven't seen him since Saturday, when I took three orgasms from him and then skipped out at the first sign of dawn, but we've texted nonstop. He doesn't know that he's earned himself an official spot in my phone contacts, and I'm not going to tell him, but *I* know, and that actually excites me.

Alex: How was your smoothie?
Me: Delicious and refreshing.
Alex: What did you get?
Alex: No wait.
Alex: Let me guess.

I smile and watch the bubbles dance on the screen.

Alex: Wild Berry Blast with bananas and an energy shot.

I blink at my phone.

The fact that he's so close surprises me. How does he keep surprising me?

Alex: I'm right, aren't I?
Me: You're very close. I didn't add banana. Banana is too overpowering for a smoothie. I only like it in baked goods and certain cereals.
Alex: Do I get cool points for getting the rest right?
Alex: *praying hands emoji*
Me: Sure, Butch. I'll give you cool points.
Alex: Yesssss.
Alex: Do you work tonight?
Alex: Wanna get together?
Alex: I want to see you.

By the time I reach the student parking lot, my cheeks hurt from smiling. I can't get up with him tonight, but I like how badly he wants to see me. I'm thrilled at how badly I want to see him. It's been a while since I've felt this kind of giddy excitement about someone, and a lot longer since I've actually acknowledged it. A sneaking insecurity flares in the recesses of my mind, reminding me the risks of trusting someone, of letting them in, but I stamp it out.

Me: I do work tonight, but I can't meet up. I got some stuff to do early tomorrow that will take most of the day. Tomorrow night, though? I'll text when I'm done.
Alex: Def.
Alex: What if I come to Bar 31 tonight and keep you company while you're working?
Me: No. If you come in tonight, I'll end up going home with you and I can't do that. I'll see you tomorrow night.

Plus, it's a Friday night. I don't need company. Fridays are crazy.

I mean it, too. The last time he came into Bar 31 while I was working, I ended up shoved up against the wall outside immediately after my shift with his hands down my pants, and then tangled up in his bed sheets until early morning the next day. As great as that night was, I cannot have that distraction tonight. Not right before this contest. It's too important.

Alex: Ok. I'll see you tomorrow night.
Alex: But no standing me up.
Alex: I've got plans for you.
Me: Yeah? What are they?
Alex: It's a surprise.
Alex: But they involve my tongue, my dick, and my fingers.
Alex: And your pussy.

Jesus lord, I cannot. I breathe in and out slowly and clamp my eyes shut in an attempt to tame the chills skirting over my body and the butterflies lapping my insides. The things this man does to me.

Me: Looking forward to it.

* * *

I haven't slept.

I got home from work at quarter to three, took a few hits from my bowl to calm my shit down, then convinced myself that the six dozen cookies I had prepped for the contest weren't good enough, so I baked another two dozen.

Ivy waited up for me, thank god, because if she hadn't been home to distract me, I definitely would have gone off the rails. Gotta hand it to my bestie—she's definitely become an expert at wrangling anxiety. She's like my very own Mr. Miyagi of coping mechanisms.

By the time my alarm goes off, I'm already drinking coffee from the pot V programed the night before. She's asleep, having turned in around four, but she's letting me borrow her car so I don't have to take the cookies in my backpack on Baby.

She's an actual angel on Earth.

I'm wearing a pair of maroon pixie pants and a black button-down blouse. This contest is going to be broadcast live on *The Morning Show* on Channel 5 News, so I figured a band tee and ripped jeans weren't a smart choice. I am wearing my Docs, though. I need something familiar.

I pull up to the bakery, park, and turn off the engine, then close my eyes and do some of Ivy's breathing exercises. I recite the mantras we came up with last night, and I do as Jesse instructed. I *manifest*, even though neither he nor I have any real clue what the hell that means. I'm desperate enough at this point that I might even resort to praying.

I have to win this contest. I'm banking on it. Literally.

I made one-hundred and twenty-three bucks last night, but only forty of it went into my Crisco can. But with this prize money...

I've got two weeks.

Two weeks to be able to say it's happening.

Two weeks before I can tell him, *assure* him, that I'm following through. That I'm not letting him down. I can't start the ball rolling until I have the money, and I won't have the money in time unless I win this contest.

I will win this contest.

I grab my cookies from the passenger seat and head into

Bakery On Main where the contest is being held. Channel 5 News is already inside setting up cameras and lighting, and a young woman meets me at the door with a clipboard and a smile.

"Name?" she asks by way of greeting. Her pen is poised, ready to check me off her list of contestants, no doubt.

"I'm Bailey. Bailey Barnes."

She takes a second to scan the page, scribbles something down, and then meets my eyes with a smile once more.

"Perfect! Follow me. We'll get you all set up back here."

She turns and weaves through the people, stepping over drop cords and smiling at everyone on the way. In the back of the room, there's a long counter with five stations set up. Three contestants are already standing at the counter, setting their cookies on the provided display stands. On the side wall is another table, which I'm assuming is where the three judges will sit. Currently, the table is empty but for three name tags. From what I remember, one of the judges will be Suzette Carlier, the owner of Bakery On Main, but I'm not sure who the other two will be.

Bakery On Main isn't a small space—it's a decent-sized cafe, and students are usually in here studying or socializing any day of the week. Today, though, the store is closed to patrons, and with the camera equipment and banquet tables, it seems tiny. Closed-up. Tight.

I can't even imagine how it will feel once the contestants' guests arrive. There are five contestants including me, and each of us were allowed to invite up to four guests to watch the competition from inside the café. I only needed three of my guest tickets, but I have no idea how many people the other four contestants invited. I'm already feeling jumpy.

I try to ignore the ominous nerves swirling in my stomach.

Everything is going to be fine. I am prepared. I am ready. I will win.

The woman leads me to a back table and has me turn in my recipe card and sign a release form, then she hands me a nametag and tells me to take my cookies to the contestant table. I thank her, and head toward my competition.

"Hey," I say as I set my cookies down in the fourth spot on the counter. "I'm Bailey." I give the three strangers a small smile that probably looks more like a grimace, and they return it in kind. They each say their names, but I don't actually retain them. I think one was Joe? Joanna? Whatever. They're my competition. I'm not here to make buddy-buddy. I'm here to win.

I do a quick sweep of the room in search of the fifth contestant, but I don't see anyone, so I get to work displaying my cookies. I'm placing one cookie on each of the three small plates for the judges when I hear a giggle. I look up, eager to see who my final rival will be, to find an absolutely gorgeous brunette.

She's taller than me, with soft, subtle curves, and a lithe sort of grace. The caramel-colored highlights in her hair look like they probably cost as much as our rent payment. She's dressed in a green blouse, sleek dark skinny jeans, and a pair of nude pumps. I bet her outfit alone could fund my mission and then some. I'd be able to get rid of my Crisco can and still have enough to get a new tattoo.

I'm surreptitiously surveying her when another body catches my attention, and when I flick my eyes to the movement, my heart jumps and I gasp.

Alex.

I can't hold back the smile that takes over my face.

I was feeling so nervous, so damn scared, but seeing him puts me immediately at ease. And he looks good, too. Black dress slacks, grey fitted button down, and his hair is pulled back in a neat bun. Quite a sight for my tired eyes. I drink him in.

How did he know I would be here? Did he get my extra ticket from Ivy? I bet she reached out to him. She's so fucking observant. Or it could have been Jesse. Him and his matchmaking. God, I'd be pissed at his meddling if I weren't so damn excited. I heave a sigh of relief and wave a bit to catch Alex's attention.

When he meets my gaze, my smile is huge, but his eyes widen in surprise.

Like he's shocked to see me here.

I scrunch up my nose and cock my head to the side, giving a little *what's up?* shrug, and I watch as his eyes jump to my cookie display, and then down to something he's carrying.

Wait.

He's carrying a container. Of cookies?

He looks back at me, face still in *small animal stuck in headlights* mode, and while I'm just as shocked to see him here, I can't understand why he looks nervous. Scared, almost. Guilty?

No. No way.

He breaks eye contact when the same woman who greeted me at the door steps up to him, and I watch as they exchange words, and she checks something off on her clipboard. When she walks away, I wait for him to look back at me, but he doesn't.

Okay.

Okay, so he's a contestant.

That's not a big deal. I didn't really know he was into baking, but whatever. I mean, funfetti cupcakes? But I guess I know at least one of the other contestants isn't a threat. I hope he'll be cool with me beating him. My stomach clenches at the thought that he might hold a grudge, and I feel a brief moment of concern. But then I remind myself of my priorities, that winning this contest is essential. Plus, Alex and I have a connection, I think.

No, I'm certain.

I don't know what it is, but we've got *something*, so I'm almost positive he won't be angry when I beat him.

I take a breath and watch as he walks to the table with the release forms. When he's finished there, he turns and heads in my direction, eyes glued to the container in his hands, and a prickle of ice skates down my spine. I keep my gaze on him, willing him to look at me, but he doesn't. Not until he's setting his container down at the station next to mine.

"Hey," I say with a small laugh. "Sooo, this is surprising."

"Yeah," he chuckles nervously, busying himself with putting his cookies on his display stand, "surprising."

He's acting so strange. Like he doesn't want me to be here. Is he competitive? Is that it?

"Hey, so, no hard feelings when I beat you," I joke. I mean, I'm serious, but I say it playfully enough. "We're still on for tonight no matter what, yeah?"

He looks up at me then, finally, and he opens his mouth to speak but doesn't get the chance before we're interrupted. The hottie with a body from earlier stands next to Alex and puts her hand possessively on his forearm, and my jaw clenches.

His body is rigid, her smile is blinding, and I just stand there and gape at the train wreck of an encounter that plays out in front of me.

"Riggs, you forgot your nametag," she says, her voice sweet and lilting, and I want to vomit. Who *the fuck* is Riggs? Alex stares at me, eyes wide, until the woman tugs his arm to turn him in her direction.

"Here we go," she croons, and presses the nametag to his chest, just over his right pec. Then, leaving her hand on his chest, she puts the other on his waist, and I swear I can't breathe. "We have to make sure the judges know whose name to call when you win, right?"

He gives her a tight-lipped smile. "Thanks, Tal."

"Kiss for luck?"

No. No, please, no.

But nope, I'm not that lucky. I watch in slow motion as the girl—this absolutely gorgeous girl—slides her hands up Alex's chest, rests them on his shoulders, and leans in for a kiss.

She's aiming for the lips, but Alex turns his head so the kiss lands on his cheek, but it's enough to wake me from my nightmare. I inhale violently, discovering that I had been holding my breath, then turn and walk calmly to the bathroom.

I barely make it inside before I burst into tears.

Shit.

Damn it all to hell.

I swear, I wouldn't be crying if I'd gotten some sleep last night, but... but...

But how could I... How did he....

I run every encounter from the last month, every text and word and kiss, through my memory searching for a sign. Searching for any hint. How did I not see? How could I let him make a fool of me?

To pursue me. To text me constantly. To sleep with me repeatedly. All while having...a...a...a *Tal*. And I was *the other woman*.

I grasp and find nothing. I'm wasting time and energy. Right now, the last thing I need to do is lose my shit, but god, this feeling. Like a panic attack. Like a *heart* attack. I wet a paper towel and run it under my eyes and along the back of my neck. I do Ivy's breathing exercises in an effort to calm the violent urges in my head.

Because do I ever want to pop off. I want to punch him in

the throat. Kick him in the dick with my Docs. Shave his stupid fucking gorgeous head of hair.

I have a brief moment of weakness where I contemplate ripping out *Tal's* expensive ass highlights, but then I remind myself that it's not her fault that Alex is a dirty, lying fuckboy. It's not her fault my heart is aching in my chest. It's not her fault I fell for his act. If I thought I could do it without causing a massive scene on local television, I'd march out there right now and tell her that her boyfriend is a cheater. Girl code, you know?

But no.

Right now, I have a contest to win. I have a promise to keep.

So instead of acting on my anger, I breathe. Fortify. Harden.

Then I put on my poker face and walk back to my station. This man will never fool me again.

"Bailey," Alex whispers beside me. I ignore him. "Bailey."

"Shut. Up," I whisper through clenched teeth. "I don't care."

"It's not how it looks," he pleads, and I whip my head toward him.

"That woman. Did she or did she not come here with you?"

He blinks and swallows, then nods.

"Did she or did she not kiss you just now?" He opens his mouth to speak, but I cut him off and go for the jugular. *My* jugular. "Are you dating her?"

"Talia?" He startles, then stutters, before answering, "It's complicated."

"Fuck off," I growl.

"Jesus, Sundance, just let me explain." Alex grabs for my hand, but I snatch it away.

"*Don't* touch me. And do not call me that. Don't call me anything. Ever."

"You really think I'd do that to you? You *know* me." His voice is begging, his expression half-offended, half-pleading. I feel nothing but anger. When my eyes catch back on his nametag, I let out a sardonic laugh.

"Yeah? Do I?" I drag my attention from his nametag back to his face. "Do I know you, *Riggs*?"

The look on his face is one of guilt. Guilt and defeat. And before he can lie some more, Suzette Carlier starts to speak. We're given instructions, and in her thick French accent, she explains the basic schedule for taste-testing, judging, and announcing the winner. At some point before the filming starts, Jesse, Ivy, and Kelley walk in. They're wearing matching t-shirts that say #TEAMBAILEY on the front and are covered in puff-paint cookies. I watch as Jesse hands them some sort of knitted headbands, and they all put them on.

Honestly, they look completely ridiculous, and for a brief moment, I feel happy. These people matter. These people are here for me. They're supporting me. They're honest with me.

They matter.

People like Alex—or Riggs, or whatever his name is—do *not* matter.

I'm just about to wave at my friends when Jesse jumps up and down and causes a scene.

"Go beast mode, Bailey," Jesse shouts as he flexes his biceps and points to the B on his headband. "Hashtag Team Bailey!" He flexes again, and before he can bring any more attention to us, I shake my head rapidly at him.

"*Stop it,*" I mouth at him with a scowl. Then I drag my index finger across my throat, threatening murder if he doesn't get his crazy ass in line. Jesse's eyes go wide in mock terror, and he clutches his neck, and I have to stifle a laugh when Kelley grabs Jesse's bicep and pulls him behind him. Like a scolded child, Jesse kicks his feet and accepts his punishment with a pout, and I send Kelley a small look of gratitude. He flashes me two thumbs up, Ivy blows me a kiss, and I take a deep breath.

This will be fine.

But as the contest moves forward, I can't seem to ignore the man next to me. When we introduce ourselves, it's a punch to the gut hearing Alex state that his name is actually Riggs Stanton. When we present our cookies, I feel completely deceived at how professionally he describes his recipe and baking process. He made *palets de dame aux raisons.* A French cookie made with rum-soaked raisins, and I fume when I remember that Suzette Callier, a judge and the owner of Bakery On Main, is originally from France. Riggs sounds knowledgeable, experienced, like a real baker. Not like the boy who needed help baking funfetti cupcakes from a boxed mix. My eyes keep flitting back to his girlfriend, and the adoring look on her face just hammers home how shitty I feel. She's in love with him, and I'm a total idiot.

By the time the judges are finished, everything else in the room is a low buzz, and all I can hear are Alex—no, Riggs—all I can hear are Riggs' shallow breaths and jerky movements. When they announce the winner as Riggs Stanton, I'm shocked. I'm numb.

For about thirty seconds, I feel absolutely nothing.

And then I'm hit with a wave of emotions so strong, I sway on my feet.

Betrayal. Hatred. Despair. Guilt.

I'm seeing red. I want to scream. On the inside, I'm a mess.

I keep my face neutral, fight to keep my breathing steady, but all I can see is the date on the calendar. All I can think of is the deadline I won't reach, and the promise I'm going to have to break.

I let my guard down. I let someone in. And in doing so, I let *him* down. The only person worthy of everything good, and I've let him down. *Again.*

Tears burn the backs of my eyelids, welling up and threatening to spill, but I won't let them fall. I've had years of practice turning my outside to stone.

The man beside me shifts, and I can feel his gaze on me. His pleading gaze with his dark, chocolate brown eyes. I see his hands moving in my peripheral, his big fingers fidget, and despite his size, the movement is delicate. I know how those hands feel on my skin. I know how soft his touch can be.

I try to fight it, the way my heart clenches and aches. I try to focus on my anger, on the betrayal. I try to keep my sadness for the boy I've let down.

But deep down, I know the truth.

Underneath the fury, buried under the newfound hatred, is loss.

Loss and longing.

Mourning for the man beside me, the man I thought I knew. The man who is not at all who he led me to believe he was.

SIX

SHIT.

Fucking shit.

This wasn't supposed to happen.

The look on her face—absolute disgust.

The first full, unbidden, carefree smile I've gotten from her —the kind I've been craving for weeks—was ruined after only minutes. Replaced with something hard and dark. Something like hatred.

By the time Madam Callier announced me as the winner and presented me with a giant check for two-thousand dollars, Bailey wouldn't even make eye contact with me anymore. She acted like I wasn't even there. Like I was fucking nothing to her.

Then she left with some big guy's arm draped over her shoulder.

I've texted her five times in the last hour since leaving Bakery On Main. The first two were read, and then the rest got nothing.

If she'd just fucking let me explain.

"Earth to Riggs," Talia giggles from the opposite side of the booth. "The server wants to know if you want to order an appetizer first, or just stick with the pizza."

Talia insisted on us going out to celebrate my win. I said yes because I've got nothing else to do. It's not like I can chase after Bailey. I don't even know where she lives.

I send the server an apologetic smile before saying, "Just the pizza. I'm not that hungry." He writes down the order and scurries away.

"Since when are you not hungry?" Talia asks with a laugh. "Usually, you'll eat the whole pizza without even saving me a slice. I have to fight for it."

I shrug. "It's my off-season. I'm not training as much, resting my arm, so I don't want to overdo the calories."

It's a shit excuse, but she buys it. The truth is, I can't get my head off Bailey. My gut is swirling and anything I put in it is at risk of coming right back up.

"You did so good today," Talia beams. "You worked so hard. You should be proud! Why are you acting like someone stole your favorite baseball mitt?"

I shrug. "Just feeling off, is all. It's fine."

Tal reaches over the table and places her hand over mine. I grit my teeth and resist the urge to move it. "Is it Odette?"

"No," I cut her off quickly. "No, it's nothing like that."

Her gaze is warm and concerned, and I feel a stab of guilt. Talia cares, she does. She doesn't deserve this, so I smile. "It's fine, Tal. Seriously." I put my other hand over hers and give it a squeeze before pulling both of mine away. "No worries, okay?"

"Okay." She's unsure, but for my sake, she'll drop it.

"So," she chirps, changing the subject with an upbeat voice and a wide smile, "what are you going to do with the prize money?"

"Dunno. It's not like I need it. Maybe I'll donate it to the rec center or my mom's charity."

"Those are both great ideas." Talia is glowing, her eyes full of hero worship and reverence. She thinks she knows me, thinks I'm still the same guy from our childhood, but I'm not.

Hell, I'm not even the same guy from last year.

My mind strays back to Bailey. Yet another woman I've deceived. Tricked. Betrayed. I tell myself it was unintentional, a product of miscommunication, but deep down, I know that's a lie. I had plenty of opportunities to open up, but I chose not to. Just like she stayed tight-lipped about herself.

But if she would just let me explain...

The server comes by with our pizza and refills our pops, and luckily for me, Talia's attention shifts off me. I get her talking about her classes, her dance recital prep, the charity gala her mom is planning. I keep the focus on her, so by the time I drop her off at her apartment, I can almost pretend that everything is okay.

But then I check my phone and see that my last three texts are still unread, and like an asshole, I send one more. Hoping like hell she hasn't blocked me. Because I just need a chance to explain.

I'm supposed to meet the guys at the baseball house for a party, but I'm just not in the mood, so I head back to my townhouse. I kick off my shoes, grab a beer from the fridge, and I call my mom to report on the contest. I end up having to leave a message with Ms. Beth, and I make her promise to have Mom call me back when she gets it, no matter what time.

Then I text Bailey once more, but when that text goes unread like the last three, my emotions go from worried to irritated, apologetic to offended. Who is she to just blow me off like this without giving me the benefit of the doubt? I know how it looked, but I thought I'd earned at least a little consideration over the last few weeks. I guess not.

And this is why I don't fuck around.

If she's gonna shut down and make assumptions, then fine. She brought some third-string baller to the contest, and she's gonna act like this about Talia?

Fine.

I'll let her.

Good fucking riddance.

* * *

I wake up early and hit the training gym.

It's technically the off-season, and a lot of the team are taking it easy, but as the star pitcher, I still have to train. Pitchers are made in the off-season, after all, and I didn't get this good by being lazy.

Even though I'm itching to throw, Coach Elbin will have my ass in a sling if I even think about touching a ball before November. So, I go for the next best thing—squats and dead-lifts. And luckily, I know it's unlikely any of the guys will be in this morning. There was a party last night at the baseball house that I decided to skip, partially because I wasn't in the fucking mood to pretend to enjoy beer bongs and bro talk, and partially because I'm nervous as shit that any of them caught the cookie competition live stream on *The Morning Show*. Chances are slim —none of those idiots watch *The Morning Show*—but it's still got me feeling anxious.

I knew it was a risk when I entered, but I took it because it would make my mom happy. Talia let me use her apartment to test out recipes, so I was able to fly under the radar. The only reason the KitchenAid mixer was at my house the night Bailey first came over was because I had just gotten it, and since I knew my roommates wouldn't be home, I hadn't hidden it at Talia's yet. Then yesterday, I told the guys I was hanging out with Tal, and they didn't ask questions. I had every intention of showing up at the party to keep up appearances, but when everything went down with Bailey, I just couldn't muster up the energy.

Fucking Bailey.

She still hasn't read my last messages. The one I sent around midnight last night, because I had a dumb-ass moment of weakness, doesn't even say delivered. She probably blocked my number. I could try to message her on social media, but then she'll see my carefully curated profile and likely jump to more conclusions.

I keep trying to be angry with her, but I just end up pissed at myself.

I did this.

I made my bed, and now I have to lie awake and stare at the ceiling in it.

Turning up my gym playlist, I step up to the squat rack. I start every set with "Drop" by G-Eazy, and as soon as the beat hits, my head clears of the bullshit.

I'm halfway through my second set of heavy squats when the gym door opens and in walks Xavier, one of my room-mates and my catcher. Of all the guys on the team, I'm closest to Zay. I gotta be. He's my partner on that field. But even with that connection, I still wouldn't call us *close*—not since last year, at least. I have to keep all my plays close to the vest these days.

My nerves jump. I wasn't ready to face one of them yet, and I watch him closely as he heads in my direction, scanning for any sign that he might know *something*. He's wearing his team sweats, his Beats are already on his head, and his face is a bored mask. He steps up to the rack next to me, nods in my direction, then starts stretching. When he begins his set without saying a word to me, I release a relieved breath and get started on my final set.

I'm on my first set of light deads when Zay finally strikes up a conversation.

"Missed the party last night," he says, eyes on his reflection in the wall mirror.

"Yeah," I nod, focusing on putting more chalk on my hands, "wasn't feeling it."

He just grunts. Face still bored. Tone still nonchalant. He positions himself under the bar and starts a set of squats, so I step back up to my bar and start a set of deads.

We finish our sets at the same time, and when I step back to take a breather, he drops a bomb.

"There was a cool live stream on *The Morning Show* yesterday."

I freeze, and my eyes snap to him. He's still facing the wall mirror, arms folded on top of the racked bar, but he's looking right at me.

I keep my face neutral. "Yeah?"

"Yeah." He positions himself back under the bar and readies his stance for another set of squats. "Some cookie competition for that café on Main Street."

I swallow and say nothing.

"I was at the house. Watched it on my phone." He meets my eyes in the mirror once more. "None of the other guys were awake yet."

I nod, and he starts another set, leaving it at that.

When I finish my deadlifts, I head to the mats for some core work, and twenty minutes later, I'm packing up to head out. I swing by Zay, where he's moved to the deadlift bars.

"Since when do you watch *The Morning Show*?" I ask as he drops the bar and steps back for a rest. He shrugs and takes a drink from his water bottle.

"Since sophomore year, I think." He flashes me the faintest of smiles, super rare for Zay. "Carmen Fredricks is hot, and I like when they do the 'About Town' segments. Found some cool local places that way."

"Cool." Zay really is a man of mystery. "Welp, I'm gonna head out. See you at the house."

"See ya."

"My dude!" Dylan yells as he comes through the front door later that evening. I can hear him kicking off his shoes on the mat and the jangle of his keys being hung on the hook. He comes down the hallway, sees me sitting at the kitchen table, and slaps me on the shoulder in greeting. "Riggs, man. Missed a banger of a party last night."

"I bet." I laugh at the sight of him. Pretty sure he was wearing those same clothes when I saw him on Friday, and he looks like he's about to pass out. "You look like shit."

"I feel it." He rummages in the fridge and pulls out a beer. "Gotta get my partying in before preseason. You know coach will flip shit if we go crazy once training starts."

"You mean your dad will flip shit."

"Yeah, don't remind me, bro." Dylan's dad is one of our assistant coaches, and he's definitely tougher on Dylan than the rest of the team, which is saying something, because Coach Neal is a hardass. I'm lucky I spend most of my time with Elbin, the pitching coach. I'd have a constant headache if it was Coach Neal in my ear all season.

Dylan pops open the tab on his beer and takes a swig. The front door opens again, signaling the arrival of Xavier. He comes strolling into the kitchen and nods at us, me sitting at the table with my notebook and laptop, and Dylan leaning against the counter gulping down his beer. I watch him from the corner of my eye. Is he going to say anything about seeing me in the gym?

"Missed quite the party last night," Zay says to me, no inclination that he'd already said those words to me just a few hours earlier.

"I heard." I tap my pen on my open textbook.

"Thought you said you were gonna come out." Zay eyes me and then pulls two more beers out of the fridge. He's gonna pretend we didn't see each other. Thank fuck.

"Yeah," I shrug, "wasn't feelin' it."

"Were you feelin' Talia?" Dylan jokes, and jabs Xavier's shoulder. Zay just brushes him off, hands me a beer, and heads toward the living room.

"Nah." That's all I give him, but flash him the suggestive smirk I know he's expecting. I let them think what they want. I play into it, sure, but the assumptions are theirs.

"Then it was that little punk rock pixie emo chick." I choke on my beer. Dylan's sporting a smug grin and lifts his eyebrows as if he's uncovered a huge secret. "The one with the green hair and the bike."

I can feel Zay's eyes on me when I set my beer down and hit Dylan with a glare. "How do you know about her?"

"Saw her leaving last weekend at like four in the morning. At first, I thought I was drunk and seeing things." He snorts, and my heart kicks up. "Like a little fairy sprite skipping across our lawn and climbing onto a fucking motorcycle."

"Fairies and sprites are basically the same thing," Xavier says from the couch.

"Shut up, dude. You know what I mean. She's tiny and has green hair."

"It's turquoise," I say without thinking, which makes Zay and Dylan swing their attention back on me. Dylan is smirking like an ass and Zay just looks...bored. Like usual. "What? It's turquoise. Learn your fucking colors"

"So, you *are* boning her." Dylan is such a douche. "No worries, dude. We won't tell Talia. Bro code."

"Past tense," I say, my irritation with Bailey from yesterday making a powerful resurgence. She's read all my texts but hasn't responded. "*Boned*. She's old news." The words taste bitter on my tongue, and it takes all my strength to keep my smirk from turning into a scowl.

"Dick down and dash," Dylan raises his beer in salute. "My man."

I smirk and shrug, but Zay butts in. "Sounds like she was the one dashing."

I send a glare his way, but he's not even looking at me. He still looks bored, his attention now on the flat screen as he skims through channels.

When Dylan cracks up laughing, I decide I've had enough.

"I'm out." I start gathering my shit and shoving it back into my backpack.

"Bro, it's only eight."

"Tired," I huff, and walk to the stairs.

"I bet Talia's tired too," Dylan calls from behind me, but I ignore his dumb ass and head up to my room.

I drop my backpack on my desk chair—no use trying to study now—and head into my en-suite bathroom for a shower. Perks of my dad owning the townhouse—I get the master. I'm going to shower and pass out. I'm over this weekend.

I'm jolted awake by my phone, the ringtone I saved for my mom sounding from it loudly. I take a breath, momentarily paralyzed, and then give my head a shake. She didn't call yesterday, I remind myself. She's checking in. I grab the phone and answer.

"*Maman?*"

"*Mon étoile.*" Her lilting voice greets me, and I slowly release my breath.

"Hi, Mom," I say with a smile. "How are you feeling?"

"I'm fine, darling. How are you?" She dodges the question, but I won't press. This is a call for happy news.

"Good, good. I've got a surprise."

"Oooh, do tell." I can hear the excitement in her faint French accent, and it's almost enough to hide the slight slurring.

"Remember how I told you I was entering that baking contest? The one for that café on campus?"

"*Bien sûr.*"

"Well, I made the *palets de dames aux raisons* that you like. I used your recipe."

She *ooohhs* softly and I can tell she's pleased. It makes me smile and my heart swell. I love her happy.

"And how did you do?"

"I won, Mom."

"Oh, that is wonderful! Congratulations!"

My smile is bigger than my face one second, elated that I've made her proud, but it immediately falls when I hear a small gasp.

"You sure you're okay, Mom?" I ask, trying to keep my tone calm. "I can come home."

"I am fine, Alex. Do not worry. I will see you soon."

"Okay." I inhale and exhale. "Okay, Mom. You get some rest. It's late."

"Tell Talia I send my love."

"I will. We'll video chat with you soon."

"*Je t'aime, mon étoile.*" Her voice, while full of love, is weary. I close my eyes and force yet another smile.

"*Je t'aime, Maman.* See you soon."

When I hang up, on impulse, I check my text thread with Bailey.

Nothing. Of course, nothing.

I shoot off a text to Talia, letting her know we need to

schedule a video chat with my mom, and then I lie back on my pillow. Talia won't respond until morning. Bailey won't respond ever. My mother is...well. She is what she is.

When I finally fall back asleep, it's with a frown on my face.

85

SEVEN

bailey

FIRST THING MONDAY MORNING, I make the call
I've been dreading to Flannagan's. When Mrs. Flannagan
answers the phone, I clamp my eyes closed. It's reality, now. My
failure. It's unavoidable.

"Flannagan's, this is Josie, how can I help you?" Her raspy
voice fills my ear, and I force a smile, thinking maybe she'll hear
it over the phone.

"Hi, Mrs. Flannagan. It's Bailey Barnes."

"Ah, Bailey. How's school?"

"Oh, um, it's good. I was actually calling because—"

"Hon, you need me to grab Michael?"

I sigh and nod slightly. "Yes, please."

I know I sound meek. Tired and quiet. I can't muster enthusiasm today. Not when I have to own up to yet another failure. I
zone out in self-pity while on hold, the dulcet jazz music lulling me
into a false sense of calm. A murky, sad calm, but calm, nonetheless.

"Bailey, what can I do ya for?" Mr. Flannagan says by way of
greeting. He seems chipper, but he knows. I know he knows.

"Hey, Mr. Flannagan. I was just calling to let you know I'm

gonna have to put a hold on my order again. It's just...well, some things fell through, and..."

"It's not a problem, Bailey," he says, voice soft and tinged with something I hate. "You don't need to explain. We'll hold it as long as you need."

I blow out a breath and squeeze my eyes shut again. "Thanks, Mr. Flannagan. I appreciate it."

"You just call and let us know when you're ready, alright? We won't set a date. We'll just wait till you say go."

I know it's for the best, but I wilt some more at the idea of not having an official deadline. What can I do, though? It's not like I can keep having them put me on their schedule only to shove it back again. They've got a business to run, after all.

"Sure thing, Mr. Flannagan. Thanks again."

"You take care of yourself, Bailey. No getting into trouble with them Hoosiers. Don't get comfortable there."

I snort a laugh. As if my Podunk hometown in central Illinois is more desirable. "No worries, Mr. Flannagan. Bye."

I hang up with Mr. Flannagan and then make a call to Jada, my manager at Bar 31. She's been wanting me to pick up serving shifts at Cheap Seats, the campus sports bar. It's owned by the same guy that owns Bar 31 and sometimes we trade staff. I've always turned her down because: a) serving requires way more schmoozing than bartending, and b) I freaking loathe sports. Too loud, too many people, too much shit I don't care to understand.

Sure, we get customers in to watch games on our bar televisions, but it's nothing compared to Cheap Seats. That's where the fanatics go. I just...*ugh*.

I'm desperate. There's no other way around it. So, I bite the bullet and pull up her contact, the very action sending a pang of surrender through me.

The call is short, and when I hang up, I've agreed to pick up a serving shift this Wednesday.

As in, Wing Wednesday.

Fifty-cent wings draw almost as big of a crowd as football.

Fuck me.

* * *

I hate Wing Wednesday.

Not only do I have to wear this ugly blue Cheap Seats t-shirt that's two sizes too big, but I've only been here two hours and I've already had half a pint spilled on my jeans and ketchup dropped onto my shoe. And, *of fucking course*, I forgot my non-slips, so the ketchup is on my checker-board Vans. No way I'll be lucky enough to find another pair of those at the thrift store, so that ketchup better come out or I will riot.

"Bailey," Sarah shouts from the hostess stand. I can barely hear her over the buzz of conversations and the drone of the music, but I see her wave me over, so I weave through the crowd and high-top tables until I'm in front of her.

"What's up?" I fidget with the loopy bow of my apron strings.

"I need you to take table 32. It's not in your section, but Erika just got sat with a fifteen-top and she's in the weeds." Her eyes are all business. Sarah runs a tight ship.

"I don't know what any of that means, but sure."

She rolls her eyes at me and turns to greet some new customers. While I'm waiting for her to check them in and put them on the waiting list, I readjust my ponytail, then grab a napkin from the stand and swipe it over my forehead and the back of my neck. It's hot as shit in here.

Sarah turns back to me as I'm tying my giant t-shirt up on the side with my extra hair tie. An inch of my stomach shows, and you can just see the crescent moon tattoo on my hip peeking out of my jeans. I'm doing it so I don't sweat to death, but if it also gets me tips, I'm cool with it.

"Fifteen-top means a table with fifteen customers. In the weeds means she's busy as fuck. Table 32 is the big corner booth in the back of Erika's section." I nod and she shoves five menus at me. "Go with God."

I snort a laugh and head to table 32, swinging by the drinks station to get five ice waters first.

As I approach the corner booth, I recognize a very familiar head of hair tied into a half-bun, brown scruff on a strong jaw, and tree trunk-like biceps. *Riggs.*

Next, I recognize a familiar brunette beauty, with expensive highlights and a *Vogue* cover model face, who just happens to be draped all over Riggs. *Talia.*

Awesome.

I've blocked his number and so far, have avoided looking him up on social media. I almost caved last night. I have a feeling this encounter will make or break my restraint. I steel my resolve, put on a sugary sweet smile, and walk up to the table.

I don't give a shit.

"Hey, guys," I chirp as I set out the ice waters. "Welcome to Cheap Seats. I'm going to be your server tonight."

I stand tall and lock my eyes on Riggs. He's staring at my hip, right where the crescent moon tattoo is peeking out, and I can feel the heat radiating from where his eyes are focused. I hate the pang of longing that prickles over my skin. I clear my throat loudly and his attention snaps to my face. He knows I caught him; his body is stiff as stone, but his face is an impassive mask. I raise a brow and take a minute to look him over before dropping an impromptu bomb. "My name's *Alex.*"

So much for pretending like I don't give a shit.

Riggs's eyes flare slightly, and then I look at the rest of the table. Talia is squinting at me like she knows something's up, but the other people at the table—two more guys and a girl—are completely clueless.

"Our special tonight is fifty-cent wings. That includes nuggets—I mean boneless. Can I get you guys started with something to drink besides water?"

I'm passing out the menus when one of the guys at the table—blond, fit, probably one of the jock roommates—calls me on my shit.

"Wait," blondie shouts, "your nametag says Bailey."

I widen my eyes at the guy, the picture of innocence, and say with a fake surprised giggle, "Oh! It does." Then I look back at Riggs, drop the smile, and deadpan, "my bad."

Everyone is quiet for a minute as Riggs and I have a stare off, but then Talia slides her perfect hand down his shoulder and draws my attention to her.

"We'll start off with two pitchers of Miller Lite, please." She's all smiles, but I can't stop thinking about her slender fingers and elegantly manicured nails gripping on to those familiar biceps. "We'll need a minute for our food order."

I nod and give her a tight-lipped smile, then turn on my heel to put in their drink order.

I grab the pitchers from the bar and enlist the help of one of the bussers to bring the glasses since I don't trust myself with a heavy tray. I'm still a novice at this serving thing and I'm not trying to spill a shit-ton of beer or break a bunch of glasses, especially not in front of these jerks. Riggs Stanton will never catch me off my guard ever again.

They're talking about me when I head back to the table. I can tell from the way their heads are bowed and their eyes keep shifting toward me. Of course, their conversation stops when I step up with the drinks, but I grit my teeth and swiftly get to work, setting up the glasses and pouring the first round of drinks into the pints. It's dumb that we have to do this—I'd much rather drop the pints and pitchers and be done with it—but the manager requires us to pour the first round, so I do it. Because I also am not trying to piss off the boss.

I'm pouring the fourth beer when the blond jock speaks up.

"Hey, Pixie Girl, you ride a motorcycle?" I can tell just from the way he says that sentence that he's drunk. They all probably pre-gamed before coming to Cheap Seats.

I nod. "Sure do."

"See, dude! I told you it was her." He smacks the shoulder of the guy sitting next to him with a laugh.

"Shut it, Dylan," Riggs warns through clenched teeth. His voice is low and calm, but there's an undercurrent of tension that piques my curiosity.

I glance at Riggs as I ask the friend, "And just who do you think I am?"

Riggs's mask has slipped now, and he's staring daggers at his friend, but the friend is oblivious.

"The mysterious little sprite that Riggs was boning," he shouts with a laugh. "With the green hair and the motorcycle."

My heart clenches and my stomach swirls as Dylan and the random girl sitting next to him have a laugh at my expense.

He was talking to his friends about me? Telling them that I was *someone he was boning*? Jesus, this guy just keeps surprising me, but no longer in a good way.

"Someone he's *boning*, huh?" I keep my tone bored and my brow raised, but my hands are closed tightly around the last pint glass and the pitcher handle. If I let go right now, I won't be able to hide how violently they're shaking.

I take a minute to glance at Talia—poor girl looks sick—and I want to tell her that I didn't know, that I'm sorry her boyfriend is a run-of-the-mill fuckboy, and that she definitely deserves better. I almost do, but then I look at Riggs and he's shooting murderous looks at his friend, which just infuriates me more.

He thinks he's going to keep me a dirty little secret? Going to minimize me into a girl he tricked and *boned* and fooled into catching feelings, then joked about with his douchey friends?

Well, newsflash, Riggs Stanton.

I'm no one's conquered conquest.

I'm the hero in every single one of my stories.

"Bon*ed*," Dylan clarifies. "Past tense. Right, Riggs?"

"Shut the fuck up, Dylan," Riggs growls again, louder this time.

"Dude, you're wasted. Just stop talking," the guy sitting beside Dylan says with a roll of his eyes. He looks bored as he picks up his pint glass and takes a drink.

"What!" Dylan shouts. "You were there, Zay. Riggs said *boned. Past tense.* Said the fairy girl is *old news.*" Dylan actually looks affronted, as if he can't understand why he's being chastised for telling the truth. "Shit, sorry, Tal," he adds as an afterthought, flashing her one of those *whoops, my bad* grimaces.

I survey Riggs. His big body is vibrating with anger, and Talia's hands are still clutched onto him, squeezing tightly enough that I can see white imprints where her fingers are digging into his arm. I'm barely hanging on to my composure, but when he has the balls to look at me with a bullshit apology on his face, I lose it.

"Move over," I growl at Talia. She stiffens and furrows her brow while the other girl at the table gasps.

"Excuse me?" Talia spits out.

"I said move. Get off him."

Rigg's eyes are comically wide, the rest of the table is silent, and Talia is sputtering.

"What? No. Just who do you think you are?"

"I warned you," I say, and then dump the pint glass and the rest of the pitcher I'm holding over their heads. Dylan howls with laughter as I soak Riggs with Miller Lite, and Talia squeals and launches herself backward, trying to escape the stream.

I didn't want to get her wet, but when you lie down with dogs...

I slam down the pint glass and the pitcher, splashing myself a little with the small lake of beer now standing on the tabletop. "Might want to go home and change, asshole. Looks like that shirt is *old news.*"

"Bitch!" the random girl screeches, but I ignore her and make eye contact with Talia.

"I really am sorry," I say genuinely. *For everything,* I don't add. She just blinks at me and jerks her head in a confused nod.

I hustle back into the kitchen and promise another server that I'll do all her closing work if she agrees to take table 32 off my hands. I don't care how much silverware I have to roll, I cannot face that fucking table again tonight. She agrees, but when she goes back to table 32, it's empty, completely cleaned off except for a ten-dollar bill and two singles, which is just enough to cover the cost of the two pitchers of Miller Lite.

I'm uneasy for the rest of my shift. I'm just waiting for the scolding from the manager for assaulting paying customers, but it never happens. Apparently, no one at the table complained. At the end of the night, I pocket my tips and agree to serve again next Wednesday.

I hate serving, but I made good money tonight, so I'm actually looking forward to coming back.

* * *

"How was Wing Wednesday?" Ivy asks the next morning.

I groan in response.

"Ooof, that bad, huh?"

"I dunno, depends on your idea of bad," I concede. "I walked away with decent tips, but I also had a run-in with a table of dickbags, and I might have accidentally-on-purpose dumped Miller Lite on the heads of one of those dickbags and his girlfriend."

"What?" Ivy looks at me with wide eyes, mouth turned up into a surprised smile. She sets her coffee cup down on the table and scans her eyes over my face before letting out a little puff of breath. "Would one of those jerks happen to be a Butler University star pitcher named Riggs Stanton?"

I roll my eyes. "That would be the one."

"Dang, B. Did you get in trouble?"

"Surprisingly no."

"Oh. Well, that's awesome, then. I hope you soaked him."

I look to see her mouth set in a firm line, her face serious.

"Yeah? You're not going to tell me that acting on my anger isn't healthy, or that lashing out is toxic for my soul, or whatever?"

She snorts. "Heck no. That guy is a jerk, and he deserved it. You got to exact a bit of retribution with impunity, so big thanks to the Goddess of Revenge for that gift." She gets quiet for a minute. "I do feel bad for his girlfriend, though."

I sigh. "Me too."

I ended up spilling my guts to Ivy after the cookie contest. I told her everything. How Baking Aisle Alex is actually Riggs Stanton, star of the BU baseball team and Grade A fuckboy. I told her how we were seeing each other regularly and talking daily. How much we had in common. How easy he was to be around. I even told her how I officially entered him into my phone contacts the night before the contest, only for it to all come crashing down around me the next morning.

Ivy was *livid*. She might come off as sweet and timid, but

she's the exact opposite when provoked. She can be downright scary when she goes into protective mode. She was ready to call the university athletic director regarding their star pitcher's gross misconduct before I talked her down. Then I ended up letting the story slip to Jesse and Kelley, so now BU's god with the golden arm is persona non grata amongst my found fam.

"You know what pissed me off the most?" I confess through a mouthful of cherry pop-tart.

"Hmm?"

"I still wanted him, even if it was just a little. I was jealous to see Talia's hands on him and before I could stop it, I *wanted* him. It's fucking dumb."

"I mean, it does make sense, though."

"What does?"

"That you'd have these conflicting feelings for him. You were starting to really like the guy he was pretending to be, and then you were given no warning before finding out that that guy didn't actually exist." She shrugs, pensively staring into her coffee mug. "You can't just turn feelings like those off. There's no light switch for our emotions, no matter how much we wish there was."

"Ugh. You sure you wanna be a lawyer? You'd be a great shrink." I shove more pop-tart in my mouth and hear Ivy sigh.

"I've definitely been to enough therapy," she trails off, and we're quiet for a minute. Me chewing my pop-tart and her drinking her coffee.

My mind flits back to Cheap Seats. "I bet she's perfectly symmetrical," I muse out loud.

"Who?"

"Talia."

"Hmmm. Didn't you say people with symmetrical faces were boring to look at?"

"Yeah, but I just said that because Jesse wouldn't shut the

hell up about his near-perfect facial structure, and I was going to barf if I had to see him Vogue one more time."

Ivy and I both laugh, and it feels good. It's a reminder that even though some shit might not be where I wish it was, I'm still in a good place. I'm not sinking. I'm still afloat. And that's something.

"So," Ivy says after a minute. "You really doused them with beer, huh?"

"Yep." I pop the p. "Not my finest moment."

"Well, it's not the most subtle way to get your point across, but dare I say, it was likely effective."

"Subtle has never been my specialty, V." I waggle my eyebrows at her. "I should learn to hex."

She barks a laugh as she grabs her messenger tote, readying to head out for the day.

"Goodness, Bailey, this world is in for some trouble if you ever decide to take up witchcraft."

I roll my eyes at her back as she saunters toward the door. "Love you, V!"

"Love you back, B!"

I finish off my pop-tart and coffee, grab my backpack and helmet, and head out. I've got a day full of classes and I picked up a closing shift at the bar tonight. Ivy's got her LSAT this weekend, so I likely won't be seeing much of her, but she is letting me borrow her car tomorrow so I can get some laundry done.

I'm juggling a lot of shit right now, but with any luck, I'll have enough money to give Flannagan's to go ahead on my order by next month. Fingers freaking crossed.

EIGHT

I HEAR the doorbell seconds before Dylan yells through the house.

"RIGGS! Your fiancée is here!"

God, he's such an ass. I hear Talia's nervous laughter as I pound down the stairs. She's kicking off her shoes, and when she sees me, she gives me a sweet smile.

"Hey, Tal."

"Hey."

"You ready?"

"Yeah."

I turn to head back up the stairs, Talia trailing me.

"You guys don't want to hang out?" Dylan asks, a lonely puppy looking for a playmate. He's kind of like having a Jack Russell Terrier.

"Nah, Dyl," I shout down the stairs as I shuttle Talia through the door to my bedroom. "We got plans."

As I'm shutting the door, Dylan opens his fat mouth again. "Use condoms!"

I just shake my head and roll my eyes. He doesn't know when to quit.

Talia takes a seat on my bed and fidgets nervously with her fingers. The sight fills me with regret. How did we get to this place? Where being alone together feels so foreign. How can someone's role in your life change so drastically, so quickly? How is it that no matter how hard I try, I just keep hurting the people who matter most?

"We've got about ten minutes," I say awkwardly.

She nods. "Okay. Um. Big plans for the weekend?"

"The usual. A session with Elbin, and then I'm gonna head home Saturday for a bit."

"Oh, I could come with you."

"Nah, it's cool." I don't miss the hurt in her eyes at my rejection.

We sit in silence for a few minutes, and then the call on my laptop comes through. We position ourselves in front of my desk.

"Ready?" I ask Talia.

"Yep," she says with a smile, then flashes her hands at me and wiggles her fingers. I roll my eyes playfully and return her smile. I take in a deep breath before turning back to the ringing computer. I accept the call and it connects, and my mom's face comes over the screen.

"*Coucou, mes amours,*" she greets, and my smile is instantaneous.

"*Coucou, Maman.*"

"*Coucou,* Odette," Talia chimes, her smile matching mine.

"And how is my favorite couple?" Mom asks, and I reach over and take Talia's hand in mine.

"Good, Mom," I say with as much enthusiasm as I can muster. "And how are you?"

"Fine, *mon étoile.* Tell me about your week. Tell me about your last date. I could use some romance." My mother loves a good romance, and I'll give her anything she wants.

When I look at Talia, she's gazing at me. Her big green eyes are sparkling as she takes me in, and her plump lips are pulled into a wide smile. My heart squeezes at the love I see on her face.

"We went on a picnic a few nights ago, Odette," Talia beams. "It was so romantic. Riggs made us the most delicious turnovers." She turns her smile on my mom, the story flowing so easily from her tongue. "You've raised him well. Your son knows how to treat a lady."

Another part of me breaks at just how wrong that statement is. She doesn't even know the half of it. For as good as Talia has become at faking it, I can tell I'm breaking her little by little, too. The picnic isn't just a picnic; it's a hope. A fantasy. One I wish I could fulfill for her, but I don't have the energy for any more facades.

I look into Talia's eyes and flash my most charming smile, then look back at my mother.

"It's easy with a woman like Talia," I say. "I just want to make her happy."

After the video call, I lead Talia to the door and send her off with a hug and a kiss on the cheek. I crack a joke about Hollywood, a thank-you veiled as a compliment, and she laughs it off. We'll video call Mom again next week, and we make plans to meet up for lunch in a few days.

I come back to my room to find a new email notification on my computer. It's from the Midwest Collegiate Culinary Association, which I'm only vaguely familiar with, and the subject line reads, "Congratulations on your invitation!"

I almost delete it, write it off as spam, but I remember Mom mentioning something about the MCCA, so I open it. It's—

shocker—an invitation, just like the subject line states. I scan the email and the wheels in my head start turning.

It's a week-long holiday baking competition that will take place over the winter break. I'm already prequalified, since I won the cookie contest with Bakery On Main, which I hadn't even realized was affiliated with MCCA. The winning team will take home ten thousand dollars. My excitement amps when I think of how happy Mom would be if I participate in this. Something real that I can give her. She won't even care if I win. I could talk Coach into giving me that week off of training—pull the family card—and the team would be none the wiser.

I'm just about to download the registration papers when I remember one specific word.

Team.

It's a contest for partners.

If I don't have a partner, I can enter a lottery and chance being paired with another solo contestant, but that's risky. Doable, but not ideal. I don't want to share a kitchen with a stranger for a whole week of what's sure to be stressful days.

No. A random partner wouldn't work.

And unfortunately—or maybe fortunately—for me, only one name comes to mind.

Shit.

* * *

Monday afternoon, I see her on the other side of the union courtyard, sitting at a table in front of the smoothie shop with three people, and one of them happens to be the same guy she left the cookie contest with.

Bailey looks stunning. Her face is soft, like how I remember from nights spent in my bedroom, not twisted up and harsh like I've seen it lately. She's got her hair thrown up in a bun, and the sun is glinting off it in a way that makes her turquoise streaks remind me of the clear waters of the Tenerife Sea. A red flannel falls off one of her shoulders, exposing smooth, tanned skin and a black tank top. She's thumbing through a textbook with green-painted fingernails while her plump lips are wrapped around the straw of a purple smoothie. Wild Berry Blast with an energy shot, probably.

God, why does she have to be so fucking pretty?

There's an attractive blonde girl sitting close to a guy with red hair, and from the way they're acting and touching each other, I'd say they're a couple. Which brings my attention to the big guy sitting next to Bailey. The same guy who had his arm around her shoulders after the cookie contest. The guy she left with.

Is this a double date?

I'm hit with a wave of jealousy, and as I assess him, I'm caught off guard to find that he's, uh, knitting.

Pretty sure he's knitting.

I watch him a moment longer.

Yep. Yep, he's definitely knitting.

And as much as I want to hate the fucker spending time with Bailey, I can't help but feel impressed. Maybe even a bit envious. How great would it be to show your true self out in the open and not care about the consequences? Of course, she'd be with someone like that. Someone fearless and honest.

I ignore my anger and force my feet to walk in her direction. I'm going to have to choke down all these feelings and self-pity. I've got to get her to agree to this competition, and the only way I can do that is to clear the air.

I step up to the table, give the guy a nod and grit my teeth at his smirk, then turn to Bailey.

"Hey, you got a minute?" I ask her, trying damn hard not to sound as nervous as I feel.

"For you?" She blinks innocently with those breathtaking amber eyes, and I hold my breath. "Hell no."

The guy sitting with her barks out a taunting laugh and sets whatever it is he's knitting in his lap. Then he folds his arms across his chest and watches. I flick my eyes to the other two people at the table. The blonde and the redhead are watching me closely. Something about the way the blonde is looking at me tells me I don't want to piss her off any more than I apparently already have, so I look back at Bailey.

"Bailey, I'd like a chance to explain," I try again.

"Yeah, no. Not interested, *Riggs*," she spits. The way she says my name with so much venom turns my stomach, but I only have myself to blame. She won't accept an apology or an explanation, not right now, so I try a different approach.

"Look, I have a proposition." I cringe as soon as the words are out of my mouth, and the dick with the knitting needles snorts. "No, not like that. I have a favor to ask, an idea of sorts to run by you."

Bailey sets her smoothie down and hits me with a fiery glare. "You're really gonna come here and ask me for a favor?" Her jaw tenses harshly before she adds, "Thought I was *past tense?*"

This woman is infuriating, and it doesn't help that I'm sweating under the attention of four pairs of eyes. I pitch no-hitters in front of stadiums full of people, but this group has my stomach in knots.

"Dylan is an asshole and didn't know what he was talking about."

"Yeah, he sounded really uninformed."

"Sundance—"

"—I don't *care*, Riggs. And don't call me that. Just go."

I step forward again and open my mouth to demand, but the guy grabs hold of Bailey's chair and drags it over next to him. The scraping of the iron legs on the pavement has everyone in the courtyard looking at us.

"I think it's time for you to go," he says sternly, and I stiffen at the authority in his tone. This dick.

"This is none of your business," I snarl, but the guy puts his arm around Bailey's shoulders and tugs her into his side, making me literally bite my tongue.

"Anything involving my girl is my business."

"*Your* girl?" I laugh at the thought that this firecracker of a woman could ever be anyone's anything. She belongs to herself and no one else.

"Yeah, *my* girl." He nods toward the blonde. "And that one's my girl, too." Then he gestures to the redhead. "And that sexy ginger is my guy."

The redhead just smirks at me while twirling a strand of the blonde's hair around his finger.

"My girl has a problem with you, so you and I gotta problem, which means you should leave now before I have to beat your ass."

"You honestly believe you could?" I scoff. Dude's tall, but I can easily take him. Coach would kill me if he found out, but it might be worth it to knock that stupid look off this guy's face.

He shrugs and smirks some more. "I think B believes it. Don't you, baby." He tries to nuzzle her hair, but she dodges and stomps on his toe. He doesn't even flinch, but I don't miss the muffled laughter that comes from the other couple at the table.

"Yeah, looks like it," I grind out.

"And you think she'd rather be cuddled up with you?" The guy is taunting me. It's a trap, I know it, but I can't seem to stop myself from trudging right into it.

"Yeah, fucker, I do."

The guy laughs again. "Nice try, dick. She's with me."

"How about you go back to your scarf, Grandma, and let me talk to Bailey *alone*."

"First, these are gonna be slippers, not a scarf, asshat. And second, if B wants to talk to you *alone*, she can make that decision herself. I'm not stopping her." He tugs her closer into his side and his smile stretches across his face. My blood is boiling.

"Get your hands off her," I growl.

"How 'bout you make me, Dollar Store Thor."

I vaguely hear the redhead say something, but I can't make it out clearly over the pounding in my head. I step forward with every intention of ripping this asshole's fingers off Bailey's shoulder, but she beats me to it. Then she stands and levels us with a scathing glare. Pretty sure both me and the slipper dick cower a little.

"Oh, is this what we're doing now?" She laughs, but its humorless as she shoves her textbook into her bag. "This dick measuring toxic masculinity bullcrap? Well, guess what. *I win.* If I had a dick, it'd be bigger than both y'all's. Know why? Because I'm not so insecure that I have to flex on other people just to keep the attention of a man-child. So have fun fumbling with your tape measures without me, assholes, because I'm out."

Bailey slams her cup on the table, hikes her bag over her shoulder, and rushes out of the courtyard.

"Oh shit, you pissed her off good, didn't you," the guy laughs, and I glare at him.

"*Jesse*," the blonde girl says in warning, and he winks at her.

"Me?" I ask incredulously.

"Hell yeah, *you*. Don't think for one second any of that—" he waves his finger in the direction that Bailey took off "—had anything to do with me."

I'm watching her run away when the dick talks again.

"She's tiny, but those short legs can move fast. You better hustle if you're gonna catch up."

I whip my eyes back to him. "Huh?"

"Fuckin' A, Stanton. You need me to skywrite it?" He swipes at the brim of an imaginary hat, tugs on his earlobe, then gives me a slow, exaggerated shove. "*Go.*"

I don't question him again. I just run after her.

"Bailey, wait!" I call when I get close, sliding up next to her on the sidewalk. "I'm sorry. I got jealous and stupid, and it got out of hand and I'm sorry."

"Save it for someone who cares, Riggs. Boys like you are a dime a dozen."

"Just give me two fucking minutes to explain," I growl.

"You don't even deserve two seconds." The. Most. Infuriating. Woman. I can't tell if I want to kiss her or curse her. Probably both.

"I just really want to talk to you," I try again.

"Yeah, well you know what I want? I want to talk to *Alex*, the intelligent and funny guy I met in aisle 6 who likes funfetti cupcakes, and talks to me about young adult fiction novels, and adores his mother. That's what I want, and the person standing in front of me right now? He ain't it. So do us both a favor and lose my number, forget my name, and fuck all the way off."

It's not the anger in her eyes that stops me short. It's the sadness. It's the subtle cracking of her voice. I didn't just piss her off, I hurt her, and I didn't even consider that.

Fuck.

I don't fight her this time when she walks away.

"Assholes," I call when I strut through the door of the townhouse. There is a shit-ton of cars out front, and I doubt they can hear me over the music. Fuckers are having a party on a Monday?

I round the corner into the living room and see my room-mates, a few guys from the team, and a handful of girls I only vaguely recognize. Dylan's in the recliner with a girl perched on his lap, Xavier and Beck, our third baseman, are playing Madden on the PlayStation, and three of our outfielders are hanging out on the sectional entertaining a few more girls. Company is the last thing I want to have to deal with, but I flash a grin and jump into character before anyone notices my scowl.

"Guys started without me?" I laugh and dump my bag on the ground. I get a round of heys and head nods from the guys. Some finger waves and batted eyelashes from the ladies.

"Oh Captain, My Captain!" Dylan calls out. The team doesn't have an official captain, but unofficially, the guys have decided I'm it. "Grab a beer, dude. Only a few more weeks until pre-season."

"Go too hard, too fast and you'll burn your shit right out. Sure Coach Daddy will love that one."

Dylan glares at my grin. "Let me worry about that, asshole."

"Hi, Riggs." A blonde smiles shyly at me from the couch. She's wedged between Ashton and Perez, and from the way their hands are on her, I think I just interrupted something.

"Hey, gorgeous." I smile at her. "Having a good time?"

She giggles and looks away, and Perez widens his eyes at me, telling me to fuck right off. I wink at him. "I've got plans, boys. Just swung by to drop off my shit."

"You can't leave," Dylan crows. "You just got here. Quit ditchin' us for pussy."

"Sorry, bro. These plans don't like to be kept waiting." I wink suggestively and walk out to a chorus of whoops.

Then I head to the practice fields to get some laps in.

NINE

bailey

AT 11:59, I turn off my mopey playlist, tug out my earbuds, and wait.

At 12:01 exactly, there's a soft knock at my door, and my lips twitch at the sides.

"Yeah?" I call out to Ivy.

She leans through the door with a small smile.

"How's your head? You good for company?"

We always ask this—*how's your head?*—as in, *how's your mental and emotional health today?* Before Ivy, I was never conscious of the importance of mental health check-ins, no matter how small. It's amazing how much it helps. But Ivy gets it. Sometimes your dark moods beg cheering up, an anchor of sorts to keep you from drifting too deep, and sometimes you just need to be sad.

I nod at her, roll onto my side, and pat the space on the bed next to me.

She strides in, sets a small white box on the nightstand, lies down next to me, and immediately takes my hand in hers.

"Happy Birthday, Bailey."

I breathe in deep through my nose, filling my senses with her mango scent, and blink at the tears threatening.

"Thanks, Ivy." I give her hand a squeeze and hope she knows just how grateful I am for her existence.

"Heading home soon?"

"Yeah," I say quietly. I don't want to. I'd much rather be here with her, Jesse, and Kelley. I'd much rather spend the day with my friends than go back to that suffocating house in that meddling town full of hateful people and terrible memories.

But I owe it to him.

I can't leave him there alone. Not today.

"Want me to come with?" I love her so much more right now for asking. I know she means it. She'll drop everything just to make the three-hour drive into Illinois with me.

"I think I'm going to go alone this time."

"You need to borrow my car?"

I shake my head. "No thanks. I'm gonna take Baby. It'll be good for me."

I feel the bed shift with Ivy's nod.

We lie there for a few more minutes, eyes closed and hands clasped, just breathing.

Ivy is a godsend. Without her, I may never have made it this far.

"I made you guys something," Ivy says after a while, and she sits up and hands me the small box from the nightstand.

I open it to find two brownies inside. I flash her a small grin.

"You didn't."

She nods and giggles. "Jesse helped. We made weed butter. They're supposedly really good. The guys say happy birthday too."

I force a smile. They know not to make a big deal out of it, but I'll still probably be finding small surprise packages over the next couple of days.

"Where are the rest of them?" I raise a brow and give the box a little shake, already knowing the answer. She rolls her eyes.

"J took them to some party with his pre-med friends. You know how hard some of those geniuses go."

I laugh at the truth in the statement. Jesse doesn't get high much anymore, but some of his other friends can get a little crazy.

"There's two," she adds softly, "one for you and one for Brandon."

"Thank you, Ivy. Seriously." I pull her into a hug. "I hate everyone but you."

She giggles. "What about J and Kelley?"

"I hate them a little less than everyone else."

When we pull apart, she presses a kiss to my forehead. It's soft and gentle, and I feel the rest of my muscles relax.

"I love you, B."

"I love you, V."

She stands and heads toward my door, but before she walks out, she turns back to me.

"I know you want to go dark tomorrow. I respect that. You know we won't bother you. But...could you maybe...instead of turning off your phone..."

"I know, V. I'm going to mute all my notifications, but I'll keep my phone on and my location shared."

"Thank you. I just...you know I worry."

"I know. You're the mom I always wanted." I send her a smile.

"Be careful tomorrow. I'm here if you need me."

* * *

When I pull Baby up the driveway to the two-bedroom house of my childhood, my skin prickles with awareness, and I am certain there are eyes on me. Probably the nosy ass, two-faced neighbors gathering gossip fodder of the Barnes' wayward daughter and her disgraceful lifestyle.

Never mind I'll graduate from Butler University with honors. Never mind I'll likely have a job straight out of college that makes more than my parents do. Sure, it's accounting and accounting sucks, but who cares?

The point is that I'm making something of myself, but all these twats see is turquoise hair, piercings, and a shitty attitude. God, why does this small town have to be populated by so many small-minded people? It would be so homey and pleasant, otherwise.

Thankfully, I stopped about thirty minutes out of town to eat half the brownie from V, and the high is starting to set in. Bran will forgive me for starting without him. I'm not one to advocate for using substances as a crutch, but I make an exception any time I have to deal with Mr. and Mrs. Barnes. I don't need an assault charge on my rap sheet.

I take off my helmet and lock it to my bike. Then, feeling every bit like Daniel, I walk toward the lion's den. Too bad I'm not blameless. Too bad there's no one to save me.

It takes all my restraint not to gag at the *Bless These Guests* door wreath and the Joshua 24:15 welcome mat. At least they didn't repurchase the *All Are Welcome Here* mat that I stole, because that one was a flat-out lie.

I knock—because you knock at strangers' houses—then stand back and wait.

My mother opens the door wearing an apron and a huge smile. Roots peppered with grays and a full face by *Avon*. She's happy to see me, so my shoulders loosen slightly.

"Oh, my baby girl is home!" she says, and sweeps me into an awkward hug. "Come on in, baby. Happy happy birthday."

She shuttles me through the door.

"Take off your shoes. You can leave them here," she says, like I don't already know the drill. The house rules are burned into my brain. After I do as I'm instructed, she moves me around the corner into the dining room where a cake with white and pink icing sits on the table.

"I got you a cake from the Wal-Mart in town." *Town* doesn't mean our town, but the larger one a half hour from here that has actual grocery stores, a Target, fast-food joints, and more than one gas station.

"How was your drive? Oh, I'm so glad you could make it home." She hugs me again. "I've missed my baby girl."

I pat her on the back and speak for the first time since walking in.

"Hey, Ma." She pulls back, keeping her hands on my shoulders, and rakes her eyes over me as if she hasn't seen me in years. Then she frowns slightly.

"Is that new?" Her eyes are on my nose. I've had my nose pierced since freshman year of college, but she always asks this.

"Nope. Same stud and everything." I did switch out the hoop and tone down the eyeliner, though. Because despite everything, much to my disgust, I still would like her acceptance.

"Hmm," she sighs and turns away, "I don't know why you want to tarnish the body God gave you. You have such a beautiful face."

"God gave me the gift of free will, Ma." I flash her a smirk and watch as she tries to hide her smile. "With it, I chose to get my nose pierced. I think he should be happy that I'm actually using his gift instead of trying to return it for a refund."

If she knew about my two tattoos, she would flip out. Instead, she just huffs.

"You kids will be the death of me."

I watch as her body tenses, and we both pause and avert our eyes, but that's the extent of the acknowledgment. Neither of us say anything about her use of the plural noun. *Kids.* Not kid. I change the subject.

"Smells good in here, Ma."

"I'm making a pork loin in the new Crock-Pot." She smiles and hurries to the kitchen counter. "And mashed potatoes just the way you like them. And I made a Caesar salad."

She's eager to please me, and my mood thaws as my mouth waters. It's quite a change from spaghetti nights and tater tot casserole. I guess being empty nesters means they can swing for fancier food. I'm jealous. I don't want to be, but I am.

"Can't wait. I'm just gonna use the bathroom then I'll help you set the table."

"Of course, of course. Dad will be in soon."

Awesome.

I walk through the hallway, past a wall full of framed photos, and into the bathroom. When I'm done, I don't resist the pull to check out my old room. It's a smack to the chest walking through the door. It smells stale and dusty, but my posters are still on the wall, my bulletin board still tacked full of pictures and concert tickets. Even the purple bedspread on the bottom bunk of the bunk bed is the same.

It's the other side of the room that sucks the air from my lungs. I'm not surprised—it's been like this for a long time now —but it hasn't gotten easier to see.

Everything has been scrubbed clean.

The sketches. The beaded curtain. The bulletin board, almost the exact same as mine, with the same concert tickets and duplicates of the same photographs.

Even the mural on the wall has been painted over.

It's all gone.

My eyes burn, familiar anger swelling, and I walk out before I explode with it. But then my eyes catch on the wall of framed photos. I was trying to avoid this wall. Every school photo starting with kindergarten. Christmas mornings. Easter Sundays. The homecoming game where Bran and I were both on court. My eyes zero in on the family photo we got taken at the church when I was in middle school. Everyone is smiling and happy. A gold cross necklace is displayed proudly around my neck, and I'm holding hands with someone who is dressed similarly. Same outfit. Same necklace. Same smile.

I feel my mom come up behind me before I see her.

"I loved it when you two would let me dress you alike," she says wistfully. "Broke my heart when you both started refusing." She brushes her fingers across the frame, lingering on the children's smiling faces.

"Yeah," I rasp, then walk to the kitchen.

My father has arrived, and in way of greeting, he gives me a once-over and grunts something out about my hair. I ignore him. I help Mom set the table, and when we sit down to eat, my father folds his hands and bows his head to say grace.

Out of respect he doesn't deserve, I follow suit.

When his gruff voice starts speaking, I can almost picture how I saw him when I was younger. A pillar of strength. A man of God. My protector. My daddy. I try to pretend that this particular prayer is like the ones of my childhood, requesting that God watch over his children as they play sports or learn to drive or study for tests. Asking for guidance and thanking Him for his unyielding love.

I tune him out. I have no interest in hearing what he's asking or thanking God for. I doubt that it has anything to do with me. Instead, while he drones on, I mentally re-count the money in my Crisco can. I recall study guide facts for my upcoming exam. I sing to the Straylight Run song that's been stuck in my head for a few days. When I hear his voice take on the familiar cadence that signals he's winding down, I return focus to his prayer.

"We ask that you please watch out for her, oh Lord, and use your benevolence to lead her misguided soul back to your grace. In your name we pray, Amen."

I roll my eyes as I mutter, "Amen."

Seems I was wrong. I was included in his invocation, after all.

My father doesn't meet my eyes or speak to me during the whole meal. My mother is our median, speaking to us both and pretending that all is well here. He complains about work and talks about church. My mother prattles on about the same topics, as well as everyone who is having babies or getting engaged in our little community. She asks me questions about school, and I answer as politely as I can.

And no one addresses the elephant in the room.

No one ever does.

When dinner is over, I help my mom clear the table and wash dishes. They sing Happy Birthday to me, and I blow out a blaze of pink candles. After that, Mom leads us into the living room for presents.

I'm sitting on the loveseat, my dad perched on his leather La-Z-Boy throne, and my mom brings out a large gift wrapped in pink and purple sparkly paper.

"Happy birthday, baby girl." She hands me the box and I cast a glance at my father. He's watching the television, and I don't doubt for one second that he had nothing to do with whatever is in this box.

"Thanks, Ma."

As I'm tearing through the wrapping paper, the neighbor's

dog barks, and I look toward the picture window. It's then that I see a new set of framed photos on the wall. The word "FAMILY" is spelled out in wooden letters, and beneath them are pictures of us. Our *family*. My mother and father in a recent picture that must have been taken at church. My 12th grade school photo. A picture from prom. Several other scenes have been selected for the gallery wall.

But it's not the pictures in the collage that set me off—it's who's left out.

"Where's Brandon?" I blurt, and my mom stops speaking. I hear my dad sit up sharply and I bounce my glare between them. "It's a gallery wall dedicated to *family*. Where are the pictures of Brandon?"

"We don't say that name in this house," my dad threatens, and I leap up, knocking the half-opened gift box to the floor.

"That's bullshit," I spit, and his eyes flare as my mom gasps.

"You watch your mouth in this house, young lady."

"You should have photos of Brandon on that wall. He is *your son*."

He erupts then with anger that I've seen many times in my life. Anger that I've inherited.

"I don't have a son," he yells, and I swear I sway on my feet from the force of the hatred in his words. He and I face off, neither of us willing to back down. Sometimes, I almost wish that he would hit me. I can tell he wants to. I look at my mom to find her crying silently, wringing her hands in her lap. I bring my eyes back to my dad, keeping my voice low and steady, fury and truth evident in every syllable.

"You need to reevaluate your priorities, *sir*, or you won't have a daughter anymore, either."

I break eye contact and stomp from the living room, stopping at the door so I can put on my Docs. My mom catches me off guard when she rushes up to me.

"Please, don't leave, Bailey. Please. I'm so sorry." My heart aches a little from her tears. A force of habit. I used to want to make her happy.

"Sorry isn't good enough, Ma. Not anymore."

She grabs my hands when I stand. "Please, Bailey. I'm working on him. I promise. He'll come around." I shake my head at her desperation.

"Too little, too late, Mom." I turn my back on her and walk out.

My high isn't quite worn off yet, so I push Baby the six blocks to Brandon. He's the only reason I came to town, anyway. The stop-off in Hell was just a guilt driven courtesy call because I'm somewhat of a masochist.

I park Baby on the street, grab my bag, and make my way up the drive, gravel pressing beneath my boots in a satisfying and familiar crunch. When I see him, I veer off into the lawn, drop my shit, and plop down next to him.

"Hey," I say quietly. "Happy birthday."

I turn and pull the box with the brownie out of my bag.

"Ivy and Jesse made us birthday pot brownies." I laugh softly. "I ate most of mine already, though. I had to. I had dinner with Mom and Dad. If I had attempted it sober, I would have broken something. Or someone."

I lie on my back in the grass next to him and close my eyes, listening to the wind rustling. It's harsher now that the crops have been harvested. Without the cornstalks for resistance, the wind kicks the field dust up in puffs. I can smell it in the air. I can taste it.

"I listened to 'The Great Escape' on my ride over," I tell him with a laugh. "I don't think I can drive into town anymore without that song on blast because of you. Remember when you stole the keys to Principal Cary's golf cart when I was babysitting, and then we drove it around town at like 2 a.m. collecting lawn gnomes?"

I can't stop the giggles.

"Oh my god, I wish I could have seen his face when he walked out the next morning to find his golf cart parked on his lawn and filled with thirty-seven garden gnomes."

The breeze tickles my nose and blows strands of my hair in front of my face.

"Or when Craig and I broke up the third or fourth time, right before 11th grade started, and you slipped mom's root touchup dye into his 3-in-1 bottle." I squeal at the memory, tears falling from my eyes. Craig was blond and fair, but after Bran messed with his shower shit, every hair on Craig's body was the same dull shade of black. The memory has me wheezing with laughter, and it takes minutes before I can catch my breath.

When the laughter stops, the tears don't.

"I'm so sorry, Bran," my voice cracks. "I'm so fucking sorry. I know I said I would have it by now. I wanted to so badly, but shit just hasn't gone as planned." I dash away a tear. "I'm working on it, though. I'll have it soon. I'll have it finished by February. Poetic justice." I force a laugh.

I roll onto my side and brush my fingers over the dates on the grave marker. The birthdate is today, same as mine, but the death date is almost three years ago. I'm still here, but he isn't.

He didn't even want to be buried. He wanted to be cremated.

I let more tears fall.

"I miss you so much, Bran," I whisper. "There's not a single day that I don't miss you. I get so mad. You should be here with me. We should be doing all of this together just like we always have. I just don't understand. I keep trying to understand but I can't." I take a breath. Wipe away more tears. "How am I supposed to enjoy living life without my best friend since birth? How am I supposed to *live* when you can't? This should have been your time. You should be thriving and making art, being here with me."

I let myself cry.

All the tears I've held back, all the sorrow that I keep inside, I let it all pour out until I'm bled dry. Two days. I give myself two days a year to feel this pain. To wallow in it. To drown in the guilt. I lie there until I'm dehydrated and sober and almost numb.

When it starts to grow darker, I take his brownie out of the box and set it on the grave marker, then I think better of it and dig a shallow hole to put it in. This way, I'm not recklessly getting random animals baked, but if a critter takes the time to dig it up, I figure they deserve the high. Once the brownie is buried, I take a tube of paint and one of Bran's old paint brushes out of my bag. I squeeze some of the black paint on the brush, and then smear it over the headstone. The name, the etchings of angel wings and a cross, the bullshit epitaph and bible verse. I cover everything except the birth and death date. When that's done, I put the brush and paint back in the plastic container and shove it into my bag.

"You gotta stop defacing the marker, Barnes."

I jump at the voice and turn to find a familiar face. I didn't even hear him pull up. I don't know how long he's been there, and my shoulders stiffen.

He looks much older than I remember, different from the boy I loved in high school. His countenance is harder, his hair less vibrant. That's what happens to people who get sucked into this black hole of a town. They shrivel from the outside in, until they're nothing but jagged facets of the same dull existence.

We took each other's virginity, Craig and me. I gave him my entire heart and all of my trust, and he crushed it under his size twelve Wolverines, along with any belief I used to have in love. I guess he's working for the county now if he's policing the cemetery.

"What are you gonna do, Craig? Arrest me?" My voice is steel, and his face is a stern mask.

"It's a criminal offense." He crosses his arms and widens his stance, his uniform stretching over his torso.

"Fuck that." I fling an angry finger at the grave. "That's my brother."

As if that's all the excuse I need.

As if that makes the crime less criminal.

Fuck. That.

In my head, it's enough.

"You know they'll have to scrub it off." His voice is soft and full of pity now, and my heart aches with defeat.

"Give it a few weeks? Just pretend like you didn't see it or something. It's not like anyone else will be by to visit, anyway."

He hesitates, then nods, remnants of the guy I once loved flickering on the surface. A small mercy. As I walk away, he calls my name again.

"Bailey." I swing my leg over my bike and look back at him. "I miss him too, you know?"

"Yeah?" Anger erupts in my belly and spews out of my mouth like hot lava. How *dare* he? "Did you miss him in 12th grade when you outed him and made his life miserable? Did you miss him that summer when he was depressed and sad and broken? When he almost lost his art scholarship? What about at that sham of a fucking memorial service, Craig. Did you miss him then?"

Craig has the decency to wince, and I watch the muscle in his jaw tense. The pain in his eyes is obvious—the guilt and regret. *Good.* He can sit with that shit for a while. He doesn't get redemption just because Brandon's dead. His transgressions weren't erased when Bran's heart stopped. I shake my head with a sigh, suddenly exhausted down to my bones. My joints ache, my eyes sting, and my head pounds. I'm done here.

"See you around, Officer Dixon."

"Yeah," he mumbles, and I drive off without looking back.

It's past midnight when I get back to my apartment. I sent Ivy a text letting her know I was on the way, so I'm not surprised to see her waiting for me when I walk through the door.

"How'd it go?"

"'Bout how you'd expect," I tell her honestly as I kick off my shoes.

"Tattoo, piercing, or hair dye?"

I laugh and drop down next to her on the couch.

"I'd say tattoo, but unfortunately, I don't have the money for any of them, so I'll have to go with wine and weed."

"Wellllll," she drags out with a small smile. "I've held off getting you a birthday present. I can't really swing for a tattoo, but what if we go to the beauty supply store tomorrow and grab some bleach and a new color? My treat."

Ivy's been dying my hair since sophomore year. I'd mentioned wanting to do a fun color and she offered to help. She watched like twenty YouTube tutorials, did several Google searches, and in the end, I had some chunky pink streaks that I absolutely loved.

"You don't have to do that, V."

She shrugs. "I want to, so you might as well be the one to pick out the color."

"Yeah?"

"Yeah."

"Okay."

Today has been absolute shit, but at least it's ending on a good note.

* * *

The next night, after Ivy dyes my hair, I move out to the balcony for some much-needed alone time. I'm sitting in my bowl chair, jar of wine in one hand and my phone in the other with my e-reader app open when I hear a rustle, a thud, and see two hands grip the bars on the balcony railing.

I startle, then freeze, and when a figure rises up over the bars, I start to scream before I notice who it is.

"What the fuck?" I yell, but Jesse just puts his index finger to his lips and shushes me with a dramatic scowl. Then he pulls himself over the rail, so he's standing on the balcony.

I'm too confused to say anything, so I just sit back and silently watch as he takes out his phone, types, and starts playing the *Mission Impossible* theme song. Then he pulls down a ski mask, opens the balcony door, and shoulder rolls into my apartment.

He pops up quickly, turns the deadbolt on the front door, and in scrambles Kelley with a big cardboard box. He hands the box to Jesse, then salutes me with a wink before they both disappear down the hall.

In a matter of seconds, they're both rushing back to the balcony.

Kelley ruffles my hair and presses a kiss to my head, then hops over the railing of our second-story apartment and lands in the grass without making a sound. Jesse steps up, ski mask still pulled down, and moves like he's going to slap me upside the head. I bring my hand up to block him, but he fakes me out and smacks me on the other side. Instinctively, I kick my foot out, hitting his thigh and just narrowly missing his dick. I smirk and flip him off when he jumps back, cups his junk, and sticks his fucking tongue out at me— through the ski mask—like a child. I can't hold back my laugh, and he smiles in triumph.

A split second later, Jesse launches himself over the railing and I hear a thud, two grunts, and Kelley say something that sounds like "get the fuck off." When I hear the pattering of running footsteps disappear into the night, my curiosity gets the better of me and I inspect the house.

Walking into my room, I find the cardboard box Kelley carried in sitting on my bed.

No wrapping paper, no bow, no card.

They know better.

I open the giant box to find another box. I roll my eyes and pull it out, then open it to find, yep, a smaller box. Like nesting eggs, they've got six boxes stacked. Ridiculous.

When I get to the smallest box, I hear a clanking noise and raise a brow.

I open it and reach in to first pull out a set of copper measuring cups and a matching set of measuring spoons. *Kelley.*

Then I take out a...uh...knitted...potato, maybe?

A knitted potato...wearing a white knitted toupee?

With googly eyes stuck to it.

I study it for a second, give it a little squish, and finally give up. Jesse's new thing is dolls. Obviously, he's not very good at it yet.

I open our group text thread and shoot off the question that I'm certain he was waiting for.

Me: J. Wtf is this?
Jesse: *cupcake emoji*

I study it again. Huh. It does kind of look like a cupcake, I guess. If you squint, the toupee could pass for icing.

Me: I can see it.
Jesse: *kiss face emoji*
Me: Ew. In your dreams.
Ivy: *laughing face emoji*
Kelley: *clown emoji*
Jesse: *sleeping face emoji* *moon emoji* *lips emoji*

Ugh. These jokers know how much I hate emojis, but I still smile and give in. Fucking peer pressure.

Me: *middle finger emoji*
Kelley: *blue heart*
Ivy: *green heart*
Jesse: *purple heart*

I let out a laugh, my mood less surly and bleak than it has been lately. With losing the cookie contest, making the call to Flannagan's, and all this crap with Riggs, I could feel myself hovering just above darkness, threatening to drop. Like always, though, my friends have thrown me a lifeline just by existing. Just by being them.

My eyes sting a bit, but the muscles in my stomach loosen.

Me: Thanks guys.
Jesse: anytime b

riggs

MY DAD CALLS TWICE this morning.

I've avoided him long enough, so when I get out of my meeting with Coach, I pull up his contact.

"Riggs, about time you called me back." His voice booms through the phone.

"Been busy, Dad."

"'Course," he grunts. "Talked to Coach Neal. He says you've been keeping up with your training."

"You doubted I would?"

"Certainly not," he scoffs. "But what kind of father would I be if I wasn't checking up on you now and then. Pitchers are made in the off-season, you know. Your team follows your lead, and you can't afford to slack if you're going to enter the draft this year. Your attention should be on baseball, first and foremost. Jason says you've been in the gym five days a week. That's good, Riggs. Bet Jason wished his own son had your dedication."

My dad and Dylan's dad are old college buddies. Both of them played baseball for BU back when they attended here, so I can't do shit without Coach Neal reporting back. It's why I have to be careful in what I let the guys see—never know what will get spilled when, and then it all will flow right back to my dad. It's exhausting.

Dad was also a pitcher, so he thinks he knows everything I should and shouldn't be doing to train. He'd preorder my meals and handwrite my workouts if he could. Thankfully, Coach Elbin, my pitching coach, isn't in my dad's ear. A small mercy. My dad missed out on his chance to play pro when he tore his rotator cuff. He's done fine for himself, though, if owning several luxury hotels in the Chicagoland area is any indicator. Antony Stanton is a great businessman, but he can be an over-bearing dick, too.

"I know, Dad."

"I still think you should have entered last year as soon as you were eligible. You know you had several gre—"

"I know, Dad." I'm so sick of this conversation.

"You know I think it was a mistake," he doubles-down.

"And you know why I did it." I squeeze the bridge of my nose between my finger and thumb. I'm getting a fucking migraine.

"Have you been being careful with your *extra-curriculars?*" he changes the subject. By extra-curriculars, he means partying and hooking up. Doesn't matter to him that I've basically been with Talia since high school. He's of the opinion that now is the time to sow my wild oats. It's one of the reasons why I've got to wear my Douchebag Hat so often. Dad, the team—hell, half the fucking campus—all expect me to behave a certain way.

Asshole Jock. Playboy Pitcher. Cocky, confident, and horny as hell.

"Yep," I answer, monotone.

"You know it's okay to party with the team, keeps up morale and builds trust. That's why I got you the townhouse, you know. So, you don't have to always do it at the baseball house. Hosting the party shows leadership."

"I know, Dad."

"You don't have to abstain from everything. Off-season is the time to indulge a little, you just gotta be smart about it. As long as your team knows that they're your priority—"

"I know, Dad," I say again. "A bunch of us are going out tonight, actually."

"That's my boy. The whole team?"

"Most of us."

"Good boy. Remind that school who runs it."

"How's Mom?" I ask before he can wax poetic about the times when he was the big man on campus.

"She's fine, son." There's that word again. *Fine.* "Didn't you just see her last weekend?"

I grunt. A lot can change in a week, and a lot can be hidden from me from a distance of 170 miles. He wants me to focus on baseball and "getting the most out of the college experience," and Mom wants me to focus on school and Talia.

No one gives a shit what *I* want to focus on.

"I gotta go, Dad. Gotta get ready to go out."

"Have fun tonight. Maybe leave Talia at home."

I hang up on him before I say something I'll regret.

Walking down the stairs, I shout into the house, "Who wants to get fucked up tonight?"

Dylan whoops, Zay shrugs from his position on the couch, and I send a text out to some of the other guys. Dad wants me to partake in extra-curriculars? Fine. But I'm gonna make a pitstop first.

"Bar 31 for a quick pregame shot, on me, and then we'll head to Keggers."

. . .

We get to Bar 31 around eleven, and the place is packed. I scan the bar and find exactly what I came here for. Taking Back Sunday shirt tied up on her waist, black skinny jeans, and her long hair is up in a ponytail, but the ends are pink now. I catch myself staring, and quickly tell the guys to head to the back.

"I'll grab the shots."

Instead of going to her side of the bar, I slouch up to the other bartender. Jared, I think his name is. I can't stop thinking about the last time I met Bailey here, before things went to shit. I had her shoved up against the brick wall outside the second she got off, one hand palming her breast under her shirt and the other hand down her pants palming her pussy. Making her make those noises...

I shake my head and wave my card at Jared, making sure not to be visible to the other end of the bar. He raises a quick eyebrow when he sees me but pours the shots of Fireball I order without question.

I carry them back to the guys at the same time Zay walks up with a beer.

"Saw your girl," he says, and he raises his glass to me.

I shake my head subtly. If Dylan gets word, he'll go ape shit and make assholes of all of us. Zay just nods and takes one of the shots.

I wait until everyone has one and then raise mine. "Bottoms up, dickheads!" Everyone throws back their shots on my command, and then I'm met with cheers.

"More?" I shout. "More!"

I get another round of whoops from the guys as I turn back to the bar. This time, though, I go to the far end. To her.

When she sees me, she stops short and then immediately blows me off. She takes orders and makes about a dozen drinks before she finally looks back at me. When she sees I'm still there, waiting, she rolls her eyes and stomps up to me.

"Jesus," she barks. "What do you *want*, Riggs?"

I flash her the same charming grin that I use on everyone else, false bravado leaking from my fucking pores.

"Look," I begin, "I know you don't want to hear my excuses or explanations regarding our past encounters," I pause a moment and she narrows her eyes at me. "Right?"

"Right."

"Right. So. Anyway, I got this email."

I take the printed copy of the email invitation out of my back pocket and lay it out in front of her on the bar. As she looks it over, I continue talking.

"Since I won the Bakery On Main Cookie Contest, I'm automatically qualified for the Midwest Collegiate Holiday Bake Off that's taking place in Chicago over winter break. It takes place the week before Christmas, and the winning team gets ten thousand dollars."

Her eyes widen when I mention the prize money, but her mouth stays fixed in a flat line.

"So?" she questions. "You want me to wish you luck? Good luck." She turns to walk away, but I lean over the bar and place my hand on her upper arm.

"No, Bailey. I want you to be my partner."

She gapes at me. "What? No way. Why? No."

"If I go solo, they could try to place me with one of the other solo contestants, but there's no guarantee. And even if they do, I won't know anything about my partner. But if I bring you, then I'm guaranteed to work with someone whose baking style I know and trust."

"Are you forgetting that I *lost*, Riggs? Wouldn't you rather team up with a *winner*?"

"Look. I think together, we could win this. Sure, your baking lacks finesse and you could use some lessons in proper technique—"

"Ha!" She cuts me off. "And you know about finesse and technique, huh?" I've hurt her pride, but I'm not going to tiptoe around her, so I give her a serious look.

"My mother is Odette Dupont Stanton. She's a classically trained pastry chef. You can Google her. She has her *Diplôme de Pâtisserie* from *Le Cordon Bleu*. I learned from her. So yeah, I know a bit about finesse and technique."

"Oh." *Yeah, oh.*

"Anyway," I continue, "you're messy, but you've got an instinctive creative element that I'm lacking. I've been doing some research—past winners always win with something imaginative and unique. Finesse and technique matter, but they won't be enough. We'll need all of it to win."

"I dunno…" She stares down at the paper, and I can tell she's running through every possible scenario. "A week? I can't take that long off work…but for five thou—"

"Ten."

"Huh?" She snaps her eyes up to mine.

"Ten thousand, Bailey."

"No, yeah, but I mean if we split—"

"No. We won't split it. If you do this with me and we win, you can have it all. I don't want any of it."

"Are you crazy? That's a fuck-ton of cash, and you just don't want it?"

"Honestly, I don't need it. I have no interest in it. I just want the win."

She stares at me some more, blinking, and her eyes narrow. I can feel her assessing me, and I really don't want to have to get into specifics with her, but I will if I have to.

"Why does this feel like a trap?" she asks quietly.

"It's not. I swear it. Do this competition with me. One week. I'll even pay for your hotel and transportation, and when we win, you can have the prize money. All of it. My team will be better with you on it, Bailey. Together, I know we can win. When it's over, you never have to speak to me again."

Her face falls. "I don't trust you, Riggs."

And there it is.

The truth in her statement is blaring. She doesn't mince words, and once again I'm kicking myself for not just being honest with everyone from the jump.

"I know," I breathe out. "But look. Registration for the competition isn't due for a few weeks yet. So, let's just...start over, kind of."

When she doesn't tell me to fuck off, I lean farther over the bar top and put out my hand.

"Hi. My name is Riggs *Alexander* Stanton."

She pops a brow and grabs my hand, giving it a shake. "Bailey Elizabeth Barnes."

"Pleasure to meet you, Bailey," I say with a smile, then tighten my grip slightly. I can't tell if I imagine the heat that flares in her eyes. "I was hoping you would give me your phone number."

The corner of her lip twitches, and I watch as she reaches into her pocket and pulls out a Sharpie. My heart is pounding in triumph, but when I flip my hand over and give her my palm, she ignores it. Instead, she leans over the bar and brings the Sharpie to my forehead. I jerk back on instinct, but when she purses her lips at me, I narrow my eyes and lean back toward her. Now my heart is pounding for a completely different reason, but I don't pull away, not even when she puts the Sharpie to my forehead and starts writing. I don't even know why I let her do it, except maybe as some stupid fucking way to prove myself. To earn a little bit of trust back. Her nearness and the way she smells like cherries excites me, but I'm nervous as shit, too. I close my eyes and hide a chill at the feeling of her soft breath on my face.

What in the actual fuck am I letting this girl do to me?

When she's finished, she drops back down and holds eye contact with me while she puts her Sharpie back in her pocket. Then her lips turn up in a small smile.

"I'll think about it."

"Thank you," I say, genuinely grateful. "I'll talk to you later?"

She just shrugs and walks away, so I head back to the guys.

When I get to our group, they all bust up laughing. *Shit.*

"Huh," Zay says as he studies me before taking a pull from his beer. "D'you forget the shots?"

The others are acting like freaking hyenas.

"What the fuck happened to you?" Dylan shouts through obnoxious laughter. "Oh my god, this is amazing." He starts fumbling with his phone. "Hold on, I gotta get a picture. Hey! Someone take his picture."

I hustle to the bathroom before anyone can snap a photo and step up to the mirror with my eyes on my shoes. When I gather the courage to assess the damage, I can't help the bark of laughter that erupts when I meet my reflection.

A dick.

Of course.

Bailey Barnes drew a dick on my forehead.

In permanent marker.

But even with a semi-permanent cock inked on my face, I can't stop the smile from spreading. Because in that dick? In that dick, she wrote her phone number. That, mother fuckers, is progress, and with Bailey Barnes, I'll take whatever I can get.

* * *

I've texted Bailey twice this week. She hasn't responded, but the texts say delivered, which means she's at least unblocked me.

I'm not spending any more time worrying about it than I have to. Communication lines are open, and I could tell by her reaction last weekend that she's gonna say yes. She can't turn down that kind of money.

There's a costume party at one of the sororities tonight and a bunch of us are going. Zombie Baseball Players. Not the most original idea, but like Daddy Dearest says, we're boosting morale and shit.

Next week begins preseason training, which means I'm finally allowed to throw again, and the guys all have to cool it on their partying. Tonight's kinda like a last hurrah, and I fucking need it.

Wearing BU Baseball tees (Coach would run our asses off if we wore our real jerseys), we go rolling into the party like royalty. Our faces are covered in green and black paint and some gnarly fake flesh wounds that we got some kids from the art department to apply, and all eyes snap toward us.

It pisses me off that the first thing I do is scan the crowd for a tiny temptress with pink hair and eyes like honey, but I shake myself out of it. She won't be here. She works most weekends. And I don't give a damn anyway.

I grab Zay and nod toward the kitchen, and we bypass the line for the keg.

"Gentlemen," a young guy greets us, likely a freshman pledge from the brother frat. "It's five bucks a cup, but since you are who you are, you drink for free."

"Thanks, man," I flash a smile. We *always* drink for free.

Zay and I head through the crowd, and Dylan rushes up to us with Talia in tow.

"My guys," he shouts with a drunk-as-shit grin. "Look what I found!" He holds up a whole damn handle of Captain Morgan. Dunno where he stole it from, but that's Dylan for ya. "Oh, and Tal is here too. Captain for my Captain?"

I give Talia a nod, then grab the handle of rum, tip my head back, and pour two shots worth right into my mouth. I hear cheers around me, and I take a bow. Boosting fucking morale, just how Pops wants.

Talia sidles up to me. She's dressed like a slutty nun.

"Sister Eileen?" I ask, referencing the physics teacher we had at our private Catholic high school.

"The off-duty version." She shimmies her shoulders and I laugh. "This is how she dressed on weekends. I just know it."

"Nice."

She puts her hand on my chest, raises up to my ear, and whispers, "Should I stick close to you tonight?"

"Nah, it's cool." I pretend I don't see the slight fall in her features.

"Okay." She forces a smile. "I'm gonna get a drink."

"I'll come with. Get you your cup for free."

"No, that's alright." She puts her hand up to stop me. "It's a fundraiser for one of the girl's cousins. He's sick."

"No shit?"

She shrugs. "Yep. That's the whole reason for the party."

"Damn. I thought it was because it's almost Halloween." I fumble through my wallet and pull out a bill. "I'm coming with."

I follow Talia back into the kitchen by the keg, drop the hundred in the money jar, then head back off to find Dylan with his handle of rum.

Last hurrah, here I come.

bailey

I LOOK HOT.

And I better, too. If I'm gonna attend this shitshow, I better look hot as fuck. Our friend Cassie's sorority is having a costume party, and the money they make from the cup sales is going to a GoFundMe for a little boy with pediatric cancer. It's the only reason I switched shifts for tonight. Cassie's sorority sister is the little boy's cousin, and they're really close, so we're all going to show support. It's a little weird, because we met Cassie when she kind of had a thing for Kelley. It was awkward for all of 30 seconds, though, because Ivy could make friends with a literal brick wall. Now we're all cool.

I step back and check myself out in the mirror. I'm rocking an old yellowish gold prom dress that I got from the thrift store. I cropped it short, so the skirt hits just under my ass, sliced the neckline low, and cut the sleeves into thin straps. I'm wearing black fishnets and a fake nylon sleeve of colorful tattoos on my arm. My hair is in a fauxhawk, my eyeliner is thick, my lips are ruby red, and I traded out my nose stud for my hoop. Add my Docs, and I'm a the most badass Disney princess you ever did see.

Punk Rock Belle. Nailed it.

"You almost ready?" I call to Ivy in the bathroom.

She pops open the door and I grin my approval.

"Oh my god. I freakin love it."

Ivy is dressed as Punk Rock Cinderella. Cropped blue dress, nude fishnets, and the same nylon sleeve of tattoos that I'm wearing. Her hair is in an updo with a spiked, black leather headband, her earrings are guitar picks, and her shoes are black leather stilettos.

"You look hot." She grins. "Can you do my eyeliner like yours?"

"Yeah, sit down."

I'm finishing Ivy's eyeliner when both of our phones chime, signaling a text in our group chat. We grab our phones and read the text at the same time.

Jesse: We otw.
Jesse: Punk Disney Princes to the rescue.
Kelley: Be there in 10.

"Do you know what they picked?" I ask Ivy.

"Nope. Kelley wouldn't tell me."

"Me either."

Me: Hurry your asses up. We're ready to go.
Jesse: Eager to see if Thor is there? *hammer emoji*

Ivy snorts, and I roll my eyes as I type back.

Me: I don't know what you're talking about.
Jesse: U know. The dude with the Tarzan hair who was about to go caveman onur ass.

Me: Whatever. He's probably too busy lying to some poor coed and cheating on his girlfriend.
Kelley: You sure about that? Dude did seem pretty possessive of you.
Ivy: I said that same thing…

"Ugh." I look at Ivy. "Not you too." She just shrugs, eyes on her phone, and I type out a reply.

Me: He's not possessive of me. He just doesn't like not getting what he wants when he snaps his fingers. BU's Golden God is used to girls falling all over him.
Me: Classic duck boy.
Me: duck boy
Me: FUCK boy***

They waste no time. It's rapid fire.

Jesse: What the duck.
Kelley: Ducking autocorrect.
Jesse: *duck emoji*
Me: UGGHHHHHH
Kelley: What's the mallard with your phone, B?
Jesse: U quack me up B.
Kelley: You really ducked up that one didn't you.
Ivy: LOL!!!
Me: I hate all of you.
Jesse: U ducking love us

I can't hide the stupid grin on my face. They're idiots, all of them, but they're my idiots. When there's a knock on the door, Ivy and I walk to it together, both still smiling from the text exchange. When we open the door and see the guys standing there, we lose it.

"Oh my *god*," I say thorough puffs of laughter. "Punk Rock Woody and Buzz?"

"There's a snake in my boot," Jesse shouts. He's got a black fake leather cowboy hat on with a matching vest, black jeans, and he's drawn tattoos all over his chest in what looks like eyeliner pencil. "Like the ink? Did it myself."

I look at Kelley. Astronaut suit that he's cut off jaggedly at the sleeves, thick black eyeliner on his eyes, and fake tattoos all down his arms. He definitely doesn't look like he teaches social studies to middle schoolers right now.

"Did his ink, too," Jesse crows. "Took me literally two hours."

"Nice." I'm impressed. "Lemme spike up your hair real quick." I dart into the bathroom and grab some hairspray, then go back to the living room to doctor them up. When I'm done, they do look pretty badass.

"Ready to go, dorks?"

"Ready," Ivy sings.

"To infinity and beyond!" Kelley yells and sprints out the door.

"You are a child's plaything," Jesse shouts, chasing after him.

Tonight is going to be a good night.

I noticed him the moment I walked in. Dressed as a zombie, Riggs is holding court off to the side of the large living room, beer in one hand and a girl pressed into his side. A girl who is definitely *not* Talia. And the real mind blower? A girl who definitely *is* Talia is on that same wall standing very close to the blond douche from Cheap Seats. Dylan, I think he's called.

It doesn't look like Riggs is paying either of them much attention—Talia or the random chick. He's drinking and smiling, an occasional touch or brush here and there, and she's definitely flirting with him, but he's not flirting back. The relief I feel is instant, and then it's immediately followed by disgust. *Just how fast does this prick go through women?* He catches my eye, then, and I suck in a breath. He flashes me a smirk, so I flip him off, then turn on my heel and pull Ivy out of the room.

I'm outside for less than an hour before he finds me.

Kelley and Jesse went off to get more drinks, and Ivy and I are watching a beer pong game. When Riggs comes stalking toward us, I have to force myself to breathe slower. The green zombie face paint he is wearing has smudged off in a few places, and the gross fake flesh wound I noticed earlier is gone, leaving behind a clean strip of tan skin on his cheek. Even undead, he's gorgeous. I hate it.

"Hey," he says, voice low and eyes glassy. "Where is your *boy* tonight?"

I shrug off his obvious jealousy. "Around."

"You unblocked my number."

"I did."

"That's a good sign."

"Don't read too much into it."

He nods, and I feel his eyes slide over me. He reaches up and fingers the small padlock I'm wearing on a chain around my neck, then lowers his hand and brushes his fingers over my tattoo. When chills cover my skin, I swat his hand away. His responding grin pisses me off and heats my blood. I can feel Ivy's eyes on us, but she doesn't say a word.

"Punk Rock Princess?" he asks after taking a sip from his cup. My lips twitch at the sides.

"Yeah." I nod and pop a brow. "And I'm looking for my Garage Band King, not some Jester Jock in Jordans."

He chuckles and steps a bit closer. "That's a great album," he whispers, and I'm momentarily shocked that he got the reference. He can tell, too, because he continues, "Cavanaugh Park is my favorite."

I hold his eyes and furrow my brow. I'm not even sure what I see in those brown depths. Behind the glossy sheen from a few too many beers, there's something much more complicated, and he doesn't blink. Like he wants me to see it. Wants me to puzzle it out.

"You're going to forgive me, Sundance. You'll see."

The sincerity in his voice catches me off guard. I open my mouth to speak, but no words come, so I close it again and bite my lip. His eyes lock on the movement, and we're suspended there until someone throws their arm around me and jostles Riggs back a few steps.

"Thor," Jesse says with a grin.

Riggs's nostrils flare as he assesses Jesse. "What are you? Some sort of porno cowboy?"

Jesse laughs. "Porno cowboy. You're funny."

"Right." The guys stare off, and the contrast in their body language is nothing short of comical. Their height is about even, but where Jesse is lean, Riggs has more mass. And right now, that mass is as stiff as a fucking stone statue while Jesse is loose and swaying, the picture of a good time.

"I was talking to Bailey," Riggs grinds out.

"Cool." Jesse smiles bigger and bounces a little on his feet. "What are we talking about?" He flashes me a trouble-making smile. "Waterfowl?"

I hear Kelley snort and Riggs raises an eyebrow. "What?"

"You know. Waterfowl." Jesse takes a small step toward

Riggs, and I take a mouthful from my cup just as Jesse says, "Quack quack, mother ducker."

I spit out my drink.

Just shower Riggs with a spray of beer, for the second time in a matter of weeks, while Ivy and Kelley erupt in a fit of laughter.

Oh hell. I take in Riggs's wide-eyed look of shock, face dripping wet, and I don't even try to hide my smile.

"Sorry," I say on a laugh, then turn and drag a boneless, giggling Ivy back through the house, and out the front door, where I call an Uber. Within twenty minutes, we're all headed back to my apartment with plans to order Chinese food and watch *Criminal Minds* reruns until we pass out. All in all, I would say this was a pretty good night.

* * *

Kelley has a scrimmage, so I told Ivy I'd come with her to sit on the sidelines and cheer him on. She and I are just settling onto a set of bleachers when Jesse comes jogging up in front of us.

"My fave ladies," Jesse croons. "Perky and Prickly, the perfect pair."

Ivy snorts and I flip him off as he takes the risers two at a time to sit behind us.

"Whatya working on, J?" Ivy turns in her seat and asks. Jesse pulls a mess of yarn and his needles out of his backpack and lays it all out in his lap.

"Voodoo doll." He pops a brow and waggles a bundle in front of us. "This one's almost done. Just gotta finish adding the hair."

He holds up what looks like a rough little rag doll, the body dressed in BU blue, and the arms, feet and head are a sandy color. And on the head are a few strands of long brown yarn.

I cock my head to the side...*is that...?*

Hmmm.

I study it some more.

"Is that..."

"Thor!" Jesse beams, and Ivy barks a laugh. "Figure if you're gonna do that competition with him, you'll need the upper hand."

I laugh and roll my eyes. "I don't know voodoo, J."

He waves me off and focuses on adding more hair. "Minor details."

Jesse works on his Riggs doll and Ivy leans in close to me.

"How's the Crisco can?" she asks, making sure not to raise her voice. If Jesse or Kelley knew about my struggle, they'd offer the money up without thinking twice. Ivy would too, if she had it. But I can't do it that way. I have to put in the work and earn it. I shrug and grimace.

"'Bout the same," I whisper back. "I've got almost twenty-three hundred, but now I need to get new tires for Baby and my laptop needs repaired. Again." I sigh. "I feel like I get so close, only for it to slip away again."

"Have you thought anymore about..." She trails off, but I know what she's saying. This is the first I've seen her since I picked up a bar shift last night, but she's been hinting that I should do this contest with Riggs.

"Yeah," I breathe out, "more and more. But it's just risky."

I leave it at that. I don't have to elaborate at all, because she knows.

Riggs has sent me three texts in the week and a half since I saw him at the party. One was later that night, hours after me, Ivy and the guys left, and it was a link to the song he'd mentioned. Just a link. Nothing else. A few days later, he texted to say he'd finished the final book in the YA fantasy series we'd talked about. Then, two nights ago, he sent a short video of his KitchenAid mixer running. "I added cherries" was all he said.

I haven't responded to any of them.

"How's Jacob?" I ask Ivy, switching the topic to her younger brother. She practically raised him, and she gushes about him like a proud mama would. Not that I would know from my own experience with moms.

"Oh, he's doing so good, now." She grins. "Those little bullies at school haven't messed with him at all and he's just signed up to do a science fair. I think Kelley and I are...gonna..."

Her voice takes on a dazed quality and she trails off. When I follow her line of sight, I snort and shake my head. Kelley is shirtless. Of course. I grab my water bottle and nudge her in the arm with it, snapping her out of her drool fest.

"Huh?" She takes the water bottle. "Why'd you give me this?"

I shrug. "Thought maybe you'd need to hydrate. Since you're such a thirsty bitch."

Her jaw drops and she gasps, a smile playing at her lips.

"Yeah?" She shoves the water bottle back at me. "Well maybe *you* should hydrate, because you're a"—she drops to a whisper—"a *salty* bitch."

Jesse and I both fall into hysterics, laughing so hard my side hurts and Jesse has tears in his eyes. Hearing Ivy cuss will never get old.

"Kelley's a bad influence on you," I say after catching my breath.

"Oh, that's too good," Jesse says between laughs. "Hydrate, you salty bitch. Ahh, I need to get that on a sticker." He wipes at his eyes, and then barks again. "Oh, little V, you're so cute." He reaches out and ruffles her hair and she rolls her eyes.

We watch Kelley's team dominate, what with him being the grossly athletic stud that he is and all. Ivy continues to drool and assess. Jesse bounces and knits. I pick at my fingernails and jam out to the song that's currently stuck in my head. It's exactly the kind of familiar Wednesday night that reminds me that I do have a home, even if it's not in the traditional sense. Home is where you feel loved and accepted, where you feel safest, where you can be yourself without fear. Sometimes that's where you grew up with the people who raised you, and sometimes, it's something entirely different.

Sometimes home is a person, a favorite pair of jeans, a song. A pair of Docs. A motorcycle. A tub of hair dye. Sometimes it's a familiar backroad in fall with the windows down and the radio up, or a two-dollar taco Wednesday night tradition with a cherry margarita and endless laughter.

Sometimes home is a beautiful, intricate, chaotic, imper-fect mosaic of people you've collected and places you've been, held together by the experiences that have made you, and you carry that with you, adding pieces to it, for the rest of your life.

That's what these people are for me. Kelley, Ivy, and Jesse are the start of my mosaic. They are my home. It's a steadying and comforting thought.

Kelley's game is wrapping up when I notice a large group of guys running on the other side of the field. They're wearing matching sweatpants, some are shirtless, and some have on blue t-shirts with BU BASEBALL printed on them. And right there in front, leading the pack, is Riggs Stanton.

And of *fucking* course, he's one of the shirtless ones.

What the fuck is it with shirtless dudes today?

"Now who's the thirsty bitch," Jesse mock-whispers, and I swat at him.

But I don't say anything to defend myself because I was definitely staring. Color me hypocritical.

When the group comes closer, Riggs makes eye contact with

me and gives me a small, almost imperceptible nod of the head. That's it. And then he just runs on past.

"Hmmm," Ivy hums.

"How's that for a brush off," Jesse quips.

"He was running with his team," Kelley counters as he walks up and throws his sweaty arm around Ivy. "He was focused."

"Yeah, but not even a wave? A smile? That's like polar opposite from every other time we've seen him." Jesse's got his arms crossed and he's staring at the baseball team as they loop the intramural fields for another lap. "Where's the chest pounding? The ground stomping? The flaring nostrils? He didn't even look like he was considering beating my ass." Jesse pouts. "It was no fun for me."

"It was kinda surprising," Ivy adds.

"He's like two totally different guys," I muse. "I don't get it. It's like he's a completely different person when I talk to him versus when he's around everyone else."

"Is he making everything complicated?" Jesse asks, and he's got this big stupid grin on his face.

"Actin' like somebody else gets you frustrated?" Kelley chimes in.

It hits me a split second before they both shout out in an ear-splitting, horrible attempt at harmony.

"Oh my *gooood*," I cut them off. "I'm living in an Avril Lavigne song."

"Yikes." Ivy laughs, then hooks her arm in mine. "You know what will fix it? Tacos."

She tugs me away from the goons behind us who are still attempting to sing that damn song, and we head to the taco bar that's a few blocks from the intramural fields. I don't bother thinking about Riggs for the rest of the night. I force him from my head and enjoy my two-dollar tacos and my giant as hell frozen cherry margarita. Then Kelley sneakily covers our bill, which assuages my Crisco can guilt for eating with money I should be squirreling away, and I get home feeling less dark, thanks to my friends.

Before I go to bed, though, I get a text from Riggs.

Fuxboi: You look good in green.

That's all he says. *You look good in green.*

I cast a glance at the green flannel I took off and discarded by the door. It was actually Brandon's, but I kept it after he died. Without overthinking it, I text him back a single thank you, then put my phone on silent and turn off my light.

* * *

A week later, I find myself at a party, while my friends celebrate accomplishments, feeling adrift.

Kelley just ran a marathon. Ivy got her LSAT scores back. Jesse just got into another top tier medical school. And I'm happy for them. I am.

But I'm restless.

It's been radio silence on the Riggs Front since the "you look good in green" text. I saw him once on the quad this past week with a group of guys. He was strutting along, leader of the pack, with his arm slung over Talia's shoulder and his dudes trailing like puppies, and it made me want to vomit.

But.

A few days ago, out of curiosity that I disguised as research, I went to Bakery On Main and ordered Riggs's winning cookie. He named it Odette's *Palets,* which begrudgingly made me smile. Not only because I now know his mom's name is Odette, but also because I'm pretty sure most of the people ordering the cookie won't pronounce it the French way. But then I tasted it, and it pissed me off. Because damn, it was good. I didn't order more to take home, even though I was really tempted.

Ultimately, I know I can't let my feelings for him blind my decisions. The Holiday Bake Off could be a great opportunity. The experience is once in a lifetime, and it would be mostly paid for. And if we win... Ten *thousand* dollars.

I could suffer through a week with Riggs for ten thousand dollars.

I could suffer through a week of almost *anything* for that kind of money.

I shouldn't be worried about him worming his way back into my good graces. That ship has sailed. My emotional walls are up, fortified with brick, and reinforced with titanium. There's absolutely no way he's going to get to me again, and I can't pass up this opportunity. If not for myself, then for Bran.

Right?

Yes. Right. So I pull out my phone and send the text I've been debating for weeks.

Me: I'll do it. What do you need me to sign?

TWELVE

IT'S JUST after noon when I pull my Audi up to the hotel where we'll be staying for the week. The Holiday Bake Off is being held at a convention center about four miles away, so I hired a driver to take us to and from the hotel every day.

I pop the trunk, then hop out of the car to grab our luggage.

"I got it," Bailey grumbles when I reach for her duffle bag. She snags the handle away from me and tugs it out of the trunk. I grit my teeth and swallow my protest. Instead, I grab my own suitcase, then turn and drop my keys into the hand of the hotel valet.

I'm in for a long ass week if that car ride was any indicator. She had her headphones in most of the drive, and any time I tried to make conversation, she'd give monosyllabic responses. It was the most uncomfortable two hours and forty-seven minutes I have ever spent in a vehicle, and that's saying something because I travel cross country after pitching no-hitters with smelly-ass athletes on the regular.

"I'll go check us in," I say over my shoulder. She shrugs and plops down into a chair in the lobby. She's trying to act bored, but I don't miss the way her eyes widen and eat up the luxury dripping from every corner of this hotel. With the Christmas lights and decorations in full swing, it's beautiful. My father spares no expense on his hotels, and this particular one, The ParisHouse, my mom helped design and decorate, even down to the various holiday and seasonal displays. It's my favorite of them all.

"Good morning," the front desk attendant greets with a smile. "Are you checking in with us today?"

"I am. The name is Riggs Stanton."

"Oh! Mr. Stanton." Her eyes grow wide at the name. "And will your parents be joining us on this visit as well?"

"Not this time," I say with a smile. "Two suites. They should be together," I add the last part quietly. I don't want Bailey hearing that I specifically requested we be neighbors for the week. I can only imagine how well that would go over with her.

"Yes, sir, I see it right here. Two luxury suites, and we've put you on the twenty-first floor. The receipt will be emailed. Is that alright?"

"Yes, thank you."

"Wonderful. Here are your key cards." She slides two small envelopes over the counter toward me. "Check out is Monday at 2 p.m. for room 2110, and next Saturday at 2 p.m. for room 2112."

"Thank y—" *wait, what?* "Wait. Monday?" I lower my voice, check over my shoulder to make sure Bailey can't hear, then lean in closer to the attendant. "I should have both suites for the week. Saturday to Saturday. There must be some mistake."

"Oh," she gasps. "Well, let me check..." Poor woman looks like a deer in headlights as she frantically types on her keyboard. "I'm sorry, Mr. Stanton...we're all booked through. But if you wait, I can call—"

"No," I cut her off quickly. "No, that won't be necessary." If she calls the manager, then they will alert my dad, and I really don't need to deal with him. I give her a reassuring smile. "We'll be fine. Thank you for your help."

Bailey looks up from her phone when I step in front of her. "You ready?"

She stands and drags her beat-up duffle over her shoulder. "Lead the way."

It's silent in the elevator as we glide to the twenty-first floor, but I catch her looking at me in the mirrored glass doors. When they slide open, we empty out into a large hallway with stylish carpet and expensive textured wallpaper. I watch her take it all in the same way she did in the lobby.

"2112 is you." I stop in front of her door and hold out the keycard.

"And you're…" she asks with a raised brow.

I grin and gesture to the door we just passed. "2110."

"We share a wall."

I nod, and I watch as she chews on her lip. For a few seconds, we're locked in one of those stare-offs I've gotten used to. Where her gaze is drawn to mine against her will. Where we stay fixated on each other in spite of everything. My eyes seek her out the way they would a candle flickering in near darkness, instinctual and immediate, and they cling to her out of what feels like need as much as desire. It's the same for her, I think, and she hates it.

Her breath hitches, and she blinks. "Thanks." She disappears into her room, letting the big wooden door fall closed behind her.

I leave my suitcase by the door in my room and kick off my shoes. My dad used to get pissed whenever we'd travel because I don't like using the closet or dressers in these fancy hotels. If you unpack, it feels more like a home and less like a hotel, and half the fun of staying in hotels is that they're *not* your home. Mom always understood.

I head into the bathroom and crank the shower, needing to thaw the chill from my body that has less to do with the weather and more to do with a particularly icy brunette. She has the itinerary, so she knows we're leaving for the convention center at 9 a.m. for the contest debriefing and orientation. That means I have no reason to see her again tonight.

Except...

I really need to tell her about the room issue. These suites are big—equipped with king beds and couches—so it won't be terrible if we have to share. We'll be spending most of the day at the convention center, anyway, so really, we'll only need the room for...sleeping...and showering.

Fuck.

Come Monday, shit's gonna get real interesting.

* * *

The next morning, I meet Bailey in the hallway. We're going to grab breakfast at a nearby café before taking a car to the convention center. She's wearing her Docs, black skinny jeans, a big, olive green parka type coat with a faux-fur lined hood, and a purple and black knitted scarf. Despite the fact that I know it's 40 degrees outside, I scowl at the scrap of yarn.

"Did Slipper Dick knit you that scarf?"

She fingers the edges with a smirk. "Yup."

I grunt and turn on my heel.

"His name is Jesse," she says as we walk to the elevators. "I've known him since sophomore year."

"Don't care."

"He's pre-med," she adds.

"Cool." I jab at the button for the elevator.

"He's a literal genius. His IQ is like 160 or something crazy like that."

"Awesome for him."

She climbs into the elevator with me, and I watch her in my periphery.

"Yeah, he's a great friend."

My ears perk at *friend*, and I flick my eyes to her, but she's looking down at her phone. I should leave it at that, but I'm an idiot, so I don't.

"A *friend*...?"

"Mhm." She sounds bored. "Me, Ivy, Jesse and Kelley. *Friends*."

When the elevator door opens, she skips past me into the lobby, and I don't catch up to her until we're stepping out onto the sidewalk.

"There's a Dunkin' right there." She points down the block, then starts walking, but I reach out and grab her shoulder.

"Nah. We're going to one of my favorite cafés. Locally sourced ingredients, fair trade coffee, and an 80's theme." I don't miss the sparkle in her amber eyes.

"That sounds great, but also hipster expensive."

"On me." I don't give her a chance to protest.

Three blocks later, we're walking into a café with 80's movie posters and cultural paraphernalia lining the walls, rustic tables with mismatched vintage-looking chairs cover the floor, and a fucking model DeLorean is suspended from the ceiling.

"Holy shit." She bounces a few times on her toes. "This is freakin sick."

"Wait till you see the menu."

I follow her toward the counter and watch as her eyes scan the chalkboards on the wall.

"Whaaat? Everything is named after an 80's movie character. This is awesome." She scans the items and flashes me a smirk. "You said you're buying?"

I smile. "Yep."

She orders a latte, a scone, and the most expensive sandwich on the menu. The Biff, it's called, and because I know she wants it, I roll my eyes and fake offense. I could buy her the entire menu multiple times over if she wanted, but I'll let her think she's irritating me by making me buy a twelve-dollar egg sandwich.

"Poetry," she says randomly between bites of her breakfast.

"What about it?" I folded my napkin into an origami frog, but it's too floppy to bounce.

"If I owned a café, I would want it to be themed after poetry. Or writing. Books." She takes a sip from her latte, and I study her. "This 80's theme is awesome, but mine would have words and quotes and books instead of movie posters and toys."

"What kind of café?"

"Like this one. Bakery and coffee shop. Easy lunch and breakfast food. Kinda like Bakery On Main, I guess."

"But with a poetic atmosphere for writers." I finish, and she gives me a smile that quickens my heartbeat and sparks flashes of memories.

"Yeah. Or readers. Or anyone, really." Her voice is optimistic in a dreamy way. "With a homey sense of community, like a family, and cupcakes."

It's like a switch flips. Like at the mention of cupcakes, she remembers who she's with and why she hates me, and the light happiness of her features is wiped clean. In its place is a blank, emotionless slate.

"Right," I grumble. "We should probably get to the convention center anyway."

At the convention center, we're given packets, folders, nametags, and welcome gift bags, then we're told to take a seat.

Bailey and I are two of twenty-four contestants—twelve teams. We're told that the contest runs Monday-Friday, and each day, a certain number of teams will be eliminated. Tomorrow is the biggest chopping block. They'll send home four teams at the end of the day. Then every day after, two teams a day will get the boot until Friday, when only two teams are left to compete for the ten thousand dollars.

Then they get into the challenges. Monday and Tuesday, we'll be given a common bakery item and ingredients. It's up to us to make up a recipe on the fly, because we're not told anything ahead of time. We've been assigned a country in our packets, and that's what we focus on for Wednesday, assuming we advance. Wednesday, we're to make a dessert item that's popular in our assigned country, and we're allowed to do a little prep ahead of time. We can even tell the judges if we need any special ingredients for our recipe and practice making the items outside of filming.

Bailey and I flip to the backs of our packets at the same time, and our shoulders fall at the same time, too.

Bangladesh.

I know absolutely fucking nothing about Bangladesh, except that I *think* it's in South Asia. I was hoping for a softball toss here—maybe France or Italy—but didn't get it. France and Italy I'm familiar with. Bangladesh is going to require some serious internet searching.

Thursday is another surprise bakery item, and Friday, for the final two teams, is a theme to be revealed on Wednesday. The two teams on Friday will have to bake three items that fit the given theme, and one of those items has to be a re-creation of something from the past week.

It's...a lot.

I glance over at Bailey and can tell she's feeling it, too. This is overwhelming, but I guess they have to have us do more than chocolate chip cookies to offer ten grand.

The people leading the orientation go over the rules and expectations. We're not allowed to use our phones on set, and we're not allowed to post details about the contest on social media. We even have to sign NDAs. Fine with me. The whole competition is being filmed for a two-night holiday special on one of the local cable channels. Five days of filming and they're going to condense it down into two hours total. Crazy how that shit works.

Once again, I'll be on television doing something that isn't baseball related, and the risk makes me fucking jittery. I barely made it out clean last time, what with Zay seeing the cookie competition on *The Morning Show*. If the guys somehow see this one... Or Dad...

Shit.

At least the contest will be over by the time the show airs, so he can't insist I drop it.

"How you doing?" I ask Bailey as we pack up.

"This is a lot."

"Yeah."

"I just started baking sophomore year. What if I'm not good enough for this?"

"Hey," I say gently, "you *are* good enough. And we're a team, so we can fill in where the other lacks. You use your creativity to give my technical focus a boost, and I'll make sure you're not a sloppy mess." I grin at her and inwardly celebrate when her lips twitch up.

"Right." She rolls her eyes. "You think we can do this?"

"I do."

"Hey, Barnes!" someone calls, and we both turn toward the voice. Up walks a guy about our age. He's clean-shaven, his eyebrow is pierced, his hair is in some 1950's James Dean style, and he's wearing a black plaid shirt that looks like it could have come straight from Bailey's closet. My hackles raise.

"Oh my god!" Bailey squeals and launches herself into the dude's arms. Are you fucking kidding me? "Taylor. What the hell are you doing here?"

He takes a step back from the hug and gives us both a smile, but he keeps his arms on Bailey's shoulders. "Same thing as you, I guess." It's reflex that my stance squares, my arms cross, and my chest puffs out.

"I didn't even know you liked baking," she says.

He raises his eyebrow suggestively, and she snorts and swats his side.

"When did you start?" he asks her.

"Sophomore year. I needed something. After."

"Yeah," his voice is soft, and he gives her a sad kind of smile. "Me too."

I clear my throat loudly and thrust my hand at him.

"Riggs. I'm Bailey's partner."

He drops his arms from her shoulders so he can shake my hand.

"Taylor. Bailey and I go way back."

"Taylor and I went to school together before I transferred," Bailey chimes in.

"Before you crossed the state line into no man's land and fell off the face of the earth," Taylor jokes. "We miss you, little Barnes. Where you staying? Maybe we can hang before this thing is over."

"We're at The ParisHouse on State and Chicago Ave," I butt in, and relish the way the guys' eyes widen and he whistles.

"We're out of the city. Takin' the train in, then hoppin' on the L." He widens his eyes as he whispers, "My partner was random. He's a Buckeye."

Bailey groans comically, and I step up and throw my arm

around her. I ignore the way she stiffens. "Well, luckily we're not random, are we, Sundance? Nice to meet you, Tyler. Our car is out front. Enjoy the train."

"See you tomorrow," Bailey says quickly as I steer her toward the exit. As soon as we're out of ear shot, she elbows me in the side, and I drop my arm. I might be an idiot, but I do value my safety. "What *the fuck* was that, Riggs?"

"Sorry, but we don't have time for you to make kissy face with the competition. You gotta keep your head in the game, *little Barnes*."

Yeah, okay, I *sorta* value my safety. Her eyes say she might break into my room and murder me in my sleep tonight.

"You're such an asshole," she growls, stomping up to the car. "Taylor is a friend."

"Taylor wants to fuck you."

"So what if he does?"

I choke on my own spit as I swing the door open.

"So what? You're not going to fuck up our chances of winning because you want spontaneous dick." She stands on the sidewalk and glares at me. "Get in the car, Bailey."

"No."

"Get in the car, Bailey."

"I'll walk."

"Are you nuts? You're not walking three and a half miles through the city alone when it's dark and thirty-five degrees out. Get in the damn car."

She huffs and throws herself into the back seat, then scoots over and plasters herself to the opposite door. I slide in after her and nod to the driver.

"Thank you," I say smugly.

"Fuck off." And in go her earbuds.

I guess getting dinner together is out of the question.

THIRTEEN

OH, fuck. Oh, shit. Oh, holy hell this is happening.

Riggs meets me in the hallway the next morning and we ride to the convention center in silence. I'm a landmine of nerves and loose wires, and from the way he's fidgeting with his fingers, I can tell he's feeling the pressure too.

"What if we mess it up," I whisper to him as the car pulls up to the convention center.

"We won't," he says confidently. "But even if we do, in the grand scheme of things, it's just a contest."

I don't respond. To him it's just a contest. To me, it's everything.

When we walk into the convention center, I'm amazed to see twelve cooking stations set up just like they would be on one of those baking or cooking shows on television. Only what you don't see on the television shows is all the filming equipment. Cameras, lighting, giant ass microphones. It's crazy and just adds to my nerves.

We're shuffled in by a production assistant who directs us to "get make'd and mic'd up" which is basically this whole ordeal where random people throw powders and crap on our faces, then fit us with portable microphones. We have to check our coats, bags, and phones, and then we're given red aprons and matching red chef's hats. The whole process takes a little over an hour, and aside from a few wide-eyed *WTF* glances, Riggs and I don't speak.

When that's done, we're shown to our station where we're told to "sit tight and don't touch anything." Other teams are filtered in, people run around testing and moving equipment and stuff, and at one point, a guy with a camera comes up and asks us some questions. We have to introduce ourselves—names, ages, college, majors, et cetera—and we're told they'll be asking us more questions throughout the week.

I see Taylor and his partner walk in, and I wave. He smiles and waves before he's shuttled away by another PA.

"Head in the game, Barnes. Quit flirting." Ugh, his stupid growly voice is annoying.

"I was saying hello," I spit. "Are you so out of touch that you can't tell the difference between greeting and flirting?"

His grin is wicked. "People don't usually greet me without flirting, Barnes. Or have you forgotten how we met?"

My face heats. "I wasn't flirting with you."

"You were." His deep timbre vibrates over my skin as he steps closer. "And I flirted back. And then we fucked. Many, many times." He reaches up and fingers the strap of my apron, and I gasp when his knuckle drags over my collarbone. "Remember?"

For a brief moment, I'm all hormones and nerve endings, goosebumps cover my skin and lust clouds my brain. And then I do what he asked. I remember.

I swat his hand away. "Yeah, I remember, *Riggs*. Funny how you *couldn't* remember your real name or the fact that you have a fucking girlfriend."

We lock eyes, frustration evident in his furrowed brow, and

I hope he sees the hatred I feel. The utter disgust. I filter it all into my expression and try my best to mask what's underneath. The hurt he caused. The betrayal. He doesn't get the satisfaction of knowing he could have been important to me. He doesn't deserve it.

"You don't know what you're talking about," he growls, jaw tight.

"I know enough."

We break apart when one of the producers calls us all to attention. He's one of the same guys from yesterday's orientation. He gives us the breakdown of how filming will go and tells us that judges and camera crew will be walking around and observing throughout the whole process. Then we're given a box and an envelope. The envelope contains the day's challenge, the box contains the necessary ingredients—we won't have to use them all depending on our recipe—and on shelves on the back wall are what they call add-ins. The ingredients that we may want to use to make our recipe more creative and unique.

When someone shouts action, we flip open the envelopes.

Cupcakes.

Today's challenge is cupcakes.

I heave a sigh of relief. Thank god. I could bake cupcakes with my hands tied.

We flip open the box and sift through the ingredients. Flour, baking powder and soda, cocoa powder, salt, butter, white and brown sugar, vegetable oil, eggs, milk, and pure vanilla extract. I avoid eye contact with Riggs when I set the vanilla on the counter.

"No cherries," he murmurs, but I ignore him and turn to head back to the add-ins. Without thinking too long, I grab bananas and powdered sugar, then go into the cooler and grab cream cheese. When I dump it all on the counter at our station, Riggs surveys the pile and turns to me.

"You don't like bananas," he states.

"Not true. I like it in some baked goods."

"We have to be careful with that banana. It's probably going to be too dense for a cupcake recipe if you don't watch how you mix it," he says. "We should see if they have extract so we don't have to use as much actual banana."

I didn't even know there was such a thing as banana extract, but I don't let him know it.

"No. I want to use real banana." I start whipping open drawers and pulling out measuring cups, spoons, and bowls, tossing them onto the counter as I go.

He sighs. "Don't be stubborn, Barnes."

"I'm not being stubborn, Stanton. Stop trying to micromanage."

"Bananas are too dense."

"Then make something else."

"We're a *team*," he stresses.

"This is what I'm doing." My jaw is tight as I start measuring out the flour.

"Do you need a sifter?" I don't answer. "Fine," he huffs, and I ignore him as he starts banging around next to me. I don't need his stupid help. I can bake cupcakes in my sleep.

On autopilot, I dump eggs, vanilla, oil, baking powder, salt, and milk in the mixing bowl. Same as I do at home. I look at the bananas, decide to mash them up with some brown sugar, and then dump that into the mixing bowl as well. Then I use the stand mixer to make sure it's all blended together.

I'm pouring thick, clumpy batter into my cupcake tin when a judge comes up to me with a cameraman behind him. I force a nervous smile.

"Bailey, tell me about what you're baking."

"I'm making banana cupcakes." I flick my eyes to Riggs as he comes to stand next to me. "And I'm going to ice them with a cream cheese icing."

"Sounds delicious. And is Riggs also making banana cupcakes? Because it looks like you two are working on two different things."

"Oh, um—"

"I'm making a different batch, sir. Vanilla cupcakes with whipped topping," Riggs says, voice smooth and steady, and the judge assesses us.

"Two different cupcakes?" He pops a brow. "And which will you present to the judges?"

"Mine." Riggs and I speak at the same time, and the judge grimaces.

"Okay. Well. Seems you two need to discuss your game plan."

When the judge walks away, I glare at Riggs then turn my back to him. Vanilla. What a joke.

Shit.

Shit, shit, shit.

"Those are muffins," Riggs says from over my shoulder. He's right. These are too dense. Instead of light, fluffy, and moist, they're dense. A few of them are even a little too soft on the bottom, telling me they might not be cooked through. They smell divine, but they are not cupcakes, and definitely not winning material.

"I know," I murmur as I spread the cream cheese icing on them. I check the clock. We have fifteen minutes before we're supposed to present. After that, we're supposed to go through interviews, and after those, the judges announce their decisions.

I know I'm a disaster. I have flour all over my apron, egg splattered on my shoe, and from the way my cheek itches, I'm pretty sure there is cream cheese somewhere on my face. When I look at him, my face falls, because he looks perfect. Clean. Unruffled. I hate how my heart skips.

"These won't win," I admit, and he shakes his head slowly.

"They might." He breaks one of the cupcakes in half, and shoves it in his mouth. I watch his jaw work as he chews. My eyes snap to his prominent Adam's apple, watching it bob as he swallows. "It's really good."

"But it's not a cupcake."

He grimaces. "I made these. They're not creative at all, but the texture and consistency is near perfect." He hands me a vanilla cupcake and I take a bite. Damn it. It's not near perfect. It *is* perfect.

"Ten minutes!" yells a PA, and Riggs and I tense.

"If we use your banana muffins, we'll probably be sent home. They specifically said they wanted fluffy cupcakes, not hearty—"

"Yes, thank you, I know I made fucking muffins," I interrupt.

"Right," he says with a sigh. "But if we use mine, we could lose points because they're—"

"Boring?"

Surprisingly, he chuckles. "Yeah."

I rack my brain for a solution. Anything to keep us in this damn competition.

"I have an idea," I whisper and then rush to the add-ins. I come back with another banana, a bottle of banana extract, and a spice bottle of ground cloves. "Um, scrape the whipped topping off your cupcakes, okay? I'm going to put banana flavoring in my cream cheese icing, and we can use that."

Riggs nods, and I pour a tiny drop of banana extract into my icing bowl and a dash of the ground cloves. As I mix it up, Riggs dices the banana into small pieces. Just as I'm about to dump the chopped banana into the bowl, Riggs grabs my hand to stop me.

"Fold in a little at a time," he says, and though my gut instinct is to pop off and tell him to STFU, I just nod and slide the bowl to him.

"You do it."

When the buzzer sounds, announcing that our time is up, I'm just placing a thin slice of banana on the top of the final cupcake. We step back and survey our work.

Honestly, it looks good. Now we just have to hope it's enough.

For the first time since this morning, I look around the room. It's a gut punch.

"Shit," I whisper. Everyone's cupcakes are gorgeous—an array of colors that suggest a variety of flavors, and all I can do is cross my fingers that ours is better than at least four of these other teams.

Riggs and I have to present our cupcakes to the five judges, and I watch in silence as they all sample them. No one says anything. It's torture. Then we're whisked into a small room, with an overstuffed, comfortable red loveseat and a Christmas tree, and behind the loveseat is a backdrop painted to look like a picture window overlooking a snowy Chicago skyline. This is the scene room where they'll be conducting all of our end-of-day interviews about our experience. They want to know how we think the challenge went, what our process was, why we chose to bake what we did. I let Riggs do most of the talking. His voice is smooth and steady, his answers confident and clear, as if he's rehearsed them.

For a minute, I wonder if this is how he handles team interviews after a game. I've Googled him. I know he's a big deal, and that he's on camera giving interviews almost as much as he is pitching at games. When he turns his camera-perfect smile on me, I almost forget everything but him, and I'm transported back to aisle six of Quick Stop. I'm so out of it that I feel myself smile back at him. It's the shock on his face that snaps me out of it.

After what feels like a billion hours, we're assembled for the judges' decisions.

The bottom six teams will be announced, and from there, four of those teams will be sent home. They announce the top two recipes first—a mint julep cupcake and a coconut rum cupcake. I knew we wouldn't be in the top two, but I'm still disappointed. And with those fancy ass recipes, I'm even more worried that we'll be sent home.

Vanilla cupcakes and banana cream cheese icing. It's basic as fuck. Might as well have done pumpkin spice and piped *Live, Laugh, Love* on the damn things.

When our names are called as part of the bottom six, I don't even flinch. I expected it.

We're going home.

I'm so sorry, Bran.

The judges go through each cupcake from the bottom six, critiquing and criticizing. By the time they get to us, three teams have already been booted. Which means it's down to us or the team next to us who stays.

"I have to say," one of the judges says, "this cupcake was underwhelming. The cake itself has a great texture and consistency. It's moist and light. Flavorful. But—"

"But it's *vanilla*," says another judge. "We like when our contestants take a risk. Even if you would have done something with the vanilla. Cherry vanilla, rum vanilla. *Something.* You're up against some of the best collegiate bakers in the Midwest— you need creativity as much as anything else."

"Think outside the box."

Riggs and I nod. I bite my lip and will my eyes not to water as the judges volley back and forth.

"I did like your icing choice, though," says another judge, and they all agree. "The flavor, while still pretty basic, spiced up the cake nicely."

"Literally with the clove."

"Exactly."

"The banana wasn't overpowering, and the icing texture was heavy, but it worked well with the lightness of the cake."

A tiny spark of hope ignites, and I hold my breath.

Riggs's hand is clasped in mine tightly. I don't know who made the move first, and I don't care. Right now, I need his grip, his anchor, so that everything else is just noise.

"We want to see you take more risks this week. Your cake recipe was executed perfectly, and your icing was a good complement. Try for more creativity—something more unique —tomorrow."

"Riggs and Bailey, you're safe this round."

"Thank you," Riggs and I blurt at the same time.

"Thank you so much for the chance to improve," I continue. "We'll be better."

Riggs sweeps me into a hug, and I let him. For a few seconds, I press my forehead into his chest and breathe him in, making sure my eyes have dried before breaking away.

We're safe.

For now.

My nerves are shot, my stomach is in knots, and my energy is depleted. I don't talk to Riggs the whole drive back, and I'm out and into the lobby before I even notice he's not following me.

Good.

I can't face him again tonight.

. . .

When I get to my room, the first thing I do is call Ivy. She answers on the first ring.

"Hey, babe," she chirps. I can hear laughter in the background, then I hear rustling and a door shutting, and it grows quieter. "How's it going?"

I break.

"I don't belong here, V," I say through silent tears. My insecurities unleash and swell like a tidal wave, and I let them pull me under, covering me in darkness. "I don't belong here."

"Yes, you do." Her voice is full of conviction. "You belong there as much as anyone else. What happened?"

"We almost got sent home. Today. On the first fucking day."

"Okay." She takes a soothing breath and I instinctively mimic her. "But you didn't, right?"

"No. But, V, I botched cupcakes. *Cupcakes*. All these other contestants are so much more talented than me. And they know how to bake. They've probably been doing this way longer. I never even used a real kitchen until we got the apartment. Before that it was just the community one in the dorms where I had to rotate everything every ten minutes or it would burn the whole left side and undercook the right."

"Hey, you made some great stuff in that crappy kitchen." I can hear the smile in her playful tone.

"True. But none of those recipes would win here."

"Stop selling yourself short, Bailey. You're a talented baker. You're creative and imaginative and *talented*. You just had a little hiccup today."

"And what if I have another hiccup tomorrow? What if they throw me something I've literally never baked before? I'm going to fail, V. I'm going to fail and let Brandon down again."

"First, you have never failed Brandon. Ever." Ivy's voice is stern, bucking any argument. "You've told me that whole story, B, and none of it was your fault. Brandon made his own choice in telling Craig, and there is no way you could have known what was going to happen freshman year. You were and are a great sister. You have *never* failed him."

I squeeze my eyes shut as tears continue to stream out, losing the battle to stifle my whimpers.

"You're good enough to be there, Bailey. You *deserve* to be there, and I know you can do this."

"I don't feel good enough."

Ivy sighs and I hear her sniffle. When she speaks again, her voice is soft, but no less firm.

"You're thinking like a secondary character again, B," she says the thing she's been telling me periodically since sophomore year. "You're more than the token best friend or twin sister. You're more than a supporting part. You don't exist just for the purpose of moving someone else's storyline forward. You're main character material."

"I know," I whisper.

"Say it," she urges, and a small smile breaks on my lips.

"I'm the hero in all of my stories."

"Every single one of them. And this baking competition is yours, too. It's your plot, B. You're the hero in this story. Right?"

"Right," I say with a sniff, and I wipe my face with my sleeve.

"And what do heroes do?"

I choke out a laugh. "They kick ass."

"That's right. And you will, too."

"Thank you."

"I'm only telling you the truth, Bails. I love you, and I believe in you. I wouldn't say it if I didn't."

"I know. I love you back." I take a deep breath and change the subject. "This hotel is insane. I've got a shower big enough to fit all four of us, and a separate tub with jets."

"What? That's nuts. I've never been in a jetted tub."

"Me either. And the bed is like three times the size of mine at the apartment. And impossibly soft. Like sleeping on a cloud."

"Dang, I'm jealous. You said you're downtown Chicago, right? I Googled it, and that hotel is *at least* five hundred bucks a night."

"Good lord, you're kidding," I choke.

"Nope. Riggs must be loaded. Paying for the luxury and the convenience, I guess."

I snort. "Rich people convenience. Like heated bathroom floor tiles."

"And no-slam cabinet doors."

"Endless supplies of hot water."

"Nightlight wall outlets."

"Self-cleaning ovens."

"Spoons that don't bend when you try to dig into your pint of ice cream straight from the freezer." She laughs and adds, "Freezers that get your ice cream cold enough to bend cheap spoons."

"How about this one: fog-proof bathroom mirrors."

"Wait. That's a thing?"

"Shit you not, V, this bathroom mirror does not fog. I ran the shower on scalding for like an hour last night. The edges fogged, but the middle stayed clear."

"It's bewitched." She giggles. I thought the same thing. "Kelley's parents don't even have those."

"I bet Dr. and Mr. Hernandez do, though." Can't tell it from his constant bouncing, but Jesse's family is hella boujee.

"They probably do," Ivy says on another giggle.

I sigh, feeling loads better. This girl. I don't know what I would do without her.

"Thanks for talking me down, Ivy Bean."

"Anytime, Bailey Bear." I know she means it. "What are you doing for the rest of tonight?"

"Ordering a thirty-dollar burger from room service and rage dancing until it gets here. Then passing out until tomorrow."

"Sounds like a plan. Talk tomorrow night?"

"Yeah. Love you. Tell Kelley I said hi."

"I will! Love you back. Knock 'em dead tomorrow. Byeeee," she sings, and then the line goes dead.

I order room service—the burger is actually twenty-six dollars, not thirty—change into some sleep shorts and a tank, and turn on my "Fuck This Day" playlist. Then, popping in my earbuds, I dance.

FOURTEEN

GRABBING my suitcase from the front desk, I vow to give Bailey a few hours to cool down before I have to break the news to her that we're gonna be roommates.

I packed my shit and checked out early this morning before grabbing her from her room and heading to the convention center. The front desk manager has been instructed to call me if any other rooms become available, but this close to the holidays, the chances of that happening are slim.

Today was rough. I could tell from her body language that Bailey is pissed. The hug was a mistake, so I'm prepping myself for a blow up the moment she hears how badly I screwed up our reservations. I'm in no hurry to face her, so instead I grab a burger and a drink at the hotel bar. I call Mom, but Ms. Beth says she's unavailable and will have her call me back as soon as she can. I respond to the texts from Talia I've been avoiding. She wants to know how the contest is going, and I tell her fine. She wants to know if she should still come for Christmas dinner, and I say yes. My family will expect her to be there. When she rings through with a video call, I accept, because I was just texting her and ignoring it would be a prick move.

"Hey, handsome," she croons. She's sitting on her white four-poster bed in her parents' house, and it looks like she's wearing some sort of slinky silk nightgown. She's also holding a glass of wine and her grin is mischievous.

"Hey, yourself," I say with a smile. "Are you drunk?"

"I thought you liked me drunk." Her voice is a purr, her eyes dancing and glassy. I shake my head with a laugh. Talia is so buttoned-up, so proper. Every bit a prima ballerina. I don't get to see her like this much anymore—fun and flirty.

That's your fault, I think suddenly. I sigh. Yeah, it is.

We talk for a while, and when my second drink is gone, I tell Talia goodnight and march myself toward the elevator. A condemned man about to meet his executioner.

This is going to suck.

When I turn down our hallway, I'm immediately confused. There's a room service cart sitting outside Bailey's door, untouched. A warm bottle of pop sits on top, and when I lift the silver lid of the food platter, I find a cold burger and fries.

Curiosity hits me first.

Unease comes next.

I knock loudly on the door and wait.

Nothing.

I send her a text and knock again.

No answer from either.

I try to call her, and it goes straight to voicemail.

What the fuck?

Quickly, I pull out the keycard from my back pocket and fumble it to the door. My heart is racing, nervous of what I will find. Is she okay? Did she leave? I don't know what I would do in either situation besides freak out and maybe fucking rage.

It takes three tries, but when I finally get the green light, I hold my breath and swing the door wide open.

And then exhale on a laugh.

Bailey is fine.

Better than fine, apparently, if the way she's waving her arms in the air and bouncing around is any indication. Her eyes are closed, and her mouth is moving as if she's talking to herself. When I look closer, I see her earbuds are in and her phone is in her hand.

Singing.

She's not talking to herself. She's singing. And she's not just waving and bouncing; she's dancing. I say her name, but she doesn't notice me, so I step in, close the door, and lean back on it with my arms folded across my chest. If she doesn't see me in thirty seconds, I'll step closer. I don't want to startle her, but I don't want to invade her privacy any more than I already have.

Though, admittedly, I would rather just watch. I'd much rather glue my eyes to her ass and tits and face and keep them there, but Odette DuPont Stanton raised a gentleman. So instead, I count out thirty seconds in my head.

I'm at ten when she notices me.

Ten and a breath when she jumps backward, screams, and trips over the couch, falling gracelessly on her ass.

"Oh my god," I bark, half-laughing, half-concerned. I rush to her. "Are you okay?"

I grab her hand and help her up, and the minute she's on her feet, she shoves my chest. Hard.

"What the fuck, Butch! You tryin' to scare me to death?" Her voice is loud but breathy, and she rips out her earbuds. "You ever heard of *knocking*?"

She's pissed. Great. This will not make our situation any easier. But what did I expect? I broke into her room and scared the shit out of her. I throw my hands up in a *whoa, there* gesture.

"I did knock. And I texted and called. I saw your untouched room service cart and thought something had happened."

She furrows her brow and looks quickly toward the door, then down at her phone, noticing the missed calls.

"I was worried," I add. "I'm sorry for scaring you, but I was worried."

Her face softens immediately, like I spoke magic words, and I'm floored when she apologizes. Apologizes sincerely, with no malice.

"I'm sorry," she breathes. "My phone was on Do Not Disturb and I lost track of time. I didn't mean to scare you." She chuckles. "This playlist is like three hours long."

"It's fine." I smile at her. "I was just worried. I'm glad you're okay."

She nods. "Yeah, I'm good. Thanks for checking on me. You can go."

Oh, shit, right.

"Um, yeah, about that." I scrunch up my face, the picture of an apologetic innocent bystander. Though I am far from innocent in this mess. "I have some bad news."

Her eyes widen. "What? Are we disqualified? Have they changed their minds and kicked us out?" She starts to pace. "Oh my god, I knew I fucked it up."

I step toward her and place a hand on her shoulder, trying and failing to ignore the familiar warmth and softness of her skin under my palm.

"No, it's nothing like that," I rush out, and she blows out a relieved breath.

"Oh, thank baby Jesus."

"Right. But..."

She blinks expectantly.

"Well..."

She widens her eyes.

"You see..."

"Just spit it out, Riggs."

"I'm moving in with you for the rest of the week."

Her face falls and her eyebrows scrunch. "Say what?"

"Yeah, see, my reservations got mixed up and the other room was only reserved until today. Since it's the holidays, I can't get another room, so I have to room with you."

"This is a joke," she deadpans.

I shake my head and roll my lips. "It is not."

"Yeah, no. You are not sleeping here."

"It's the only option."

"Bull. Call the front desk again."

"I did that already, as well as five other hotels in the area. There are no vacancies."

"Then sleep in the hallway," she says with a scowl, and my shoulders bunch.

"I am not sleeping in the hallway, Bailey."

"You're sure as shit not sleeping here."

"Look, I didn't want to pull this card, but I'm paying for this room, and now I have to stay here. You can either stay here too or you can go crash at the roach motel in the south burbs with Trevor." My anger flares at the idea of her staying with that douche, but the threat was a bluff, and I can already tell she's gonna cave. She might be looking at me like she wants to castrate me, but I see the resignation mixing with the fury in those golden eyes.

"His name is Taylor."

"I don't fucking care what his name is."

"Well," she spits, "what about Talia?"

"What about Talia? I'm staying in your room, not fucking you on the roof deck." Her eyes flare and she grits her teeth.

"Won't Talia be pissed that you're sharing a room with someone you boned and bailed on? I know I'm *old news* and all, but usually girlfriends don't like it when guys spend time with other people who know what their dick tastes like."

I gulp hard at her words, fight off the memory of her on her knees in front of me, and grit out, "Don't really care what Talia thinks because she's not my fucking girlfriend."

She blinks. Opens her mouth, then shuts it. Then gives her head a little shake. This infuriating woman is stunned speechless briefly and if I weren't so pissed, I'd be proud.

After another moment of silence, she looks at the bed and whispers, "But there's only one bed."

"I'll sleep on the couch."

She looks at the couch and groans. "That couch is barely five-feet long. I wouldn't even fit on it. You're a gods-damned giant."

I laugh at her distress but choose not to point out that she's showing concern for me.

"I'll be fine. Promise." When she doesn't say anything else, I continue, "I really am sorry about this. I tried to get a different room, but they're all booked up."

I don't tell her that I could pull strings since my dad owns the damn place. That's not a perk I'm ready to exploit since it will ruin this whole week worse than her pissy attitude over our forced proximity problem.

"It's fine. I mean, it's not, but whatever."

She walks to the door quickly and opens it, stopping short when she sees my suitcase.

"Oh, yeah." I walk up next to her and grab the handle, rolling it in behind me. She pushes the room service cart in and sets her burger on the small table. "You can call the front desk and get a new one since that one is cold."

"And waste a perfectly good burger?" She lifts it up and takes a giant bite, then says through her mouthful, "hell no." She chews and swallows. "Where I'm from, we don't waste food just because it's gone cold. I'll use the microwave for the fries, but the burger tastes good as it is."

I nod. "Okay. Suit yourself. I'm gonna shower real quick." She keeps her eyes on her burger, but I don't miss the way her shoulders lift and her jaw tightens.

"Kay."

Yep. This is going to be an interesting week.

The lights are off. Bailey is in the bed, and I'm bunched up uncomfortably on the couch. I can hear her breathing. Every slight movement she makes, I focus on it. It's driving me nuts. Since we're both awake, I ask one of the questions that's been on my mind since we ran into Taylor/Tyler yesterday.

"When did you start baking?"

Her breath catches momentarily at the sound of my voice, like I startled her.

"Sophomore year of college. I made brownies for a study group and really liked it. Started experimenting after that... You?"

"Years ago. My mom used to be one of the top pastry chefs in Chicago, and it was kind of our thing. Me and Dad had baseball, me and Mom had baking." I chuckle. "And origami."

"I was wondering about the origami." There's a smile in her voice, and I latch onto the sound, soaking it in. "You're always folding little animals and things."

"Yeah. Helps me think. My fingers tend to fidget otherwise."

"I've noticed."

That surprises me. "You have?"

She doesn't answer, and we sit in the silent darkness for a while longer. I try to quietly readjust my position without being obvious. This couch is honestly the worst. No matter which way I lie, I'm losing sensation in at least twenty-five percent of my body, while the other seventy-five percent is in pain.

Fucking hell.

"Why are you doing this contest?" she asks out of nowhere. "You don't need the money. Is it for your mom?"

"Yeah," I admit, then give her most of the truth. "My mom doesn't work as a pastry chef anymore, but she still loves baking. And she really loves when I bake. My dad hates it, but he's kind of a prick. He doesn't think I should have interests outside of baseball. But I'm doing this just so my mom can see me doing and enjoying something we used to do together."

She hums, and we go back to silence.

"I'm doing it for my brother Brandon," she whispers after a while. "He died freshman year of college."

"I'm sorry," I say, then remember the E.E. Cummings tattoo she has inked just above her heart. "Is that who the tattoo is for?"

"Yeah," she pauses, "he was my twin brother."

"Did he...um...did he like to bake, too?" I'm desperate to keep her talking, feeding off every ounce of information she's willing to give me. So much about Bailey is a mystery. I'm drawn to her even when she hates me. Even when she infuriates me, I'm pulled to her. It's the same thing that brought me to her in aisle six of Quick Stop when I was only there for beer. The same thing that made me work for her number, for her name, despite Talia and everything else I have going on.

I need to know her. Everything about her. Even if she doesn't want to know me. Even if she can't.

Bailey is like an origami star made from the last page of a book I am absolutely loving. Beautiful and intricate and necessary. To learn her story means I have to be gentle—careful with the creases and edges, attentive to the most delicate parts. Unfold the pages just enough to appreciate what's inside, but not so much that it can't be molded back to its original shape. She's the most complex and captivating type of art.

She snorts. "Not unless you mean *getting baked*." I laugh

with her. "No, I didn't start baking until after he died. But I'm going to use the money to do something for him."

She's cryptic, but she wouldn't have brought it up if she weren't open to talking about it, right? I take the chance.

"What is it that you're going to do for him?"

She's quiet for a long while. So long that I think I fucked up, crossed a line, but then I hear her roll over. When I glance at the bed, she's on her side with her eyes on me.

"I'm getting him a new headstone."

Oh. "Oh. Is his broken?"

"No. But it should be. Bran was transgender."

She pauses and I can feel her eyes burning into me, challenging me, as if she's waiting for me to say something. When I don't, she continues, "Brandon was trans, and our parents...well...they're assholes. And they weren't accepting. Honestly, they're hateful and horrible. But Bran and I got out and went to college, and everything was okay, you know? People at school were amazing. He was flourishing as himself. We both were, but he was doing it out in the open as Brandon. As who he was always meant to be. But then when he died..."

"They didn't," I whisper, disgust filling me.

"They did. They held a big funeral service for Brielle Barnes, their 'loving and devoted daughter,' and then put that name on the grave marker. It's abhorrent. Brandon wanted to be cremated and sprinkled across Lake Michigan, so every single fucking thing about it was despicable and disrespectful. A betrayal and a spit in the face of him and everyone who loved him. It was just this huge lie carried out so my parents could save face in the eyes of the town and the God they think told them to reject him. Their own child."

Her voice is strong with anger and determination when she adds, "But I'm going to fix the part that I can. That's why I'm doing this contest."

"How much do you need?"

"I don't want your money," she bites out quickly.

"No, I know. You're going to do this without help, I get it. I was just curious."

She huffs. "For the headstone, the setting fee, and the removal and disposal of the old grave marker, I need thirty-two hundred, but I've got about two grand saved. I already have the headstone order placed. I just got to get the rest of the money."

We drift back into silence, but the air around us feels clearer, less stiff. I listen to her soft breathing and match mine to hers, thinking about what she shared with me. Our paths, different in so many ways, yet so similar in others. The biggest difference? I'm a liar, and she's not. She's strong, and I'm a fucking coward.

Before sleep takes me, I whisper into the darkness, "We'll win for Bran, Sundance. I promise."

A soft "thank you" floats toward me from the bed as I drift off to sleep, but I don't know if it was her, or a dream.

"Get up," someone growls, and something soft and heavy hits me on the head.

I startle awake, the quick motion sending agony through my stiff neck and back. I swear the resounding crack of my joints can be heard through the walls.

"Ow, fuck," I groan, and I'm smacked again with the soft, heavy thing. I let my eyes adjust to the darkness and find Bailey standing in front of me, hair a mess and pillow in hand. "Jesus, what?"

"You're folded up like a damn pretzel and snoring like some redneck's jacked-up Ford, that's what," she grumbles. "Just get in the bed and stay on your side."

My sleep-addled brain doesn't quite understand as she

climbs back onto the far-side of the bed and burrows under the covers. "What?" I ask lamely.

With her back to me, she says, "Get in the bed, Stanton. If the improved sleep posture doesn't stop the snoring, though, I'm putting you in the fucking hallway."

Oh. Well, okay then.

I don't argue. I just climb onto the bed, the empty side is cool to the touch, the sheets smooth and wrinkle-free, and I can feel her body dip toward me as the mattress sinks under my weight.

"Thanks," I say with a smile.

"Shut up and go to sleep," she grunts, and I have to bite my lip to hold back my laugh.

When I come back into the room the next morning, I'm greeted with the sound of banging in the bathroom. I drop my gym bag on the floor, just as Bailey comes out fully clothed for the day with her hair in a ponytail and a toothbrush in her mouth. The soft morning sunlight streams through the giant windows and settles around her. Like she's glowing from the inside out. The pink in her hair is extra vibrant, and when she looks up at me, her amber eyes shine like golden sunbeams. It twists up my stomach and makes me frown. She's so beautiful, the parts that she keeps hidden even more stunning, and she hates my guts.

"Hey," she grumbles around her toothbrush.

I grin. "Not a morning person?"

"Mornings can suck it. I need coffee."

"Let me change, and then we can grab some on the way."

She eyes me in my joggers and hoodie, flicks her eyes to my wet hair, and nods stiffly. "Lemme spit first."

I arch an eyebrow and smirk, but she glares at me, so I don't say anything. She disappears back into the bathroom, then returns thirty seconds later.

"All yours." She gestures behind her, so I grab my clothes and head in to get ready. Normally I would come back to the room to shower after a workout, but since I've got a new roomie and I don't want to make her uncomfortable, I went ahead and used the gym facilities. I change my clothes, brush my teeth and then my hair, throwing it all up in a bun, now that it's long enough, and walk back out to meet Bailey. It takes under five minutes.

"Good?" she asks when I step into the main room. She's already dressed in her parka jacket and dumb fucking scarf, like she can't wait to get out of this hotel room, so I shrug on my own coat, and we head out.

After grabbing coffees at the coffee shop on the corner, the car picks us up and whisks us to the convention center, and we go through the whole thing again. Check coats and phones, makeup and microphones, and Bailey talks to that fuckface Trevor. Unfortunately, he wasn't in the bottom six yesterday and I'm still butthurt about it.

"What do you think it's going to be today?" she asks me as we wait at our station.

"I don't know. I wouldn't be surprised if it's something pretty standard, though. Get the easy shit out of the way to weed people out."

"Weed people like us out, you mean? Because yesterday was a fucking disaster."

"Hey." I give her a nudge, so she makes eye contact with me. "Yesterday was rough but we're still here. Today will be different. Today will be better."

She scrunches up her nose. "Right."

"For Brandon and Odette, today will be better. Yeah?"

With that, her worry is replaced by determination. "Yeah. Better."

We're called to attention, given the same rundown we were given yesterday, then, like yesterday, we're provided with a box and an envelope. Bailey picks up the envelope and flips it in her hands.

"Here," she says, and shoves it at me. "You do it."

When we're given the go ahead, I open the envelope. Then I give Bailey the biggest smile.

"Cookies," I tell her. "It's cookies."

Her eyes light up in a way that makes me crave her happiness, and her smile is full of contagious excitement. "We can do cookies," she whispers.

"We can. We definitely can. Do you have any recipes memorized that you think will work? I don't think my *palets de dame aux raisons* will win twice. Plus, none of these judges are French."

She snorts. "I knew you picked that recipe to suck up to the French owner of Bakery On Main."

"That and my mom is from France," I admit. "So both."

"Yeah, whatever, cheater," she says, but it's jokingly. No accusatory malice. Just a playful jab. Then she smiles at me again. "I have an idea!"

bailey

WE MAKE CHERRY CHEESECAKE COOKIES.

I make a graham cracker cookie dough and a brandied cherry topping with fresh cherries. I was so excited when I saw the bottle of brandy on the add-in shelves that I actually squealed.

While I fret over that, Riggs throws together a cheesecake filling mixture, but he does it "his mom's way." He uses ricotta cheese, egg whites, and lemon zest, in addition to the standard ingredients that I use (cream cheese, sugar, and egg yolks), and the way he alternates between beating to whipping to folding so seamlessly makes me jealous and turns me on. The fact that the man can make my nipples hard by beating eggs is ridiculous. Who knew baking could be so sexual? I hate it.

We roll the cookie dough into balls, using a rounded teaspoon to form them into little bowls. When I move to spoon the cheesecake mixture onto the cookies, Riggs stops me and suggests we pipe it in. Damn stupid genius. So, he does that, making the cookies gorgeous and neat, and we bake them. When they come out of the oven, they're almost perfect. Once they have cooled enough, I delicately spoon a single brandied cherry onto the top of each one.

We're finishing the last cookie when a PA tells us we have five minutes left, and I'm fucking proud of us.

"Did we just crush this task?" I whisper to Riggs, as we stand back and watch the other teams scramble.

"I think we did." He looks at me with a smile that takes over his whole face, and I die a little once more at how grossly attractive he is.

And also at how clean he is.

I look from his apron down at my own and huff.

"How the hell do you stay so *pristine*?" I whine.

He shrugs and chuckles. "You're a mess, Sundance. You were making me dizzy with how many times you spun in circles today."

My chest warms and my eyes narrow. "Don't call me that."

The large timer buzzes before he can respond, and we move through the whole judging process again. This time, Riggs encourages me to speak during the interview, and I find myself giddily explaining our choices. Yesterday's dark doom and gloom feeling is completely drowned out by the light of today's excitement. It's such a good feeling, and I'm vibrating with it.

When they announce the bottom three, we're not in it. We don't have the day's top recipe, but we don't get sent home, and that's huge.

Taylor's team does get cut, though, and Riggs is so damn smug that I'm pretty sure he's happier about Taylor's loss than our kind-of win. He's such an alpha asshole, thinking he needs to flex on Taylor or pee on me like I'm some sort of possession. I let him assume, though. It's none of his business how I know Taylor, or that Taylor and Brandon were kind of seeing each other right before Bran died. It's one of the reasons I didn't keep in touch with him after I transferred. Seeing Taylor used to hurt too much, made me feel too guilty, and I couldn't handle it.

Seeing him now, though? It felt good. I missed him and didn't even realize it. I missed knowing someone who knew Brandon, and I would have liked to hang out with him and catch up, but Riggs was too busy being a dickhead.

It irks me, a lot, but it's not enough to bring me down from the high of not being cut.

We're staying.

I'm gonna do it, Bran.

"Hey," Riggs says after I say my goodbyes to Taylor, "What do you say we go get dinner and strategize for tomorrow? I've saved a few recipes for Bangladesh. I already requested a few things we'll probably need, but we have until midnight to send any other ingredient requests to the PAs for tomorrow."

I nod right as my stomach grumbles. "Sounds good. But we can't go anywhere crazy expensive. I'm cool with finding a McDonalds or a Subway or something."

Riggs's eyes widen, and he grimaces. "Are you fucking kidding? I'm not getting fast food when we're in one of the best culinary cities in America. I'll pay for you."

"No. Hell no, Riggs. You're already spending an obscene amount of money on that boujee ass hotel. You're not paying for my food too." I plant my feet on the sidewalk, once again refusing to get into the car. He scowls.

"We're not arguing over this."

"Seems like we are."

"Get in the car. I'm starving. I want to get dinner."

"I'm not stopping you."

"You're infuriating."

"You're overbearing. And annoying." Despite my insults, he grins at me, and I bristle. "And you're a pain in my ass."

Riggs sighs and rolls his damn eyes at me. "What about we split a pizza? Have you ever had Chicago deep dish?"

I scoff. "I'm from Illinois, Riggs. Of course I've had Chicago style pizza. Jesus, you think I live in a cave?"

"Wait, you're from here?"

"Yep. Well, not *here* here, but from Illinois, yeah."

"Why didn't I know that?"

I shrug at him and break eye contact. "We didn't do a whole lot of talking."

We're quiet for a moment, no doubt both thinking about all the things we did instead of talking, and I shiver. It has nothing to do with the windchill.

"Get in the car, Barnes. We'll split a pizza."

I release an exasperated, dramatic sigh. I'd rather spend five bucks on value menu nuggets and a pop, but I'll splurge fifteen for half a pizza and a water. We're in Chicago, after all, and we did just survive day two of the contest. I climb into the back seat and Riggs slides in after me. He tells the driver to take us to a place on Ohio and Wabash that I've never even heard of, and my stomach grumbles again.

"So, where you from, then?" Riggs asks after about a block.

"'Bout three hours south. A small town just off Interstate 57."

He looks at me with a raised brow. "Did you transfer to Butler from UIUC?"

"Nah. From the community college in the same town, though." I clear my throat and force away the tears that want to prickle my eyes. "The plan was for me and Brandon to transfer to UIUC after two years at the community college. But after he died, I couldn't stay in that town anymore, so I transferred to Butler. Took on more loans than planned, but whatever."

He's looking at me. I can feel his eyes on the side of my face, but he's not speaking. He doesn't have to. I know what he's wondering.

"Just ask it," I say to my lap. When he doesn't say anything else, I look over at him and hold his eyes. "Ask it, Riggs."

He nods, his brow furrowed. "How did he... was it...?"

Suicide.

That's what he wants to ask. *Was it suicide?* It's what everyone always thinks, and as much as I hate it, it's not an unreasonable assumption. The suicide statistics for transgender youth are harrowing. I shake my head.

"No. Brandon didn't die by suicide. Though I was scared for him before we left home—shit was bad senior year of high school. If we hadn't gotten out..."

I squeeze my eyes shut at the old fears that creep up. Unwarranted now, but my body still remembers them. Isn't it strange how muscle memory can apply to emotions? Even years later, my body reacts to the fear and worry as if it were fresh. As if we were seventeen again and Brandon was right in front of me. All it takes is a song, a scent, a place, some unknown trigger, and suddenly the trauma is exploding before my eyes all over again, and I feel *everything.* I take a breath.

"When we graduated and left, things got better. We got an apartment together and he was involved with the LGBTQ+ Student Center. Outside of the toxicity that is our hometown, Bran was able to focus on making art and transitioning and being *him.*" I smile at the memory, but it quickly falls into a frown. "We both got strep throat. The health center told us it was pretty common for freshman students—all the new germs circulating in close proximity or whatever. Anyway, we treated it and thought it was fine. But he developed myocarditis. It was such a freak thing. And we didn't even know until..."

"I'm sorry," Riggs says softly, and when he takes my hand

and gives it a squeeze, I let him. I don't let go until we pull up to the pizza place.

We order a twelve-inch deep dish. It's supposed to feed four to five people, but Riggs has already hoovered two-thirds of it. And here I thought I'd get to bring home a doggie bag.

It's great pizza, though. I'm almost uncomfortably full, wondering if I can pop the button on my jeans under the table without him noticing.

"So, we're going with Chum Chum, then?" Riggs asks after finishing up his pop. I nod. Chum Chum, also called cham cham sweet or chomchom, is a traditional Bengali sweet that is popular throughout South Asia, and specifically in Bangladesh and West India. From the recipes we've been seeing, it's typically made by curdling whole cow's milk and shaping the curds into thick cylinders, cooking those in a boiled sugar syrup, then rolling them in dried coconut, stuffing them with something called mawa, and topping them with a variety of things. We've seen recipes top them with pistachios, some with tutti-frutti candies, dried fruits, and, in our case, cherries.

"Yeah, I think that's the one we should go with. It will be a little tricky because we'll have to curdle the milk, and I've never even heard of mawa before, but the rest of the ingredients I'm familiar with." I shrug. "And we can top it with cherries, so that's a win for me."

"I already asked the PA to grab us some of this stuff just in case. I'll send an email to see if they can get us mawa, but if not, we'll at least have the stuff to try and make it." He pulls out his phone and starts typing, sending an email from his app, probably. "It shouldn't be too hard. It looks like mawa is just coagulated milk. This says we can make it with milk powder, ghee, and a few other simple pantry items."

"I've never used a cheesecloth in my life," I murmur, mostly to myself, as I scroll back through one of the recipes Riggs shared with me. The idea of jumping into this recipe without any sort of practice makes me extremely nervous, especially with so much riding on the final product. The *what ifs* start circulating through my brain, and I'm a split second from spiraling into an anxious mess when Riggs sets his phone down and interrupts my thoughts.

"I have an idea."

When I look up from my phone screen, he's studying me with a blank face. I put my phone down and fold my hands in front of me. "Okay."

"What if we go to my house and practice a few times."

"We're allowed to do that?"

"Yeah. That's why they gave us the country on Sunday during orientation. We're allowed to prepare, and that includes practicing the recipe if we need to. I'm sure a lot of the teams will have trouble finding a kitchen if they're from out of town, but it says in the contract that we could even use the cooking stations if we wanted."

My mouth gapes. "I didn't know that! Why didn't you say something sooner?"

"I thought you'd read the contract."

I look away and shrug. "I started, but it was overwhelming, so I decided to take the contest one day at a time."

"Well, lucky for you I've read it about eight times. We're allowed to practice this recipe and whatever we decide to do for Friday, assuming we make it through tomorrow and get assigned the theme."

Well, damn. Maybe I should have read the contract.

"Okay. So why don't we just go back to the kitchen stations at the convention center?"

His grin is huge. "My mom is a renowned pastry chef, Barnes. Our kitchen and pantry are next level."

"Your parents won't care?"

"Nah. My dad is actually out of town until Christmas, and my mom is probably sleeping." He checks the time on his phone. It's only a little after eight. "What do you say?"

"Let's do it." I glance around for our server. "Let's pay the check and head out."

"Already took care of it."

"You what?"

"I already took care of the check," Riggs repeats. "I gave the server my card when we ordered." He looks so damn smug. I want to smack him.

"We agreed we'd split it," I grouse, and he shrugs. Like a *too bad, so sad* kind of shrug. Asshole.

"I ate more than you did, anyway." He stands and slides on his pretentious black peacoat. "Stop pouting. Let's go."

"I'm not pouting, you jerk. I'm angry." I huff and stand up, putting on my own coat. When he turns to walk out, I follow him.

"You look like you're pouting."

"Screw you, Stanton."

"Been there already, haven't you, Barnes?" His eyes twinkle when he swings the car door open for me, and the smirk playing on his plump lips stops me in my tracks. I hold my breath as I scan his face. The thick scruff. The strong jaw. The sensual mouth. I feel the attraction everywhere. Sometimes, when I catch him looking at me like that, when he flirts, I can *almost* forget. *Almost.*

But then I remember, and the moment is broken.

I accidentally on purpose elbow him in the gut when I get into the car, and I don't hide my smirk when he grunts at the impact. He's the enemy, I remind myself. A liar. A thief.

I'm just here to win this contest, and then I'll be done with him.

When Riggs said he lived in a condo, I was picturing something like what Kelley and Jesse live in. An apartment, but a little bigger and little nicer. When the driver pulls us into a parking garage beneath a condo high-rise off the Chicago River, I have a feeling my assumptions were wrong.

"Is that a doorman?" I ask Riggs, gesturing to the guy wearing a suit standing just inside a glass vestibule which holds a reception desk and an elevator.

Riggs glances where I'm pointing and smiles. "Yeah. That's Mr. Williams. He's been here since I was in high school."

"Huh."

We sit in the idling car for a moment, neither of us making a move to get out. When Riggs turns to me instead of reaching for the door handle, my shoulders tighten.

"What?" I ask flatly.

"Well, there's probably something you should know before we go in there."

Oh hell. I knew something was off with this guy. Like, who the hell can book a hotel for five hundred bucks a night and then still doesn't want any cut of the winnings from this contest? People that rich gotta be corrupt.

"Is your family in the mafia?" I ask seriously. "If I go inside with you, will I be added to a list?"

He pauses for a second, then his eyebrows shoot up. "No. What? A list?"

"Yeah, you know, like a list of potential threats or, um, assets for the rival mafia. And then I'll be surveilled and kidnapped and taken hostage by your enemies because they mistakenly thought I could be used as leverage against your family but, plot twist, you guys don't actually care about me, so the rival mob is going to kill me but then, plot twist—"

"Another plot twist?"

"Yeah. Plot twist, the rival mafia don's son falls in love with me and then I'm forced to marry him and then your dad kills my new father-in-law, making me and my new husband the new leaders of the rival mafia. Making *us* rivals." I gesture from my chest to his. "Which means, you'll probably be tasked to kill me, but my husband is obviously smarter and stronger and a better shot, so he'll kill you first. Is that it?" Riggs's face is a portrait of confusion before he shakes his head slowly.

"Yeah, no, that's not even remotely close to reality."

"Huh. Damn." *Damn.* "Could have been hot, though. Now I want to read a book like that."

He laughs. "Weirdly enough, me too."

I snort and he rolls his eyes at me. "No, my family is not part of the Outfit, as far as I know. But I do need you to know about my mom." He levels me with a serious look. "Remember how I said she's not a pastry chef anymore?"

"Yes."

"That's because she was diagnosed with amyotrophic lateral sclerosis about a year and a half ago. Do you know what that is?"

My gut twists and my brow furrows.

"Yeah," I say quietly. "ALS. It's a disease of the nervous system that affects muscle control." I don't say any more than that. That there's no cure. That it's fatal. The look on his face tells me he already knows.

"That's right." He never takes his eyes off me. "You probably won't meet her. When I texted my mom's nurse to let her know we were coming, she told me my mom is already asleep. Mom sleeps a lot these days. But just in case, I wanted you to know. She's in a wheelchair now, and she has limited use of her arms."

"Okay, yeah. Thanks, um, for the heads up."

"Sure. Well, let's do this." In a flash, the serious expression on his face morphs into the confident grin I'm so used to seeing, and he slides out of the car without another word.

I climb out after him and he walks us toward the elevator. He introduces me to Mr. Williams, they chat briefly about sporting something or other, and then we're in an elevator rocketing up, up, up.

"What floor are you on?" I ask, while fiddling with my phone.

"Thirty-second."

"How many floors are in this thing?"

His grin is cocky. "Thirty-two."

My jaw drops. "You grew up in a penthouse apartment?"

"Penthouse *condo*."

"Good lord. No wonder you're such a pretentious ass."

"I am *not* pretentious."

"Maybe not," I wave him off and continue, "but you're definitely overconfident in all things and don't understand the word no." I side-eye him. "All signs of a spoiled brat."

He just smiles and takes a step toward me. "I wouldn't say my confidence is unreasonable, Sundance. I seem to remember a few times when you benefited from my *cocksure* attitude."

He accentuates the *K* sound, drawing it out like it's two words, and my breath catches. I'm just about to pop off when the elevator opens into an elegant foyer with marble flooring and a small table with a large crystal vase holding a bouquet of colorful flowers.

Riggs leads me toward a coat closet, and I take off my shoes and jacket just like he does, hanging the jackets on hangers and placing the shoes on a little shoe shelf. *Cute.* When he heads down a long, wide hallway, I follow, taking time to study the large, greyscale family portraits that hang on the walls.

On every canvas, the Stantons look magazine-level perfect. Happy, smiling, gorgeous. Riggs as a boy, wearing a turtleneck and tiny chinos. As a teen, a button down, tie, and slacks. His eyes glittering, his straight white teeth showing. His mom's smile is exactly like his in every photo. It's obvious to see where he gets his looks. His chocolate brown eyes, his dark wavy hair. His full lips. Only the strong jaw and broad-shouldered build are from his dad. Everything else is all Odette DuPont Stanton.

My eyes land on the last canvas and stick—Riggs wearing a Butler University baseball uniform, standing on the pitcher's mound, and a stadium of people blurred out in the background. His firm ass is outlined in his uniform pants in a way that makes my nipples tighten. His arm is bent, his bicep bulging. His hair is short, curling out just over his ears under his ball cap, and his profile is serious. He's focused. He's determined. He's fucking sexy.

Damn it all to hell.

A throat clears to my right, and I'm jerked out of my reverie. I whip around to find Riggs watching me with his arms crossed, stupid cocky smirk on his full lips and heat in his eyes. I hold his gaze for a moment before the backdrop catches my attention.

"Holy shit." I walk to the floor-to-ceiling windows and look out at the sparkling buildings, across to the lakefront, then to the Chicago River below. "This view is incredible."

"Wait till you see it from the terrace."

"You have a flipping *terrace*?" Jesus Lord, this is how the top one percent lives, huh? I look around at the huge living area and the gorgeous Christmas tree with white lights and red ornaments. "This has to be like a million-dollar piece of real estate."

"Try six."

Record. Freaking. Scratch.

"What! Now I don't even want to touch anything. Six

million freaking dollars? Your living room is bigger than my whole damn house back home. It's like a sky mansion."

He laughs at me. "You want a tour?"

"Hell no, I do not want a tour. I'm hyperventilating just from this. If I see the rest of it right now, I might pass out."

Part of me wants to ask why we're staying in a hotel when he lives in a castle, but I hold my tongue. If it's because of his mom's illness, I don't want to put him on the spot, and if it's because he just doesn't want me in such a personal space...well, I'd rather not know. It's probably better anyway, because at least at the hotel I'm not afraid to touch things.

I'm brought out of my thoughts by Riggs's laughter. His booming, rolling voice vibrates right through me, and his eyes are shimmering with water. I feel that laugh in my gut, and I have the weird desire to breathe it in. To drink it—to rub it onto my skin like lotion. My mind wants to be captivated by him, and it pisses me off.

"Shut up," I growl. "Just show me the damn kitchen."

He jerks his head to the side, then turns and walks in that direction. I trail after him, and when we turn a corner into the kitchen, I literally cannot breathe. Like, all the oxygen in the room is gone and I'm just a gasping, gaping lunatic.

"Oh my *gawd*," I whisper, and run my hands over the smooth white countertop of one of the islands. Because there are freaking two. "Is this granite?"

"Quartz."

"Hmmm." I walk between the islands, identical except one of them has a sink and a six-burner cooktop. The cabinetry is white with silver finishes, and the french door refrigerator and dual double ovens are stainless steel. I'm admiring the clean, white subway tiled backsplash when I feel Riggs come up behind me.

"You gonna come just from touching it, Barnes?"

I swallow hard, then force a laugh and step away from him to hide my reaction. "You wish."

He just hums, low and long, and I refuse to look at him.

"Should we get started?" I say to my hands. His chuckle pisses me off yet again.

"Yeah, let's do it."

Surprisingly, or maybe not at all, Riggs's pantry has almost every ingredient on our list. Not mawa, but we have everything we need to make it.

I'm stuffing our homemade mawa into eight fresh Chum Chum when a woman, probably in her forties, comes into the kitchen. She's wearing purple scrubs, her black hair is pulled into a bun, and there's a tired smile on her face. This must be Riggs's mom's nurse.

"Riggs," she greets, "I thought I heard you still out here."

"Hey, Ms. Beth." Riggs smiles back then gestures to me. "This is Bailey. She's doing the holiday baking competition with me."

"Nice to meet you," Ms. Beth says to me, and her words are warm and genuine. I like her.

"You, too. Thank you for letting us use the kitchen."

She laughs. "Oh, it's not mine, but I know Odette loves the idea of Riggs out here putting it to use."

"Is she up?" Riggs asks, and I note the hint of excitement in his voice.

"She is." Ms. Beth's smile is still present, but it's different now. I can't quite place it.

Riggs quickly washes his hands and takes off his apron, then turns to me. "I'll be right back, okay? If she's up for visitors, I'll come back for you."

"Yeah, sure." I smile awkwardly. The nerves I feel all of a

sudden are intense and strange. He takes off around the corner, leaving me with Ms. Beth.

"So, you go to school with Riggs?"

"I do. We, um, both entered a cookie contest a few months ago."

"Oh, yes. The one he won with Odette's recipe?"

"That's the one." I bristle.

"She was so proud." Ms. Beth laughs. "She talked about it for weeks."

Hearing that, my animosity regarding the cookie contest fades, and I'm surprised to find that I'm not even that mad about it anymore. I don't know when it happened, but my anger has tamed, and now it's just a dull annoyance.

"Riggs says she was a pastry chef. Studied at *Le Cordon Bleu.*"

"Mhm. She wasn't just *a* pastry chef; she was *the* pastry chef. She was the executive pastry chef at *Temetum.*" She waits for my reaction, but I don't have one. I just nod lamely, because I have never heard of this *Temetum* place.

"Wow," I force out with a smile. She sees right through me and laughs.

"It's okay. I didn't know what it was until I started working for the Stantons. It's not exactly in my price range."

"Yeah, I'm more of a two-dollar tacos and frozen margaritas kinda girl," I say with a smirk.

"Mmmm, me too. *Temetum* is the only three-star Michelin restaurant in Chicago. People pay a pretty penny to eat there, and when Odette was the pastry chef, she won the James Beard Outstanding Pastry Chef award and the national ACF Pastry Chef of the Year award."

"Wow," I say again, but this time I mean it. "I had no idea she was such a badass."

Ms. Beth nods. "The baddest."

Riggs comes back into the kitchen, then, and his smile kicks up butterflies in my belly.

"You wanna come meet my mom, Barnes?" I must look terrified, because he and Ms. Beth both laugh at me. "She's mostly harmless," Riggs jokes.

"Your mom is culinary royalty, Riggs," I hiss. "Why didn't you tell me that? I'm covered in flour and curdled milk. There's no way I can meet her like this."

I start frantically brushing at the white spots on my jeans. Even wearing an apron, my clothes look like I just went to an orgy in a crack house. White powder and mysterious looking wet spots cling to the fabric and I am freaking out.

"It's fine," Riggs says, and he places his hands on my shoulders, halting my brushing. "She's spent her life in kitchens. Guarantee she's seen worse than this."

I huff. "Not from you. You look perfect." His grin grows, and I roll my eyes. "You know what I mean, asshole." I flash an apologetic glance at Ms. Beth. "Sorry."

"Oh, it's fine." She winks at me. "I knew what you meant." *Hm.*

"C'mon, Barnes." Riggs hooks my arm in his and starts walking me down a hallway off the kitchen. "She's gonna want to sleep again soon."

I drag my feet. Stupidly, I think if I walk slower, I'll have time to calm my nerves. But that's impossible with Riggs's giant strides and how my heart beats faster and faster with every door we pass. When he slows, I squeeze my eyes shut and give myself a pep talk.

She's just a person. Pastry Chef of the Year or not. Riggs Stanton's mom or not. Billionaire Queen of the Castle in the Sky or not. She's just a person.

When we walk through the door, I hear a soft whirring and a quiet, rhythmic beeping. I see the big four-poster bed in the center of the room before I see the tiny body sitting up in it. The room is grand. Whites and greys with expensive, elegant accents. There's even a damn chandelier and a wall of windows overlooking the sparkling skyline.

But then I notice other things.

The origami stars that hang from the canopy beams above the bed.

The large, white bookshelf teeming with books.

The canvas photos of Riggs on the walls.

When I finally gather the courage to look at Mrs. Stanton, she's smiling softly at me, her head slightly tilted to the side and her eyes curious but warm.

My first impression of Riggs's mom is that she is small. I knew she would be from the photos I've seen, but she's much tinier than I expected. Odette DuPont Stanton is petite and delicate, but from what I've learned, she's also a force.

Or she was.

Before.

My second impression of her is that she is intelligent. Her eyes are sharp and sparkling, so much like Riggs's, and I can tell she's missing nothing. Not the kitchen mess on my clothing. Not my rapid pulse fluttering in my throat. And not the way my breath catches when I stand too close to her son. She sees it all.

When Riggs walks closer and sits in a chair at her bedside, I see that a safety rail has been installed. The harsh, clinical appearance is in direct contrast to the soft elegance of the bed. There's a breathing machine on the bedside table with a nasal mask resting on a hook next to it.

"*Maman,*" Riggs says, taking hold of his mother's hand, "this is my friend Bailey."

Her deep brown eyes haven't left my face, but her soft smile grows when she greets me. "*Bonjour,* Bailey. Alex has told me about you." Her words are slurred slightly, but her French accent is still beautiful, and I don't miss that she called Riggs, Alex. *Hm.*

She glances at her son, love and playfulness in her eyes. *"Bien qu'il ne m'ait pas dit que tu étais belle."*

Riggs's cheeks color pinkish, and he flicks his eyes toward me.

"Mom, you're making her nervous." His mom laughs lightly in response, and I fidget awkwardly.

"Nice to meet you, Mrs. Stanton." I step up next to the bed and stand by Riggs's side.

"Please, call me Odette. Riggs said you are a wonderful baker."

"Um, I don't know about that." I snort. "I'm still learning. He's much better than me."

"Don't listen to her, *Maman*," Riggs cuts in. "She's brilliant. She has sharp instincts and she's creative just like you." I feel his eyes on me, but I don't look at him.

"Oh, I love to hear that. You should bake something for me sometime." Her eyes crinkle with her smile, and I pretend not to see Riggs rub his thumb over the back of her hand. It's so intimate, so loving, and my eyes sting at the sight. Their bond, the love in this room, it's something I've only ever experienced with one person, and he was taken from me. My heart breaks to know Odette will be taken from Riggs, too.

"Sure," I say with a smile, and I look at Riggs to find his eyes locked on my face. "We can do that, can't we, Butch." His eyes flare and a smile twitches on his lips at the nickname.

Odette laughs and glances at her son. "Butch? And where is that from?"

"Yeah. You know Butch Cassidy?" I arch a brow mischievously, and Riggs narrows his eyes.

"Nope. Cover your ears, Mom. *Elle raconte des histoires.* She's fibbing."

"No, no, no," I laugh. "You can't sweet talk your way out of this one, Riggs." I widen my eyes at Odette playfully, then lower my voice to a mock-whisper. "When I first met your son, he was *not* being an upstanding citizen."

"Alex," she gasps with a smile. "You were being a naughty boy?"

I nod. "Very naughty."

"Sundance is just angry because my hands are faster than hers," Riggs jokes, and I scoff.

"Sundance?" Odette questions, and when she studies me, I feel naked.

"Oh, yeah," I stutter out. "You know, The Sundance Kid? He's Butch Cassidy's—"

"*Son partenaire de crime*," Odette says. "His partner in crime." She looks back at Riggs, and I can't help but notice how he averts his eyes. "That is a very cute story," Odette says, breaking the silence.

"All lies, Mom." Riggs laughs awkwardly.

Odette laughs a little, too, and then she sighs.

"We'll get going and let you rest." Riggs's voice is soft, and my heart squeezes when he lifts Odette's hand and places it on his cheek. "We'll come back and see you in a few days."

"*Je t'aime, mon étoile,*" she whispers.

"Do you need help?" he asks as he sets her hand down, then gestures to the breathing machine.

"No. Just send Beth back in," Odette says with a sad smile. He leans over and kisses her on both cheeks.

"*Je t'aime.* See you soon."

"Nice to meet you, Odette," I say as I step toward the door.

"Pleasure meeting you, Bailey." One last smile, then Riggs places his hand on the small of my back and leads me out.

"She's wonderful," I say to him.

"She is."

"Was that an oxygen machine?"

"BiPap. For when she sleeps. She doesn't need it all the time."

"That's good, right? That she doesn't need it all the time, I mean."

"It is," he says with a nod. "She had a feeding tube placed a couple months ago, but she can still eat some. She likes to taste, you know?"

"Yeah. She's a baking boss babe, so I can see why," I say with a laugh, and he smiles in the exact way I was hoping for. "Thanks for letting me meet her."

"Thanks for being willing to meet her. And for acting..."

"Yeah," I force a smile. "Of course."

He doesn't have to say it. Thanks for acting like everything was normal. For not acting like she's got a terminal disease. For not acting like her son and I are enemies. Thanks for *pretending*.

This whole situation sucks.

"Why does she call you Alex?"

"She just always has. She likes it more than Riggs. My dad wanted Riggs and they couldn't decide, so they flipped a coin for it. Mom lost, so they made Alexander my middle name and she's just always used that." He laughs. "She's the only person who calls me Alex. Well, until you..."

I don't say anything, and an awkward tension blankets us. *Until me* because I called him Alex. Because he told me his name was Alex. Before I learned that his name is actually Riggs. Unease starts to unfurl in my belly, but Riggs changes the subject.

"Feel confident about tomorrow?" he asks as we walk back into the kitchen and start cleaning up.

"I do, actually." I wipe down the gorgeous countertops, and Riggs places the Chum Chum in a glass storage container. "I think practicing was just what we needed."

I let Riggs give me a tour of the rest of the condo. Both stories, the other three bedrooms, the terrace and balcony, the home gym and a friggen theater room. We talk strategy as he shows me around, and he tells me little stories about his childhood. Memories of things that happened in each room.

I'm relaxed as we head back down the spiral staircase. I'm feeling light and even, dare I say, happy. I'm smiling to myself as we head through the hallway that leads back to the foyer, and I continue to smile the entire drive back to the hotel.

SIXTEEN

FOR THE SECOND morning in a row, I awake to find Bailey's soft body plastered against me and my arms wrapped around her. Today, our legs are even tangled together, which makes slipping out that much more difficult.

There's no doubt in my mind that if she wakes up in my arms, she will be livid, and all the progress we've made toward a ceasefire will be firebombed to hell. It won't matter to her that we're on *my* side of the bed, which means she had to have been the one to cross the invisible line dividing the mattress down the middle.

Nope.

She'll just use it as another reason to spit daggers at me from her eyes.

In between the moments when she's looking at me like she wants to devour me, that is.

I swear, this infuriating woman has my head spinning in circles. Most of the time, she hates my fucking guts. She won't listen, she purposely goes against me at every opportunity, and she finds any reason possible to snap at me with that damn sassy mouth. But other times, I can tell she wants me. Craves me. Craves the way I make her feel. Because I do know how to make her feel good, and she can't deny it. I see the memories burning in her eyes when she thinks I'm not paying attention. But I'm always paying attention, even when I don't want to be.

Last night messed with my head more than I expected. It was never the plan to let her meet my mom; the situation is just too complicated, and I didn't want to have to explain Bailey to my family. When I suggested we could use the kitchen at my parents' condo, I was prepared to feel a little off-kilter, having her in such a personal space. I didn't even think we'd see my mom, but when she woke up, I suddenly wanted Bailey to meet her. I wanted *her* to meet Bailey. Having her in the home where I grew up was an intoxicating kind of intimacy, and I craved more of it. When Bailey met my mom, though, I wasn't prepared to feel so fuckin' bulldozed. There was something strange about seeing them interacting, getting along, joking. In another life, Bailey and my mom would have been friends. If I had met Bailey sooner, if I hadn't fucked up so royally, she could maybe even be more, and then they would be more.

I change into a pair of joggers and a hoodie, then grab my bag, which is full of freshly laundered gym clothes, thanks to the hotel guest services. I slip on my shoes and glance back at Bailey one more time. She's out cold. I don't know how this girl snuck out on me so many times when she sleeps like the dead herself. The nights that she stayed at my townhouse, she must have never fully relaxed. One eye must have always been open and trained on the door. The only reason she's sleeping now is because she has no other choice. But before, there was another choice. A better one. And it wasn't me.

I shake my head.

No wonder it was so easy for her to hate me. She never even let herself like me.

The realization is a line-drive straight to the fucking chest.

I shut the door softly on my way out.

I send my workout videos to Coach Elbin after my shower, and he gives me a call the minute they go through.

"Sup, Coach?" I say into the phone.

"Stanton. Reps are looking good. How's your arm feel?"

"Feels good. The tension bands are helping, but I'm ready to throw again."

He grunts. "You'd be throwin' plenty if you hadn't fucked off to the city."

"Yeah, I know. I'll be back on it after the holidays."

"Neal was asking about you." His voice is leading. *Fuck.*

"Yeah? What's Coach Neal want?"

"Wanted to know what you were up to and why you weren't at practice."

Double fuck.

"I got the feelin' he was askin' for your dad," he adds.

I grunt. "What did you tell him?"

"That you had family shit."

I stay quiet.

"Any reason your dad would be asking after you if you've got *family* shit?"

"He's outta town until Christmas." I shrug it off, even though he can't see me, and I hear him huff on the other line.

"Lies always come back to bite you in the ass," he states clearly. I don't respond to that either. He sighs. "Take care of your shit, kid. I'll keep Neal off your back."

I let out a relieved breath. As long as I'm keeping up with my training like I'd promised, Elbin will cover for me. "Thanks, Coach."

"Right. You looked like you had more in the tank yesterday.

Do another arm set tomorrow," he says, referring to the workout videos I sent him yesterday.

"Yes, sir."

"Talk to you soon, Stanton." And he hangs up on me.

I walk back into the room to find Bailey in the same position she was yesterday. Banging around in the bathroom with a toothbrush in her mouth.

"Mornin," I say, giving her a charming grin. She really is a sight in the morning. Makes my chest warm and ache, all at once.

"Wh'uhn guh?" she mumbles.

"Huh?"

She rolls her eyes and holds up a finger, then hops into the bathroom. I hear the water run, then she comes back a second later without her toothbrush.

"Where did you go? This morning and yesterday, you were gone when I woke up." She eyes me suspiciously, and my face splits into an amused grin.

"Not used to being the one left, are you, Barnes?"

She rolls her eyes again. "Fine, forget I asked. I don't care what you do." She turns her back on me to dip back into the bathroom. Infuriating woman.

"I went to the hotel gym," I call out, and she pops her head back out of the bathroom, her nose all scrunched up like she smells something rancid.

"Why?"

I walk toward her and lean back on the wall across from the bathroom.

"One of the conditions Coach gave me to allow me to skip out on training to come here." She hums, and I watch as she brushes out her hair and starts pulling it back into a bun. "I have to do his preapproved workouts and film them every day, then send them to him. Since we never know what time we'll be done at the convention center, it's easier to get up at five and do them in the morning."

She's lining her eyes with eyeliner, one eye closed and mouth half-open. When she finishes one eye, she looks over at me. "Ew. That's gross."

I chuckle. "It's part of being the best, Bailey. I didn't get to be the best by sitting on my ass." I sound like my dad, but it's true.

She's moved on to her eyelashes now, and I watch mesmerized as she swipes a brush over both eyes. Her lashes are already thick and full and the blackest of black, but when she puts this stuff on, her amber eyes glow. It's almost paranormal, how hypnotizing they become. The first time I saw her, even under the fluorescents of the Quick Stop, her eyes grabbed my attention, and I couldn't let go.

It's why I followed her into aisle six like a stalker.

Why I listened to the muffled sounds of Fall Out Boy streaming from her earbuds as she mentally deliberated over the items on the shelf.

Why I made the split-second decision to grab for the vanilla just before she did.

It was those damn amber eyes first.

Then the way she strutted when she walked. Like she was fearless.

And then the bored, mysterious, almost haunted look on her face.

I had to *know* her.

"Well, Golden Boy, let's hope you bring some of that champion energy into the kitchen today, because we need this W."

"You talkin' sports to me, Barnes?"

"Whatever gets through to your dense athlete brain, Stanton." She tries to hide her smile as she puts on her jacket, but I see it. "Coffee first?"

"Coffee first."

The PAs were able to get mawa for us, but Bailey made the executive decision to make our own. She says it will make our final product more impressive, and I don't disagree. She also chooses to add rose water to the sugar syrup, something she read about and practiced last night, and the end result is phenomenal.

By the time we've rolled the Chum Chum in the coconut and stuffed them with our homemade mawa, they look amazing. After we top them with the diced cherries, they look even better. Even as perfectly executed as our recipe is, I still am floored when they name our Chum Chum the winner of the day's task.

As soon as the cameras are off, our arms are around one another. I don't even know who initiated it; all I know is this hug is now in my top five hugs of all time.

"Oh my god, we did it." She smiles up at me, and I can almost see her body shake with excitement. It's contagious.

"We should celebrate and talk strategy for Friday."

"Right. Yes. Yes, we should. Just because we won today doesn't mean we can slack now. *Chicago is for Lovers* is such a weird theme."

"I was expecting something more festive. Christmassy. Not so—"

"Romantic?"

"Well, yeah."

"Sorry, Butch. You're gonna have to channel your inner lover for this one. Table the bat-swinging caveman mentality."

"You know damn well I can be a lover, Sundance." I drop my voice low and keep my attention on her, so I don't miss the rapidly fluttering pulse in her throat, or the way she tries to swallow down the lust she feels.

"Shut up, Stanton. You know what I mean."

"Hmm." Unfortunately, I do. "How about we head back to the hotel and grab something from the rooftop bar. Maybe eating under the stars will help set the mood, so we can come up with some suitable ideas."

"Sounds good," she chirps as she slides into the car.

Once I'm buckled in next to her, the driver takes us back to the hotel. We head straight up to the rooftop bar, and even though it's cold, the retractable glass barriers and the outdoor heaters make it warm enough that we can shed our outer layers.

"This is gorgeous," Bailey says, and she snaps a photo of the cocktail she ordered. I watch as she types on her phone. "V is gonna flip." She looks up at me, her eyes dancing. "Too bad we can't really see stars, but the Christmas lights are a decent second."

"Yeah, stars aren't something we get to see much of in the city. Too much light pollution." I look up at the night sky. "Some of them break through, though."

"The brightest, most determined ones," she says, her voice almost reverent.

She's beautiful. The soft shine of the Christmas lights, the glow from the heaters, they all seem to hit her just right, illuminating her in a way that makes it impossible to look away. Brighter and more vibrant than everyone else out here. I'm staring, I know I am, and when she catches me, her eyes flit away quickly, and she fidgets with her scarf.

"So, *Chicago is for Lovers*," she says into her cocktail glass before she takes a sip. "We could play up the things about Chicago that people tend to love. Sports. Pizza. Stuff like that. But I kind of want to take a more elegant, romantic approach."

"Okay."

"I feel like we can do some fun stuff with silvers and golds, maybe a little pink and white. Maybe something with champagne. Something sparkly. Not really kitschy like Valentine's Day, boyfriend/girlfriend Hallmark stuff. More like engagement proposals or weddings. Baby showers. Timeless love."

"I like it. We could probably do something with cheesecake since that was part of our cookie recipe."

"Oh, yeah, maybe." She pulls a pen and a small notebook out of her bag, then starts writing notes. "How are you at decorating cake?"

"I'm actually pretty good," I say, after taking a sip of my own drink. "I can do basic stuff like roses and cursive script. And I can manipulate fondant pretty good, too."

"Nice. I've never messed with fondant, but the rest I'm pretty good at."

A server comes and takes our food orders, and I tell him to charge it to our room before Bailey can argue. She tries anyway, once the server leaves, but I shut her up by telling her she can pay me back after we win.

We eat and talk, some brainstorming, some natural conversation. She tells me about her friends. How two of them recently got together after years of mutual pining. How she and Slipper Dick teamed up to make it happen. I tell her about baseball and my team, some stories about growing up in the city. It's nice, and when it starts to snow, it's perfect.

"Oh wow," she whispers. "It's so pretty." I watch her put out her hand and catch a snowflake on her finger. It starts with light, delicate flakes, but within minutes, the snow comes down in clumps, clinging to our hair and clothes. We grab our stuff and wait in line for the elevators, and without thinking, I reach out and brush some snow out of Bailey's hair, then push a strand behind her ear. She shivers.

"Your fingers are cold," she whispers. I smile in response.

We ride to the room in comfortable silence.

"I'm going to take a quick shower to warm up," she says, after discarding her jacket and kicking off her boots.

"Sure." I don't look at her as I take off my own coat. She grabs something from her bag, then darts into the bathroom. I hear the shower turn on a minute later.

While she's in there, I grab some paper and keep myself busy. The door opens fifteen minutes later, steam billowing out behind her. She's wearing shorts and an oversized Brand New concert tour shirt, her hair twisted up in a fluffy white towel. Her face is scrubbed clean, her cheeks tinged with pink, and something about her makes me want to swallow my tongue.

She's so fucking pretty.

"It's all yours," she says, and I blink. *What?* "The shower, I mean."

Oh right.

"Right," I say, and move to the bathroom just to do something other than sit on my ass and ogle her. "I'll be right out."

The moment I cross the threshold, I'm knocked on my ass by her smell. Vanilla and fruity, and permeating the air with the steam, and I'm immediately hard. I strip and get in the shower, and it takes all of ten seconds before I crank the knob to cold.

This girl is fucking with my body and my head, and I need to get my shit under control. The best way to undo all the progress we've made is to walk out there with a massive boner. I snort out a laugh at the thought. I can only imagine how Bailey would react. She'd probably threaten to cut my dick off. *Ha.* She might even try to do it.

I finish soaping up, wait until my dick is fully deflated, then turn off the water and climb out. I pull a fresh towel from the shelf, dry off my body, then drop it and reach for my clothes.

The clothes I didn't bring into the bathroom.

Shit.

She's going to kill me.

I dry off my hair as best as I can, then wrap the towel around my waist. Have these towels always been this small? I check the rack to make sure I didn't grab one of those small floor mat towels instead of a body towel. Hm. I check myself in the mirror one more time. Everything is covered, so maybe this towel isn't that small? I just feel naked, is all.

Christ.

Okay.

With any luck, she'll be asleep, and this won't make things awkward.

I swing the door open quietly and step lightly into the main room, eyes trained on my suitcase, when Bailey turns from where she's standing by the bed. We lock eyes, and for a second, we just stare at each other.

"Sorry," I rasp. "I, uh, forgot my clothes. I'm just gonna—"

My words halt when I notice Bailey's eyes trailing down my torso. I can feel them on my chest, and I flex my pecks on instinct. I watch her face as her gaze falls lower, and I know the instant they land on my dick. Her breaths quicken, she bites her lip, and I immediately sport a semi. I know she can tell, because her eyes widen, and I get even harder. When the head of my dick brushes on the fabric of the towel, I groan, and she gasps.

"Sundance," I grind out, "I know I'm not your favorite person right now, but if you keep looking at me like that, I'm gonna have to do something about it."

"Like what," she asks, eyes still on the growing bulge under my towel.

"Like throw you on the bed and make you come on my cock."

Her eyes shoot to mine and she whimpers, then she slowly starts to walk toward me.

"This doesn't mean anything," she whispers.

"Nothing."

"It's just sex," she says as she gets closer.

"Got it."

"I still hate you."

"You hate everyone."

"I hate you most."

"Fine," I growl and grab her hips, pulling her into my erection. "Then fuck me like you hate me."

I lift her up and she wraps her legs around me at the same time our mouths connect. God, the fucking mouth on this girl. She bites my lip and grinds herself on me, and I squeeze her ass.

"Fuck, wait," she gasps out, then pulls back sharply. "Tell me the truth. Are you with Talia? And I don't just mean she's not your girlfriend. I mean, are you fucking her, are you together? I am not trying to break girl code and be a soap opera plot line."

"I'm not with her. I'm not dating her. I'm not fucking her." I meet Bailey's eyes and say it again clearly. "I am not with Talia or anyone else."

"Okay," she says, then attacks my mouth once more. I drag my teeth down her jaw and over her earlobe, then suck on the soft flesh of her neck.

"I'm gonna make you pay for taking this pussy away from me," I say against her shoulder before I bite her.

"Shut up," she says, then she pulls hard on my hair, forcing my head up, licking up the column of my throat. When I groan, she reaches between us and grips my dick, giving two firm tugs before I literally toss her tiny ass onto the bed. She pops up quickly and whips off her shirt the same time that I drop my towel. I'm on her in a breath, pushing her onto her back and sucking a nipple into my mouth.

"Fuck, I missed these." She arches into me, and I push my

hand into her shorts. "You wet for me already, Sundance?" I slide a finger through her pussy and then rub her clit. She moans into my mouth. "Mmhmm, you missed me, too."

"Stop talking," she growls, grinding on my hand while chasing my lips with hers. I slip two fingers inside her and press the heel of my palm to her clit.

"Tell me you missed this," I demand, as I pulse in and out of her. She moves her mouth to my neck, sucking and biting.

"No," she bites out. I slip in a third finger, and she moans loudly into my shoulder.

"Tell me you missed the way I make your pussy feel," I rasp.

"Fuck, fine," she gasps as I pull my fingers out of her pussy and rub her clit. "Fine, I missed this." She reaches down and palms my dick. "I missed your fingers in me. I missed your mouth on my clit. I missed your cock stretching me, filling me." I groan as she moves her hand up and down my shaft. "I missed the taste of you on my tongue."

"Jesus." I sit up and pull her shorts and underwear down her thighs, then toss them off the bed. Her legs fall open immediately and my mouth waters. "You want to come, Sundance?"

"Yes."

I fall down next to her, then grab her hips and lift her, so she's straddling my torso.

"Fuck my face."

"What?" Her mouth falls open and she blinks at me, excitement and shock mixing on her features.

"Climb up here, put your thighs on my fucking ears, and ride my face with that pussy. Fuck my tongue until you're coming down my throat."

Slowly, she scoots forward until her legs are on either side of my head and she's sitting on my chest. I squeeze her ass cheeks. "Up."

She rises up on her knees and braces herself on the head-board, so her dripping pussy is directly above me.

"Fuuuck," I groan, then I grab hold of her ass and pull her down on my face.

She's stiff at first, but by the second swipe of my tongue, her body grows loose and pliable. When I suck her clit into my mouth, she starts moving on me until she really is riding my face, grinding down so hard at times, it's difficult to breathe. It's fucking amazing, and while I'm tonguing her pussy, I have to reach down and stroke my dick because it's so hard it hurts.

Fuck, I've missed her taste. Her body. Her smart mouth. Her smiles. I've missed all of her.

When her movements speed up and I can feel her quivering, I reach up and pinch both of her nipples while I suck hard on her clit. She comes undone, gasping and moaning, until her hands are on my head halting my movements, and she's scrambling off me.

"Holy shit," she cries, "holy shit."

I chuckle. "Catch your breath, baby."

Bailey turns her head toward me and smirks, then she rolls onto all fours and works her way down my body. I watch with rapt attention as she fists my dick and brings it to her lips, then licks up my shaft.

"Fuck yes. Let me see your lips around my cock."

She swirls her tongue around the head of my dick.

"You want me to suck you off, Riggs?" she asks with a bat of her eyelashes, and before I can answer, she pulls me into her mouth. I groan as she works her lips lower and lower on my shaft, as she laves her tongue on the sensitive skin of my dick. *Fuck*, her mouth.

I could close my eyes, grip her hair, and let her go to town. I could thrust into her mouth until I'm spilling down her throat. Fuck, do I want to. But I want to be inside her more. Just the thought makes me want to come, and suddenly, I'm cursing my decision not to beat off in the shower.

"I need to be inside you," I tell her, and I feel more than see her smile around my dick.

Slowly, she removes her lips from me. "Isn't that where you are?"

Smart ass.

I laugh and tug her up next to me, capturing her mouth in another deep kiss. Our tongues tangle as I maneuver our bodies, so she's beneath me and I'm suspended above her. I run my fingers back through her slick folds, and then I freeze.

"Fuck," I groan and drop my forehead to hers. "Fuck."

"What?" I feel her lips moving over mine. "What's wrong?"

"I don't have a condom."

Fuck.

"Fuck," she breathes out. "Don't you carry condoms?"

"No," I release a strained laugh. "Believe it or not, Bailey, I don't just expect to get my dick wet at random, unplanned times. There's literally never been a reason for me to carry a condom."

She snorts and pushes lightly on my chest. When I lift off her, she rolls out of the bed, and I watch as she waltzes her gloriously naked body to her purse on the table. As she rummages through her bag, I keep my eyes on her ass, on the subtle curves and soft skin. Even now, my fingers itch to touch her.

"Eureka!" Bailey whisper shouts, and she holds up a foil packet. "Tonight is your lucky night, Butch."

I watch her hips sway as she sashays back toward the bed, and she tosses the condom on my chest. I recognize the package as the exact kind we used months ago. The kind I had at my townhouse. The kind she started carrying, too. I raise an eyebrow at her.

"Don't even with that look. I just haven't cleaned out my bag in a while."

I take the condom from her and tear it open.

"I've only got the one," she says as I roll it on, "so you better make this good."

I move myself over her again and throw one of her legs up on my shoulder.

"I'm gonna make it the best you've had yet," I promise, then I line up and slide in. "Fuck, I missed this pussy." I rock in and out of her slowly, watching her mouth fall open and her brow furrow. When she moves her eyes from my face to my cock, so she can watch where we're connected, I speed up. "You want a show, baby?"

"Yes," she says on a moan. She flicks her eyes back to mine with a challenge. "Show me what I was missing."

I kiss her, slow and deep at first, but when she bites my lip, I growl, and speed up my thrusts.

"Oh fuck," she gasps, and I tilt my hips to the left, hitting her in a spot that I know will bring tears to her eyes. "Yes. Just like that."

"Nobody else fucks you like this, do they?" I grit out, pounding into her rhythmically. "Nobody treats this pussy as good as I do."

She squeezes her eyes shut and clamps her teeth down on her lip, so I kiss her again until she's panting. I break the kiss and shove my thumb into her mouth, making her suck on it just enough to coat it in her spit, then I move it down to her clit and rub. Tight, fast circles is what she likes. I circle her clit roughly until she's just about there, then I press hard, and she comes with a strangled cry.

The way she clenches around my dick makes me see stars.

The way her face twists up in pleasure is a mesmerizing thing of beauty.

I drop her leg from my shoulder, and she immediately wraps her thighs around my waist, locking her ankles at my back. When she moves her hips, matching my thrusts, I let out a groan that sounds almost pained.

"Fuck, Sundance, when you move like that. You drive me crazy."

"Yeah?" she croons, her amber eyes are locked on mine and dance wickedly. "Nobody fucks this cock like I do." She speeds up her thrusts, fucking me as I fuck her, and damn if she isn't right.

"No one," I growl. *"Baise-moi comme ça."* She moves her hand between us and rubs her clit, never losing the rhythm of her thrusts. When she clenches tightly around me, I groan again.

"Bailey, fuck it, I'm gonna come," I pant. "Keep moving like that and I'm gonna come."

"Yes," she hisses. "Give it to me. Come for me, Riggs."

Jesus fuck, she doesn't have to tell me twice. I still, spilling my release into the condom, but she keeps moving, rubbing her clit and moving on my dick a few more times until she's coming, too.

I pull out and drop down next to her. We're both panting and damp with sweat.

"Shit," she whispers after a few minutes. "That was an ab workout." She rolls onto her side and props her head on her arm. "Think if I keep doing it like that, I'll have a six-pack like yours?"

"Eight."

"What?"

I laugh. "It's an eight-pack, Barnes."

She swats at my chest. "What the fuck ever. I have to pee."

She hops out of the bed and heads toward the bathroom. My eyes are glued to her naked form, my dick already getting hard again. She looks back at me and takes on a serious expression. "Stop looking at me like that. We only had the one condom, and this is never happening again anyway."

Then she stomps into the bathroom and shuts the door.

I get up, wrap the latex in Kleenex, and drop it in the trash can.

We only have one condom *for now*, and if she thinks we're not doing this again, she's not thinking straight.

bailey

"SHHH," Riggs whispers when I reach for him. "I've got to hit the gym."

"What time is it?" I mumble into my pillow.

"Almost five."

"Ugh, gross, go away."

I hear him laugh, the bed shifts, and then a light touch runs down my naked back, fingertips ghosting over my forehead and the shell of my ear.

"Sleep, Sundance."

It takes about ten minutes after he leaves for me to sit up and freak out.

Oh hell.

Oh. *Hell.*

I snag my phone off the charger and call Ivy. She answers on the fourth ring.

"Bailey? Is everything okay?" Her voice is scratchy from sleep, but she's alert.

"Yeah, sorry for waking you. Everything is fine." I wince. "Well, it's not *fine*, but I'm not, like, in physical danger or anything." I wince again. "Well, not *serious* physical danger…"

The line is quiet for a moment, just the sound of deep breathing, and then I hear bedsheets rustling, low whispered voices, and a door clicking shut.

"You slept with him." It's not even a question. She's that freakin' good.

"How *the fuck* do you do that?"

She giggles. Damn her.

"Well?"

"Well, what?"

"Well, how do you feel?"

"Sore."

She snorts out another laugh. "No, I don't mean how your vagina feels. I mean how's your head? How are we handling this?"

I love how she does this. Every obstacle, every complication, it's *we*. How are *we* going to tackle this issue, how are *we* going to solve this problem, because with Ivy in your corner, you'll never have to go through anything alone unless you want to.

"I have no idea," I answer honestly. "I don't regret it, but now I'm worried that I want to do it again."

"Is that a bad thing?"

"Hell yeah, it's a bad thing," I squeak. "He's a liar, V. I can't let my head get all wrapped up in him again."

"Your head or your hear—"

"Nope. Don't say it."

She hums, then switches her approach.

"So, the sex was good, then?"

"Phenomenal. I fucking hate it." I groan. "I don't know if I want to choke him to death with my bare hands or choke myself to blackout on his dick. It's very inconvenient for me."

Her tinkling laugh makes me smile, and I groan again.

"What the hell am I gonna do, V?"

"Only you know what's best for you, Bails. If you want to

sleep with him again, and you think it's something you can do without risking your, um, *head*...then do what you want, you know?"

"Yeah, maybe."

"You're the hero here, B. This is your story."

"So, what you're saying is if I want the D, I should take the D," I deadpan, and she laughs again.

"If you want the D, then take the D. Just, you know, be careful." Her voice drops. "Make sure he's worth it."

"Worth what?"

"Worth the risk."

And that's the ten-thousand-dollar question, isn't it?

"Pie tins? Today's task is...pie tins?"

Riggs and I share a glance, then look back into our box, which only contains a variety of pie tins. Today there was no envelope telling us which baked good we'd be making. Instead, all we got was the box. And in it...

...pie tins.

"So, they want us to make a pie?" Riggs questions, and I shrug.

"If they want us to make a pie, then why not just put PIE in the envelope? Why do this all cryptic and shit?" I look around at the other three teams. They've all already started gathering their ingredients. "It looks like the others are doing pie."

"We could do cherry pie."

"We could."

"Or something a little less common. Like...pear?"

"Hmm. Ginger pear? Chai spice pear."

Hmm.

"What's going on in that brain of yours, Sundance?" I can

feel his eyes on me as I squint at the pie tins. "I can tell you're coming up with something."

I tap my fingers on the counter. "What if we just have to make something *in* the pie tin, but it doesn't have to be *actual* pie?"

I look at him to find a big smile on his face, and immediately, a matching one stretches over mine. "Take the lead," he says, and the words make my belly tingle and my chest tight. *Take the lead*, he says. So, I do.

We make a classic French fresh fruit tart.

The crust is made of buttery shortbread, the filling is *crème pâtissière*, which is just a sweet vanilla custard, and we top it with an assortment of berries and kiwi. Honestly, the trickiest part is making myself be patient, because our recipe requires a lot of cooling time between steps. If not for Riggs, I definitely would have rushed through and messed it all up.

Since we're working with a pie tin and not a traditional tart pan, I show Riggs my trick of using parchment paper to carefully remove the tart crust from the pie tin. You learn a lot of hacks when your resources are limited.

I would have filled the tart with a mascarpone cream because it's easy, but Riggs insists on making the custard. Which, good thing he does, because I have no idea how to do that shit. Then, when it comes to topping the tart with the berries, Riggs completely floors me with his attention to detail. He wasn't kidding when he said he was a master of technique. After I arrange the strawberries, blueberries, and raspberries on the top, Riggs makes a kiwi flower for the middle. Like, an actual rose formed out of sliced kiwi. Watching him slice the fruit and shape the delicate flower with his big, dexterous fingers has me panting and sweating in a way that could have almost been embarrassing. Then, when he shows me how to use apricot preserves as a glaze, I almost come on the spot.

Why does he have to be so good at everything?

Well. Everything except telling the truth.

But...maybe I've jumped to conclusions? His mom calls him Alex. He says he and Talia aren't together. As I stand back and watch him gently brush the glaze over the fruit topping, I wonder if maybe I've been overreacting.

I let Riggs hold my hand all through the judging process. When it's announced that we've, once again, survived the chopping block, that we now have a chance to compete tomorrow and actually win the whole competition, I let Riggs lift me in a hug and spin me in a circle.

Then, when we're in the car and he asks if we should stop by a drugstore, I enthusiastically tell him yes. Because what the hell, right? I've basically forgiven him. I might as well enjoy my last few nights in the city before we part ways for good. It's not like I'm at risk of getting hurt again. It's not like he's Craig, anyway. It's not like he's done any *real* damage...

"Wanna grab food and then head back to my parents' place to finish off plans for tomorrow?" Riggs asks after climbing back into the car, a brown paper bag peeking out of the pocket of his pea coat.

I can't help it. I smirk at it.

"That's a big bag for a twelve-pack, Butch."

He arches an eyebrow, pulls the bag from his pocket, and tosses it into my lap.

"That's because it's not a twelve-pack, Sundance."

Heat prickles my skin from the fire in his eyes. I take a breath, so my voice is steady, cool, and then cock my head to the side.

"You think you're gonna need more than twelve condoms?"

His grin is wicked. "I think *we're* going to find out, won't we?"

I laugh it off, but my body is burning up, so I change the subject.

"Food sounds good, but I'm paying for my own this time, so it has to be like under eight bucks."

He pulls out his phone and taps something out, then flashes me another heartbreaking smile.

"How about empanadas? There's a food truck not too far from here. They're not always out after it snows, so we're lucky."

"Empanadas sound amazing."

"Driver! To West Town!"

I laugh when he taps on the roof of the car, and I laugh even harder when the driver laughs at his antics. Everyone likes Riggs, even when he's being an ass, and it's as annoying as it is charming.

We find the food truck in one of Chicago's more residential neighborhoods and get a variety of empanadas to take back to the condo. After hanging our coats and stowing our shoes on the cute little shoe shelf in the foyer closet, he suggests we take our food out to the terrace. Apparently, rich people pay other not-as-rich people to clean the snow off their outdoor entertaining areas, and they also pay for heating lights and towers, just in case they decide that they want to sit outside in thirty-degree weather to eat their dinner.

Rich people convenience is fucking weird.

But of course, I agree. Because when else am I going to get to eat food truck empanadas on a thirty-second floor terrace in the middle of winter?

"Oh my god, this is amazing," I say with my mouth full of a macaroni and cheese empanada. Mac and cheese is one of my favorite comfort foods. Mac and cheese wrapped in a warm and flaky handheld crust? Even freakin' better.

"Right?" Riggs says between chews. "Here, try this one. It's bacon, dates, and goat cheese." He passes me the half-eaten empanada, and I take a bite.

"Oh my god, that's amazing too. Like a tastebud orgasm. What else did we get?"

He digs through the bag. "Chicken curry, mushroom and blue cheese, something with egg, and..." He pulls one out and looks at it.

"Oh, banana and Nutella!" I make grabby hands at him. "Gimme."

"Hold up, Barnes. This is a sweet one for *dessert*. You've not even finished a whole savory one yet." He gestures to the plate on the lounge chair in front of me with three half-eaten empanadas on it.

"There's too many good ones. I want to try them all." I put my mac and cheese empanada down on the plate. "Besides, life is too short to abide by arbitrary sweet and savory meal course rules. If I want a dessert dish for dinner, that's my prerogative as a grown-ass woman."

His lips twitch with a smile. "You don't even like banana."

"False. I like banana in *some* things. Maybe I'll like it in empanadas. Won't know until I try." I put my hand out again, wiggling my fingers and raising my eyebrows.

Slowly, he sets the empanada in my hand, touching way more of my palm with his fingertips than necessary. I swallow back a sigh, then take my time unwrapping the food. When a corner of the empanada is bare, I hold eye contact with Riggs as I take a bite. The moment the flavor hits my tongue, my eyes flutter shut, and I hum.

"Oh. My. *God*." It's so damn good.

I'm about to insist Riggs try it, but my words die in my

throat when I open my eyes and catch him looking at me like he'd rather have *me* for dessert. I swallow, and his pupils dilate as he watches my throat contract with the action. I lick my lower lip and he groans, reaching out and taking the empanada from me, then taking the plate from my lounger and setting it somewhere on the ground.

"Sundance," he rasps, his voice jagged and tight, "have you ever been fucked on an open-air terrace thirty-two stories up?"

I shake my head slowly and clear my throat. "Can't say that I have."

"Would you like to?"

"Yes." *Duh.*

He's on me, then, big hands in my hair and up my shirt, tongue in my mouth, teeth on my neck. He's everywhere at once and it's still not enough. I rip at his clothes until he's shirtless, so I can drag my fingernails down his chest and back. So I can grab onto his biceps and squeeze.

I go for the button on his pants next, and he lets me wrap my fingers around his hard cock before he groans and flips me onto my stomach. He tugs my jeans down my thighs, pulls me up onto my knees, and then shoves his tongue into my pussy from behind. All I can do is whimper and moan, white knuckle the lounger and urge him on.

I've never, ever, been touched like this.

The places I can feel him are new and strange and oh, so good. He bites my ass cheek hard, and I let out a cry. Then his tongue is back on me, in me, lapping at my clit and making me squirm. Any self-consciousness I may have felt is off the balcony and plummeting into the river below. I flatten my chest on the lounger so my ass is straight in the air and I can press back onto his face with more force. I know it's what he wants, because he wraps one of his big hands around my thigh and pulls me closer, then uses his other hand to palm and massage my breast.

"I'm close," I cry, "I'm so close." He takes my tight clit into his mouth and sucks, and within seconds, I'm coming so hard I can feel it dripping down my thighs.

He stands briefly and I feel a cold breeze on my backside. I hear his pants drop, a soft grunt, and then he's plunging into me with a force that shoves my cheek into the cushions. I wouldn't be surprised if I have a fabric imprint on my face when this is done. Totally worth it.

He pumps a few times, then pulls me up so my back is to his chest and his mouth is on my neck. I twist so I can kiss him as his thrusts slow, pulsing in deep and pulling out slowly, so I can feel every ridged inch of him. One of his big hands holds me in place by my hip, and the other slips under my shirt and cups my left breast, fingers splayed over my tattoo. I know he can feel my heart racing. I can feel his thumping on my back.

His mouth never leaves me, not when I come for a second time tonight, and not when he finds his release moments after.

"I like your boobs," Riggs says randomly about an hour later. I couldn't move my legs after his assault on me, so he brought a blanket out to the terrace and wrapped us both in it. Now I'm tucked in his arms with my head on his chest, watching snowflakes fall from the sky and melt before they hit the ground.

"Ugh." I snort out a laugh. "Don't say boobs. I hate that word."

"Tits?" he asks, reaching down to cup one of the *boobs* in question.

"Surprisingly, I can do tits. Or breasts."

"I can't do breasts. Makes me think of baked chicken." I laugh loudly at his tone.

"I guess it's tits, then," I say, and he chuckles.

"Okay, well, I like your tits. They remind me of holding a baseball."

I shoot up and turn to look at him. "The fuck?"

The *fuck*? This dude just compared my tits to a baseball?

He sits up straight, his smile big and his eyes playful. "No, hear me out," he says. "When I've got a baseball in my hand, it feels perfect. The perfect size and shape. It's like the baseball was made specifically for me to hold it. It just...*fits*."

"Okay..."

"So basically, your tits fit my hand perfectly. And they're even better because they're softer and smoother and warm. Like my hand was made to hold your tits. Your tits were made for my hands. Fucking sexy."

I roll my eyes and flop back down on his chest. "Good lord, that's ridiculous."

He moves both hands over my chest. "I might just hold your tits instead of your hand next time we're out."

"Ha! Then I'll hold your dick."

"Is that supposed to be a bad thing? It sounds amazing."

I can't hold back my laugh, and soon, I'm giggling so much my stomach hurts and I have tears in my eyes. "Oh my god, shut up," I gasp, catching my breath. "You're seriously fucking ridiculous."

He shrugs, and I feel him smile into my hair. "I know what I like."

We fall back into a comfortable silence, and my eyes drift shut as he runs his fingers lightly up and down my arm. It's not until he starts speaking softly that I wake back up.

"She was diagnosed in June of last year," Riggs whispers. I don't say anything, but I take his hand in mine, so he knows I'm listening. "She was having trouble holding piping bags and measuring cups and stuff. Like she couldn't quite keep a grip. Then she had a fall at work—not a slip, just tripped over her own feet—she went in for testing."

"That must have been scary."

"Yeah. It seemed like she got worse kind of fast after that. She was using a wheelchair just six months later." He sighs and my heart squeezes for him. "Only recently has she had difficulty with her arms."

"Is that why she's got the feeding tube?"

"Yeah. In her stomach. Lifting her arms to feed herself was tiring her out. She won't say it, but I think chewing does, too. They didn't tell me about the feeding tube until a few weeks ago, and only then it was because I felt it when I moved her from her bed to her chair." I can hear the anger in his voice.

"Why wouldn't they tell you that?"

He shrugs. "My dad doesn't want me taking my focus off baseball. Wants me to go to the pros. I think my mom doesn't want to worry me. She doesn't want to interrupt things with…well, school and stuff."

I don't ask how much time Odette has. I Googled it on my phone Tuesday night. It could be a few months or another year. I don't want to make him talk about anything he doesn't want to, so I don't ask.

"Sometimes I feel like I'm doing all this other stuff for everyone else, and I haven't really had a chance to think about what I want." His voice is low and kind of dreamy, like he doesn't realize he's saying it out loud. If he weren't running his fingers through my hair, I'd think he'd forgotten about my presence all together. "Baseball, the draft, school, and—" he stutters, and I feel his body jolt. "Just everything."

"You don't want to enter the draft?" I trace my fingers on his chest, over the t-shirt he's put back on. "You're a really good pitcher."

I feel his smile in my hair. "You checkin' up on me?"

I scoff. "As if. I don't live under a rock, Stanton. I hear people talk."

But also, I have Googled him numerous times. I don't tell him that.

"I used to want to go to the pros." He sighs again. "I used to want a lot of things that I don't anymore."

I lift his hand to my lips and kiss his knuckles, and he hums.

"Tell me about Brandon."

My smile is instant.

"He was just like me, but nicer." We both laugh. "I'm serious. Nicer, and more talented. He was a brilliant artist. He was good at everything—drawing, painting, sculpting—but he loved digital art. He wanted to go into graphic design. He helped design the LGBTQ+ Student Center's website for our Community College. In high school, he painted a mural on one whole side of our bedroom. It was just of us doing random shit. One of the scenes was of us in front of the Bean at night, the whole skyline lit up in the reflection."

"The Bean at night is amazing."

"It is. We used to come to the city for concerts and stuff, and it was always our first and last stop. Day Bean and Night Bean, he called it." Riggs kisses my head softly, and it makes tears prickle my eyes.

"He sounds like he was a great person."

"He really was. I know people tend to romanticize others after they've died. 'Their smile lit up a room,' 'they made friends with everyone,' that sort of stuff. But that was actually Bran. He was legitimately one of the friendliest, kindest, most genuine people ever. Everyone loved him." I choke back the surge of anger that flares in my chest. "Everyone who mattered, anyway."

"I think it's really good of you to replace his headstone with the one he deserves, Bailey. It's thoughtful and caring, and I admire you a lot for it. A lot of people wouldn't even bother."

"I owe him at least that." The guilt is evident in my tone, and I swallow it down. When I open my mouth next, the story falls from my tongue so easily. The only other person who knows it all is Ivy.

"I was the reason stuff got bad for him in high school," I confess, my voice a whisper. "I was dating this guy. Craig Dixon. I had been dating him since 9th grade, off and on. He was a constant fixture in our house. He was always hanging out with us. I thought...I dunno. I thought he loved Brandon like I did. When Bran came out to me, I was just kind of like 'okay, cool,' and when we were in private, I used his pronouns and name. But, you know, Brandon wasn't out yet. He wanted to wait until we graduated." I swallow the brick in my throat. Work to wet my bone-dry tongue. "I fucked up. I fucked up so bad."

Riggs tightens his hold on me. "You don't have to tell me," he whispers, but I shake my head.

"I told Craig. It was an accident. I was talking about Homecoming and mentioned Brandon going with us, and Craig thought I was talking about one of the football players from a rival school. Craig was our wide receiver. Anyway, he got pissy and started trying to say I was trying to cheat on him, and then Bran overheard and stepped in to defend me. He ended up coming out to Craig. We'd all been friends forever. Since kindergarten, really. I thought he loved us. Loved *me*... I...I didn't think he would..."

I start crying. Big, fat, tears leaking down my cheeks.

"He outed Brandon at school the next day. Stood on one of the tables in the cafeteria during lunch and announced it to everyone in there. Just…threw him to the wolves and sneered while he did it. He led a campaign to make his life miserable for the rest of our senior year."

God, it was terrible. The pranks, the name calling, the vicious bullying. It was like the guy I was in love with didn't exist. I'd been completely blind to the kind of person Craig truly was, and my brother paid the price for it.

"And to make it worse," I continue in a whisper, "our parents didn't even try to stop it. They weren't at all supportive. If anything, they made it worse by dragging us to church and trying to request prayer chains." I squeeze my eyes shut and swallow. "I was so scared for him."

"I'm so sorry he went through that. Nobody should ever be treated like that." Riggs's rumbling voice is muffled as he speaks into my hair. "But he got out. You both did. You said he was doing well at college. That dickhead Craig, your parents, that whole fucking town— they didn't win, Sundance. They didn't succeed in breaking him."

I take a few steadying breaths and let his words wash over me, seeking out the warmth in them.

"Yeah," I rasp. "He was doing so well. And he said he didn't blame me for any of that shit, even though I know it was my fault. And then," my voice cuts off on another sob, "and then, when he got sick, I left him at the apartment, so I could go see a stupid band play. I should have stayed with him. We were supposed to make dinner that night and hang out because we'd been so busy, we hadn't seen much of each other, but this band I liked was playing a surprise show, and Bran didn't want to go, so I ditched him. If I had been home, if I had gotten to him sooner…"

I can't say it, but I know Riggs knows. If I had been there to call 911, Bran probably would have lived.

"That's not your fault," Riggs says fiercely. "You can't blame yourself for that. There's no way you could have known."

I just shake my head and cry. It doesn't matter how many times I hear it, I will never believe that. But I can still do one last thing for him. Not to assuage my guilt—nothing will ever wipe me clean of that, and I have accepted it—but to give him the respect he deserves, especially in death.

When my tears have dried, Riggs moves us to the kitchen. We tweak our recipes and do some trial bakes. We laugh and smile and crack jokes, and it's exactly the release I need after my cathartic confession on the terrace. When Riggs has the car drive us back to the hotel, we shower together. He washes my hair and jokes about having enough flour in it to make a small cake. When we move to the bed, we have sex, and it's languid and intimate in a way I've never experienced before. He kisses me like he means it, and it's terrifying, but I still fall asleep with my face buried in his neck.

The next morning, after he's left for his workout, I wake to find a delicate, perfectly crafted origami star on his pillow, and my heart stutters in my chest.

Crap. I think I'm falling for the asshole.

Again.

EIGHTEEN

"HOW DO YOU FEEL?" I ask Bailey as we wait to present our display to the judges. "Confident?'

"Yeah, actually." She smiles up at me, eyes sparkling and teeth showing. She's glowing, and I want to bask in her light. "I think we have a serious chance. Literally everything turned out perfect."

It's true. I couldn't have dreamed up a better outcome. We didn't have a single hiccup. And while Bailey is still covered in half of the pantry, we managed not to spill anything important on the floor or in the oven.

"Riggs and Bailey," the judge calls. "What have you made for us today?"

Bailey looks at me with a tinge of fear in her eyes, and I squeeze her hand. Then we grab the tray of plates we've arranged, and hand them out to the judges.

"Well," I begin after the plates have been delivered, "we decided to highlight three popular desserts that are unique to Chicago, we chose each dessert because we felt it, in some way, embodied a concept of love."

"We can't wait to hear about it," another judge says. "The

presentation is beautiful, I have to say. I love the silver sugar and strawberry heart garnishes."

"Thank you," Bailey and I say at the same time. She flashes me a shy smile.

"What do you want to start with?"

I glance at Bailey. We discussed who was going to present what last night. I did the intro, and she'll do the first and third items, so we trade off talking time.

"We'll start with the cupcakes, which is our redo item from the week." She winces playfully when she says *redo*, and the judges all chuckle. "We went with a white chocolate raspberry champagne cupcake. Both the cupcake batter and the raspberry buttercream icing use the most popular sparkling wine from Pops Champagne, here in Chicago, and the wine is actually made by Illinois Sparkling Company. For the white chocolate ganache, we used chocolate from Chicago's own Veruca Chocolates on Halstead."

Bailey stops talking to watch the judges cut into their cupcakes and inspect the ganache filling, and we both stare as the judges take their bites. Just like all the other times, they give nothing away. I see her swallow, but she continues on.

"We went with champagne and chocolate because, well, they're sexy flavors, quite frankly." Her shoulders loosen when everyone laughs. "Champagne and chocolate make us think of romantic dates and dinners, and that fits perfectly with the concept of romantic love."

"Very nice," a judge says after wiping his mouth with a cloth napkin. "And how about this one?" He uses his fork to point at the next item on his plate.

I clear my throat. "Those are traditional buttermilk donut holes, similar to the ones you'll find at Do-Rites, but with our own Chicago twist. If you'll cut into them..."

I watch as they each cut into their donut holes, finding

different flecks of color inside. Bailey and I planned it so each judge has a different color scheme.

"Since we modeled our cupcakes after romantic love, we took a different approach here. What do Chicagoans love fiercely, loyally, and will go to battle for?" I ask, and immediately one of the judges speaks up.

"Deep dish and beer!" Everyone laughs, and I nod.

"Okay, yes, that too." I chuckle. "But also, Chicagoans love their sports teams. No matter how much they may break our hearts, we stick by our teams through thick and thin. And let's be real, usually it's thin." More laughter.

"The color schemes inside your donuts—red, white, and blue; blue and orange; red, white, and black; black, grey, and white—represent each of the big sports teams here in Chicago."

"Hey, wait," one of the judges yells. "I got a Cubbie one." He looks at the other judges' plates. "Give me yours," he says, gesturing to the judge who has the black, grey, and white sprinkles.

"See?" Bailey cuts in with a wry grin. "Exactly our point."

"The sugar sprinkles we used melted into the donuts when we cooked them, coloring the donuts without messing with the traditional flavor or texture."

Again, Bailey and I watch as they sample their donuts. This time, though, I notice that a few of the judges ate their whole donut and went back for more of their cupcake. The longer we talk, the emptier the judges' plates become. I look at Bailey to see if she notices what I do, and the way she rolls her lips to try and hide her giddy smile tells me she does.

"The final item on your plate is a chocolate strawberry French silk parfait," Bailey says after the judges ask about our third dessert. "We made the chocolate pots de crème, once again, using bittersweet chocolate from Veruca Chocolates, and we layered that with vanilla Chantilly cream, and topped it with fresh strawberries."

"I recognize this dessert," one of the judges says, and I can't hold back the pride in my smile. Bailey beams as well. "Is this the dish they serve at *Temetum*?"

"It is," Bailey says with a smile. "Chicago's only three-star Michelin restaurant."

"Wonderful," one of the judges mumbles as he tastes the parfait. "And how does this fit with your love concept?"

"Well," Bailey says, then clears her throat and blinks a few times. "We chose this recipe to represent the familial bond, the unconditional love you get between a mother and child."

I have to hold my breath and count backward from ten in French to keep from tearing up.

"This recipe was created by Odette DuPont Stanton, who happens to be my partner's mom."

The judges are all smiles, and I force one of my own. Not many people know why my mom retired from *Temetum*. We've kept it quiet at her request to avoid attention, and I'm grateful for that now. There's no sympathy on the judges' faces. Just appreciation for a well-executed recipe and a thoroughly connected theme.

There are a few more *mmm's* and whispered praises, and then we're ushered to the scene room for our interview. Bailey can't stop bouncing, I can't stop wringing my hands, and I would give my left nut for a few pieces of paper so I could fold a crane or a butterfly or a dinosaur or something. I don't even remember what I say in the interview, and when we're finally moved back into the main room for the announcement of the winners, I could fucking jump for joy.

"Is it just me or did that feel like forever?" Bailey groans once we're back at our station.

"It did. It really did." I look at her to find that she's gnawing on her fingernail, so I reach over and take her hand in mine. "I know this isn't what you want to hear, but even if we don't win, we still did an amazing job."

She huffs.

"I'm serious, Bailey. There wasn't a single minute from this week that I wasn't completely in awe of you."

"Really?"

"Yeah. Really." I lift her hand to my lips and kiss her knuckles. "You're sensational."

"Okay, are we ready to begin?" a PA calls, and the judges tell her yes. The PA barks a few more orders, then we're told the cameras are rolling.

The judges take turns talking, going over our desserts and the other team's desserts, and I tune almost everything out. Some things jump out at me, like "delicious" and "perfect" and "creative," but I don't know who they're praising. Instead of paying attention to them, I watch Bailey.

Her facial expressions dictate the entire judging ceremony for me. When she grins wide and her eyes light up, I know they've said something good about us. When her lips tighten and her mouth falls into a polite smile, I know they've praised the other team.

It's not until her eyes start to well with tears that I start to worry. I squeeze her hand, but she won't look at me, so I tear my gaze from her and return my focus to the judging panel.

"Honestly, this was an extremely difficult decision to make," a judge is saying. "Both teams pulled off some seriously talented baking today."

"Su and Parker, you made one of the best cheesecakes I have ever tasted."

Bailey's shoulders sag.

"Agreed," another judge says, "it melted on my tongue."

"My favorite item of the entire week was definitely the

French silk parfait from Bailey and Riggs," adds another third judge.

Bailey sucks in a breath and flicks her eyes to me. Hope.

"But unfortunately, only one team can be the winner and take home the ten-thousand-dollar grand prize."

"Since all the desserts presented to us were wonderful, we couldn't decide based on that alone."

She's bouncing now, and my stomach is in my throat.

"So, it came down to the theme."

I squeeze her hand again.

"Parker. Su. Your decision to create traditional Valentine's Day desserts was a great one."

"All three of your desserts complemented each other brilliantly."

She squeezes my hand back, and I can tell she's trying desperately not to shake.

"But Bailey and Riggs..."

Her back shoots ramrod straight, and she's squeezing my hand so hard I can't feel my fingers.

"Your take on the *Chicago is for Lovers* theme was perfect."

I wrap my arm around her shoulder and pull her in tight. I don't think she's breathing. I certainly am not.

"Your desserts were the embodiment of Chicago."

"Congratulations, Bailey and Riggs, you've won the Holiday Bake Off."

She squeals and launches herself into my arms, and we're both laughing as I spin her around. When I set her back on her feet, she faces the judges with tears rolling down her cheeks.

"Thank you so, so much for this opportunity," she says. "Thank you so much."

They hand us one of those giant television checks and have us pose for pictures. The judges all shake our hands and tell us what a great job we did. We're interviewed again. And then, finally, we're allowed to leave.

"We have to tell your mom," Bailey says as soon as we're in the car. Technically we're not supposed to tell anyone yet, but fuck that, we have to tell my mom.

I text Ms. Beth and she tells me my mom is sleeping, but she will call me the minute she wakes up. *No matter the time*, I tell her. I make her promise.

"What should we do in the meantime?" I ask Bailey.

"I don't know. I'm so buzzed. I just want to celebrate."

"Want to go to the Night Bean?" The smile on her face tells me everything I need to know, so I ask the driver to take us to Millennium Park.

When we get there, we take about one hundred photos in front of the Bean. Some with ridiculous faces in the distorted reflective surface of the sculpture, some of us each posed in front of it, some selfies with our arms outstretched, and a few together that we got some random people to take for us. In every picture, the buildings are lit up against the night sky, the Christmas lights twinkling like fake stars on a movie set. In every picture, Bailey's smile shines the brightest. Her happiness a beacon for my own. Her luminescent eyes my Polaris, guiding me back to myself.

"*Regarde-toi, tu es magnifique,*" I say earnestly, and she smiles, bemused.

"What did you say?" she asks, and I shrug in response. She narrows her eyes at me playfully. "Teach me something. Teach me something in French."

"*Mon aéroglisseur est plein d'anguilles,*" I say, trying to hold back a laugh.

"Moan ay oh glee surly planohghee," she says.

Her accent is absolutely terrible. She literally said nothing.

"Great job," I say sarcastically, and she rolls her eyes.

"Ass. What did I say?"

"*You* said nothing." She swats at me.

"Fine, what did *you* say?"

"My hovercraft is full of eels."

She barks a laugh, and then another, until we're both full-fledged cracking up and I'm pretty sure these tourists think we're drunk off our asses.

"You're crazy," she says after catching her breath.

I just nod. "*Pour toi.*"

In this moment, bundled in our winter clothes, laughing with tourists and sipping hot chocolate, I feel like *me*. For the first time in years, I know who I am and what I want.

And what I want is her.

This fierce, intelligent, wicked, infuriating woman who challenges me and makes me laugh and lights me up on the inside. Who protects her heart with a dry sense of humor and emotional Kevlar because it is, by far, her most valuable asset. Who is beautiful in her vulnerability and her strength.

I want this woman. Bailey Elizabeth Barnes. My Sundance.

And I'm going to make her mine.

I WAKE to the smell of coffee and something sweet. When I pop open one eye, lifting my head slightly off the pillow, I see a room service cart sitting next to the table with a coffee carafe and a few silver-domed food platters. My stomach grumbles.

I sit up slowly and swing my legs over the edge of the bed, then I snag Riggs's shirt off the nightstand where we tossed it last night. I slip the shirt over my head, covering my naked body, and walk to the room service cart. When I lift a coffee mug, another origami star falls out, and my stomach fills with butter-flies. The giddiness is ridiculous, I know it is, but I still take the star and tuck it safely into my duffle next to the other one.

Before I can pour a cup of coffee, I hear the shower kick on, which means Riggs must be back from the gym. It was probably him bringing the cart in that woke me up. I lift the lid on one of the food platters and find the most delicious looking Belgian waffle topped with cherries and whipped cream.

He ordered this for me.

Ugh, why is he so damn good?

I let out a little moan and press my thighs together, before stripping the shirt back off and walking into the bathroom. Waking up to fresh coffee and cherry topped Belgian waffles the morning after winning ten grand makes me feel very generous. Is there a better way to start a day than in the shower kneeling in front of a gorgeous man while gagging on his cock? Right now, I'm thinking probably not.

After shower head (for both of us), then breakfast, then table sex, Riggs and I are dressed and ready to head out. He doesn't have to check out until four, so we're going to go visit with his mom for a few hours, then come back here and use the bed one last time before heading back to campus. I freakin' love this bed.

Since it's Saturday, I can't ring up Flannagan's and give them the go ahead on my headstone order, but I'm buzzing with excitement for when I can finally make the call on Monday. I did, however, call Ivy and gush to her, and then I texted the group chat, and I've been fielding congratulations messages all morning. They're planning something, I can tell. The sneaks.

"All set?" Riggs asks as he grabs the handle on my duffle.

"Yep. You sure your parents won't mind us coming by? I know she was tired last night."

"Nah, Dad won't be back for another few days and Mom's good. She's stoked to celebrate the win. She wants to see us before I take you back to campus."

"I feel bad making you drive me all the way back."

"It's seriously not a big deal." He pulls out his phone and silences a call. The third one he's ignored this morning.

"You need to get that?" I arch an eyebrow as we step into the elevator.

"Nope. Not important." Then he takes my hand in his, and I melt a little. Stupid boy. Stupid heart.

When we get to the condo, we hang our jackets and take off our shoes, then move into the main room. Odette and Ms. Beth are already there, Odette in her wheelchair and Ms. Beth sitting on the couch. Riggs's mom looks beautiful. Her hair is curled and her makeup is impeccable. If I didn't already know about her diagnosis, I'd think she was the picture of health.

Her eyes light up the moment she sees us.

"*Mon étoile,*" she calls to Riggs, "my darling. I am so glad you're here." She looks to me, then, with the same smile on her face. "Bailey, *belle fille*, wonderful to see you again."

"Hi, Odette. Ms. Beth," I greet. "Thanks for having me over again."

"You look beautiful, *Maman*." Riggs swoops down and kisses his mom on both cheeks. "Ms. Beth," he says as he hugs his mom's nurse. When he stands, he gestures to the breathing machine attached to the back of his mom's wheelchair. "I thought that was just for nighttime? When she sleeps." He looks from Ms. Beth to his mom, and Odette flutters her fingers at him.

"It is," she says with a warm smile. "Just for comfort. There is nothing to worry about."

"We just finished working out," Ms. Beth explains, and I assume she means range-of-motion exercises. "We brought the machine out just in case."

"I could have done the exercises. You should have waited for me."

"Nonsense," Odette laughs. "I wanted to spend time with you both." She looks at me with excitement in her eyes. "I hear congratulations are in order."

My smile blooms instantly. "Yes! We kicked a—uhm, butt." I scrunch up my nose. "We kicked *butt.*"

"So, I heard," she says with a laugh. "And you made my French silk. How did that turn out?"

"Perfect," Riggs answers. "Bailey really crushed it, Mom. You'd be proud." His smile for me is full of reverence. I blush a little and look away. "Definitely would have promoted her in your kitchen." He winks at his mom. "Might have even made her your protégé."

"I wish I could have tasted it," his mom says wistfully, and Riggs and I share a conspiratorial grin.

"Well, actually..." I start. "We might have brought you something."

"Go ahead," Riggs nods toward the kitchen, "go get it."

I bounce into the kitchen and pull a white box from the big refrigerator, then I grab the plates and spoons we set out last night. When I bring it all back into the living room, Odette gasps.

"*Ouah*! I am so excited." She looks from me to Riggs. "I would say you didn't have to, but I may have been hoping for this."

Riggs sets everything up on the coffee table—two cupcakes and a parfait. We couldn't snag any donuts. Surprisingly, those were all grabbed up by the staff. We were lucky to get the cupcakes and the parfait. I watch as he cuts the cupcakes in half, then hands Ms. Beth and me a spoon.

My heart squeezes as he digs into the parfait and gathers a small amount of silk and Chantilly crème onto the spoon, then looks at Odette. "Okay. This was all Bailey."

"That's not true." I narrow my eyes playfully at Riggs, then look at his mom. "Odette, your son and I split the baking. He had just as much of a hand in this as I did."

He chuckles and mock whispers, "I just did what she told me to do."

"Smart man," Ms. Beth jokes.

"*Absolument,*" Odette agrees.

"Ready?" Riggs asks, and Odette nods. As he places the spoon in her mouth, my heart squeezes and my throat tightens. Odette's eyes fall shut and she hums. Then she looks at me with a smile.

"Perfect," she says with a grin. "Well done. Now that." She gestures at the cupcake.

I tell her about the recipe and why we chose it, and Riggs, once again, fixes a small sample on the spoon. I don't miss the way he carefully gathers a small bit of every element of the cupcake. A bit of the cake, a small amount of the ganache, and a little of the icing. It's not a large amount, I notice. It would barely require chewing. From what Riggs told me, Odette can eat and swallow, but it's tiring for her, and too large of bites, or tough to chew foods, are a choking hazard. The care with which he is feeding her warms my heart and makes me want to cry all at once.

"That is perfect as well," Odette says after she's finished. "Tell me about your week," she urges, and we tell her. Riggs continues to feed her small samples of the parfait and the cupcake, and Ms. Beth and I also try some. Everyone agrees that the desserts are delicious, and I cannot help but puff up with pride.

We fucking did it. I fucking did it. I've never felt like I accomplished something this big before. Sure, I've got great grades and I receive a small scholarship as a result, and I've worked my ass off to cover everything else I need. I've managed to support myself without the help of my parents since I started college, but this has all been out of necessity, and I've never really felt accomplished because the job is never really finished.

When you're working double time just to stay afloat, just to make ends meet, it's difficult to see the value in your effort. When you don't have much to show for it, it's easy to feel like you're fighting a losing battle. But this contest—I've never worked this hard for something this big and succeeded. And knowing that I can finally do something for Brandon that he deserves? That feeling is unparalleled.

At one point, after we'd been at the condo for a couple hours, Ms. Beth has to take Odette back to her bedroom.

"Girl things," Odette says with a smile. The moment they're out of the room, Riggs has me pinned down on the couch, kissing my lips and my neck like a fiend.

"God, I cannot get enough of you," he says against my lips, and I run my hands over his shoulders.

"You need to try," I say with a giggle and give him a shove. "Your mom and Ms. Beth could be back any second."

He shakes his head and kisses me again, working his hand over the button of my jeans. "They'll be at least twenty minutes. I can make you come in ten."

I gasp when he makes contact with my clit over my panties. Even through the fabric, his big fingers sliding over my slit has me panting.

"Will you let me make you come?" he growls and bites my nipple through my shirt. I'm so thankful I'm wearing a thin bralette and not something padded. His teeth on my flesh is heaven.

I pull him up and kiss him fiercely. "Fast," I say against his lips, and he smiles before kissing me again. He slips his hand into my underwear and swipes through my slick folds, then rubs my throbbing clit. I gasp and hum, and if it weren't for him moving his mouth from my neck to my chest, I wouldn't have heard the door in the foyer open and shut.

Riggs goes rigid, and I shove him off me. I sit up quickly, straighten my shirt and fix the button on my jeans. When I flick my eyes to Riggs, he's got a wicked grin on his face, and then he sucks his fingers into his mouth. My eyes flare, and he removes them just as footsteps enter the main room.

"Riggs," a man's voice rumbles, and I turn on the couch to see Riggs's father. I know him from the canvas portraits. Riggs has his strong jaw, height, and broad shoulders, but otherwise, the resemblance is minimal.

"Dad," Riggs says as he stands up. "You weren't supposed to be back for a few more days."

"New York is expecting a winter storm, so I left early." He moves his piercing grey eyes to me, but continues speaking to Riggs. "And this is?"

His voice is strange. Not warm, like Odette's, but dismissive. He's not rude, but I get the feeling he doesn't particularly want me here.

"This is Bailey Barnes, Dad."

That's it. That's all he says. I clear my throat lightly before speaking.

"Nice to meet you, Mr. Stanton." I'm not surprised when he doesn't correct me and tell me to call him by his first name. "You have a lovely home."

He grunts and looks me over, then his impassive face morphs into a charming smile. I have to blink a few times, because I've seen that smile on Riggs's face. I've come to think of it as his fake smile, though I never would have known had I not spent so much time with him this week.

"Thank you. Pleasure to meet you, Bailey." Mr. Stanton looks at Riggs. "And why are you two here? Didn't the team have training all week? You shouldn't be here until tomorrow."

Huh. I widen my eyes at Riggs. His Dad didn't know?

Riggs squares his shoulders and meets his Dad's eyes. "I wasn't at training this week. Bailey and I participated in the Midwest Collegiate Holiday Bake Off. We won, actually."

Riggs's dad looks livid. His throat is tight, his shoulders stiff, and I have a feeling he would be popping off real bad if I wasn't standing here to witness it. Before Mr. Stanton can say anything, Riggs speaks again.

"I squared it with Elbin. He gave me an independent training schedule for the week that I had to record and send to him every day."

"Did you throw?"

"No sir, but Elbin isn't worried. I'll get the throwing time I need after the holidays."

Riggs's dad looks at me quickly then back to him. "You should have talked to me about this first."

Riggs shrugs. "Mom knew, and my *coach* was fine with it." They stare off for what feels like an hour, and I fidget awkwardly, because what the hell else am I supposed to do? I about weep with joy when Odette and Ms. Beth come back into the room.

"Antony," Odette says brightly. "You are back early."

His smile for her cracks my heart right in two. He may have been cold with his son just now, but there is nothing but warmth and love for his wife.

"*Ma chérie,*" he says before placing a gentle kiss on her lips. "You look beautiful."

Odette laughs him off and whispers something that I can't hear, then she looks at me. "Did Alex tell you about the baking contest that he and Bailey have won? I am just so proud." She beams at us and Antony puts his hand over hers.

"Yes, he's told me. So happy for them."

"If you had gotten here a few hours earlier, you could have tried their desserts." Odette smiles at me again. "They made my French silk!"

"It was delicious," Ms. Beth chimes in.

"Next time, then," Antony says to his wife.

Antony moves to sit in the chair next to Odette's wheelchair when a melodic bell tolls through the house. I jump and look up at the ceiling, trying to find where the noise came from, and everyone laughs.

"That's the doorbell," Ms. Beth clarifies, then stands and heads toward the foyer. "I'll see who it is."

"Oh." I say lamely. "Of course, it is." I watch Riggs stifle a laugh and I narrow my eyes at him. He winks at me, then looks to his parents.

"Are we expecting company?"

"Not that I know of," Antony says, then glances at me. "What are your plans for the holidays, Bailey?"

I start to answer when Ms. Beth walks back into the room with a familiar body trailing her. A tall, lithe body that moves with a dancer's grace and a model's confidence. Riggs goes stiff, Odette lets out a tinkling laugh, and Antony stands from where he was sitting and moves to greet her.

"Talia, my girl," Antony says, "I thought you weren't coming until tomorrow." I watch, speechless, as he pulls her into a hug. Her wide eyes flit from me to Riggs and back.

"Well, um, since Riggs was already here..." She looks at Riggs and raises her eyebrow.

He still hasn't said anything.

Talia walks over to Odette and kisses her on the cheeks.

"Hi, Odette," she says with a smile, then gives Ms. Beth a hug. "Hi, Ms. Beth."

"Talia, darling," Odette says with a smile. "So glad you can join us."

Talia looks back at Riggs then. "Um, you weren't answering your phone." As if that explains everything. I'm still in the dark. She looks at me once more, and I realize I must be staring like a lunatic. I blink a few times because my eyes are dry, and then glance at Riggs.

He's still stiff and not speaking. When he moves his eyes

from Talia to me, I feel like I've been punched in the gut. That look. The same one I saw at Bakery On Main the day of the cookie contest. The same one from Cheap Seats right before I dumped beer over his head.

Oh shit.

I look back at Talia, but she's still staring at Riggs, and then Antony's voice breaks in.

"Bailey, have you met our future daughter-in-law, Talia?" He gestures from her to me. "She goes to school at Butler, also. A dance major."

My voice is a broken rasp. "Daughter-in-law?"

"Yes, Riggs's fiancée." He smiles at Talia who is now grimacing. "Still haven't set a date, but we're hoping to convince them to do it soon."

My heartbeat is pounding in my ears. The ground is moving under my feet. Is that an earthquake? Is the high rise collapsing? My eyes find Talia's left hand, and sure as shit, there's a big stupid shiny diamond on her ring finger.

I look slowly at Riggs. "You're engaged," I whisper.

His mouth opens, then shuts. He looks from me to Talia, to his parents, then back.

"I... Bailey, I..."

I choke back a sob, my face flames, and I squeeze my eyes shut. I cannot cry here.

"I have to go."

I turn and hightail it out of the living room, out the foyer door, and into the elevator. When the doors slide shut, the tears fall. As soon as my feet hit the concrete, I speed walk down the block, so I'm out of sight of the high rise and order an Uber. As I wait for the car, I call Ivy.

"Hey, B!" she chirps when she answers. There's music playing in the background. "If the guys were to be making something delicious for dinner tonight, and I'm not saying they are, but *if* they were, would you wan—"

"Ivy," I sob, cutting her off.

"Bailey, what's wrong?" Her voice is urgent. "Are you okay?"

"Can you guys come get me?"

"Yes, of course. You're still in Chicago?"

"Yeah."

I hear her say something to the guys, then there's a door shutting and fabric rustling.

"Bailey, do I need to call the cops?"

"No, no, it's nothing like that." I swipe my face with my sleeve. My cheeks are wet and freezing now, thanks to the cold. "I just need a ride. I can't..."

"Okay. It's okay. We're coming. We'll be there in—"

"Two hours and forty-two minutes, barring traffic," I hear Kelley shout from the background.

"Two hours and forty-two minutes," Ivy repeats. "Call me if you need anything. Will you be at the hotel?"

"I'm heading back now to get my stuff." I sniffle and take a deep breath. "I'm not gonna stay there, though. I'll probably go to a pub or something. I'll text you the location."

"Okay. We'll be there soon."

"Thank you."

"Hey, B. We love you."

"Love you back."

I hang up as the Uber pulls up to the curb of the hotel, then rush inside. I'm shoving my last few items of clothing into my duffle when the door swings open and Riggs steps in.

"Go away," I growl as the tears start again. "I don't want to hear it. I don't want to see you ever again."

"Bailey, please, it's not at all what you think," he pleads, and I laugh at him through my sobs.

"Are you engaged?" I ask.

"Not anymore," he says softly. "Not for almost a year."

I jerk my head back. "What?" I shout. "Your parents think you're engaged, Riggs. They want you to get married *soon*."

He nods. "I know. Tal and I used to be engaged, but we're not anymore."

"Does *she* know that?"

"She does, yes."

"But your parents don't?"

He shakes his head slowly. "No."

"So? You're just *lying* to them? Like you lied to *me*?"

"I never lied to you," he insists, and it pisses me off.

"Bullshit," I shout. "You certainly didn't tell me the truth." I release a shuddering breath. "Oh my god, I let you fuck me on their terrace, and they think you're fucking engaged to another woman!"

"Sundance—"

"Don't call me that," I shout. I must look like a wild animal, the way he approaches me. I feel wild. Rabid. "You don't get to call me that anymore."

"I'm sorry," he says, water rimming his eyes.

"So, what, you're just letting your parents think that you and Talia are engaged? For what reason?"

"Tal's been in my life since we were kids," he says in a low, sad voice. "We got engaged about six months before my mom was diagnosed. Everyone was so happy. My mom was ecstatic. I think she always wanted me and Tal to get married. She always wanted a daughter."

Fuck, I don't want to hear this. I can't stop crying. But I just need to know. For fucking once, I want to know the whole truth.

"After a while, though, Talia and I both realized we didn't want to get married. We love each other, but we aren't in love. We decided to break the engagement, but then Mom started getting worse... I just...I couldn't take this away from her when she's already losing so much else."

"So, you just *lie*? You and Talia. You're pretending to still be engaged...until what? Until your mom...until she..."

I trail off because I can't say it. He and I both know his mom's fate.

"I don't know, Bailey," he whispers. "I never really thought it through that far. Not before you. I just wanted to keep her smiling any way I could. I wanted to give her some sort of light."

I squeeze my eyes shut and take a few deep breaths. When I'm confident I can speak without my voice cracking, I open my eyes and hold Riggs's gaze.

"We all have our shit. I'm not going to hold that against you. I understand what it's like to want to do everything in your power to lift up the people you love. I forgive you."

"You do?" His lips quirk up into a ghost of a smile.

"Yeah. But I can't be part of this anymore. You have your shit, but I have my own shit, too, and I don't have the emotional capacity to deal with yours on top of it."

"Bailey, no." He shakes his head, his voice desperate. "No, I just need time."

"I can't give you that," I say firmly. "It was only sex, anyway."

His laugh is dark and so out of place. "Now who's lying, Barnes?"

"I'm not." I shake my head. "None of it matters. We weren't dating. We weren't anything."

"Bullshit," he spits. "If you're gonna get on my ass for not telling you the whole truth, then you better step back and reevaluate. You've been lying this whole time, Bailey. From the very beginning. Every time you were in my bed, it was with one eye open and one foot out the door. You won't even be honest with yourself."

"Fine!" I shout. "Fine. You want the truth, Riggs? Fine. Yeah, okay, I liked you. I don't do relationships, and I don't hold out hope for happily ever afters, but I was drawn to you. I *wanted* you. Right away. More than I should have. And then we started hanging out and I liked you more. I liked how you made me laugh. How you looked at me like you saw something special. I liked the way you made me feel…"

I squeeze my eyes shut, fighting the tears flooding my lashes and streaming down my face. I rake my fingers through my hair and take a deep breath. My heart is being carved from my chest, so the act of inhaling burns, but I continue despite the cracks in my voice and chest.

"So little by little, I let my guard down for you. I let you in. This week, I wanted to hate you. I wanted to hate you so badly, but I just couldn't, even after everything. So yeah, this was more than sex for me, Riggs. A lot more. Because I let you in not once, but twice. I gave you *two* chances when most people don't even get one. And you know what? You hurt me both times. How's that for the fucking truth?"

"Let me fix it," he pleads. "Please, Bailey. I don't want to lose this."

"Would you marry Talia?" I ask abruptly, and he startles. "Would you two carry this charade all the way to the altar?"

"No," he says fiercely. "Not anymore."

"But would you have?"

He doesn't have to answer. The look on his face is enough. He would have. He would have married Talia just to make his mom happy.

Fuck. I can't even be mad at him for that because I get it. It hurts so much, but I get it.

"And Talia?" I ask.

He just nods, and my tears are a constant waterfall soaking my cheeks, chin, and neck. I clamp my eyes shut again and take a few steadying breaths.

"I have to go. It hurts," I choke out. I lower my voice to a whisper. "You're hurting me. My heart can't take any more."

"Your heart?" he asks, and all I can do is laugh sardonically at this stupid, beautiful man. This stupid, beautiful, selfless man who is breaking my heart by breaking his own. "Your *heart*, Bailey?"

"Yeah, Butch. My heart." I open my eyes and look at him again. The pain in his face, the tears in his eyes, they gut me. It's like my chest is caving in, my lungs are collapsing. "I have to go. Please don't follow me."

I brush past him and walk out the door without another word. He doesn't follow.

When I get to the street, I pick a random direction and walk. When my fingers and toes start to tingle from the cold, I find a pub and order shepherd's pie and a beer. I text Ivy my location, and about an hour later, she texts that they're outside.

I pay my tab and walk out to find Kelley's Jeep idling at the curb with Ivy in the passenger seat and Jesse hanging out the back window. All three of them smile when they see me, and for the first time this afternoon, I smile back.

"Get in, loser," Jesse shouts, "we're going drinking!"

TWENTY

I DON'T KNOW how long I stand in the empty hotel room, but I'm certain it's well past checkout. By the time I leave, the sun is setting, the air is colder, and there is fresh snow on the sidewalk.

I pull out my phone and scroll through my missed calls and messages, then I pull up Talia's number and call her back.

"Riggs?" Talia answers right away, her voice tight and full of worry.

"Hey, Tal. Are you still at the condo?"

"I am."

"Okay, I'll be there soon."

She's waiting for me in the foyer when I walk through the door, and she immediately wraps me in a hug. I lean into the familiar comfort of her arms, breathing in the minty scent of her shampoo. The same shampoo she's used since high school.

"I'm so sorry, Riggs," she says after she pulls away. "I tried to call, but you weren't answering. I didn't know this would happen."

"I know, Talia. It's not your fault. I should have called you back or texted or something." I scrub my hand down my face. "I just wanted one more day, you know?"

"Bailey. Is she...?"

"Yeah," I say. "Yeah, that's her."

"Damn."

"Yeah."

"What are you going to do?" Talia asks, and her eyes search my face.

"I don't know. I fucked it up." God, did I ever fuck it up.

"Are you in love with her?"

My heart jumps and my brow furrows, and then all I can do is stare at Talia.

"What?" Her question has stunned me. Why would she ask that?

"Bailey. Are you in love with her, Riggs?"

I know the answer immediately, but I'm so caught off guard that I can't say it. Instead, I run through every memory, searching for how I could have missed it. Fuck.

"You are," Talia says for me, and I nod.

"I think I am, yeah."

"I think we need to tell Odette, Riggs." I look at Talia and hold eye contact, my breath stalled in my chest. This is exactly what I was coming to tell Talia, and I was prepared to break her heart if I had to, but if she's saying it too....

"Your mom loves you. She'll love anyone you love. You know she will. I don't think it has to be me. I've been thinking about this a lot..." Talia sighs. "This whole time we've been worried about hurting her because she wanted us together, because she was so happy when we were engaged, and we didn't want to take that away from her when everything else started getting bad. But, Riggs, I think she was just happy that we were happy."

"Where's this coming from?" I shake my head, and she can see confusion on my face.

"I'm not in love with you, Riggs," Talia says with a sad smile, "but no one wants to be trapped in an affectionless relationship." She shrugs, tears welling in her eyes. "So, I tried. I thought you were my future, so I tried to make it one I was happy with. It's not like I could just date around. If word got back to your dad that you were messing around, he wouldn't care. He wouldn't tell Odette or my parents. But if it were me?"

She lets out a sigh, leaving the implication hanging. She's right, and I'm angry for her. Bailey's the only other person I've been with, but I didn't even think twice about pursuing her when I saw her. I wasn't at all worried about the consequences. But Talia wouldn't have had that privilege, and the double standard—and the way I benefitted from it—makes me sick.

"I'm so sorry, Tal," I say, and grab her hand. "I had no idea. I had no idea how much this was hurting you." She squeezes my hand, then wipes her eyes.

"I think we had good intentions, but it's gone on for too long," she says. "I think maybe our methods were misguided. I don't want to lie anymore. It's not just hurting me, Riggs, it's hurting you, too. And I think... I think Odette would want to get to know your *real* future, not just the one you think she wants for you."

My *real* future. Meaning Bailey. Bailey is my real future. The one I choose.

God, I'm such a fucking idiot.

"You're right."

"When?"

"Now." I've wasted too much time already.

"Do you want me to come with you?"

"No, but I'll let you know when I'm finished, in case you want to come talk to her."

"I'd like that. Thank you." Talia gives me another hug and then kisses me on the cheek.

"You're a good person, Riggs."

"You are too, Tal. Thank you for being such a great friend through all of this. I don't know how I would have handled the last year and a half without you."

"Well, that's good, because you're never getting rid of me. We're family."

Talia waves goodbye as the elevator doors close, then I turn on my heel and head into the house. Mom's been moved to her bed for the night, so I head toward her room and knock on the door. She's sitting on the bed with her back propped against the headboard, and my father is in the chair by her bedside.

"Alex, you're back," my mom says, her voice tired and concerned. "I was worried. Is Bailey alright? She took off so quickly."

"She's upset with me, *Maman.* But I'm going to fix it." I move my attention to my father. "Dad, can I have a few minutes alone with Mom?"

"Of course," he stands and sets the book he must have been reading to her on the bedside table. "Come get me when you're finished." He pats me on the shoulder on his way out, and I take over his spot in the chair.

I take my mother's hand in mine and bring her palm to my cheek. It's something she used to do a lot when I was growing up—place her palm on my cheek and then caress my face with her thumb—and it's one of the little things that I will miss the most.

"I have something to tell you."

"Alright," she says, and I feel her thumb brush gently over my cheek. "What is wrong, *mon étoile?*"

"I haven't been honest with you lately. About Talia and me."

She's quiet, her eyes searching my face, but there's no judgment in them. No anger. Just concern and love.

"Talia and I aren't engaged anymore," I say into her palm. "We haven't been for a while."

"For how long?" she asks, and I swallow my guilt.

"About a year now." Her eyes flutter shut and my heart clenches in my chest. This is what I wanted to avoid. This look on her face.

"And you lied for me." It's a statement, not a question. "Because you didn't want to disappoint me."

"I didn't want to *hurt* you," I clarify. "I know how happy you were when Talia and I got engaged. You were so excited about finally having a daughter. I didn't want to take that from you."

"Oh, *mon étoile,*" she shuts her eyes again, and I watch as a tear falls down her face. "I want you to be happy. I would never want you to put your life on hold for me." My mom opens her eyes and hits me with a look so full of love that it's almost painful. "I want you to be true to your heart, my love."

"I know that now." I swallow back the lump in my throat. "I'm sorry for lying to you for so long. I'm so sorry, Mom."

"And Bailey?" she asks, and I blink at her sudden segue. "She is who your heart wants."

"*Elle est ma lumière, Maman,*" I say earnestly, and she nods, a small smile on her lips. *"Mon étoile Polaire."*

"She is lovely," she says, and rubs my cheek with her thumb. "You do light up around her. You glow."

"I'm in love with her."

"And now she is angry with you. Because you were dishonest."

"Yes." A few more tears trickle down her face, and I wipe them away gently with my fingers.

"Then I cannot forgive you," she whispers, and my heart plummets. "Not until you make things right with Bailey." Her eyes shimmer with tears, but her lips quirk up into another soft smile. "You know how much I love romance, Alex."

I laugh at the mischief in her tone, and my smile brightens.

"It's the French in you."

"You are French, too. Do not forget," she scolds playfully, and I feel her fingers twitch slightly on my face. "Go," she says sternly. "Bring me a love story worthy of your blood. Make it worthy of song and story. That you will tell your children. Bring me a romance that will live long after I am gone."

"*Je t'aime, Maman*," I whisper, my voice strained.

"*Je t'aime, mon étoile.* Go get your light."

Bailey won't answer any of my calls, but my texts are still saying delivered, which means she hasn't blocked me. Yet.

When I get to campus, I head straight for her apartment complex. I picked her up from here before we left for the contest last week. Christ, how has it only been a week? I don't know which unit is hers—she made me get her from the damn curb— but there's only about twenty apartments in this complex.

I start with unit one.

I knock, I wait. Not many people answer. There are only a few days until Christmas. I'd be worried she went home, but I'm keeping my fingers crossed that she didn't.

When someone answers, I ask about Bailey. Tiny, feisty, colorful hair and a sharp attitude.

I get to the second unit on the second floor when a guy answers. Tall, thick glasses, and obviously stoned. I ask about Bailey and he cocks his head to the side.

"The chick who rides the bike? Got kind of a girl-at-the-rock-show meets girl-next-door thing going on, but kinda also looks like she might shank you?"

I release a sigh of relief. "Yes, exactly her. What's her unit?"

"Right behind you, man. I pass her every morning."

"She here?"

"Yeah, her and the tall guy and the dude with the auburn hair and her roomie."

"Thanks. You can go back to your bong."

"Dude, it's a vape pen." He laughs. "But thanks. Good luck."

He shuts the door and I turn around. There's a mat that says, "Welcome-ish" and a knitted flag thing on the door that has a wine glass on it. I smirk. Slipper Dick.

I take a deep breath and knock. I can hear talking inside, and it sounds like maybe the television is on. When there's no answer, I knock again. Then I hear rushed movement, the door jostles, and someone says, "oh shit." I look up at the peephole and lift a brow.

Another minute goes by before the door opens. Slipper Dick and the Ginger are standing with their arms crossed like some sort of security brigade, but it's the blonde roommate who steps out to face me and shuts the door behind her.

"Riggs," she says sternly.

"Ivy." I know who she is without her having to tell me. Bailey has talked a lot about her.

"She doesn't want to see you." Her stare and voice are both pointed, bucking argument.

"I know."

She arches a brow, and I start to sweat under her scrutiny. Damn. She's intimidating. No wonder she's gonna be a lawyer.

"Look," I start. "I know I fucked up big."

"You did."

"Right, I know." I release a breath and scrub my hand down my face. "I want to make this right. I need to." I meet her eyes and lay it all on the line. "I'm in love with her, Ivy."

She doesn't give an inch. "Have you told her that?"

"Not yet. That's why I'm here. I have to see her."

Still, she doesn't say anything. Her face is expressionless, but her eyes are hard, assessing.

"Does she hate me?" I ask, fear evident in my tone.

"She might," Ivy says softly. A slight wince is the only emotion I've seen from her. *Sympathy*. Fuck.

"Fuck," I mumble, and squeeze my eyes shut. When she sighs, I open my eyes and meet hers.

"Hate is a passionate emotion, just like love. They're separated only by circumstance. If she feels hate, there's hope. It's when she moves to indifference that you have to worry."

I furrow my brow at her, breath lodged in my chest.

"What are you saying?"

"I'm saying change your circumstance. If you want a chance for her hate to grow into love, change your circumstance."

She moves to go back into the apartment, but then she turns back to me. "I'm not doing this because I like you. Right now, I don't, and I'm not sure you deserve her, but I do know she deserves happiness. She deserves big love, Riggs. The biggest. You think you can give that to her?"

"I'll spend every day of my life trying."

Can she hear the desperation in my voice? Can she see how much I love her? How I'll do anything for her? Ivy nods, and hope blooms in my chest.

"I'll talk to her," she says. "Go home. Give her a little space, but don't give up just yet."

Then she turns and leaves me standing in the hallway—speechless and breathless, but for the first time in hours, there's a spark of light on the horizon.

I pull out my phone and send another text.

Me: I'm not giving up, Sundance. You mean too much to me and I can't lose you. I'm keeping you, ma lumière.
I'm not going anywhere.

The message says delivered. I go back to my townhouse and make a sandwich. Drink a beer. Text Ms. Beth to check on my mom. It's not until hours later, in the early light of dawn, that I see the text has been read, and there's a response.

Sundance: Okay

I go home for Christmas, but not before dropping off a package at Bailey's door. I text to let her know it's there, just a little gift that I snagged for her the night after we won the contest.

She texts me back an hour later. A simple thank you with a picture of my gift sitting on her desk. A small snow globe with a sculpture of the Bean inside. But it's not the snow globe that makes me smile, that makes my heart stutter in my chest, it's what is sitting next to it. Two origami stars, the ones I left for her in the hotel, an origami crane made from a Bar 31 napkin, and the floppy origami frog from the 80's café in Chicago. She kept them all, and that means something. That means *everything*.

You're mine, Bailey Elizabeth Barnes.

I'll be here when you realize it.

bailey

CHRISTMAS COMES AND GOES. I've exchanged a few texts with Riggs. A Merry Christmas. A thank you for his thoughtful gift. A few grumbles about my parents making me want to pull my hair out. A short rundown of his father's reaction to the news that he doesn't plan to enter the draft.

Each text lifts a weight. Each exchange repairs a little crack in my heart. Bolsters my confidence a tiny amount. Removes a brick from my partially reconstructed wall.

I could be foolish. I could be making a huge mistake.

He could just hurt me again.

But...

I don't know.

Something quiet inside of me whispers that he won't. Not again. A small but strong voice keeps telling me to take the chance. Because if I'm being honest, I never truly let him in. Not really. Not all the way. And if I want that courage from him, then I should be brave enough to do the same.

Two days after Christmas, after I've already returned to my apartment at BU, I have to turn around and go back home. I wasn't expecting *Flannagan's Headstones & Monument Company* to return my call, given that it's the holidays, but two hours after leaving my voicemail, Josie Flannagan called me back and invited me to the shop.

I pull up to the building in Ivy's car. She went home with Kelley for Christmas and left me the keys. "You shouldn't be driving Baby in the snow," she'd scolded, ever the mother hen. I told her it wasn't necessary, but I'm thankful for it now. Midwest winters can fucking suck it.

"Hi, Mrs. Flannagan," I say when I walk in. She's sitting at the front desk, and just like the last time I was here, I have to suppress a shudder. It's so strange being surrounded by these empty headstones and grave markers. I get that they need display pieces, but it just reminds me of Bran's cemetery, and without him there, it's cold and dark feeling.

"Bailey," she greets with a warm smile. "Hold on, I'll grab Michael."

I fidget as she walks to the back, my debit card burning a hole in my wallet. I swear, I can feel the reverberations through my crossbody purse all the way to my heart. I'm excited and scared all at once. It's happening. *It's happening, Bran.*

"Bailey," Mr. Flannagan says as he steps through the door. I smile at how his greeting is the same as his wife's, and I wonder if that will happen with my partner later in life. If we'll adopt each other's mannerisms. A brief picture of Riggs flashes through my mind, and I shake it away. *Not now.*

"Hey, Mr. Flannagan," I say with a nervous smile. "I wanted to go ahead and give the green light for my order. I guess you wanted me to come by so I can pay for it?" I dig through my purse and pull out my wallet. "I've got the money now."

"That's great, Bailey." His smile is warm. "I can have Josie ring you up. I want to show you this first." He motions toward the back, and I assume he wants to go over my order one last time.

"Sure," I chirp. "Hey, do you know about how long it will take? Before it's finished and can be erected, I mean." I walk toward him, and he winks, a funny little glint in his eye.

When I follow him into the back, he walks me to a table, and I see a large slab of black granite lying flat on the worktable. It's a little larger than the one I ordered, but the color and basic shape is the same.

When we get a little closer, I get a better view of the front, and I can't breathe. Tears immediately fill my eyes and I let out a sob. I reach out and run my fingers over the smooth surface, then trace them over the etchings there.

Brandon Barnes
Beloved Brother & Friend
"To be an artist is to believe in life." –
Henry Moore

It's exactly how I envisioned it, except in the upper corner, there is an additional etching. I'd admired this image in the catalogue, but I didn't order it because, at the time, I couldn't afford it. It's a paint pallet with little splatters of paint on it and a paintbrush lying next to it.

It's absolutely beautiful.

"It's perfect," I whisper.

"I'm glad you think so," he says softly. "We went ahead and upgraded the size to the largest the cemetery allows, and we added the etching that you originally were admiring. And I upgraded your sealant. It will last longer this way, and these are all at no additional charge. It's on the house."

"Thank you." I can't say anything else. His kindness means more than he can ever know. It's the kindness Bran should have been afforded when he first came out, and I hope, wherever he is, he can feel it.

"It's our pleasure, Bailey. We're so happy you're doing this for your brother. We want to help any way we can."

"Do you think we can have it erected by February 9th?" *The day he died.*

"I think we can, as long as you get the paperwork squared away."

I wince. That's going to be the next hurdle. Pretty sure it's my dad's name on the deed for the cemetery plot.

"Right," I croak. "I'll take care of it."

The paperwork is nestled safely in my bag in Ivy's car. I square my shoulders. I've got another stop to make while I'm here, and it's not going to be an easy one.

When I walk through the front door of my parents' house, I'm met with my mother's wide eyes. I didn't knock like usual. I haven't entered this house without knocking for a long time.

"Bailey," she breathes, before jumping from her seat and coming to me. "What are you doing here? I thought you had to be back on campus for work?" She ushers me out of my jacket and over to the table. I don't have a chance to take off my shoes, so I'm tracking dirty snow through the house, but she doesn't seem to notice.

"I'm glad you're here," my mother exclaims. "Did you change your mind about spending New Year's with us?"

"No, Mom. I still have to work. Is Dad here?" She blinks at me, and I don't miss the way her face falls.

"He is. I'll get him."

I wait while she gets my father, and they're back within minutes. He's standing in front of me, broad stance and stern face, and for the first time in maybe my entire life, I don't feel an ounce of fear in his presence. Dad was never cruel to us growing up, not until Brandon was forcefully outted, but we were always raised with this "fear is love, love is fear" mentality. It was drilled into us at church and at home. My relationship with my father received the brunt of that mentality—respect came from fear because I knew no different.

But now, looking at him, respect is gone and with it the trepidation and submission. All I feel is indifference, and deep down, pity.

"I need you to sign this," I say as I hold out the papers. He takes them and looks them over, and I know the moment he realizes what they are. "I had a new headstone made for Brandon. I've paid for everything and it's to be erected in February, but I need you to sign this because you're the owner of the grave plot." His hand drops and his eyes flash with anger, but I don't back down. "I also need the deed."

"No," he growls, "I will not allow this."

"Too fucking bad. It's happening. Even if I have to force it."

I have no idea how I'll force it, but I have to try.

"There is no way I can condone this. It's a spit in the face of God. It is disrespectful and I won't support it. I will not let it happen."

I don't hold back my mocking laugh.

"You're such a hypocrite, Dad. What about not casting judgment? What about loving your children unconditionally? You have so much hatred in your heart that you can't even see how much damage you've caused."

"You won't talk to me like that, young lady."

"You don't get to tell me what to do. You were supposed to protect us and keep us safe. You were supposed to love us no matter what, support us, and you fell short. You failed Brandon and you're failing me. I'm not putting up with it anymore. You can take it up with your god."

"Bailey, please," my mom cries.

"No, Mom," I grind out. "You make a decision now. You

either sign those papers, you do this, and you give Brandon the respect he deserves, or you lose your only other child. I will be done with you. No holidays. No birthdays. When I get married, you won't be invited. When I have a child, you won't even know them. I mean it." I take a deep breath. "This isn't an empty threat. I don't need you. I haven't for a long time, and I don't need your toxicity in my life."

"Eric," my mom pleads with my father. "Eric, think this through."

"Get out," my dad growls, and I try not to let my shoulders fall. I refuse to let him see my defeat. Instead, I nod, turn on my heel, and stalk out.

Arguing erupts behind me, but I don't stay to listen, even though my mother's voice has risen louder than I have ever heard it. It was always my father with the booming, frightening voice, never Mom. But from her tone, she's not playing the devoted, doormat wife anymore.

I have no idea what I'll do now. I don't know the next step. Can I buy the deed? Can I petition something? Do I have to wait until my father dies? Can I buy my own plot and have the headstone erected in his memory?

I'm lost in thought as I buckle myself into Ivy's car, and I'm starting the engine when something bangs on my window. I jump, whipping my head to the passenger side to see my mother.

"Open the car door, Bailey. Please."

I swallow down the lump in my throat, close my eyes, and take a few deep breaths. Then I click the unlock button. My mother climbs in, and my car immediately smells like her floral perfume.

"Bailey, I am so sorry," she says, and I won't look at her. The waterworks won't work this time.

"It's too late," I say. "Please leave."

"Here," she says, and she nudges my arm with something. "Here, Bailey. My name is on the deed. It's from the Karras side, not the Barnes," she says, referring to her maiden name.

I look from her to the items in her hand. A stack of papers and a manilla envelope.

"Here. I signed them. Please. Please just take them," she cries. "I've been a terrible mother. Let me try to make up for it."

"I won't come back here," I say as I take the stack of papers. "I'm done with him, Mom."

"I know," she nods frantically. "I know. I won't ask you to. I'm....well, I've looked into filing for divorce. I should have done it a long time ago. I never should have let any of this happen. I should have taken up for Brie—for Brandon." Her use of his name gives me pause, and I have to squeeze my eyes shut. "I should have been there for him. I know that. I knew it then, but I was a coward."

I search my heart for a softened area, for some kernel of forgiveness or sympathy, but I can't find it. Not yet. Not today. But I am grateful for this, for what she's doing. It's taken a lot of courage. I'm not denying that.

"Thank you," I say clearly, and I mean it.

"I'm sorry, Bailey." She says again, one hand on the doorhandle. I'm relieved she doesn't expect a hug or anything else from me.

"I know, Mom." This isn't atonement, but maybe it's a start.

I text Ivy an update about my trip home. She's supportive and brilliant and every bit the best friend I need. Then, after a glass of wine and bit of weed, I text Riggs. He rings in with a video chat immediately.

"Hey," I say when I answer.

"Hey," Riggs says back, his gruff voice sending chills down

my spine and sparks in my tummy. His chocolate brown eyes roam my face, taking in every inch of it, as if he's searching for something. "I'm sorry today was so hard. Do you want to talk about it?"

I shake my head. "No. But thank you for asking. I got the paperwork signed and everything is paid for. I'm focusing on the W's today."

He grins at my sports reference. "You talkin' sports to me, Barnes?"

"I think I am, yeah."

He sighs, his charming smile faltering.

"I miss you, Sundance," he whispers. "I need you to know that I told my mom everything. My mom, my dad, Talia's family. Everyone knows. And not just that we're not engaged, but that we haven't been for a long time."

My stomach twists with something strange, my breath catches in my throat. My eyes, my throat—everything stings.

"Are you okay?" I whisper, and he nods.

"I am. Not everyone was understanding, but it was necessary. They'll get over it."

We're quiet for a moment before he speaks again.

"I also told my dad I'm not going to the pros," he confesses. "This is my last year playing baseball."

"How did he take it?"

"Not good," he says with a resigned chuckle. "He exploded. Threatened to stop paying for college, and I told him to go ahead. I've got one semester left. Then he threatened to kick me out, sell the townhouse, and I told him to do that, too. I won't be forced into a future I don't want. It's not good for anyone."

"I'm sorry he took it so bad," I say, and he shrugs.

"Despite being an overbearing ass, I know he loves me." Riggs smiles before he adds, "and anyway, my mom will chew his ass out if he doesn't come around eventually."

I laugh lightly, then ask the question that's been plaguing me. "Are you happy now?"

His smile drops. "Not yet," he whispers. "But I hope to be soon."

"Yeah? Why's that?"

"There's this girl. I'm crazy about her. But I messed up. I hurt her, and now I need to win her back."

"That sounds rough." Our voices are low, as if we're trading secrets. Like if we speak too loudly, the bubble we're in will burst and we're afraid of what will happen if it does. I feel like I'm hiding from something, but I don't know what. I don't know a lot of things right now.

"It is. It fucking sucks. But I'm not giving up." His eyes bore into mine, laying himself bare at my feet. Showing me everything. "I'm not going to lose her. I'm not going anywhere until she's mine again."

I blink away my tears and swallow, but my voice is still dry and cracked when I finally speak.

"Good."

* * *

On New Year's Eve, a text from Riggs buzzes through five minutes before midnight. I could say I don't know why I kept my phone on me instead of putting it in my locker, but that would be a lie.

This text. The text from him. That's why I kept it.

He sends me a picture of him and Odette, both wearing silver sparkly party crowns, and Riggs is raising a glass of champagne. I notice they are in her bedroom, she's propped on the headboard, and she's got her nasal cannula in. She looks tired, but her smile is genuine and warm.

Riggs: Happy New Year, Sundance.

Riggs: I hope this one is filled with love, laughter, and happy memories.

I smile at his message, then snap a picture of me in my jeans and band tee, a maraschino cherry between my teeth. It's not until I hit send that I realize there's a couple sucking face at the bar behind me. *Awesome*. Then I send him one of my favorite New Year's quotes.

Me: "May your coming year be filled with magic and dreams and good madness. I hope you read some fine books and kiss someone who thinks you're wonderful, and don't forget to make some art -- write or draw or build or sing or live as only you can. And I hope, some-where in the next year, you surprise yourself."

Riggs: Neil Gaiman.

I shake my head with a grin. Of course, he knows it. Of course, he does. I'm about to respond when another text from him comes in. Another Neil Gaiman quote, and my heart squeezes.

Riggs: "Whatever it is: art, or love, or work or family or life. Whatever it is you're scared of doing, Do it."

Me: Happy New Year, Butch. Give Odette a hug from me.

Me: Talk soon?

Riggs: I'll be waiting.

Two nights later, I'm sitting on the balcony, bundled in a blanket with a cup of hot cocoa, when my phone rings. I smile at the name on the screen. I haven't spoken to him since our text exchange on New Year's Eve, and I've been trying to work up the nerve to call him.

Seems he's beaten me to it.

"Hello?" I answer, but I'm met with silence. I furrow my brow. "Hello? Riggs?"

"Sundance," his voice cracks, and my stomach bottoms out. He sounds utterly broken.

"Riggs, what's wrong?"

"Can you come here? It's Mom... it's bad. I'm sorry to ask—"

"No, I'm on my way. Are you at the condo?"

"No. Northwestern Memorial."

The hospital.

"I'll be there soon."

"Thank you."

TWENTY-TWO

PNEUMONIA.

That's what the doctors have said. She has pneumonia in both lungs.

She was fine days ago, and now...

I'm so angry. And scared. I want to blame someone, anyone, but I'm not sure who or what or why. We've been careful. We've done everything right. But she still got sick.

She's in the ICU, hooked up to IVs and monitors, and they say that all we can do is wait. I stayed with her on and off all day yesterday and last night, but I kept having to trade off with Dad, since only one of us is allowed in there at a time.

I was crawling out of my skin out here in the waiting room. I couldn't read, I couldn't watch TV. Talia was here, but she went home early this morning, and she's not who I want to draw comfort from anyway.

I can't stop thinking about the last conversation I had with my mother. She knew. She knew something bad was going to happen. I told her I loved her. I told her to keep fighting, to stay strong.

"We're in one of the best hospitals in the country," I said. "They'll heal you."

She just brushed my cheek with her thumb. Slowly. Her movements were so slow. She would blink, and it felt like hours before she would reopen her eyes.

"Tell me about how you met Bailey," she said. Her voice raspy and her words slurred. "Tell me the love story you will tell my grandchildren."

So, I did. I told her about Quick Stop. About tracking Bailey down at Bar 31. I told her about the cookie contest. I even told her about the beer shower and the dick Bailey drew on my head. Her eyes were closed as I spoke, but every so often, she would hum, or tsk, or let out the faintest, weakest of laughs. I didn't know I was crying until her thumb moved gently on my cheek, catching a tear.

"She will forgive you, *mon étoile*," she whispered, and though her voice was weak, her surety was strong. "She will forgive you, and I will watch your love story from the stars."

"*Maman*, don't say that. You're going to heal and be home before you know it. And then you'll be part of our love story. You'll see it all."

My mom hummed again, a pleased but tired sound.

"*Merci d'être ma lumière, mon étoile,*" she whispered to me after a few shallow breaths. "You are my greatest accomplishment. Have brought me the most happiness. I'm so lucky to be your mother. *Je t'aime, mon étoile.*"

"*Je t'aime, Maman,*" I whispered back, pressing a kiss to her palm. "I love you."

She fell asleep after that, and I sat with her for a while, watching her sleep. Watching her struggle to breathe, even with everything the hospital has been doing. The vests and the medicine and the monitors.

I left to find some coffee and texted my dad that he could sit with her. He was sleeping in a chair in the waiting room, but I went down the opposite hall to avoid him. When I came back, I settled into a chair and counted the tiles on the floor.

Then later, around 10 p.m., they had to put Mom into a medically induced coma.

They found abscesses in her lungs, and she turned septic.

I lost it. And then I called Bailey.

When she arrives, I almost weep with relief. She's the most wonderful sight, and when she pulls me in for a hug, I bury my face in her hair and breathe her in. She tightens her arms around me, like she could hold me up if needed. Like she would bear my weight to lighten the load on my heart.

"Thank you," I say into her hair, clamping my eyes shut to stop from shedding more tears. I feel like I've cried myself dry.

"Of course," she says into my chest. "I'm yours for as long as you need me."

I pull back and look down at her, searching her amber eyes for a reflection of what I feel. Does she realize what she said? I will always need her. I will keep her forever if she lets me.

"Do you want to get some coffee?"

"I'll do whatever you want, Butch." She smiles softly, and it's sad and sympathetic, but still absolutely beautiful.

We go down to the cafeteria and get coffee. Then we get sandwiches and pick at them. She asks about my mom, and I lose hours talking to her. Telling her all about my childhood. About our trips to France to visit with my grandparents and cousins. Playing travel baseball in high school. Skipping school to dick around in the city with Talia and our friends. Learning to drive a car on Lake Shore Drive.

She's the perfect listener. Laughing and smiling, chiming in periodically, and her amber eyes never leave mine. When I get a text from my dad to come back up to the ICU, I'm lighter. I'm sad, I'm worried, I'm fucking terrified. But somehow, even with all of that, I'm *lighter*.

And then it all crumbles.

bailey

IT'S pitch black in the bedroom when I'm jostled awake. The clock on the bedside table says it's just after four, just two short hours since we went to bed, and the pillow beside me is cold. I know I fell asleep with his arms around me, but judging from the temperature of the sheets, he's been gone for a while.

I crawl out from beneath the covers, but instead of trying to find my clothes, I move to the dresser and dig through the drawers until I find some sweats and a t-shirt to pull on. It's quiet in the condo when I step foot in the hall. I check the home gym and the theatre room, but both are empty.

Unease unfurls in my belly as I make my way down the cold, marble staircase. The other bedrooms are quiet, Odette and Antony's door is closed, and aside from the small glow of lights from the wall outlets, the kitchen and living room are dark and empty as well.

I stand in the middle of the large lower level, holding my breath, but hear nothing.

Slowly, I make my way back up the staircase to get my phone, but when I reach the landing, something out on the terrace catches my eye.

Snow.

It's snowing again.

And despite everything that's happened over the last week, I have to admit that it's beautiful. I walk toward the floor-to-ceiling windows to marvel a moment, to soak up as much of it as I can, and then I see him.

Riggs, in shorts and a t-shirt, his head in his hands and a bottle of whiskey at his feet. He's sitting hunched over on the lounger, and I rush to him.

"Riggs," I call when I step outside, hissing a bit as my feet hit the freezing stone floor. He doesn't even have the heat lights on. "Riggs, you're going to freeze."

I put my hands on his shoulders and crouch to eye level.

"Riggs, please come inside."

"No," he grumbles into his hands. "No."

"Please. Let's go inside. Please." He's silent, unmoving, so I plead again. "Riggs."

"No," he says louder, shoving my hands off his shoulders. When he looks at me, his face is haunted. Broken. Nothing but sorrow and sadness and loss. "No," he says again, and starts to cry. "You don't call me Riggs. You call me Alex. She called me Alex," he sobs. "I don't want to be Riggs anymore."

My heart breaks.

"Oh, baby," I whisper. My cheeks sting from the tears meeting the frigid air. "C'mon, Alex. Come inside with me. Come lie down with me. Please."

He moves then, but sways on his feet when he stands, and I have to wrap both my arms around his torso and inch our way into the condo. He's shivering, teeth chattering and lips blue, when I set him on the bed.

"I'm going to get us in the shower to warm up, okay?"

He nods but stays silent. Tears are still falling down his face, a steady stream wetting his cheeks and lips. Staining his t-shirt.

I hurry into his en-suite bathroom and start the shower, making sure to keep it on the cool side of warm at first. I'll turn it hotter once his cold body adjusts. When the temperature is how I want it, I pull some fluffy towels and a washcloth out of the linen closet, then head back into the bedroom.

"Okay, I need you to stand up with me," I say as I take his hand. "Help me out."

He grumbles and then stands, swaying a bit, but steadier than before. With my arm wrapped around his middle, I walk him into the bathroom, then sit him on the edge of the separate, jetted tub.

"I'm going to take your clothes off, okay?" I say to him, and he nods, putting his arms up like a small child. Gently, I grab the hem of his shirt and tug it over his head, then I go for his shorts. "Can you stand?"

He does, and carefully, I slide them over his backside and down his thighs. When he's naked, I strip my clothes off quickly, then guide him into the large shower. As soon as the water hits his skin, he hisses.

"Is it too warm?" I ask, reaching for the knob.

"No," he rasps, and takes my hand and brings it to his chest, holding it close and tight, like a lifeline. "It's good."

His eyes stay closed, his tears mixing in with the stream of the shower, and I press a soft kiss just above his heart. "Can I wash you?" I ask softly, and he nods.

I put bodywash on a washcloth, then gently soap him up. His torso, his arms, his powerful thighs. I hope that my touch is washing away the hurt, just a little, and reminding him that he is loved. I am here, and he's not alone.

You're not sinking, I tell him with my touch. *You're still afloat.* And that's something. That's *everything*.

When I'm finished, I grab the shampoo.

"Want to sit?" I ask, and he slowly maneuvers himself to the floor just out of the stream of the shower head.

He starts shivering again, so I turn up the heat of the water before kneeling in front of him, straddling one of his thighs. With his eyes on me, I put some shampoo in my palm, then work it into his hair. I lather the long strands, taking care to massage his scalp with my fingertips. He groans and his eyes flutter shut as he drops his head back.

I study his face as I wash his hair. His full, downturned lips, cracked from the cold and dehydration. The thick, dark scruff, unkempt and messy, covering his strong jaw. His smooth skin and sharp cheekbones, usually sun-kissed, but now eerily pallid. His eyelashes, thick and long, shadowing the circles under his eyes from a week of restless sleep.

Even in pain, in the darkest, most difficult moment in his life, he's still a beautiful sight to see. I take my thumbs and brush them over his cheekbones, then run them over the edges of his jaw. His eyes squeeze tighter, and he releases a quiet, almost imperceptible whimper. Barely discernable over the sound of the running water.

"I don't know how to handle this," he whispers. "Everything is so dark. I'll never find my way out."

I blink away my own tears and place a soft kiss to his lips.

"Sweet boy," I whisper against his mouth, then press my forehead to his, "some of the most beautiful flowers bloom only at night."

"How do you deal with it?" he asks, his eyes searching mine as he places his palm over my tattoo. "The pain. It's so big, I feel like I'm drowning in it. It's going to swallow me whole."

"Honestly," I say with a sad smile, "it never goes away. It never gets easier. But eventually, it won't be the first thing you think of when you wake up in the morning, and it won't be the reason you cry yourself to sleep every night. Maybe not soon, but someday, you'll be able to think of her without feeling your heart break all over again. You'll be able to say her name with a smile instead of a sob. It might happen gradually, where you can feel the cracks in your heart fusing back together bit by bit, or it might happen suddenly, where one day you wake up and the fond memories are the first ones you recall. But it will happen, Riggs. I promise. And I'll be here with you through all of it."

"What if I can't do it? What if I'm not strong enough?"

I kiss him again, his lips, his cheeks, his eyelids. I kiss him until his tears are mixed and blended with mine, until I'm wrapped up in this pain with him, so he doesn't feel alone.

"You've made it through one-hundred percent of your hard days, Riggs. You have a perfect record—you haven't given up a single hit yet. You'll pull through this one, too."

For the first time in days, a small smile forms on his lips, and it's like the sun breaking through the clouds. I half expect to see a rainbow form in the steam.

"You talkin' sports to me, Barnes?"

"Whatever gets through, Stanton."

* * *

The funeral is on a Tuesday, and there are so many people that they have to stream the ceremony into an overflow room in a banquet hall down the street. It's absolutely beautiful, and surprisingly lighthearted.

I've been to two funerals in my life, and both were depressing and sad. Odette's funeral is the opposite. It's a celebration of her life, instead of the mourning of her death. Her family flies in from France, and people from all over the country come. People she's worked with and went to school with, people she traveled with in her twenties, people whose kitchens she's blessed and tummies she's filled. She's touched so many lives, and I know for certain that she is another person whose beauty doesn't need to be romanticized in death. I wish so much that I could have gotten more time with her, that I could have gotten to know the woman who is loved by so many.

Riggs's eulogy is short. A few sentences about how he'll miss his mother, and then he reads the final stanza of E.E. Cummings' poem "i carry your heart with me (i carry it in."

Talia's eulogy is longer, and wonderful, and there's not a dry eye or a frowning face in the place when she's finished. After everything, I'd expected to feel some animosity or maybe jealousy, but there's nothing there except sympathy and a strange fondness. Talia, like Riggs, was in a difficult position, and all she wanted to do was keep someone she loved happy for as long as she could, even if that meant sacrificing her own happiness. I can't fault her for that. In fact, just like with Riggs, it makes me respect her more.

When Riggs is shaking hands and speaking with family members, Talia surprises me outside of the bathroom. Her body language suggests she's unsure of how to approach me, so I offer her a smile and a small, awkward wave.

"Hey, Talia," I say. "Your eulogy was beautiful."

"Hi, Bailey," she says with a soft, genuine smile. "Thank you. It wasn't difficult to write. Odette was a wonderful person."

"I wish I could have gotten to know her better," I confess. "She must have been pretty special to have you and Riggs love her so much." Talia nods and wipes away a few tears.

"She was." Talia takes a deep breath and then smiles again. "I, um, I actually have something for you," she says, and holds out a silver envelope that I didn't realize she was holding.

I take the envelope and study it, arching a brow.

"I hope it's okay," she whispers. "Odette wanted me, well, she asked if I would help her write you a letter. She dictated and I wrote." She swallows, wiping away a few more tears. "I was going to mail it, but she got sick so quickly after that, I..."

"It's okay," I whisper. "Thank you."

"You have to know," she starts and bites her lip. "I do love Riggs, but not like that. I haven't been *in love* with him for a long time. I'm not sure I ever was, to be honest, and we just got engaged out of some naïve, misplaced sense of duty, you know? My parents aren't...they're not..." Talia shakes her head and squeezes eyes closed, her face blurry through my tears.

"Riggs is my family. Odette and Antony. *They* are my family, and at the time, I didn't know any other way to keep them. But the way I love Riggs isn't like the way you do. Or the way he loves you. You guys...you just," she stutters then takes a deep breath.

In her pause, I'm rocked by her words. I *do* love him. And he loves me?

"You two just fit," she continues, "and I want you to know that I am so happy to see it. Just like Odette was." Talia gestures to the envelope, which I nearly forgot about. "I hope, that eventually, you and I can be friends."

Instead of replying, I surprise us both by stepping forward and embracing her. She squeezes me tightly, and we hug for a moment, crying into each other's shoulders, until we both start laughing and pull apart.

"Sorry if I got snot on your dress," I joke, wiping off my cheeks.

"No more than I got on you, I'm sure," she says back with a smile.

"Thank you," I tell her. "Truly. Thank you."

She smiles once more and nods, then gestures again at the envelope. "Read that somewhere private."

Talia heads back into the main room, and I decide to take her advice and sneak into another empty room before opening the letter. It's on heavy, personalized stationery, with a cursive O. D. R. embossed at the top in silver print. The handwriting—Talia's, I realize—is small, slightly slanted to the right, and impossibly elegant. I smile. It's so fitting.

When I see my name written, I take a deep breath and ready myself for what's to come. When my heart has slowed, I read.

Belle *Bailey,*

It was a pleasure meeting you. I'm sorry our time together ended the way it did, but I am hopeful that we will meet again soon. For any hurt you have been caused, I am sorry. It was done on my behalf, out of love, and I cannot help but feel responsible.

I cannot speak for Alex, but I would like to apologize for the part I played in your heartache. You see, I know now that I put too much pressure on my son, and on Talia, to fuel my happiness. In the dark times after my diagnosis, I held on tightly to any promise of light for the future, and one of those things happened to be the desire to see my son happy and in love. I wanted to leave this world knowing that Alex's soft heart was protected. That he had found his partner, and that someone would love him in the way that he loves—endless, unconditionally, and with his entire being.

It was in my desperation that I did not see his and Talia's situation for what it was—a misguided, albeit selfless, attempt at giving me hope for that bright future. The future that they knew I would not be able to experience.

It did hurt to learn that he and Talia were not together, but not for the reason you might expect. It hurt because they felt the need to keep up the charade for so long, and in doing so, they neglected their own happiness.

When I saw Alex with you, I knew he had found in you a heart to partner with his. You light him up in a way I have never seen. The way he smiles when you're around radiates a love so bright that it illuminated all of my shadows. I've only been in your presence for a short while, but I see your strength and beauty, and you're exactly the soul I would want for my Alex. Mon étoile. *My star.*

I do hope that you can forgive him someday for the pain he has caused you. I hope you will let him heal the cracks in your heart that he has made, and that you can help heal his. That you can heal and grow together. And I hope, too, that I will see you soon. You are a lovely girl.

All my love,
Odette

By the time I put the letter back in the envelope, I'm full-on sobbing. Heaving, chest-wracking, breathless sobs, and I can't help but also laugh at what a mess I've become. Odette was grace and elegance personified, and I'm over here covered in snot and tears. But damn. I do love her son. She saw it, Talia saw it. I bet Ivy, Jesse, and Kelley saw it. Now that I see it, I think Riggs deserves to see it, too. Because he is just as his mother said. A soft, beautiful, worthy heart, and I am in love with him.

. . .

When the funeral is over, and everyone has said their condolences and given their hugs and shared their favorite memories, I take Riggs back to his condo and we watch 80's films. We're finishing up *Ferris Bueller's Day Off* when he pauses the movie.

"Sundance, I have a favor," he says, running his fingers up and down my arm as I lie on his chest.

"Anything."

"Well, it's more like I want to ask your permission."

"Sure," I say slowly, then roll over so I can prop myself on his chest and make eye contact. "What's up?"

"Your tattoo. The one on your chest." He moves his hand to the place just above my heart and grazes his fingers over it. His touch lights me up even through the t-shirt.

"Yeah?"

"I was wondering if I could get one, too. The same one. For my mom."

"I think that is a beautiful idea," I say earnestly.

"You wouldn't mind?"

"Of course not. When do you want to go get it done?"

"Tomorrow?"

"Then let's do it tomorrow."

"Sundance," he whispers again a while later. We're lying on our sides now, our legs tangled together, our breaths mingling, listening to the movie credits roll.

"Yeah, Butch," I say with a smile on my lips.

"I'm in love with you." His eyes are locked with mine, love and reverence and a hint of fear swirling in his brown irises. My stomach tingles and my heart speeds up. "*Dans mes heures les plus sombres, tu es ma lumière.* I'm in love with you, Bailey. I'm keeping you. Forever."

"I'm in love with you," I rasp as happy tears fill my eyes. "And that's good, because I'm keeping you, too. Forever."

His kiss is soft at first, but it deepens quickly, feeding every ounce of love he feels from his lips into mine. And I take it all. I swallow it, and share mine with him, until it's blended, and we're connected, and this time, I'm never letting go.

TWENTY-FOUR

"ARE YOU NERVOUS?" I ask Bailey as we walk, hand in hand, through the cemetery.

It's a surprisingly beautiful day for February in Illinois. Clear blue skies and a high of 55 degrees, when just last week it was below freezing and icing. It's almost like it was handcrafted for this day, this event. A new memory painted by a talented artist.

"I'm not sure," she says, twirling the bouquet of white flowers in her other hand. "I think so. I think I'm also excited and scared."

"Why scared?"

"This is something I've been working toward for so long, and it kept falling just out of reach. I guess I'm still worried it's not real. Like I'm waiting for the other shoe to drop."

I halt our walking and turn her to face me, then pull her hand to my mouth, kissing her knuckles.

"It's real, Sundance. It's happening. Enjoy it. Be proud."

She smiles up at me, the fucking galaxy in her amber eyes, and when she raises on her tiptoes, I pull her close and kiss her with everything in me. Because that fear? I understand it. It's exactly how I felt about her, how I still feel. Like it's all too good to be true. Like I'll somehow fuck it up again.

She must see something in my expression because she takes my hand, opens it, and presses my palm to her cheek.

"It's real. I'm here. I'm yours. Be happy."

I kiss her again, until we're both a little breathless, and then we resume our walk. The others have already gathered around the grave. I didn't even notice they'd passed us. When we join them, Ivy wraps her arms around Bailey and rests her chin on her shoulder.

"It's perfect," Ivy says, and everyone agrees. "It's absolutely perfect, B."

"It is, isn't it?"

"I like the paint pallet and the brush," Jesse says. "It's badass."

"The quote is great, too," Kelley chimes in. "You picked a good one."

"Thanks, guys," Bailey says, and she steps forward to place the flowers on the grave. Then Jesse pulls something out of his jacket pocket and hands it to Bailey. She barks out a laugh, and I look to Ivy and Kelley, who are bundled up together and smiling like fools.

Bailey turns to me and flashes the small item at me.

"Pot brownie," she says and rolls her eyes. Then she kneels and digs a little hole off to the side of the headstone. Weird. I'll have to ask about that later.

As I'm watching her, Jesse steps up next to me and eyes me with his hands in his pockets.

"Dollar Store Thor," he greets with an arched brow.

"Slipper Dick," I say back, and we stare at each other, unblinking, until we break into laughter at the same time.

"I *cannot* with Slipper Dick." Jesse chuckles. "It's like cock sock but make it geriatric."

I snort. Despite our rocky start, I really like Jesse. I really like all of Bailey's friends. The few weeks after my mom died were rough, and they came through and showed up for me as if we'd always known each other. They've even welcomed Talia into the fray, which was admittedly awkward as shit at first.

I mean, my ex-fiancée and my future fiancée hanging out like best buds?

Fucking strange.

But the weirdness wore off pretty quickly, and now it's just comfortable and familiar. It feels kind of like we've all been together forever.

After Ivy places her own bouquet of flowers down, she hooks her arm with Bailey's and they turn back to the cars. They start whispering, voices too low for me to hear, so I fall back in line with Kelley and Jesse.

"What are they scheming now?" I ask the guys.

"Fuck if I know," Jesse shrugs. "I've stopped trying to figure out Perky and Prickly. They're complex individuals."

Kelley chuckles and shakes his head at his friend.

"It really could be anything," he muses. "My guess is it either has something to do with Jesse's recent med school acceptance, my birthday, or something with Cassie. They've been texting her a lot since we got back from winter break."

"Yeah, they even made a new group chat and won't let us in," Jesse adds. "Rude."

"Does Slipper Dick feel left out?" I joke.

"Yes, he fucking does," Jesse snarks, and then sticks his tongue out at the girls' backs. Kelley and I both laugh at him.

When we get to the cars, Ivy and Jesse climb into Kelley's Jeep, and Bailey and I get into my Audi.

"We'll follow you guys?" Kelley asks through the rolled down window.

"Yeah," Bailey answers, and we back out of the parking spot. "You remember where to go?" she asks, and I flash her a smile.

"Your town is like five streets, babe. I think I can find it."

She rolls her eyes, and I head in the direction of the Legion Hall that Bailey rented for today. We decorated the inside and let in the caterers this morning, but when we pull up, Bailey's eyes widen and her jaw drops.

"Oh my god," she gasps, and then she turns to me. "Did you know they were gonna do this?" Her smile is huge and she's bouncing in her seat. "Oh, the bigots are gonna fuckin hate it," she giggles. "I feel like someone should stand outside and record anyone who drives by just to get their reaction."

I laugh and take it all in.

"Taylor asked if they could get here early to drop off a few things, but he didn't tell me what," I answer her. I knew they were bringing some decorations, but I had no idea they would be doing this.

We climb out of the car and stand on the sidewalk, gazing at the American Legion Hall. Seconds later, Ivy, Kelley, and Jesse walk up next to us, and Jesse lets out a low whistle.

"This is brilliant," he marvels. "Absolutely brilliant."

"Right?" I say, and Ivy takes out her phone to start snapping pictures.

The front of the Legion Hall has been decorated with Pride flags and posters. On one side of the door hangs a large Progress Pride Flag, and on the other side hangs a Transgender Pride Flag. There are rainbow balloons tied to stakes in the grass, and smaller flags fluttering in the breeze.

When we walk inside, Taylor is waiting to greet us, and he gathers Bailey into a hug, then pulls me in for one, too. In planning this event, I've gotten to know Taylor better, and he's grown on me. He's a cool guy, and his friendship is important to Bailey. He's even shared some great memories of Brandon with me, and I love knowing more about Bailey's life, about the people she loves.

"What do you think, Little Barnes?" Taylor asks. "Is it too much?"

"Are you kidding," Bailey beams. "It's fucking perfect." She's grinning up at him when the art prints catch her eye, and she gasps.

All along the sides of the banquet hall stand easels filled with picture collages of Brandon, and amongst the collages, are large prints of artwork Brandon had done before he died. Taylor was able to get them from the art department at their college, as well as some work he'd done for fun at the LGBTQ+ Student Center.

"Oh my god," Bailey gasps. "Taylor, this is..."

"C'mere, Little Barnes. I got one more thing to show you before you turn to mush," he says with a sly grin, and he winks at me. I'm beyond excited for her to see this. She's gonna fucking flip. He hooks his arm in hers and leads her to the back of the hall. They step up on the raised platform where people will stand to share their favorite memories of Brandon, and later, where a DJ will play. Off to the side of the platform stands another easel, but whatever is on it is covered with a sheet.

"Unveil it, Barnes," Taylor says and gives her a nudge. Slowly, she walks to the easel and pulls down the sheet. The moment the print is exposed, everyone gasps, followed by hushed statements of awe and praise.

Bailey starts to cry big, loud, hiccupping sobs, and I gather her in my arms and pepper her face with kisses.

"It's beautiful," she says, then she looks to Taylor. "How did you find this? Where was it?"

"It was on his computer at the Center," Taylor says, tears forming in his eyes as well.

"Thank you," she whispers.

She hasn't taken her eyes off the print, a digital portrait of her and Brandon in front of the Bean. The words "Night Bean" are scrawled in cursive along one curved edge of the sculpture, and the city skyline glows in the reflective surface. Bailey and Brandon are sporting matching grins, twin pairs of eyes lit up with happiness. It's absolutely breathtaking.

I knew Taylor was bringing this, but seeing it in person brings a whole other level of appreciation. Brandon was extremely talented, and I'm already scheming a way to get this framed so we can hang it on a wall in our future house.

"Ready to celebrate Bran's life, B?" Ivy says from beside us, and Bailey turns to her with a smile mirroring the one in the portrait.

"Hell yes."

Hours later, after we've cleaned up the American Legion Hall until it's in pristine condition and taken pictures of our work to avoid any *suspicious* damage charges that they may try to sneak on us, Bailey and I drive back to campus in comfortable silence.

She's got her phone hooked up to the Bluetooth, she's humming along to a Jack's Mannequin song, and our hands are clasped over the center console.

"Why'd you tell me your name was Alex?" she asks, breaking the silence. "That first text."

"You didn't know who I was," I say honestly, "which meant you didn't have to see me as BU's star pitcher with the MLB future. I just wanted to be, I dunno, *me. Just* me. And at the time, I didn't know how to be me without separating all the different facets of myself. I was fractured in so many different places, being a different version of myself for everyone in my life, it was exhausting. But when I met you, it was a blank slate. So, I gave you a name that wasn't known on campus, and I went in without pretense."

She's quiet, rubbing small circles on my hand with her thumb, so I swallow and continue.

"I wasn't expecting you, Bailey," I admit. "I don't know what I was expecting, actually. Maybe nothing. All I knew was that I had to know you, *all* of you, and I wanted you to know all of me. *Just* me. Not the person I was pretending to be for everyone else."

She rolls her head on the headrest so she's facing me, and I feel her eyes roam over my face.

"I liked you right away," she admits. "I tried to pretend like I didn't. Acted like you were just going to be a hookup. But I was hooked the moment you tugged out my earbuds and flashed me that stupid, sexy smirk." She lets out a laugh. "God, I was so stupid, too. I wasn't fooling anyone but myself."

"Yeah?"

"Yeah. I mean, V sees everything, so that's not surprising. But even Jesse could tell how deep I was in it. And I hate when J knows something I don't. He's so gloaty and smug."

I chuckle at that because I can picture Jesse's reaction. Hell, I've seen it firsthand, now.

"You liked me right away," I repeat, and I don't hide my grin.

"I did," she admits again. "And you liked me right away."

"I did." I pull her hand to my lips and kiss her knuckles. "I'm never letting you go again, Sundance. From now on, we're doing everything together."

"Everything?"

"Every damn thing," I stress. "You're never getting rid of me."

"Hmmm," she purrs softly. "And what if I said I wanted to

turn off this highway and onto a secluded, dark, side road, so we can fuck in the back seat of your Audi?"

I flip the blinker immediately and turn onto the next road, which just happens to be surrounded by nothing but barren fields and telephone poles, the nearest streetlight shining a few miles away.

"Everything, Barnes," I say as I pull off the road and flip the lights. "Get in the back seat. I'm going to eat your pussy first, and then you're going to ride me until you're coming on my cock."

She lets out a tiny, excited squeak, and then scrambles into the back seat. I'm out the door and into the back before she can even get her jeans unbuttoned, and she's coming on my tongue before the song changes on the radio. By the time we're finished, the windows are thick with fog, she's come three more times, and we've gone through every track on the *Everything In Transit* album and have started on *The Glass Passenger*.

"Damn," Bailey says as we lie tangled up with each other, catching our breath before we have to get back on the road. "I think I might need to make a sex playlist, Butch. You keep outplaying my albums."

I laugh, drawing little hearts on her naked back with my finger and watching as goosebumps prickle and her breath catches. I don't think I'll ever tire of witnessing the effect I have on her body.

"What would you put on it?"

"Only the sexiest shit, obviously."

"Like 'I'll Make Love To You?'"

She snorts. "More like 'What's Your Fantasy.'"

"Oh yes," I say with a grin. "Nothing sexier than Ludacris."

She giggles and presses a kiss to my chest.

"I have a confession," I say to her, and she widens her eyes comically.

"Oh boy. Lay it on me."

I press a quick kiss to her lips, and then say, "I wasn't at the Quick Stop for vanilla. Just beer."

She gasps and pushes my chest lightly. "Then why did you steal it from me?"

"Didn't steal it," I correct, and she rolls her eyes.

"Whatever. If you weren't there for vanilla, then why'd you snatch it?"

I shrug. "I wanted to know you."

She props herself up on my chest and laughs. "So, you *stole* from me?"

I scoff playfully, then kiss her again. "Worked, didn't it?"

She grows quiet for a minute, amber eyes searching mine as a small smile plays on her plump pink lips. "Real talk, Butch."

"Let's hear it, Sundance."

She scans my face once more before saying, "I've never been happier than I am right now, right here, with you."

The statement gets me. Right in the chest, in the stomach, in my fucking toes. I feel it everywhere. I slip my hand into her hair and bring her mouth to mine, and I kiss her lips with all the love I feel for her. From the moment she came into my life, she's made it better. More interesting. More rewarding. Better in every single way.

"Every minute I spend with you is the happiest I've ever been," I say when we break apart. "Every single one is better than the last. It's all better with you."

"*Je t'aime*, Riggs," she whispers against my lips.

"*Je t'aime*, Sundance," I whisper back. "*Je t'aime, ma lumière.*"

Two and a half years later

SHIT.

I'm going to be late.

How could I forget about the game? And not just any game, either, but the tie-breaking third game of the Crosstown Classic. These streets are bumper-to-bumper. Chicagoans don't fuck around with their baseball rivalry. At this rate, it's going to take me forty-five minutes to make what would normally be a ten-minute trip.

Fuckin' sports.

I should have done this yesterday. Or tomorrow. I should not have done it today, of all days. This is what happens when I get excited and try to be cute. Damn it.

I pull my phone out of my pocket and check the time. 12:30. I have thirty minutes to get there, and I have multiple text messages from multiple people asking me where the fuck I am. Ugh. It feels like I've only moved two blocks in the last hour.

Putting my phone back in my pocket, I scan the traffic behind me, then do a quick glance up ahead. Things look clear, so I start to slowly weave Baby in between the cars. Any space I can find, I squeeze through it, at some points popping up onto the sidewalks, too. I take as many alleyway shortcuts as I can, never stopping, until I'm pulling Baby into the familiar gravel lot and parking her next to the dumpster.

I'm locking up my helmet when I hear the door to the building open. When I look up, Riggs is standing in the doorway, looking every bit as gorgeous as the day I met him. He's so freaking hot. It's gross how attractive I find him.

"You made it," Riggs says with a smile, then bends down to kiss me when I'm within arm's reach. "I was worried you were getting cold feet."

I snort. "Can't get cold feet now, Butch. Won't be able to outrun these loans."

He chuckles and shuttles me into the back room where I drop my bag.

"I'm gonna change quick, okay?" I say to him, and he nods, then disappears through the swinging door. I duck into the bathroom and switch out my ratty jeans and band tee for something a little more professional—teal pixie pants, a white silk tank, and a black blazer—but I leave my Docs on. For familiarity. As soon as the cameras are off us, I'm switching back into my jeans and t-shirt anyway. Don't want people to get too comfortable with the buttoned-up version of me.

I run a brush through my purple ombre hair and pull it into a bun, then reapply my eyeliner and mascara. After a swipe of tinted lip balm and a few extra swipes of deodorant (because it's hot out and also because I'm nervous-sweating like crazy), I slip through the swinging doors after Riggs.

Entering the front room, I see Ivy and Kelley first, in front of one of the display cases. They're both dressed up and looking gorgeous, but it's the little nugget in Ivy's arms with the biggest green eyes you've ever seen that gets my attention. I rush them with a huge smile.

"Thank you so much for coming," I cry, and pull Kelley in for a hug first. "Sorry I'm late! I forgot the stupid baseball game today and traffic was insane."

"We wouldn't miss it," Kelley says. "You know that."

"*Stupid* baseball game? Really, babe?" Riggs chides with a smile, and I roll my eyes.

"What? If you were their pitcher, *obviously* I would make more of an effort, but since you're not..." I wink at him and move onto Ivy next, kissing her on the cheek and then stealing the baby.

"Hello, you adorable little monster," I coo, then look at V. "Jesse is here?"

She smiles big and waggles her brows just as the man in question rounds the corner scrubbing at his button down with a washcloth.

"J," I shout, elated to see him. "I thought you couldn't get off?"

"*Psh*," he says, and hooks me in a one-armed hug. "You know I run that place." He presses a kiss to the top of my head. "We wouldn't miss this for the world, B."

"Did it come out?" Ivy asks, gesturing to the wet spot on Jesse's shirt.

"Yeah, enough." He looks at me. "Spit up. Kid's got some impressive reach."

I snort, but when he moves to take the baby back, I turn away.

"Not yet," I say with a grin. "I need to up my bonding time if I'm going to be the favorite auntie." Ivy giggles and I stick my tongue out at her. "Where's Jocelyn?"

"She and the kids are upstairs," Ivy chimes in. "I showed

Jude the chalkboard wall, and Riggs let them have some cupcake samples."

"Jude is quite the food critic," Riggs says with a wry grin. "I might be more worried about him than I am about the *Trib* now."

"Yeah, try packing his lunches," Jesse says, exasperation and humor in his tone as he shakes his head. "We gotta buy nitrate-free lunchmeat. When I was his age, I ate pizza Lunchables and Uncrustables."

"I still eat Uncrustables," Kelley says, and we all laugh. "The team loves it when I bring them to practice, too. Ives orders us a shit-ton from Costco now."

Kelley and Ivy live here in Chicago. Ivy is in law school and Kelley teaches history and coaches soccer at one of the local high schools. Being in the same city, Riggs and I get up with them at least once a week, but with Jesse in med school, we don't get to see him nearly as often. It's nice to have all of my favorite people together.

A reporter from the local news station approaches and asks us if we're about ready, so I reluctantly hand the baby back to Jesse. Jesse, Ivy, and Kelley head out into the café's dining area and I watch as they move to stand by Riggs's dad and my mom. A few moments later, Jocelyn and the kids come down the stairs, and I stifle a laugh at the suit Jude is wearing.

"He even kind of looks like a food critic," I whisper to Riggs.

"I know, right?" Riggs laughs. Jocelyn's six-year-old son is a crack-up. No wonder he and Jesse get along so well.

"Okay," the reporter interrupts, "we're going live in ten. We'll ask the prepared questions, then cut the ribbon, and then you can be open for business. We'll be here for about an hour or so interviewing customers, though, as long as that's still okay?"

"Yep, we're good with that," I say with a smile, nerves fluttering around like mad in my belly.

I still can't quite believe this is happening. This time last year, I was in Indianapolis working for a CPA firm, Riggs was taking extra business classes online while working remotely for his dad, and we were both restless. Happy with each other, but with not much else. Then, one night, after some good wine and phenomenal sex, we started talking crazy. Big, dreamy, impossible things.

Riggs asked me what my ideal life looked like for us.

"If we could do anything in the world, what would it be?" he asked.

"Anything at all?" I pressed my lips to the ink of the tattoo just above his heart.

"Anything. No limitations."

His eyes sparkled and shot sparks of desire through my body. His brown eyes always get me; so deep and full, it will take me a lifetime and then some to discover all the magic they hold. So I, drunk on drink and love, started rambling.

I said we'd live in Chicago—a brownstone in Lincoln Park, specifically. We'd have brunch with Ivy and Kelley every Sunday morning. We'd visit the Night Bean once a month, and we'd bake something new together once a week. And we'd own a coffee shop. A multi-level coffee shop, where the baked goods and beverages on the menu were named after poets and popular fiction characters, and spoken word open mic nights were hosted monthly, and shelves of used books lined the walls for customers to take and read as they pleased. We'd display art from local artists, decorate the ceiling with white Christmas lights and origami stars made from book pages, and play 2000's pop punk and indie rock playlists from my personal collection.

And we'd do it all together. Every day. We'd work and play and create and live together, every day, for as long as we could make it last.

"Forever," he said. "We'll make it last forever."

The next morning, I was hungover as hell when I trudged into my CPA firm, but my step was light, and my heart was full. When I got home from work, Riggs told me he'd made some calls to commercial realtors he knew in Chicago and asked if I wanted to maybe go look at a few properties with him the following weekend.

From there, things just started happening. Good things. Amazing things. Some small hiccups here and there, but mostly the ride has been thrilling and wonderful, and I still can't quite believe this is my life.

We live in a two-bedroom apartment in a renovated brownstone in Lincoln Park. We have a cat named Pierre-Boo (who admittedly wasn't part of the original plan, but he was too cute to say no to), we have brunch with Ivy and Kelley almost every Sunday, and we bake something new every week. We've been to the Night Bean six times just this month alone, and today is the grand opening of our new café, The Poet's Keep.

It's two levels, with the upper level being a loft that houses two couches, a handful of bistro tables and chairs, and a chalkboard wall for customers to make art on.

The lower level has more tables and couches, several "Love a Book, Leave a Book" bookshelves, and two hundred and fifty-seven origami stars (and one origami dinosaur) are hanging from the ceiling. I know exactly how many because I helped Riggs fold them. I also know exactly where the origami dinosaur is hiding, and I'll never tell.

The display cases are teeming with delicious baked goods, the menus above the cash register are full of clever and creative literary references, and right now, The Shins are filtering through the shop speakers.

And on one of the walls, there is a large, black and white canvas picture of Riggs and Odette from when he was about six or seven. They're wearing matching chef's coats, and she's teaching him how to pipe whipped créme fraiche onto a tray of tarts. It's my favorite thing in the entire café.

It's all even better than I imagined, ten times better than I could have even hoped for, and I say as much during our interview with the reporter, which takes about fifteen minutes. We're so insanely busy that the day flies by in a blink, and our display case is almost empty when we flip the sign to CLOSED. The plan is to donate any unsold items to the homeless shelter, but it looks like tonight, we'll only have enough to wrap up and send home with family members.

"It went so well," Ivy says from the sink where she's currently washing dishes. We have a dishwasher and a staff to do things like this, but Ivy can't *not* help. The baby was getting fussy, so Jesse left with Joss and the kids, but V and Kelley stayed the whole day.

"You were so busy today, B. You should have seen the line! It wrapped around the block a few times. I made sure to take pictures." She wipes her hands on the towel she has tucked into her apron. "How's your head?"

"In the clouds, V," I say through a huge smile. "I didn't even know I could feel this happy." I blink away a few tears, and she wraps her arms around me.

"You deserve it all, Bailey Bear," she says as she squeezes. "All the happiness. All the success. All the warm and fuzzies and the biggest, biggest love. It's all yours, B."

"I think I might finally be starting to believe it," I whisper, then break away with a laugh. "I fucking love you, V."

"Love you back, B." Her grin is wide, dimple popped, blue eyes dancing, when she lowers her voice and asks, "and the other thing? How do we feel about that?"

I meet her eyes and share her conspiratorial grin. "We feel good about it."

"Think we're done out here," Kelley says as he walks into the kitchen through the swinging doors, carrying an empty bus tub with a towel slung over his shoulder.

"Yep," Riggs says from a few steps behind him. "And everything for tomorrow is prepped so we should be good to head out."

"Perfect!" I look at Ivy and Kelley. "You guys wanna go out and celebrate?"

"Oh, I'd love to, but," Ivy stutters, "I've got this case writeup that I need to—"

"Yeah, and I have forty more essays to grade," Kelley chimes in, and I wave them both off with a tired smile.

"Fine, whatever, losers, just go." We exchange hugs and goodbyes, and as Riggs walks them back out into the front to unlock the door for them, I slip into the back bathroom to change.

"Jesus," I grumble as I look in the mirror. Why didn't anyone tell me I was such a disaster? Thank god, I was wearing an apron. I tug off my outfit and slip back into my ratty jeans and band tee, then take my hair out of the bun and shake it out. I clean up my eyeliner smudges with a piece of wet paper towel and apply a little more ChapStick. "We did good today," I say to myself in the mirror. "Enjoy this. Bask in it. You're main character material." One last smile at my reflection, then I step out and turn off the light.

Riggs is waiting for me in the kitchen when I walk in. He's leaning on one of the stainless-steel work tables, his arms folded across his chest and his eyes trained right on me. Damn, he's so hot. I'll never tire of looking at him.

"Stop looking at me like that, Sundance," he growls.

"Or what," I purr back.

"Or I'll have to fuck you on this table, and then we'll have to re-sanitize the whole kitchen, which means it will take that much longer to get home where I can fuck you on our bed."

"Hmmm." I bite my lip and pretend to think as I strut toward him. "Could be worth it."

He grabs my waist and pulls me against his erection.

"Definitely would be worth it," he says before tugging me in for a deep kiss. I hope he always has the power to knock me on my ass with just a kiss. Our tongues tangle and my thighs clench. I can feel him growing harder against my hip, but when I reach down to palm him, he grabs my hand and stills it.

"Wait," he says, his voice pained. When I whimper, he chuckles. "Wait just a second, Sundance." I pull back just in time for him to lift me up and set me on the counter.

"I'm in love with you," he says, eyes pinned on mine. "I've never loved anyone the way I love you. Every night, I go to bed thinking there's no way I could love you any more than I do, but every morning, I wake up and it's like my heart has grown, because my love for you has doubled. I want to spend every single day of the rest of my life loving you, and every single morning I want to wake up to find that I love you more than I did the night before."

He kisses me, and my lips are wet with the tears I didn't realize I'd started crying. He places his palm on my cheek, his thumb rubbing gently over my lower lip as he pulls a velvet box from his pocket and opens it.

"You're my Polaris, Bailey, guiding me through the darkness. My Sun, dancing on the horizon, shining light on a hope for better days. My life, my future, my heart. It's all better with you in it. *Veux-tu m'épouser?* Will you marry me?"

"Yes," I say, then crush my lips to his. "Yes," I say again between kisses. I pull back just long enough for him to slide the delicate ring onto my finger, and I gasp at how beautiful it is.

"It's an oval moonstone on a platinum band, and the accent

diamonds are lab grown because I know how you feel about the diamond industry," he says to me as I marvel.

"It's perfect," I whisper as more tears fall down my cheeks, then I throw my arms around his neck and kiss him again. *It's perfect.*

"Let's do it now," he says against my lips, and I laugh. "I'm serious, Sundance. Life's too short. We've waited long enough. I want to marry you right now, tonight."

"It's after eight! Is there even anywhere in the city that can marry us this late?"

"Tomorrow, then?" Riggs asks, and his voice is giddy. My face hurts from smiling. "We'll go to the Cook County Clerk's Office tomorrow and get a license."

"Okay."

"Okay?"

"Yes," I say on a laugh. "Let's get married tomorrow!"

He kisses me once more, then pulls me off the counter and leads me through the kitchen and into the front of the café. The music is still playing softly, and the twinkle lights on the ceiling are casting a beautiful glow around the café.

"She said yes!" Riggs shouts, and we're met with a chorus of cheers. Ivy, Kelley, Jesse, Jocelyn, my mom, and Riggs's dad are all standing under the twinkle lights, smiling and clapping. I laugh again, dashing away a few happy tears just as Jesse pops open a bottle of champagne and Kelley starts handing out glasses. These tricksters. They were waiting for this.

"You know," Jesse says as he pours me a glass of champagne, "I'm an ordained minister."

"What," I screech. "You are not. Since when?"

"Since we all got wasted on that guy's weekend last month and Riggs told us he was going to propose," Kelley chimes in with a smile. "He also drunkenly promised Jesse he could officiate your wedding."

"If you're okay with it," Riggs adds. "I said he could officiate *if* you were okay with it."

"Well?" Jesse raises his eyebrows at me, a small smirk on his lips.

"Fine," I huff playfully. "But we're getting married tomorrow, so if you're not—"

"I am! I will! I'll be there. I'm gonna marry you guys." Jesse's goofy grin is contagious, and I can't stop the silly giggles that keep bursting out of me. I feel like I swallowed the sun, or a whole night sky of stars, for how glowy and bright I feel.

"A toast," Riggs's dad says, then raises his glass.

"Oh!" I blurt. *Oh shit.* "Wait. I have something for you," I say to Riggs, then I look at Ivy with wide eyes. She's biting her lip, trying not to laugh when she hands me the origami figurine and takes the champagne flute from me. She must have known this would happen. Always so prepared, that one.

"Um," I say, the moonstone on my ring sparkling in the twinkle lights as I fiddle with the origami heart. "Here." I thrust it at him, and he takes it with a bemused smile.

"Thanks, babe," Riggs says as he inspects the heart, but when he moves to put it in his pocket, I stop him.

"No. Open it."

His eyes flick back to mine and widen. I know the exact moment he realizes something is up, because his breaths quicken, and his fingers start to tremble.

"Open it, Riggs," I whisper again with a small smile, and he slowly begins to unfold the paper. The room is absolutely silent —the only sound is the soft music coming from the speakers— as Riggs flattens out the paper and begins to read it.

"Is this..." he starts. "Is this...what is this?"

He looks at me, eyes shining and blinking rapidly.

"It's a blood test," I say, and he blinks a few more times.

"Does this say that you're... that we're..." His smile stretches over his face, and his voice drops to a low whisper. "Sundance, are you pregnant?"

"Bun in the oven," I say on a laugh, and he just stares at me for a few more breaths as his smile grows and his eyes shine. He steps closer and puts his palms on my cheeks and kisses my lips softly.

"We're gonna have a baby," he says, and I nod. He pulls back and looks at our audience. "We're gonna have a baby!" he shouts to them. "I'm gonna be a daddy!" And cheers erupt once more.

"You're sure this is okay?" I ask. "We've not even been here a year yet. We just opened the café. It's going to be really challenging."

"People have kids in the city and work all the time. Everyday. It's going to be challenging, yeah, but it's going to be so worth it. And we're lucky—we've got this family and a strong support system."

He kisses me again, and I glance around the room at all the people I love. They're smiling and laughing, and I'm filled with so much happiness. They're here for us, and I realize that Riggs is right. We've got the best people in the world backing us. Even my mom, though our relationship is still rocky, she's proven herself many times over the last two and a half years. She left my dad, she moved out of that town, and every time I've needed her, she's been there for me. For *us*. These people lift me up when I'm low, and sometimes when it's necessary, they lie down at the bottom with me until I'm ready to get back up.

"Don't be scared, Sundance. We're gonna do this together, if it's what you want."

"I do," I say quickly. "I do want this. I love you so much," and then I say to the room, "Thank you all for coming tonight. For being here. I love you all big, big."

"We love you, too" comes from Mom and Antony, and a

crooned, off-key chorus of, "love you baaaaack," comes from Ivy, Kelley, and Jesse. Even Jocelyn blows me a kiss, and my heart could burst from all the love it's soaking up.

It's the perfect ending to a perfect day, and the perfect beginning to what's sure to be a wonderful, beautiful, challenging, never boring, love-filled life.

And I can't wait to live it, because every day will be better than the last.

Better with my found family, who came to me when I was at my darkest and filled me with light. Better with Riggs, who stole my heart in aisle six of the Quick Stop and has held it close ever since. Better with Pierre-Boo, our adopted alley tabby, who really does nothing except ruin our furniture, hiss at visitors, and knock shit over just to be a dick (but I know he loves us).

I splay my hand over my still flat tummy. And now, it will be better with you, *mon étoile.*

Je t'aime, mon étoile, I whisper. *Je t'aime.*

The End

"Bro, we're out of beer." Dylan groans as he pulls his head from the fridge and shoots me a scowl. "Wasn't it your turn?"

"Yeah, but I thought since it's a fucking *Wednesday* we wouldn't need it," I answer without looking up from my phone. I don't have to see him to know the kind of face he's pulling. "I was planning to grab some tomorrow."

"It's almost preseason, though," Dylan argues, as if that's answer enough. Once preseason training starts, the guys will have to chill on their partying. Dylan is apparently trying to squeeze in as much as he can while he still has time. Idiot.

"Dyl, just go get some fucking beer, then," our other roommate, Xavier, yells from where's sitting on the couch, his eyes never leave the book he's holding.

"It's his turn," Dylan grumbles, and I roll my eyes. I need the breather anyway.

"Fine, I'll go grab some now," I say as I stand. "But you're fucking flipping the dishwasher."

"Deal," Dylan beams as Zay coughs something that sounds like 'pushover' into his paperback. I narrow my eyes at him, but he's paying me no attention.

Dylan shouts his thanks, and I don't say anything else as I slip on my shoes and grab my keys. There's a grocery store just a few blocks up the street that I could easily walk to, but I start up my Audi and point it in the direction of Quick Stop instead. The convenience store is about fifteen minutes away, and I need the time out of the house.

A respite.

From my roommates, the team, everything. *Everything.* It's all weighing heavily on me this week. I just need a few minutes where I don't have to be *on* for anyone. Where I can just *be* and have that be enough.

The parking lot is empty except for the clerk's beat up Chevy S10 parked by the dumpster. I roll up next to it, park, and head inside. The door chimes with my entrance, but after a quick glance in my direction, the clerk bows his head and goes back to flipping through the pages of a magazine. Thank fucking god. At least I know I won't be asked to sign a napkin or a lotto ticket or something. I can keep the charming smile and cool jock demeanor in my back pocket for now.

I go into the walk-in beer cooler and grab Dylan a case of the piss water he prefers, then grab a six pack of a local fall lager for me and Zay. The whole switching off weeks buying beer thing makes zero fucking sense when you consider how much Dylan drinks in the off season compared to Zay and me, but his finances are nothing compared to mine. Buying a fuck ton of beer every three weeks makes hardly a dent in my wallet, so I don't bitch. Same reason I buy more than my fair share of the groceries.

As I'm walking out of the cooler with both hands full of beer, the door chimes again. I swing my eyes toward it, hoping it's not signaling the arrival of someone I know and will have to make nice with, and my shoulders fall with relief when I don't recognize the girl who walks in.

Instead of making my way to the cashier to check out, though, I watch her, and a weird warmth blankets my body, followed by a tingling sensation. Like a hot shower after pitching in ice cold rain. That feeling of going from freezing and uncomfortable, with my baseball uniform sticking to my skin and my muscles aching, to complete and utter relief. When my body loosens, my eyes flutter shut, and a sigh drifts past my lips. It's that feeling, but instead of closing my eyes, I can't unglue them from the girl.

She stands just inside the entrance for a moment, thumbing through a phone that's connected to the earbuds already popped in her ears, and I take the opportunity to study her. She's petite, with turquoise in her dark hair and a faded Green Day shirt hugging her body. Her black skinny jeans are tight and ripped at the thighs and knees, and she's wearing a pair of black, lace up combat boots. When she slides her phone into her back pocket and looks up to scan the aisle, I catch a glimpse of sparkling amber eyes, and something punches me right in the chest. The expression on her face is blank, bordering on annoyed. But her eyes...they hold something entirely different. Something I can't quite pinpoint, but it feels familiar.

Before I realize it, I'm putting the beer on the floor and following her as she heads into one of the aisles. When I round the corner, she's scanning the shelf. On light steps, I walk closer, until I'm three feet from her and can hear the low hum of music floating from her earbuds, but she hasn't noticed me yet. Probably because her music is loud enough that I can definitely tell she's listening to a Fall Out Boy song from their first album.

The girl goes up on her tiptoes and reaches for something, then halts, hand suspended in the air for a split second, before she drops her arm back to her side with a slap and her heels to the floor with a thump. I feel a smile creeping over my lips as she props her hand on her hip, but when she releases a small growl, I have to stifle a laugh.

I look to the top shelf and try to gauge what she's studying. I'm pretty sure she's trying to decide between the two options of vanilla extract—pure and imitation. Then her hand reaches up again. I don't think it through. I just push my hand over her shoulder and grab the bottle of pure vanilla extract before she can get ahold of it. From the way she whips around, eyes trained on my hand, I know I guessed right which one she was going to choose.

Her eyes flash with anger and her nostrils flare, and my body tenses into defense mode. I might have just fucked up, and I'm working out my apology in my head when her attention slowly drifts up my arm, pausing on my bicep before crawling over my shoulder then chest. I can feel it, her gaze, as light as a feather and as powerful as a stacked barbell all at once. My muscles flex on instinct, and the corner of her mouth hitches up in the slightest, smallest smirk.

This girl is checking me out.

Shamelessly and blatantly checking me out.

I chuckle that the realization.

"Prince Harry," she mumbles to herself, and I let out a confused laugh.

"Prince Harry?" I ask, and her eyes dart to my mouth, so I repeat myself.

"Huh?" she says, and cocks her head to the side. Her confusion, for lack of a better word, is fucking adorable, and I laugh again as I reach up slowly and tug out one of her earbuds.

"You said Prince Harry," I tell her, and she rolls her eyes.

"No, I said prince-*haired* Harry," she argues, as if I'm supposed to know what that fuck that means, "and I didn't realize I'd said it out loud."

"Oh," I say, and I try not to smile at her pissed off expression. She's intimidating for her size, but she's also fucking hot. "Are you okay?"

"I'm fine," she spits out. *Oh, this is fun.*

"I wasn't sure. You're kinda just standing there staring," I say, deciding I'm going to milk this, see how much she'll engage with me.

"I was sizing up my new enemy," she states, and pulls out her other ear bud. I stand taller at that, take it as a sign that she's committing to this conversation. She slides the earbuds into her pocket.

"Enemy?" I question, and another laugh bubbles out of me. A real laugh. Not the kind I have to force around the guys, or the half-assed types I let out around Talia. It's a real laugh coming straight from my stomach, and I latch onto the feeling.

"You just stole that vanilla from me. I don't make it a habit to befriend thieves."

"I didn't steal it. I just got it before you."

"I was *clearly* here first," she argues as she puts her hand back on her hip, popping it out in a way that makes me swallow hard. "I was *clearly* reaching for that bottle when you jumped out of nowhere and snatched it." She raises her eyebrows at me accusingly, giving me that *what do you have to say for yourself?* look that I used to get from *Maman* anytime I did something stupid growing up.

"You were here first, yeah. But you were standing there surveying the shelf for a pretty long time." I smirk at her, and I don't even hide the fact that I'm flirting. "Some of us have places to be. It's not thieving to just sneak past ya and grab what I need."

"It's line jumping, which everyone knows is poor social etiquette, and it is thieving, because that bottle is mine."

"Poor social etiquette?"

"Mmhm."

"Is it poor social etiquette to blatantly check out a stranger at the grocery store, too?" Her eyes flash briefly at being called out, but she covers it well with a scoff.

"*Please.* I was not checking you out. I was surveying you for weaknesses in case I have to resort to violence."

When I laugh again, her lips twitch into a small smile, and the surge of triumph I feel surpasses the one from last year's Division I Championship win. Okay, maybe this particular social interaction isn't the worst.

"Resort to violence? I'm like twice your size," I tease.

"The bigger they are, the harder they fall. Don't underestimate me," she warns. "It could be your undoing."

Noted.

I take the moment to look her over. Now that I'm within arm's reach, my eyes don't want to leave her face. The dark, arched eyebrows. Her amber eyes lined with thick black lashes. There's a small, silver hoop in her nose, and a smattering of freckles cover her tan cheeks. And her lips...*fuck.*

"So, Butch," she interrupts my thoughts like she knew where they were heading. "You gonna hand over my property or do I have to overpower you and take it myself?"

"Butch?" *Butch?*

"Butch Cassidy? Train and bank robberies? A famous *burglar.* Don't tell me you're a thief *and* uncultured."

I give her a shrug and feign ignorance, but of fucking course I know Butch Cassidy. I'm surprised she does.

"Just a pretty face, then. Such a shame." She shakes her head with a sigh, but I zero in on her words.

"You think I'm pretty."

"I have eyes. Doesn't change the fact that you're a criminal."

I barely hear her. I just focus on the fact that she finds me attractive, and I decide that I have to see this girl again. This feeling she's giving me, the exhilaration and excitement—more fun than I've had in a long ass time—is addicting, and I want more.

"I'll tell you what," I say. "I'll trade you for the vanilla."

She purses her lips, then asks, "What do I have to give?"

"I'll trade you this vanilla for your number."

"I told you before that I don't associate with criminals."

"But if I give you the bottle, then I wouldn't be a criminal. I'm not stealing; it's all just one big misunderstanding," I argue. She's not going to make this easy. I've known her for all of five minutes, yet that doesn't surprise me at all.

C'mon, girl. Just give me your number.

"And what if this isn't your first offense? How do I know you're not trying to trick me? Get my number, then make off with the vanilla? You could be trying to set me up for a bunch of cold calling campaigns. Or planning to put my number on a billboard or a bathroom stall. How do I know you can be trusted?"

Fuck, she's hot. This whole exchange has me keyed up, what with her sass and snark and the way she's sparring with me. And her eyes. What the hell is it about her eyes?

"You bring up good points," I say slowly. "I don't suppose you'll take my word for it."

She laughs and rolls her eyes like I'm an idiot, but I'm not offended. I'll take one hundred more eye rolls if I can keep talking to her. If I can see her again.

"I'll let you buy it first?" I try again, deciding against offering to buy it for her. Something in my gut tells me she wouldn't like that. "You can buy it and put it in your car, and then give me your number."

She pauses, taps her finger on her lips, and thinks it over. It takes all my strength not to cross my fingers and chant "please, please, please."

"If we do it that way," she says after the longest fifteen

seconds of my life, "you'll stay on the sidewalk until I've secured the vanilla, and then I'll shout my number to you."

"Deal. Shake on it?"

She squints at my outstretched hand, then mimics the face I must be giving her, before sliding her small hand into my much larger one. Her hand is soft and warm, and her fingers are delicate. Lightning shoots from my palm to my toes and I tighten my grip slightly with the strange desire to never let go. When her eyes flare with heat, I know she felt it too. Whatever it is.

After she pays for the vanilla, I follow her out the door, and she busts my balls some more. Every word out of her sassy mouth hooks me harder, pulls me deeper. I want to keep her talking, and the farther away from me she walks, the stronger my need to bring her back grows.

I watch her walk through the small parking lot, and I notice seconds too late that the lot is empty but for my Audi, the clerk's S10, and a motorcycle. I don't even have a chance to wonder if she took a bus before she's stuffing the pure vanilla extract into a saddle bag and unlocking a helmet from the backrest.

She rides a fucking motorcycle. My dick hardens and I fist my hands at my sides.

I have got to get to know this girl.

I clear my throat before calling out to her.

"Is the package secure?" I shout, and she pats the saddlebag.

"Snug as a bug in a rug."

"Okay. I held up my end of the bargain. It's your turn to hold up yours."

"Hmmm, what was my end, again?" she teases, and I do my best to hide the giddy feeling that bubbles in my stomach. Like Christmas morning, like my first starting game, but better.

"Your number," I state clearly.

"Oh yeah. Thirty-one."

"Thirty-one?"

"Thirty-one," she repeats, and even from here I can see her lips twitch from the force of the smile she's hiding.

"Thirty-one is not your phone number," I say. *What's this girl playing at?*

"It's not," she says slowly. "But you didn't specify what number you wanted. Thirty-one is the number you get."

I'm stunned speechless for a breath. It could be a brush off, but it doesn't feel like it is, so before she climbs onto her bike and rides off into the darkness, I throw out my last playable card.

"Sundance," I call out, and when she whips her attention back to me, the pleased smile of surprise on her face tells me I played it right. "I didn't get your name."

I brace myself for it. I know it's coming as certainly as I know my next move. Sure as shit, she smirks and then shrugs.

"Bummer for you," she says, then she cranks her bike to life and cruises out of the lot.

And I'm left standing there, dick half-hard and smiling like an idiot, staring at her shrinking taillight until the rumbling sound of her bike fades to nothing.

Thirty-one, she said.

I asked for her number, and she said *thirty-one*.

It could have been a brush off, a round-about way to tell me to fuck-off, but I know it's not. I don't know how I know, but I do. This is a challenge, a test, and I don't fail.

The whole drive back home, I'm running possibilities through my mind, and when I pull into the driveway of my townhouse, I think I've got an idea.

There's a bar on campus. *Bar 31*. That's where I'll start.

Because I have a feeling Sundance wants me to find her, and I'm not going to let her down. Not with this challenge, and not with any other. Because once I catch her, I'm keeping her for a while.

I'm lost in my thoughts, mouth tipped into a bemused smile, when I unlock the door and traipse into the townhouse. When I round into the kitchen, I'm met with Zay and Dylan's questioning faces. Zay's eyes are narrowed with curiosity as he studies me, and I wipe my expression back to neutral, but Dylan looks annoyed. It takes me a minute before I realize why.

"Dude, did you forget the beer?" he asks, and I let out a sigh. The beer.

I don't respond, I just turn around and head back out. This time, I walk the few blocks to the grocery store, and the entire time my mind is on only one thing.

Sundance.

I can't wait until I see her again.

I'm not usually one who needs an engagement or a baby in my HEA, but with Bailey and Riggs, both felt *right*. I think, with all they've been through and all they've lost, they'd waste no time doing the things that make them happy. And with Bailey and Riggs, what makes them happiest is each other, and everything that comes along with that.

This book touched on some difficult topics, one of which is trans death rights. Unfortunately, Brandon's story isn't unique, and too often, the identity and end of life wishes of trans and gender non-conforming people aren't honored in death. While writing *Better With You*, I came across an article by Rebecca Roberts Galloway titled "End-of-Life Planning Tips for the LGBQT+ Community," which pointed me in the direction of several resources that LGBTQ persons could use to ensure that their end of life wishes are protected in death. If you think you or someone you know could find them useful, check them out. Trans death rights are human rights, and they deserve protecting.

Lambda Legal
LGBTAging Center
@Transdeathcare on Instagram

NOTHING FEELS BETTER

CHAPTER ONE EXCERPT

JESSE

Kelley pulls up to the curb a block down from Riggs's townhouse. I can already hear the music pumping from the building and see people stumbling around on the front lawn.

Riggs Stanton, Butler University's star pitcher, has been dating Bailey since around Christmas. They had a rocky as fuck start, but things are going good now. He even hangs with me and Kelley on nights when Ivy and Bailey are doing secretive girl shit that we're not invited to.

"Fuck, did they invite the whole campus?" Kelley muses as we hop out of the Jeep. He slings his arm over Ivy's shoulder, and we make our way to the house. "Bet Riggs loves this shit."

I snort, because we all know Riggs does *not* love this.

If Riggs could go the rest of his life without having to attend another raging house party, he gladly would. Bummer for him, his roommate Dylan was selected to play in the MLB Draft

League, so the whole baseball team decided to throw him a party. And since Riggs is the unofficial team captain and campus stud, he's hosting. Dude's fucking *thrilled*. Not.

When we walk into the house, Bailey and Riggs meet us at the door.

"Hi, guys!" Bailey shouts over the music, then she links her arm with Ivy's and starts to pull her away.

"Kelley. Dr. Hernandez," Riggs greets as he shuttles us in.

"He's not a doctor yet," Bailey shouts over her shoulder. "If someone gets hit by a car, we're still calling 911." I roll my eyes, and she sticks her tongue out at me as she and V disappear into the house.

"This place is fuckin' packed," Kelley says, and he gestures for my coat, so I shrug it off and hand it to him. "You want these in your room?" he asks Riggs.

"Yeah, just toss them on the bed." Kelley heads up the stairs with our coats, and I follow Riggs into the kitchen, weaving in and out of the crowd of people on the way.

I'm reaching into the fridge and grabbing one of Riggs's fancy beers when someone bumps into me. I step back to find Riggs's roommate Dylan, blitzed off his ass and grinning like an idiot. It's his party, and he's living it up.

"Jesse!" He shouts, and pulls me into a drunk bro hug.

"Hey," I say with a smile, giving his back a few pats before pulling away. "Congrats on the Draft League, man. That's fucking awesome."

"I know, right?" He slurs. "And what about you? You got into Harvard Med!"

I can't resist the in, so I grin and say, "What, like it's hard?"

Dylan scrunches up his face in disbelief. "Yeah, bro. It's fucking *Harvard*."

"*Legally Blonde*?" I ask, brows raised and eyes wide. Is he fucking with me?

"Dude." He blinks. "This is my natural hair color."

"Never mind, man. Super excited for you." I pat him on the shoulder once more as I shuffle around him. "I need your autograph before you leave."

An hour later, I'm sitting in a lawn chair in the smallish back yard with Kelley, Ivy, and Xavier, Riggs's other roommate. Riggs and B disappeared a while ago and I doubt we'll see them for the rest of the night. It's cold as shit out here, but the fire pit in the middle of our lawn chair circle helps fight off the chill.

When Xavier gets up to head inside, I briefly cast my attention across the fire toward Kell and V. Their eyes are closed, and she's perched on his lap with a blanket draped over their legs. He's running his fingers through her hair, and they're probably nice and toasty and comfortable and content. In more ways than one.

I fight off a pang of something like envy. Not because I've got feelings for either of them—nothing but the strongest platonic love for my friends—but because of that *thing* that they have.

That Bailey and Riggs have, too.

That I *don't* have.

My gentle foot shaking switches to quick leg bouncing, my hands move like they're holding my needles, and I start to sink deeper into my thoughts. When something stabs me in the arm, my whole body jerks with alarm.

"Ahhh," I shout, and swing my head in the direction of the fucker who jabbed me. I'm expecting Dylan or another of the drunk goons from inside, but instead I see a tiny human dressed as a pirate.

The kid's just a smidge over three feet, so he's probably around four years old, and he's wearing a black plastic vest and Spiderman underwear. On his head is a plastic pirate hat, on his feet are a pair of Spiderman rain boots, and in his hand is a fucking sword.

It's made of cardboard, but it's still a fucking sword.

And the kid is scowling at me. What the hell did I do? He's the one who stabbed me. With a fucking cardboard sword.

"Ahoy there, Dread Pirate Roberts," I say in my best pirate voice, but the kid doesn't say anything. I don't even know if he's blinked yet, but his eyes are kind of big. They're definitely the biggest thing on his face. "How fare the seas?" I try again. "Cap'n Blackbeard says he saw some merpeople off the coast... of...somewhere..."

He blinks!

"Seriously, though, kid, aren't you cold?"

Nothing.

"Where's your, like, parents? Or grandparents? The people in charge of you, where are they?"

He still doesn't speak, so I stand and start to shrug out of my coat.

"Here, kid, take my jacket and we'll find your, uh, crew? First mate?" I move to drape my coat over his shoulders when a woman comes rushing up behind him.

"Jude," the woman yells, voice equal parts anger and relief. Then she drops down on her knees in front of the kid and throws a blanket over him. "Jesus, Jude, you're gonna freeze your toes off." She stands and picks him up. "What did I tell you about leaving the house?"

"Not Jude," the kid growls, and I watch as the woman closes her eyes and takes a deep breath.

"Captain Meatball," she says tightly, and I have to hold back my laugh. "What did I tell you about leaving the house?"

"Don't do it without you or Doonie."

"Correct. So why are you out here? It's eleven at night and forty degrees. You're supposed to be in bed."

Captain Meatball shrugs and points to the fire pit behind me. "I wanted 'mores."

The woman looks up to see what he's pointing at, but her eyes run straight into mine, because I'm staring hard. Her eyebrows shoot up, as if she didn't even realize I was standing here until just now, so I give her my most reassuring bedside manner smile. The one I use on patients when I'm volunteering at the hospital. She visibly relaxes, and my smile grows.

The orange flames from the fire pit create just enough light that I can make out her features. I can't tell what color her eyes are, but they're big, just like the kid's. Her face is shaped like a heart, and her upper lip looks like it's got a perfect Cupid's bow. Her nose is tiny and slightly upturned. When she blinks, her eyelashes add to the shadows on her cheeks, and her dark hair is thrown up on top of her head in one of those crazy bun-things that Bailey and Ivy like. I quickly let my eyes scan the rest of her. She's wearing a huge purple hoodie, grey sweats, and flip flops. Basically, she's dressed like most of the students of campus during finals week.

"Sorry, ma'am," I say smoothly. "Meatball didn't mention he wanted s'mores. I could have found him some."

"No," she stutters, then squeezes her eyes shut and gives her head a little shake. "It's fine. I'm sorry if he bothered you."

"I didn't!"

"He didn't." The kid and I protest at the same time.

"Still," she says, "he shouldn't be out here."

"It's fine, really," I assure her. "I've never met a real live pirate before." I flash the kid a grin and he gives me one right back, nose scrunched up in that fucking adorable way only kids can pull off.

The woman laughs, and the sound hits me deep in my chest. It's not a tinkling sound, like Ivy's giggle, and it's not a sarcastic bark like Bailey's. It's more...I don't know. *Full.* Musical. And kind of raspy. And kind of tired. She only does it once, and I have to swallow the urge to make her do it again. She gave me one note, but I want a whole scale.

"Right, well," she says on a sigh, "Meatball needs to go back to bed." She nods toward the fire. "Enjoy your night."

The woman, with the miniature pirate still hoisted on her hip, turns and walks toward the neighboring townhouse—not the one Riggs's house is attached to, but the one just across the yard. The kid waves at me with his sword, and I salute him. His smile makes me chuckle.

I watch until the woman reaches the dimly lit cement patio and opens a sliding glass door. She steps into the house, and just before she slides the door closed, she smiles softly and sends me the wave that I didn't know I was waiting for. I smile and wave back, then sink down into my lawn chair.

"Who was that?" Kelley asks, and I look up to find him and Ivy watching me. Ivy's got a little smile on her lips, which has me realizing I've got one on mine, too.

I shrug it off. "Captain Meatball and his first mate."

"She was pretty," Ivy adds.

I hum in response, just as Dylan comes stumbling from the house and throws his drunk ass into a lawn chair.

"Dyl, who is your neighbor?" Kelley asks casually, gesturing to the townhouse across the yard.

Dylan squints toward the house. "You mean the hot mom?"

"The hot mom?" I repeat. It didn't register that she could be the kid's mom. I assumed babysitter or something, but the eyes... Those big eyes that they both had. It makes sense.

"Yeah," Dylan pushes out as his eyes drift closed. Dude's gonna pass out. "Moved in last month. Zay and Riggs helped her unload a U-Haul."

"Huh," I say, and flick my eyes back to the house. The lights are off but for a soft glow coming from a second-floor window.

I bet that's her room.
The hot mom.

* * *

Jesse's book, the third standalone in the *Better Love* series, is available now on most retailers!
Add it to your TBR on Goodreads now!

acknowledgments

My second book EVER. This is bananas. I don't even know what to say except wow.

Truthfully, this book flowed quickly. I had the idea for it even before I finished *Love You Better*, and writing Bailey was easy because she has so much of me in her. I'm not naïve enough to believe every book will be this easy, or that my turn-around will be this snappy, but damn was it nice to experience for this one.

I have several brilliant, amazing, wonderful, don't-know-what-I'd-do-without-them people to thank, and at the top of the list is my husband. Dude, you're so clutch. I can't even express how crucial your support was for this book. I never, ever would have gotten it done so quickly AND been able to focus so much attention on it if it weren't for you. Thank you from the bottom of my grumpy little heart. I love you.

To the ARC readers, bloggers, and bookstagrammers who decided to ONCE AGAIN take a chance on a noob and picked up this book. Thank you a billion times over. Every page read, every review posted, every like, share, and comment are so very appreciated. You've made this journey fun and rewarding, and I adore you for it.

To Murphy Rae for knocking this cover out of the damn park. I love it so much. You brought Riggs and Bailey's story to life, and I am so, so grateful. I will sing your praises to any and everyone who will listen.

To my editor, Rebecca at Fairest Reviews Editing Services,

for your patience and kindness and keen eye, thank you so much. You've once again helped elevate my work to the highest quality possible, and my appreciation for you and the work you do cannot be stated enough.

To my proofreader, Sarah at All Encompassing Books, thank you for being you. I value you not just as a proofer and essential member of my team, but also as a friend. You go above and beyond every single time, and I hope you realize how grateful I am for you. Love you, friend.

To my sister, thank you for inspiring me every damn day, IRL and in fiction. You're the Bailey to my Bailey, and I wouldn't want it any other way.

To my beta team, Caitlin, Dawn, Haley, Brook, Brianna, Jenna, and Kara, you guys are so brilliant. I cannot express how important your feedback was to me. You are the reason Bailey and Riggs shine so brightly, and I cannot thank you enough. My books are *better with you* on my team (*see what I did there?*). I love you, I love you, I love you.

Extra special thank you to Dawn and Kara for pushing so hard for a letter from Odette. We have you two to thank for those extra tears shed. Jerks. (JK I love you.) The energy you ladies brought to this story gave me life, for real, and I couldn't have done it without you.

Caitlin, for your unparalleled ability to spot a plot hole from ten chapters away, thank you. My story runs more smoothly because of your keen eyes. Never, ever leave me.

Brianna, your beta notes are exactly the kind of WattPad comment vibes I need in my life. So helpful and ALSO entertaining. Thank youououououou. (And Gooby Goo, too.)

Haley, thank you for complimenting my ability to write steam scenes. You have no idea how much I needed that confidence boost. I might get it tattooed on my arm.

Jenna, your honest feedback and suggestions were so very

helpful. Thank you once again for going out of your way to read my manuscript. I don't deserve you.

Brook, you have no idea what your praise meant to me with Bailey and Riggs. I appreciate your feedback more than you probably realize. Thank you for always being honest and thorough.

And last but not least, to Harry Styles, whose Chicago *Love On Tour* concert was partially my motivation for getting this book done on time, thank you so much.

And Lil Nas X, thank you for MONTERO. It has nothing to do with this book but hot damn I fucking love that album.

Until next time, friends,

-J-Brit

Brit Benson writes romance novels that are sassy, sexy, and sweet. She likes outspoken, independent heroines, dirty talking, love-struck heroes, and plots that get you right in the feels.

Brit would almost always rather be reading or writing. When she's not dreaming up her next swoony book boyfriend and fierce book bestie, she's getting lost in someone else's fictional world. When she's not doing that, she's probably marathoning a Netflix series or wandering aimlessly up and down the aisles in Homegoods, sniffing candles and touching things she'll never buy.

f facebook.com/britbensonbooks

instagram.com/Britbensonwritesbooks

goodreads.com/authorbritbenson

pinterest.com/authorbritbenson